ALSO BY JILL SMOLINSKI

*The Next Thing on My List*

*Flip-Flopped*

# objects
# of my
# affection

## JILL SMOLINSKI

A TOUCHSTONE BOOK
Published by Simon & Schuster
New York   London   Toronto   Sydney   New Delhi

Touchstone
A Division of Simon & Schuster, Inc.
1230 Avenue of the Americas
New York, NY 10020

First Touchstone hardcover edition May 2012

TOUCHSTONE and colophon are registered trademarks of
Simon & Schuster, Inc.

For information about special discounts for bulk purchases, please contact
Simon & Schuster Special Sales at 1-866-506-1949 or
business@simonandschuster.com.

The Simon & Schuster Speakers Bureau can bring authors to your live
event. For more information or to book an event contact the Simon &
Schuster Speakers Bureau at 1-866-248-3049 or visit our website at
www.simonspeakers.com.

*Designed by Joy O'Meara*

Manufactured in the United States of America

1   3   5   7   9   10   8   6   4   2

Library of Congress Cataloging-in-Publication Data
Smolinski, Jill.
Objects of my affection : a novel / Jill Smolinski.
p.  cm.
"A Touchstone book."
1.  Single mothers—Fiction. 2.  Compulsive hoarding—Fiction. I. Title.
PS3619.M65O25  2012
813'.6—dc23                                        2011039107

ISBN 978-1-4516-6075-3
ISBN 978-1-4516-6078-4 (ebook)

*For Mary Jo Reutter,*
*who, as best friends go,*
*is forever in my "keep pile"*

objects
of my
affection

# chapter one

I remind myself as I enter the coffee shop that it's actually a *good* thing I sold my house and, for that matter, almost everything in it. Sure, some may find my situation pitiful—a thirty-nine-year-old woman reduced to sharing a bedroom with her best friend's preschooler daughter. But for purposes of this particular job interview—I pause to look around to see if anyone is looking around for me—it makes me even more of an expert. Will Meier is going to be downright *impressed* that the woman he's thinking of hiring to clear out his mother's home barely has a possession left of her own.

Not that I'll mention anything about it to him.

A man at the counter orders one of those ridiculous coffees that sound as if you should get a cake with several people around it singing "Happy Birthday" rather than something in a paper cup. Then he turns his attention to me. "You must be Lucy Bloom."

This is my guy. "Hi, and you're Will Meier! Nice to meet you," I say, shaking his hand. He's tall, fortyish, clean-cut, and wearing a business suit with the sort of ease that makes it clear he doesn't usually waste his mornings hanging out in coffee shops.

"I recognized you by your book." He points toward the copy of *Things Are Not People* that I'm clutching. "What can I get you to drink?"

"Coffee, black. Thanks."

Maybe my spartan drinking style will be another check in the yes column for me. *The woman is amazing! Even her beverages aren't cluttered!*

The coffee shop is only half-full this late in the morning on a Tuesday. We grab a table near a window.

"So what have you been told about the position?" Will asks.

I take a sip of my coffee to buy myself a few seconds to think. Then I list off some of what the woman at the referral agency explained to me. "You need someone to help you clear out your mother's home. I'd be supervising crews and working directly with her to determine what stays and what goes. And it's important the job get done in a timely manner."

What she said that I elect not to mention: Your mother, besides being renowned artist Marva Meier Rios, is a monumental pain who has either frightened away or turned down every organizer they've referred to date. Also, the contents she's managed to cram into one house could in fact supply an entire third-world nation if there were a way to ship it there . . . that is, if most of it weren't junk.

"It needs to be done no later than May fifteenth," Will says.

Just shy of two months. "Sure." It seems like a generous amount of time, and I can't help but wonder what the catch is. "Of course I'll need to see the house first," I say in a tone that I hope disguises how desperate I am to get this job. "May I ask why your mother wants to do this now?"

He gives a shrug. "Don't know." Pulling his cell phone from his pants pocket, he snaps it open. "Although she's had health issues. Smokes like a chimney. Diabetes. Been hit with some chronic infections—miracle she's hung in there this long." He looks at the screen. "Hold on a sec. I need to return this text."

It's all I can do to hide the disgust I feel. Could the man be any colder? Talking about his mother's failing health as if he's commenting on the weather! It's weird how quickly Will Meier morphed from being a man who'd initially struck me as rather good-looking in a

Clark Kent sort of way to one who *could* be but isn't due to an apparent lack of a heartbeat.

Tucking the phone back in his pocket, he says, "I assume the agency described the pay structure?"

I nod. Although I'm supposed to charge by the hour, Will is offering a weekly salary that, truthfully, isn't great. But there's a big, fat bonus if I bring the job in by the deadline—enough to make my eyes roll in my head and make that *cha-ching* sound like an old-fashioned cash register.

More important, it would be enough to start my life over again.

Will smiles, but I see there's a challenge in his eyes. "Tell me, Lucy, why should I hire you?"

My mind immediately flashes to the list of credentials I'd mapped out while preparing for the interview.

1. I've always been good at letting go of things. Back in grade school when they were collecting toy donations to raise money for the starving babies in Africa, I didn't give them old, broken junk (like some brothers of mine I could name)—I even fixed up my outgrown Sting-Ray bike to add to the pile.
2. On a recent trip to see my parents in Arizona, I managed to talk them into throwing away their entire collection of empty margarine containers, which took up two cupboards.
3. Anyone who can convince her nineteen-year-old son to go away to a drug rehab will have no trouble strong-arming some lady into giving up stuff.
4. I really, really, really need the job—rehab costs a fortune—so I'll work hard out of sheer desperation. . . .

I pull out the copy of *Things Are Not People* that I brought. "You should hire me because I'm organized, efficient, and an expert in the field of de-cluttering," I say as I hand it to him. "This is for you. I would have autographed it, but that seems so pretentious."

"I'll admit, I was intrigued when the agency mentioned you'd written a book on clutter. Interesting title."

"The book is part how-to, but it's also an exploration of the way people tend to get attached to things—you know, if Susan gives you a mug, and then Susan moves away, you can't let go of the mug because it reminds you of Susan. The mug *becomes* Susan."

"What inspired you to write it?"

"It started as an article on assignment for a magazine—I did a bit of freelancing when I worked for a PR agency, before I opened my own organizing business." I fish my résumé from my bag and hand it to Will. "The article was supposed to be tips for de-cluttering your home, but as I researched it, it grew into something different. The editor liked it so much, he suggested that I shop it as a book."

"How'd it sell?"

Why do people always ask that? Can't they just be awed by the fact that I got a book published at all? Does success always have to be based on how many copies it sold? "Quite well . . . for that type of a book."

Truthfully, after I got laid off from the PR agency, I'd hoped that writing a series of books about organizing would become the next step in my career. That idea hasn't panned out since the first book was such a flop. A few months ago, with my unemployment and much of my savings having run dry, I earned a possibly bogus online degree as a professional organizer and decided to try my hand in a new field. My first client was a former neighbor who needed help running a garage sale, which I did for the fee of him helping me run mine. Then, unable to drum up any other business—and too broke to rent office space and hang my "open for business" sign—I stumbled across a referral agency that specializes in placing organizers. Will Meier is the first nibble I've had from them.

He sits back in his chair and levels a look at me. "You know who my mother is?"

"I'm familiar with her work, of course." Originally, I'd planned to gush a bit at this point—mention how Marva Meier Rios practically pioneered the neo-Expressionism movement back in the 1970s, how one of her paintings, *Woman, Freshly Tossed,* is considered one of the greatest works of art of this century, how she used to hobnob with celebrities from John Lennon to Liza Minnelli, and other fun facts I'd looked up on the Internet (never having heard of her before). Given Will's chilly attitude toward his mother, however, perhaps understated was the way to go.

"You're aware she can be difficult," he says.

"Who could blame her? She's sick. She's elderly."

"You want to see how difficult she can be, try calling her elderly to her face."

"I'm only saying I can roll with the punches."

"There might be a few of those, too."

"You're joking. I get it."

He leans in. "Look, here's the deal: I don't have time to baby-sit this project. I'm out in Hinsdale, and the drive here is a hassle. Meanwhile, I've got a crew of guys ready to work, and everything's at a standstill because the client—my mother—is being uncooperative. They can't get rid of a thing unless she says so. I need somebody in there who can make it happen."

"I can definitely do that." I feel a strange urge to leap to my feet and salute.

"She'll need to meet you first, give her okay, before I can say 'you're hired.'"

"Of course."

"Well then"—he stands, tossing his cup neatly into a trash can—"let's go face the firing squad."

As I follow Will Meier's car the two or so miles from the coffee shop to his mother's house, I find myself humming along with the radio to calm my nerves. It's playing one of those cookie-cutter pop songs that my son, Ash, and I used to make fun of—him because he was far too hip for pop music, and me because I wanted him to think I was hip, too.

It's been a month since Ash left for rehab in Florida. Rough deal, huh—*Florida?* Staring up at palm trees sure sounds like more fun than looking up at this gray, drizzly Chicago sky. Almost makes it seem ridiculous that anyone could feel sorry for him.

But I do. Feel sorry for Ash.

Or at the very least, feel sorry *about* him—that his life got so horribly derailed—that instead of being at college pulling all-nighters and playing pickup soccer, he's sitting in a circle, sharing war stories with a bunch of other drug users.

Plus he's fair-skinned and burns easily—I know he won't always remember to wear sunscreen. The sun there is so much stronger than it is here.

And, yes, I do realize how stupid it is to worry about something that minor, considering the circumstances. At least I didn't call his therapist at rehab to ask if he could remind Ash to use an SPF 30. Although I don't believe an e-mail on the subject would be entirely out of line.

Anyway, I would say that sending my son away was the hardest thing I've ever had to do, but I've officially stricken that phrase from my vocabulary. Hear that, Universe? I am no longer making proclamations as to what has or has not been the hardest thing. You can quit upping the ante now. The first time I was foolish enough to say it was twelve years ago when Ash's father and I divorced. I naively thought *that* was the height of my bottoming out, so to speak. "This is the hardest thing I've ever had to do," I sighed to myself again, years later, as I explained to an eleven-year-old Ash that his already infrequent visits with his dad were being suspended altogether because they made the new family "uncomfortable." By the time Ash and I had battled our way through his later teen years, I'd worn the phrase down to a nub. I'd hardly felt a thing these past couple months while selling my home and cashing in my savings to pay the rehab's outlandish fees.

It'll be worth it, though. I gave up everything, and I'd do it again if it means that I'll have my sweet boy back, instead of the pasty, sullen, almost unrecognizable one I sent away. The one who refused to let me accompany him and the interventionist to the airport.

Like that song, Ash said he didn't need rehab, no, no, no, but nonetheless he went. It was with checkered Vans sneakers digging into the ground all the way . . . but he went.

And now here I am.

As I drive down a densely tree-lined street, I can't help but get excited about the prospect of working in this neighborhood. Oak Park is one of those eclectic, artsy areas of Chicago where you can have a funky bungalow right next to a house personally designed by Frank Lloyd Wright. It's about a thirty-minute drive from where I'm staying now, depending on traffic, which of course in Chicago you can never depend on.

Will pulls into a curved driveway and parks his car, and I follow. Like the other houses on this block, Marva Meier Rios's house is set back from the road, with plenty of yard and foliage surrounding it. It's Craftsman-style in a warm brown with absolutely gorgeous woodwork on the windows. From the description the agency gave me, I half-expected there to be a couple of cars on the lawn jacked up on cement blocks and a refrigerator on the porch.

"Looks perfectly respectable, doesn't it?" Will says as we get out of our cars and walk toward the porch.

"It's nice. Is this the only property?"

He snorts a laugh. "This is it. My mother would never invest in anything as bourgeois as real estate. She inherited this from my grandparents."

"Did you grow up in this house?"

"I grew up in a lot of places." He pulls out his phone, punches in a number, and says, "We're here. I'll give her the tour." A look of annoyance crosses his face. "Let's see if she runs screaming before we get into all that."

My stomach does a flip. That doesn't sound promising.

Will starts to unlock the front door, then turns to me. "I feel I ought to say something to prepare you for this."

"Don't worry about it. I've seen messy places before. I have a teenager."

"The mess. Right. Yes, it's bad. I meant more to prepare you for meeting my mother."

Okay, now I'm definitely nervous. "I'm sure she'll like me."

"No, she won't. But she doesn't need to. She only needs to be willing to tolerate you."

"She won't like me? Why won't she like me?"

The question was meant to be rhetorical (I mean, *everybody* likes me!), but Will gives me a slow once-over. "You're too . . ." I can tell he's searching for the right words to express my inadequacy. I'm tempted to supply some—just toss out a few random adjectives—but I find myself intrigued to see what he might come up with on his own. "You look like you used to be a cheerleader," he says finally. "You know, too blond. Too girl-next-door. Your clothes color-coordinate. I guess that's what it is."

I cross my arms, the ones warmly covered by the brand-new on-sale J.Crew sweater set I splurged on for this interview (because it went so well with my favorite pants). "I wasn't a cheerleader."

"Forget it, I shouldn't have said anything."

"I happened to have been in the National Honor Society, thank you very much. Yearbook editor. *Student government.*"

"It's just . . ." He lets out a sigh, then does that thing that my ex-husband used to do, squeezing the bridge of his nose to collect himself. "Marva would like nothing better than to hire someone exactly like Marva, only that person could never get the job done. I am moderately confident that you can." Another sigh. "I am so sick of dealing with this. The only reason I got involved in the first place is because I don't trust her to be discreet if she handled the process herself. The last thing I need is for the media to get hold of this and start reporting on how the great Marva Meier Rios is living in squalor. It would turn into a circus."

I pause to consider what he's said. "That *would* be bad."

"Exactly. I've got a business and a reputation to think about. In this crap economy, I don't need that kind of negative publicity working against me."

Ah, *your* reputation. "I see. Got it."

"All right. Let's do this." Will pushes open the door and we step inside.

I'm braced for what I might see, but what hits me before anything else is the smell. Although that's probably because it's so dark that relying on my sense of sight is pointless. The smell isn't horrible. We're not talking rotting corpses or anything. It smells . . . dense. As if I need to breathe in deeper to get enough air. I wonder how long it's been since anyone's drawn the drapes and thrown open the windows.

As my eyes adjust to the light, or the lack thereof, I see what I'm about to be up against. I swallow from the shock of it. How does the woman move around in here? We're standing in what I assume is the living room, but I'm basing this only on the room's proximity to the main entrance, not on any furniture I can identify. It's probably there somewhere—a couch and love seat, maybe a coffee table—beneath mountainous piles of bags and books and vases and papers and knick-knacks and framed art and sculptures and boxes and who knows what else. It's impossible to take it all in, much less categorize.

"Okay," I say, trying not to sound as shocked as I feel. "This is . . . um . . . not that . . . um . . . okay."

Will merely replies, "This is the living room. Through that way is the kitchen and dining area. Let me show you the upstairs first."

There are stairs? Right in front of me, as it turns out, and I couldn't see them. We pick our way along a twisty path. I wonder if Marva left this path or if it's been previously cleared with a machete by her son.

"Bedroom . . . bedroom . . . bath . . ." He rattles off the names of the rooms, barely giving me enough time to peek into each one. Doesn't matter. Every room is much the same. I can't see the beds in the bedrooms. Or a toilet or bathtub in the bathroom. It's as if I'm walking through a storage facility—everything is mishmashed together with no sense of order or purpose, other than to cram it in to the rafters.

I stall to get a better look at the last of the rooms. Like the others, it's a floor-to-ceiling jumble of boxes and trash bags, mixed in with loose objects of every size and type. There are silk pillows, religious artifacts, what appears to be a sculpture constructed of bicycle parts, a disco ball, lamps, baskets, suitcases, a guitar, frames, a ceramic duck with a giant crack in it, and stacks upon stacks of loose paper—enough to fill a dozen filing cabinets if they were filed, which of course they aren't. I get the impression that Marva started out with proper intentions. I see plastic bins with lids and labels—as if at one point she decided to organize. Then I imagine how she needed to find something—could be anything, a photo, a pair of scissors. She did a bit of rifling, things got shifted, boxes were opened . . . moved . . . toppled . . . and next thing you know, it looked as if people had ransacked the place. Only instead of stealing, they brought in even more stuff.

"So there are four bedrooms and a bath and a half up here," Will says. "There are another two bedrooms downstairs that are much larger. One is where my mother sleeps, and the other she uses as an office."

I nod, trying not to let my slipping confidence show. The more I see, the more I worry about working for Marva Meier Rios. My only real experience as a professional organizer was writing the book—and that was advice for managing ordinary clutter, such as messy closets and overstuffed cupboards. Being here in her home, I realize I'm out of my depth in more ways than one. Because Marva doesn't need an organizing expert—she needs therapy. Seriously. It's not *normal* to have so many things. That she's been willing to squeeze herself into a tiny space so her belongings can take over makes me wonder how hard it will be to get her to let go now. I mean, she has a box of doll heads! What could she possibly be saving them for? And why would she have them in the first place?

We make our way back downstairs, through a dining area. Or at least that's what room Will tells me it is. "Now around this corner here is the kitchen. . . ."

I steel myself. The kitchen. Surely it's going to be crammed with congealing food and trash and, I shudder, possibly bugs and rats and . . . "Hey!" I say, not hiding the surprise from my voice as we walk in. "This room isn't so bad." Granted, stuff is piled up on the countertop, and the kitchen table is buried beneath clutter—but the mess is nothing like I'd feared. The stovetop is covered with stacks of magazines, and costume jewelry dangles from the ceiling rack where pots and pans would normally hang. "Guess she doesn't do much cooking, huh?"

"There's a part-time housekeeper. She brings in my mother's meals. Special diet. So you ready?"

I'm busy imagining what a housekeeper could possibly do in here—if you dusted the place, it'd create a sandstorm—and then I realize Will is asking me if I'm ready to meet Marva. "Sure," I say, and turn to head down the last hall before I can lose my nerve, but Will doesn't move.

Instead, he pulls out his phone again. All he says into it is "We're out here."

After he hangs up, I say, "I won't be seeing the last few rooms?"

"You can see from here the mudroom that leads to the backyard, and there's a laundry area through there." He points to a door off the kitchen. "All that's left is a bedroom and a bathroom. An office. Bungalow out back. More of the same."

With that, I hear a door slam, followed by the sound of steps, and a thumping noise. Grumbling . . . words like "damn knees . . . taking forever . . ." More steps, more thumping.

I straighten, ready to meet Marva—then remember how cheerleaders are known for their posture, so I go for more of an attentive slouch.

Will leans close. "She's going to try to intimidate you. Grill you down. It's how she operates. Don't let her or it's over."

Marva Meier Rios emerges from around a corner, leaning heavily on a cane. As soon as I see her, I feel like a fool for having imagined her elderly and frail—especially since I knew from my research she's only in her midsixties. In her heyday, she was quite the striking brunette. Now the hair is peppered with gray and tugged into a careless bun, and the once-smooth olive skin carries some wrinkles and sags a bit, but she has the sort of strong bone structure that defies time. While not much taller than my five feet four inches, her air is imposing. She's wearing a brightly colored cape that on anyone else would look like a superhero costume but on her seems regal, and her black eyeliner and red lipstick are expertly applied. The crazy-lady appearance of the house does not extend to the woman herself.

Will does the introductions—I notice he calls his mother Marva. Weird . . . I can't imagine Ash calling me by my first name. Then again, when the drugs were talking, he called me lots of things.

"It's an honor to meet you," I say.

"Lisa is it?" she says.

"Lucy."

Irritation flickers across her face. "Luuuuuuucy," she says, and draws it out to make it clear how inconvenient it is for her to shape her mouth into the *u* sound. "Tell me. Are you easily offended?"

I barely pause to wonder why she'd ask such a question before I think, With what I've been through in the past year? Is she kidding? I almost have to laugh.

"I prefer to think I'm easily amused."

Marva stares at me without expression. I swallow over the dry lump that's formed in my throat. I've blown it. Why did I have to be glib? I couldn't have simply said, *No, I'm not?* I want to explain to her that's what I do when I'm on edge. I crack stupid jokes. Please don't take it seriously. Please understand that I need this job, even if I am entirely unqualified for it—even if I'm only a laid-off PR writer and hack author parading herself as an organizational guru. Give me this chance and I swear I'll—

Marva turns away, and the thump of the cane makes it clear she's going to leave.

I'm still silently pleading when Marva says, "Fine." She flicks a hand dismissively toward Will. "I suppose this one will do as well as any other."

# chapter two

When you hold on to everything in case you might someday love it/
want it/need it, you block the path to what is truly valuable to you.

—Things Are Not People

It's 2:00 a.m., and I'm lying here while Abigail digs her feet rhyth-
mically into my side. For a four-year-old, she can really go at it with
force. She's managed to wriggle herself so she's lying horizontally on
the bed, wedging me into the crevasse between the bed and the wall.
Rather than attempt to push her away, I climb over her to the mattress
on the floor, where her mother—my friend Heather—tucked her in
earlier. Won't do me much good. Abigail is a pixie-haired, green-eyed
heat-seeking missile. She'll find me again.

Ah, well. It's not as if I'm going to be able to sleep anyway. I'm too
busy worrying.

I'd feel better about my first day on the job if I had an idea of what
to expect. I want there to be a lady from HR, greeting me with an

employee packet and a video on sexual harassment in the workplace. Seems instead I'm on my own.

Will and I did talk awhile after Marva left as he walked me to my car. Although at first, all he could do was utter variations on "I don't get it. Why you?"

It went on long enough that I felt compelled to ask if he had a problem with me.

"You're fine. But she didn't even talk to you. As far as she knows, you could be a serial killer."

"Or perhaps," I pointed out, speaking slowly, "she trusts that her son wouldn't bring someone inappropriate into her home."

He stared absently toward the house. "No, that's not it."

Whatever. I'm to report to work at ten o'clock, although I'm free to arrange different hours with Marva. I can use the bungalow outside as an office. I don't have to do physical labor; there's hired muscle for that. Will's already hired an art expert, whom I'm to coordinate with to take any valuable art and high-end items to auction. The rest—the majority—is either trash or for a yard sale. Anything that doesn't sell will go to charity.

"Your mother certainly has a nice, big yard for a sale!" I said. "And this neighborhood will draw in the customers. People love—"

"You will *not* conduct the sale *here*," Will snapped, as if I'd proposed running live nudie shows on the roof. "Do I need to explain the importance of *discretion*? I've rented a storage unit. Anything to sell is to be transported there. You will oversee the estate sale *there*, at the *facility*, when the job is complete."

Boy, somebody got himself worked up mighty quickly. "Sounds like a plan!" I said, eager to prove he hired the right woman for the job.

"Naturally, you can't get rid of a single thing here without my mother approving it."

"Nothing?" I'd already mentally been wielding an ax and smashing that ugly, cracked duck statue upstairs to smithereens.

"Nothing. I may have hired you, but she's the one paying your salary. And she decides where each and every item goes."

"You don't mean what's obviously trash."

"I mean everything."

I picked up a crumpled potato chip bag. "This."

"Yes, that."

The objects in the house seemed to suddenly glow and dance and mock me. I'm no math whiz, but even I can figure out it's going to be impossible to personally handle all of what's in Marva's house in the span of time available to me. I have less than eight weeks—fifty-two days to be exact, and some of those are weekend days when I won't be working. It seemed doable when I thought I'd merely be pointing to entire piles and telling the work crew, "All this goes." But piece by piece by piece . . . multiplied by a bazillion? The paperwork alone! I'm screwed. Her house is huge. Even my dinky two-bedroom house took some time to dismantle after I sold it.

My house.

Siiiiiigh.

It's been a week since I packed up the last few things and drove away—seven days of playing musical beds with Abigail and being an awkward add-on to Heather's perfect family until I get back on my feet. (And I'm not exaggerating about the wonderfulness of her family. Her husband, Hank, is the poster husband for a nice guy. Their son DJ's only fault is being close in age to Ash, so every time I see him do normal high school things, it's a stab in the gut.)

To think a year or two ago I had what appeared to be a good life. A house, a job, and a son—things that at least let me pretend it all wasn't falling apart. I also had a boyfriend, Daniel, whom I was wild about and who I thought loved me back. That was, until he dumped me . . . and for a reason that hurt more than anything I could have foreseen. I'd rather it have been another woman than what it was.

Now all I have left is a closet-size storage unit and what I've brought with me here, which isn't much. Clothes, sundries . . . the bare essentials. The one precious item I've kept is a photo of Ash, which I keep tucked in my wallet. It's his senior portrait. He'd had the flu the day it was taken, although now I wonder if he wasn't sick at all but hungover. Still, I love it. Ash is giving his usual smirk . . . the smile that tips more on the left side. His blond hair is falling into his eyes the way it always does. He has a slight sunburn across his nose. For the split second that the photographer clicked the shutter, Ash looks like any high school student with his whole future ahead of him.

I roll over onto my stomach, determined to get some sleep. Maybe I'm fretting over nothing. Will told me his mother is ready to do this. She might need prompting—a hand to hold hers and lead it ever so gently to release whatever's clutched in it—but I can do that.

I'm sure it won't be the hardest thing I've ever had to do.

Marva is sitting on the front porch smoking a cigarette when I pull up. I'm hyperaware of the rattling of my car's engine. It's long overdue for a tune-up, but I'm afraid to take it in because they're going to tell me what else is wrong with it. I drive a classic cherry-red 1971 Ford Mustang convertible that I've had for twelve years—although the top is broken so it's technically not a convertible anymore. As cars go, it's not "me," but that's exactly why I bought it. It was my "F-you, Billy" purchase after my divorce, once my money was my own and I could afford to flip him off with the car he'd always coveted. I was surprised to find how much I actually grew to love it—the feeling of driving a car so sexy. Even when running errands around town, the Mustang suddenly made me feel as if I weren't the mom with her hair shoved back in a ponytail but, rather, the girl who dared wear black fishnets to the wedding. It brought out a side in me I didn't know was there. That's why, when I'm financially flush again, I plan to restore my car to its former glory. Put the top down and ride off into my shiny new life.

But I get ahead of myself.

"Morning!" I call out cheerily as I climb from the car. Marva is wearing a fuchsia print caftan and lots of bangly jewelry. Her legs are crossed, and I can see she's in flip-flops, though it can't be more than fifty degrees out. I grab the carry bag of organizational supplies I brought and head up to the porch. "Looks like it's trying real hard to be sunny out today."

She takes a drag on her cigarette and gives a noncommittal nod.

"It's been so rainy lately."

When there's no reaction from her, I say, "I'm Lucy. I'm here to—"

"I know who you are."

"Okay, great then."

Not certain how to proceed, I make a show of noticing a bush off to the side of her porch. "Does that flower?"

"Please don't feel that you need to make chitchat. I quite enjoy the morning quiet."

"It is nice, isn't it? So peaceful. I remember once when I lived right off a busy street and I'd wake up every morning to—"

Marva is barely suppressing her irritation as she looks away.

Oh. Right.

Slinging my bag over my shoulder, I say, "Do you mind if I show myself inside and take another look around? You can let me know when you're ready to get started."

She waves her cigarette in the direction of the front door, which I take to mean go on in, so I do.

Squeezed into the living room, I'm startled all over again by the squalor. How does anyone get used to this?

For the next hour, I poke in any closets, drawers, and cupboards I can manage to wriggle into. It's funny what you can learn about people by what they keep. For example, I am learning that Marva might be a pack rat, but she's not a slob. There is a difference. Although there's a ton of stuff here, it isn't garbage. No food or dirty bowls or snuffed-out cigarettes, at least that I've seen. Then again, anything could pop up. My toes scrunch at the idea of mice scurrying across them.

At one point I am wedged beneath the dining table—butt in the air reaching for what I thought might be a huge diamond ring but turned out to be a broken piece of a chandelier—when I hear Marva: "May as well get this show on the road. What's your plan, Princess?"

"I have one!" I say, overeagerly I realize as soon as the words are out of my mouth. I drag myself from beneath the table and face Marva, who is seated in the one cleared chair in the kitchen. "I have one," I say again, calmly this time, choosing to ignore the sarcasm in her little nickname for me. "A plan on how to proceed. I believe you're going to be very happy with it."

I pull the organizational system I spent much of last night devising from my bag, setting it on a tiny cleared space on the kitchen counter. I feel like an advertising exec giving a pitch to a client—but that's fine. Marva needs to be on board or it's not going to work. So I need to sell, sell, sell. The lucky news: I'm using Post-its. Who doesn't love an organizational system with Post-its?

"To start, I'd like to free up space, so that means clearing out some of the larger items first. I have these"—I hold up a handful of Post-its in a variety of colors—"so we can tag where each item is to go." Then I hold up the chart I designed on the computer—a *pie chart*, because who doesn't love pie charts? "As you see here, pink is for anything that's trash, yellow is recycling, blue is charity, purple is yard sale, orange is auction—"

"Charity should be orange," Marva says.

"Excuse me?"

"Charity. I've always thought of it more as orange, not blue. Blue is for recycling. Everyone knows that."

"Um . . . okay . . . we can switch that." I start rifling through my bag. If I learned anything from my years in advertising and PR, it's to placate the client. "I'm sure I have a Sharpie in here. We can make any changes you'd like. After all, you're the artist!"

"And why isn't there green?"

"Green? I just—"

"Green is a very calming color. I can't imagine going through this process, using these tags of yours, and not one of them being green."

"No problem. I can get green. For now we can substitute a different color that's close to green—like we could use blue and yellow together, right? That makes green." I find the Sharpie pen and wait with it poised at the chart. "What category is green to you?"

Marva grabs for her cane and uses it to hoist herself to standing. "I can't see this working as it is. Tell you what: You run get those green tabs and make the changes to your chart. In the meantime, I have other things I need to handle. Perhaps we can reconvene later this afternoon."

*Perhaps? This afternoon?* It's not as if I can get started without her. She has to approve everything I do. "We don't have to bother with the tags right now," I say. "You could point to things, and I can—"

"I'll be in my office. I don't want to be disturbed."

She goes to the refrigerator and pulls out what appears to be a boxed lunch.

Oh, no, she's bringing provisions. I could lose the whole day. "How will I know when you're ready?" My voice is a desperate squeak. I can't help myself. If day one sets a tone for how this project is going to go, it's looking grim.

"If I'm ready later today, I'll come find you," she says as she disappears down the hall. I hear a door shut.

I flop down into the chair Marva vacated. So much for diving right in.


Two o'clock. Marva has yet to emerge. I've been checking at regular intervals, peeking down the hall for signs of life. In the meantime, I bought those stupid green Post-its (and a bunch of other colors and patterns, too, just in case) and grabbed lunch.

Then to kill time, I decide to rearrange what Will called the bungalow so I can use it as an office. It's a converted one-car garage— tiny, with thankfully no car squeezed inside. I guess if you don't go anywhere, you don't need one. The bungalow is separated from the main house by two enormous oaks and accessible by a side driveway. What was once the garage door is now a wall, and there are curtained windows and a bathroom. It is potentially quite cozy. More important, it'll make a nice place to hide from Marva.

And based on the empty pop cans and fast-food wrappers I see stuffed in a trash can, I'm not the first to have this idea.

I sustain only minor injuries as I shove things around to make room, even managing to single-handedly drag down a couch that was standing on end.

Mmm, a couch.

I could use a break. It's been such a frustrating day so far. Couldn't hurt to lie down and relax. Rest my weary bones. Take a few moments to contemplate my next move . . .

The dream bubble pops above my head.

Eerf. I must've fallen asleep. My face is smashed into a couch pillow. I feel sticky and muddled and . . . ugh. What is that *smell*?

I attempt to tug my eyes open and drag myself up.

"Hey, lookit here, Sleeping Beauty is waking up." At the sound of a male voice, my eyes fly open like a window shade with a haywire spring. I'm trying to yank myself upright, only my legs keep tangling up against the guy, who is sitting on the end of the couch, eating beef jerky from a bag.

"Move already!" I snap, pushing at him with my feet.

Another man's voice: "Gee, somebody's cranky when she wakes up."

"What the—?" I practically fly to a standing position. My hands feel around on my body to see if I can tell if I've been groped. My clothes appear to be intact. "What are you doing in here?"

The owner of the second voice is sitting with his back propped up against the wall, gnawing on a giant pita sandwich (which explains the smell). They're both youngish, midtwenties I'd guess, tatted up— one of them sporting muttonchops and the other that weird strip of chin hair as if he missed a spot shaving.

Muttonchops says, "You that chick they hired?"

I glare at him. "You have no right to be here. This happens to be my office now."

"So I'll take that as a yes."

A toilet flushes and a third guy walks out of the bungalow's small bathroom. I whip around to him. "You didn't wash your *hands?*"

He gives me that deer-in-the-headlights look. "Uh . . . yes, I did."

"You did not! I didn't hear water running!"

"Um, okay, well, I can—"

"No," I say, sensing my hysteria rising. "It's too late now. All of you get out. In fact, even better, where is your supervisor? He ought to hear how"—I narrow my eyes at the guy on the couch, who is chuckling—"his workers find it so *funny* to sneak up on innocent women while they're *resting* and do *God knows what.*"

"Whoa, hey, babe, chill."

As if I'm going to take that from a guy with filthy hands. "I will not *chill.* I—"

The bungalow door opens, and *another* guy walks in, this one scribbling on a clipboard he's holding. He must be the one in charge. "Oh, hey, you're awake, cool," he says when he glances up.

"No, it is not," I say. "It is not the slightest bit *cool* to wake up surrounded by a bunch of . . . of . . ."

He looks at the others while I search for a word besides *hooligans.* "You were in here while she was sleeping?" They don't answer, and he says to me, "I'm sorry. Sometimes they're idiots. Unfortunately, they're also my cousins and they work for me. By the way, I'm Niko Pavlopoulos—and you must be Lucy."

He extends a hand for me to shake, which I reluctantly accept. Niko is about the same age as the others, but at least he doesn't sport that fresh-from-prison look that they do. In fact, he has a nice face . . . good brows, and the kind of lashes that make the ladies grumble what a waste they are on a man.

"They scared me half to death," I say, not entirely ready to let go of my fight.

Niko tips his head toward the door. "Guys . . . out. I picked up the pipes for the basement. Start on that." Surprisingly, they gather up their food and cheerfully file out.

After they're gone, I drop back down onto the couch. "Basement," I say, groaning, "I forgot about the basement. I'll bet it's a nightmare down there."

"You're in luck. Pipes busted—that's why Will brought us on in the first place. Water damage was so bad, we had to haul everything straight to a Dumpster. Even then, Marva was trying to stop us, tell my guys it wasn't wrecked that bad." Niko settles onto the arm of the couch. "That's why I'm so glad you're here. Somebody needs to get this project moving."

I don't sense sarcasm from him, even though moments ago I'd been caught drooling into a couch cushion. "I'm usually more a woman of action than you saw here today," I say, sheepish.

"No worries. So how's it going so far?"

"With Marva?"

"Yeah. I brought all three guys with me today figuring by now you'd have stuff for us to haul out."

I look at my watch—it's almost six o'clock. There's no point in lying. I've blown the whole day. "I didn't get anywhere. Marva sent me out to buy Post-its, and then she locked herself in her office."

"Post-its?"

I explain to him my organizational system, and how Marva thought the colors should be different, and green should be represented, and you know these artists, how temperamental they can be, and the best thing is to humor them so they believe they're getting their way and . . . and . . .

Niko is laughing.

"What is so funny?" I ask.

"Man, she saw you coming."

"And what exactly is that supposed to mean?"

"It means she played you."

"She did not!"

"You spent your day buying office supplies."

"Those Post-its happen to be an integral part of my organizational system."

"Whatever you say."

I'd like to hit him with a snappy comeback, but I'm haunted by the image of Marva walking away this morning as I was too cowed to say a thing, and I slump in defeat. "You're right. I let her totally manipulate me."

I want to cry—it's Ash all over again. It's Ash, telling me some elaborate story about how it wasn't his pipe or his stash or his pills— he was only holding them for this guy he hardly knows. And me being a sucker and believing it, time and time again, because I didn't want to think about what the truth would mean.

Niko slides down so he's on the couch, facing me. "Don't feel bad. None of us have been able to get her to do anything for weeks now. Her own son couldn't do it. That's why he had to bring you in." He pauses. "This was only one day. You'll get the hang of it."

"There's just so *much*."

"We could wipe out everything in that house in less than a week if it weren't for her. It's only a big job because she's making it that way. As much as she wants it done, she doesn't want to do it."

"Well then," I say, putting on my brave-girl face, "I'll have to use my awesome powers of persuasion."

His mouth pulls up in a smile. "I look forward to seeing that."

Niko leaves to join the crew in the basement. Out of sheer stubbornness, I'm tempted to stay and wait Marva out—even if it takes all night—but I have to be at Heather's son's birthday party in half an hour. Instead of skulking out defeated, I screw up the courage to go to Marva's office, where on the door is taped a note: *Do not disturb.* The blocky forward-slant of her handwriting seems aggressive enough that I hesitate. When it dawns on me that I'm such a pushover that I'm even intimidated by this woman's *writing*, I make myself knock.

I hear Marva call for me to come in. As soon as I open the door, it's as if I'm walloped by a cyclone of color. The walls are covered with paintings of every size, and canvases are stacked up against them, pulsing with such intensity that it's overwhelming. "Wow, are these yours?"

"What is it you need?" Marva asks. She's sitting in front of a desk, making some sort of notes in a book that's set on top of a pile of papers. "Are you finally ready to get back to work?"

*Me? Finally ready?* I want to pull one of those paintings off the wall and clobber her over the head with it.

"I thought you didn't want to be disturbed."

She doesn't glance up. "That being the case, why are you willing to disturb me now?"

A red painting with orange and yellow swirls exudes a sense of violence, plus it looks real heavy. That's the one I'll hit her with.

"I wanted to say good night."

"Good night."

This is where I should leave, but I find myself lingering. A portrait of a morose young girl who vaguely resembles Marva stares at me. It's done in the style I recognize as hers: realistic, yet exaggerated, as if she purposely colored outside the lines.

Marva stops writing. "Yes?" Although typically a positive word— *yes!*—the way she says it is better translated as "Why are you still here?" Or, more accurately, "Don't be here."

I turn to go but then stop myself. "The painting behind you, is that a self-portrait?"

"Only egotists do self-portraits."

"So, then I take that as a no?"

She graces me with what could almost be called a smile—it's achieved mostly through a lift of the eyebrows rather than a curve of the lips. "Touché. Now good night."

This time I take the hint and leave, although not without first telling Marva that we'll start tomorrow morning at ten o'clock sharp. She'd better be ready to roll up her caftan sleeves and get work done because I'll be cracking the whip something fierce. Okay, maybe I only confirmed the time and stopped there, but I believe the rest was implied.

▪ ▪ ▪

I get to the bowling alley in time to help Heather's husband, Hank, carry pitchers of pop from the concession stand. It's one of those new, glossy bowling alleys with the high-tech video screens and pulsing music. Tonight is eighties night, and Cyndi Lauper is reminding us how girls just want to have fun.

"I can't believe DJ is eighteen. I'm the father of an adult," Hank says, setting the pitchers down on a table next to a cake and a pile of gifts. "I'm barely an adult myself."

"They grow so fast when you feed them," I say. "So where is everybody?"

"The kids are bowling. The moms are hanging by the bar."

"Who's here?" I keep my voice nonchalant, but Hank picks up on my tension. Or more likely, Heather has prepped him, reminding him of how I've been avoiding people for a reason. She must have told me a dozen times I didn't have to come tonight, but that's like when people invite you to Tupperware parties and say you don't have to buy anything. They never mean it.

"Don't worry, we kept it small. Let's see . . . DJ invited Zac, Nicholas, Samantha, and of course Crystal. So that means mom-wise we have—"

"My worst nightmare?"

"Nah, merely a few of your dearest, closest friends." He chucks me under the chin. Hank is an ex–college football player, gone soft over the years, and the master of the gentle gesture, having one too many times not known his own strength. "You'll be fine. Nobody's going to say anything about it."

*It* being Ash. *It* being rehab. *It* being the talk of our suburb for a while, although never to my face.

Hank excuses himself to go drag little Abigail away from the teenagers before she picks up any new words. I mentally dress myself in armor and head to the bar area.

As I approach, Mary Beth Abernathy gives a wave from the booth where they're sitting. She's in her uniform of mom jeans, sneakers, and a sweatshirt advertising one of her kids' sports teams—her bangs a tad too short, as if she cut them herself. "Why, look, Heather, here comes your roommate now!"

Impressive. She didn't even give me time to get a drink before she managed to embarrass me about having to bunk with Heather's family.

Heather rolls her eyes. She doesn't like Mary Beth any more than I do, but their sons have been best friends since grade school. They're practically in-laws.

Janie—who is the mom of DJ's girlfriend, Crystal—pours a margarita from a pitcher on the table and hands it to me. "I hear today was your first day on a new job. I'm guessing you need this."

"Straight tequila might be more appropriate."

"That bad?" Heather asks, scooting over to make room for me. Heather has been my best friend since we met in college, and I swear she hasn't aged ten minutes since then. She still has that sleek, coltish, coed look—as if she spends her days playing tennis and lunching with the gals, instead of what she really does, which is take care of everybody and everything.

"I'm joking," I say. "It was all right." I turn to Mary Beth, eager to change the subject to something other than me. "So has Nicholas decided on a college yet?"

And off they go—I'm free to sit back and enjoy my drink while the three of them go back and forth about SAT scores and graduation and college choices and the higher-education prep I didn't get to go through with Ash. I'd always thought I would. Ash is smart, as in "I don't have to study but I still ace the test" smart. Although he's a year older than DJ, they used to hang out in the same crowd—nice kids with great grades that managed to sidestep being tagged as nerds. Of course, once my son got into drugs, the lifelong friends went by the wayside, along with the grades. His new crowd looked as if he'd pulled them out from under a collapsed building.

From where I'm seated, I can see DJ and the others as they bowl. Samantha—whom Ash briefly dated in his junior year—throws a gutter ball. Then she skips to her seat, high-fiving as she goes. I take a bite of a tortilla chip from a basket on the table, wondering if it will ever stop hurting seeing normal kids having a normal time.

I'm about to go for another handful of chips when Mary Beth clasps my reaching hand across the table. "Lucy. Dear Lucy. Tell me. How is Ash?"

The question came out of nowhere—or maybe it didn't. I wasn't paying much attention to the conversation. She gets my stock answer. "He's doing well."

"When I heard about, *you know*, I was so upset. I said to myself, not our Ash!"

This is awkward, and I want my hand back. Plus, yech, her hand is moist.

Janie says, "It's fantastic that he's doing what he's doing. Good for him."

I try to ease my hand toward me, but Mary Beth has a death grip on it. "Thanks, Janie," I say, and with that I make a pointing gesture at her that makes utterly no sense but provides the excuse for claiming my hand back.

Heather smacks the table so hard it jostles the drinks. "What are we, a bunch of old ladies? Sitting here when there's bowling to do? Shame on us! I've been practicing on the Wii all week—I've got some teenaged butt to kick on the lanes!"

I tap her foot with mine under the table—nice save. No awards for subtlety, but nice.

Mary Beth leans back. "Oh, let's let those kids be kids for a while." That even gets an eye roll from Janie—it's common knowledge that no one is more involved in the minutiae of her children's lives than Mary Beth Abernathy. "When's the last time you talked to him?" Mary Beth asks, turning back to me.

Ouch, straight shot to the kidneys. "I haven't yet. That's one of the rules. No outside contact for a while."

This is not entirely true, but that's the cornerstone of good lying. Stay as close to the truth as possible. Ash wasn't allowed calls his first two weeks, but he was encouraged to write to me. He never did. Not one measly letter. Not so much as a sentence, even though I sent *him* a nice letter full of well wishes and support and completely free of any hint of bitterness. Now he and I are allowed a ten-minute phone call. So far he's declined. I have been able to talk to his therapist, but those conversations are mostly me asking how Ash is doing, and Dr. Paul saying, "I'm not legally allowed to say anything, he is an adult, but . . ." Then he divulges some crumb of Ash's recovery that will have to sustain me until such time that my son is willing to talk to me.

"That's smart that they do that," says Heather, who knows I'm lying. "Total immersion. That'll make things go that much faster."

"How long will he be in . . . um . . . the place where he's at?" Janie asks.

"As long as he needs to be. That's why I picked this particular rehab," I say, using the word Janie was reluctant to say. "It's called the Willows. They have a program they run them through, and they don't release them until they're finished. It can be anywhere from a couple months to a year, or more. Although four months is the average."

"So what was he into?" Mary Beth asks, slugging down the last of her margarita. "Pot? Meth? Crack?"

Is she honestly asking that so casually? What's next—my bra size? If I've ever engaged in a three-way?

Heather says, "Oh, for goodness' sake, Mary Beth."

"What? I'm only saying, there's all kinds of drugs and temptations out there. If we as parents are afraid to dig in and find out what's going on in our children's lives, anything can happen. I don't know what I'd do if my Nicholas or Katie started messing around with any of that."

"You'd do what any of us would do," Heather says. "Whatever it takes. Now come on." She stands up. "I came here to bowl, not to wag my jaw all night."

"Potato," I say quietly to Heather as we gather our glasses to carry with us, which is code for "I love you." I don't even remember why.

She squeezes my elbow. "Potato, too."

After that, there's bowling and pizza eating and opening of presents and blowing out of candles. I do what I can to shut off my brain. The margarita helps, but since I'm driving, I can only have the one. Besides, there's something wrong about drinking to forget that your son is in rehab.

Later, I'm pushing a piece of cake around my plate to disguise that I'm not eating it—one word, *coconut*—when Samantha sits down next to me.

"Hey, Mrs. Bloom."

"Hi, Samantha." I've been exchanging barbs with the kids all evening—the usual trash talk about how I can bowl them under the table—but I haven't actually talked to any of them. "It's good to see you. Are you excited about graduating?"

"Uh-huh. I got a summer internship at my aunt's ad agency."

"That's great! Where are you going to school?"

"I got into State."

"That's my alma mater. I can tell you anything you need to know—especially the best places to meet guys. Oh, wait . . . I mean the best places to study."

She laughs, but she's wriggly in that way Ash was when he had something on his mind.

"I just wanted to say . . ." Her voice trails off. I wait. Eventually she continues, "I'm sorry I haven't written him back. Is he mad?"

"Written him back?" I instantly know exactly what she means only I wish I didn't. "You mean Ash."

"I feel so bad. I would've—only my mom? She saw the letter? And told me not to?" Her face is puffy—she's trying not to cry.

I suppose that means that my face is puffy, too. Ash wrote to Samantha. He hasn't said so much as hello to me, his mother, who sold her house to pay for his rehab. But this girl that he dated for a few weeks, a couple months at most, *she* received a letter.

This should make me happy. Ash is reaching out to a nice girl. He's not writing letters to his drug dealer, at least so far as I know.

That's the problem: What do I know? Nothing.

And what's up with Samantha's mother telling her not to write my son back? What—does he have drug cooties? Will her precious child catch something by mere association with Ash? He's in recovery, for crying out loud! That seems to me an occasion to reach out. If she were here, I'd give her a piece of my mind. Not to get on a soapbox, but something is desperately wrong with a society in which we care only about our own without regard to others—especially others whose mothers have driven your daughter places and bought her Taco Bell and clapped for her in school plays, and those sorts of things you *do* for your child's friends.

It takes effort to smooth down my hackles before speaking. "He didn't mention that he wrote to you." I can't figure out how to ask what the letter said without prying—and I don't care if I do, I just don't want her to shut me out. "Did he ask you in the letter to write him back?"

She nods.

"Do you want to?"

"I'm not sure."

I can't stand it anymore. "What did he say in the letter? If that's too nosy, you don't have to answer."

"Mostly hi. And he misses me. And he's sorry."

"Sorry . . ." I say. "Did he do . . . um . . ." I'm asking if my son did something awful to this girl, and desperately hoping I don't get an answer.

"Sorry in general, I guess. For messing up his life so bad?"

As much as I'm relieved, I'm also irritated. She gets a sorry? The boy once held an airsoft gun to my head! He stole money from me and punched holes through my walls and lied and . . . ugh . . . so much for me not showing any bitterness.

"I'm glad he wrote you," I say. "And I can't tell you to write him back because it's against the mom code for me to suggest that you disobey your mother."

Samantha picks at the polish on her nails. "But you want to."

"I want my son to get better. If I knew how to make that happen, he wouldn't be where he is right now. If he wrote to you, I'm guessing he felt it was important to his recovery."

"Forget my mom. I'm writing him back."

I put my arm around her to give her a quick squeeze. "Look, sweetie, do what you think is right."

# chapter three

Marva is reclining in a chair that looks like a big, fuzzy question mark, having an afternoon smoke in the mudroom. After allowing her enough time to puff down to the filter, I walk in, only to see her lighting a second cigarette off the first.

"Another one? I was hoping we could get started."

She blows a smoke ring. "Give a woman a break here. This is the only vice I've managed to hang on to. Let me enjoy it."

A break. Please. Her coffee breaks, lunch breaks, bathroom breaks, and now cigarette breaks have frittered away the entire morning. Instead of being busy throwing things out, all I was able to do was strategize a plan for how I'll proceed, should I ever be allowed to actually do my job. At one point, bored—and in desperate need of a shot of motivation—I ran to the office supply store to buy a calendar. The first thing I did after posting it on the bungalow wall was circle the deadline date: May 15. I wrote the number of days left on each date square, counting backward to today. Then I drew a big, fat X through yesterday, Day 52. I'm starting to worry there may be another X on the calendar before I clear so much as a scrap of paper from the house.

Still, I stay upbeat and don't even wave away the waft of cigarette smoke coming at me so as not to insult Marva. "There's lots to do today," I say, "so we need to get to it!"

"You sound just like my son," she replies in a tone that makes it clear it's not a compliment. The windows that flank the tiny room are open, and Marva is looking out over the backyard where a gardener is planting bulbs. "Life to Will is nothing but a checklist. He's always in a hurry to get this or that done. If you ask me, none of it seems that interesting."

I'm not particularly thrilled to be compared to Will Meier. "You hired me to do a job. I'm trying to do it. Now, if there's flexibility in the deadline . . ."

"There isn't," she says, taking a long, leisurely pull on her cigarette. She was probably one of those people who in college wrote their term papers the day before and figures we can clear out this house if we pull an all-nighter.

I attempt a different tack. "In my book," I say, "I recommend that any organizing effort start with envisioning the result. So I'm going to ask you to close your eyes and picture your home a couple months from now. We've finished the job, and it's exactly what you hoped it would be. What does it look like? How do you feel being in it? Can you describe that for me?"

She flicks the ashes from her cigarette into an emptied coffee can that is serving as an ashtray. "You win. We can get started."

"Great!" I say. "But it really does help to—"

"You know what I'd like to envision? Us not having this particular conversation right now."

"You got it," I say, even though I'm stung. There was no need to be rude. I'm only trying to help. "We may as well start here in the mudroom."

I pause to assess what's in the room. It's filled mostly with the sort of things that straddle the outside and inside worlds: jackets, boots, magazines, beach towels, plastic stacking chairs, a patio table, a six-foot, flamingo-shaped umbrella holder.

Climbing over stacks of boxes, I make my way to a heap of clothing that reaches the ceiling.

"These clothes. Yard sale?"

"You'll need to hold them up so I can see."

"Each one?"

"How else do you expect me to decide? Some of my clothing is very expensive."

I grab a damp corduroy jacket with ratty elbow pads. "Yard sale?"

"Keep."

"But it's in such poor condition."

"I often get a chill."

"Marva, surely you have other jackets that are much nicer than this one."

I stiffen as soon as I realize I've used her first name. It's probably expected that I call her Ms. Meier Rios, or missus, or ma'am, or something demonstrating proper subservience.

"Fine, then," she says, not mentioning the faux pas. "You may sell it."

Hmm, *Marva* it is. I toss the jacket into a trash bag color-coded for yard sale. Then I hold up another piece of clothing for her inspection. And again. And again. She debates the merits of each item so thoroughly, it takes nearly an hour to fill one bag for the yard sale. My tiny victory is that I coaxed her into getting rid of most everything she'd at first said she wanted to keep.

Still, I'll never get anywhere at this rate.

Some professional organizers are also trained therapists. Their strategy would be to get Marva to examine her psychological ties to her possessions. Take her back to her childhood, or a traumatic incident, to help her recognize why she places such importance on material things.

I've known Marva only a day and a half, but I have no doubt she'd eat one of those therapists alive.

I hold up a stained, smelly blanket. "Trash?"

"Keep."

Ugh.

"Marva, I realize it's hard to let go of things that you once cherished, but think about how much you love this beautiful house! Isn't your home—your ability to move freely through it—more important than this one blanket?"

"Keep."

If I give in on an item this bad, I fear it'll give permission for her to keep all sorts of ratty things, which is why I'm fully prepared to fight the battle of the blanket. Even though my last attempt at introducing a tip from my book was met with derision, Marva leaves me no choice but to try another. "To decide if it's truly a keep," I say, "let's apply what I call the N-Three test. Need—Now—No. If you're deciding whether to keep something, ask yourself, 'Do I truly *need* this item? Do I use it *now* or will I in the near future? What's the worst that can happen if I say *no* to it and let it go?' So, on this blanket—"

"I choose to keep it."

The woman is hopeless. "How about looking at it this way. The faster you let go and clear out things, the sooner I'm out of your hair."

"Whatever gave you the impression I don't cherish our time together?"

I can't help but burst out in a laugh. Sure, she's treating me like something on the bottom of her shoe, but you've got to hand it to the gal. She's not going down without throwing a few punches on the way.

"Oh, go ahead," she says. "Put that in your little sale."

After that, I manage to press her to decide on everything in the mudroom, right down to the last tube of expired sunscreen. One whole room tagged or bagged for the guys to clear out tomorrow. Granted, the room is not much bigger than a hallway. But progress is progress.

After the mudroom, we move on to the living room, following my plan to designate larger items that can be cleared to free up space. Post-its dot the room like an office rainbow.

I'm starting to get that buzz that comes with digging in and getting a job done when Marva says, "I believe I'll take a nap."

I'm disappointed, and I'm not ready to call it a day. "Is it all right if I stick around until you wake up? Maybe we can get more done today."

"Suit yourself."

While she's sleeping, I decide to speed up the process by presorting items in the living room. Grunting with effort, I shove around boxes and sculptures and furniture and endless piles, guessing what Marva might want to do with each item. I wish I'd asked Niko to come today. I could use some muscle, but I didn't dare risk another day of watching the crew sit around with nothing to do.

By the time Marva emerges from her nap, it's dark out, and I'm sweaty and sore.

"What's this?" she asks.

"What?" I say, hands on hips and breathing heavily. I need to work out more. I've let myself get seriously out of shape since I canceled my gym membership to save on expenses.

"You've moved things."

"I've presorted. Thought I'd use my time wisely. Now don't worry. I haven't thrown anything away. It's all here, it's just—"

"Who said you could move things?"

"Well, I figured—"

"You *figured*. Isn't that terrific. Now how am I supposed to know what's what with nothing where it's supposed to be?"

The edge to her voice would've been sharp enough to cut through my diamond stud earrings if I hadn't already sold them on eBay.

"You and I are still going to sort through it," I say. "There's no need to—"

"Remove the tags."

"What? The Post-its?" A rush of panic surges through me. "But I only shifted things around."

"I said remove the tags."

"But—"

"Now! I want them off! All of them!"

It's as if she's swelled to five times her size and her eyes have taken on a deranged gleam. Frankly, she's terrifying, like an angry Macy's parade balloon.

"Okay, okay," I say, pulling a green Post-it off a clock and holding it up for her to see. Maybe watching me obey will calm her. "You don't understand. I didn't change any of the—"

"How am I supposed to trust you now? When you stomp through my home while I'm asleep and destroy order?"

Oh my God, she's completely off her rocker. There couldn't possibly have been any order in here.

"Off," she says, as she uses her cane to climb partway up the stairs before sinking down onto one of the steps.

She stares coldly down at me like an emperor watching slaves toil, while I make my way through the living room, pulling off tags, one after another. I attempt again to explain, but she shushes me. After the living room detagging is complete, Marva frog-marches me to the mudroom, where I empty the trash bags I've filled. We're silent as I work, but it doesn't feel quiet. It's as if a sound track of misery is playing in the background, filling up the house so even the air is cluttered.

Two days and it's over. I've failed. I wanted to find a job where I could make money fast and stay in the area. Rebuild a home for Ash and me when he returns. What kept me going through it all—sending my son away, selling my home, and getting rid of all my possessions— was clinging to a picture in my mind of soon everything being normal again. That this period of having nothing was just a bump on the road map of my life. I thought for sure this job was going to set me back on course. Only now it's over before it's begun, and I don't have a plan B.

"There, done." I dump out the last bag onto the floor. Tears are pooling, but if it takes every ounce of strength I have, I won't let them fall. "I'm sorry. I never meant to—"

"Save it," Marva says. "I won't let you in the house tomorrow if I'm going to have to endure all that caterwauling."

Tomorrow?

There's a tomorrow?

I definitely heard her say *tomorrow*.

It appears that I'm not fired—not yet anyway.

"All right then," I say cautiously, backing up toward the door. "I'll see you tomorrow?" I test out the word to see if Marva objects to hearing it roll off my tongue.

She doesn't answer, so I let myself out, grabbing only my purse and leaving my stack of Post-its behind.

I call my mom on my way home, having stopped first at a convenience store to buy a box of Cheez-Its, which are serving as both dinner and emotional comfort. As my mom does nearly every time I call lately, the first thing she says after "Hello" is "You sound upset. Is there a problem with Ash?"

"Ash is fine. I, however, am about to throw myself from a building."

"Why are you throwing yourself from a building, sweetie?"

In the background, I hear my dad say, "Who's throwing themselves from a building?"

"Lucy."

That answer seems to satisfy him because he doesn't inquire further.

"It's this job I took," I say.

"With the artist? Ooh, I looked her up on the Internet after you told me you're cleaning out her house. I couldn't believe it—the one painting of hers, oh, I can't describe it, but the famous one with the naked lady in it? Rosalyn Wozniak has that very painting above her downstairs toilet. Not the actual painting of course. A print. But isn't that funny?"

"Mom, you know you can't mention that I'm working for her, right? I've promised to keep it a secret."

"Tick a lock," she says. I picture her making the gesture of turning a lock on her lips and tossing the key. "So is it not going well?"

"It's the weirdest thing. She hired me, but now it seems she wants me to fail. I can't seem to get her to let go of anything."

"I'm not surprised. The older you get, the more attached you get to what you have. It's because so many of your friends and family have died off or moved away. You want to at least have a reminder of them. You're young—you'll understand someday. Personally, I can't believe how you were able to sell all your things. I still think you should have put more in storage."

"Storage costs money. Besides, I don't miss any of it."

"How can you possibly say that?"

"Because it's true."

"But your pretty dishes! And that antique armoire you had in your bedroom—oh, you were so excited about refinishing it. Remember how you sent me all those pictures of it on the e-mail? It had to have broken your heart to let it go."

An image of my old bedroom floats to my mind. I'd spent weeks picking just the right lavender color for the walls, one that set off the whitewash I'd lovingly given the armoire. But before I can think too long about how I handed over my cotton, eyelet bedspread in exchange for a $5 bill at my garage sale, I sweep the thought away. I did what I needed to do. "It's no big deal," I say.

"I don't mean to bring up a sad subject."

"It's not. I'm fine." As long as I don't think about it, I'm fine.

Truth be told, in some ways, I'm actually *glad* to have it all gone. It couldn't get gone fast enough, in fact. I recall how the taxi carrying Ash and his interventionist had barely pulled away and I was already in Ash's room, eager to sweep through and throw away anything stashed there that was possibly drug-related. Going through every drawer, closet, and crevice, I chucked the obvious: pills and powders, baggies, pill containers, pill cutters—but then weird stuff, too, that had no place in a boy's bedroom, such as pen casings emptied of their insides and plastic two-liter pop bottles filled with murky water. A euphoria came with watching the trash bag fill up that had me buzzier and more energized than I'd been in months.

A week later at my garage sale I was still on a high—and against a deadline to move out before escrow closed. Heather, who was there helping, had to talk me out of selling some things. Just because Ash had duct-taped a hash pipe out of some of his LEGOs, she'd said—

taking a LEGO pirate ship set off the FOR SALE table and hiding it away from customers—didn't mean they all were bad. Ash had a right to his belongings.

And it wasn't only *his* stuff I was tossing. I also sold the dining room set that reminded me how we didn't eat dinners together anymore . . . the stereo that played far too many sad songs . . . the couch that my ex-boyfriend Daniel and I picked out back when we were together for the three of us to pile on to watch movies. Even things seemingly benign—a fondue pot, a corkboard—shouted at me their need to belong to someone who could give them a proper home, after I'd proved that I couldn't.

I turn my attention back to my mom, who has moved on to giving me the weather report for Sun City—hot and sunny! The poppies are already coming in! What I didn't realize was that it isn't conversation but, rather, a sales pitch.

"So if that job doesn't work out, you always have a place here with your father and me," she says, causing me to choke on the Cheez-It I just popped into my mouth. "We've got that spare room. I don't understand why you didn't come here in the first place instead of being squeezed in at Heather's. It doesn't seem there's anything holding you to Chicago. You don't have a regular job. Ash is in Florida. I don't see a boyfriend in the picture . . . unless there's something you're not telling me. Wait, *is* there a new beau?"

"No. There isn't anyone." It's embarrassing that I'm still nursing my wounds over Daniel's breaking up with me, though it's been months. It's not unreasonable for her to think I might have found someone else in this time. Yet to me, it's as if his side of the bed is still warm. Even though I sold the bed.

"So why not come here? Live rent-free!"

As I have every time she's brought up my moving to Arizona, I hold back the real answer: *Because if I had to live with my parents at thirty-nine years old, especially in the retirement community of Sun City, I would leap from a building.* Instead, I say, "Ash is going to want to come back when he's done. He'll have an easier time getting on his feet if I'm settled here, too."

"Either one of your brothers would also be glad to have you," she presses.

My brothers, Tim and Mike, still live in Wisconsin, where I grew up. They're both married with kids. While I had no doubt they'd shove over one of their offspring to make room for me, I already have a similar arrangement conveniently right here in Chicago at Heather's house.

"Thanks, Mom, but I'm going to give this my best shot." Then I quickly say my good-byes before my mother can come up with any more relatives to pawn me off on.

Niko takes it in stride the following morning when I tell him I don't have anything ready to haul out. He asks me to hand him my phone. When I do, he punches his number into it. "Call me when you need me," he says, tucking the phone into my front pants pocket with a wink.

Huh. If I didn't know better—that is, if he weren't barely out of diapers—I'd say the boy was flirting with me. Perhaps he has a thing for older women who are incompetent at the jobs they've been hired to do. If that's the case—with two days under my belt and only having made the house messier than when I arrived—I must be like a goddess to him.

Minutes later, I'm in the kitchen clearing a spot on the counter to set my lunch when I hear a man's laughter. It's coming from the direction of Marva's office.

*Please don't let it be Will.* This is too soon for him to check up on me. My mind races with excuses I can feed him for why nothing is done yet. Although I did move things around. Maybe he'll buy the old "you have to make a mess to clean a mess" excuse.

A bearded man bustles out to where I'm standing in the kitchen.

"Miss Marva darling!" he calls out when he sees me. "You have company!"

"I'm not company," I say. "I'm here to help clean out the place."

He looks away from me and shouts, "The maid is here!"

For crying out loud—my sweater is cashmere. "I'm not a maid." That's when I notice that he is wearing one of those scrubs shirts with the wacky patterns. I'm assuming medical profession—a nurse or medical technician (as I doubt a doctor would be wearing a cupcakes print). "I'm here to see Marva, but . . . is she okay?"

"Yep. Give us a few more minutes. I'm fixing her up with an IV drip." He pulls a face as he looks around him. "She says there's bottled water in the fridge. I'm afraid to look in there if it's anything like the rest of this place."

I find myself strangely defensive of Marva. "The refrigerator's fine. The house only recently got this way, and that's because we're organizing. Sometimes you have to make a mess to clean a mess."

Maybe I will use the line on Will because this guy seems to accept it. He heads to the refrigerator and opens it. "You're right, not bad. By the way, I'm Nelson." He shuts the refrigerator door. "I'll be popping in for the next few days."

"I'm Lucy, the professional organizer. Obviously, I'll be here a while. So why does Marva need an IV?"

"Sorry, that's information for family only."

"I'm working closely with her. If she's sick, I need to be aware of her limitations," I say, hoping that whatever those might be, they don't slow her pace even further. "I don't want to strain her."

He regards me as a bouncer might a pimply teen proffering a shady-looking driver's license, but eventually says, "It's a mild infection, but a persistent one. Not uncommon in people with diabetes. We've got her hooked up with antibiotics. The good news is, she'll be able to move about"—he gives another look around the house for effect—"or at least try to." He screws the cap off the water and heads toward the hall that leads to Marva's office. "Back in a jiffy!"

When Marva and Nelson emerge a few minutes later, she's walking with a cane in one hand and pulling an IV pole on wheels with the other. She's wearing a silky poncho and slacks, full face of makeup as always. That astounds me. When I'm sick, I tend to look as lousy as I feel.

Nelson gives Marva instructions on how and when to remove the IV, then he's on his way. It seems overly intimate for me to be hearing her medical instructions. It occurs to me for the first time how exposed Marva must feel. Her house and her possessions and her hoarding habit and even her health problems are splayed open for me to see. Whereas I haven't had to reveal anything, not that she'd care to know.

"Are you up for getting started?" I ask. "We can do the mudroom first since there's that nice big chair in there."

She harrumphs, which I interpret as a yes, not taking offense. I'd be cranky, too, if I had an IV port buried in my arm.

The mudroom is a few steps from where we're standing in the kitchen. With anyone else, I'd wheel the IV pole. I have a hunch I'll find it skewered through my gut if I so much as offer.

We walk over, and before she sits, Marva says, "You seem relatively intelligent. Think you can handle remembering what I'd said I wanted to keep or dispose of yesterday?"

"Sure," I say, giving her a pass on the *relatively*.

"Take care of it. I have other things to do."

Yeehaw and hallelujah. I'm thrilled I'll be able to work in peace. I don't let it bother me that it's a total waste of time that she's now trusting me to redo what she made me *undo* because she didn't trust me.

Without having to wait for Marva to debate every decision, I'm finished so fast that I treat myself to a salad at a deli up the street. I can eat the peanut-butter sandwich I'd brought with me for dinner instead.

When I get back, Marva is ready to work, which means I have to slow my pace to hers. It's like that sound of a screeching halt they always play in TV shows—*eeeeeeerch*—as Marva says, "I wonder what's in this drawer here." Next thing I know, we're sitting next to

each other on dining room chairs I swept free of piles. She's painstak-
ingly taking out each item from the cabinet drawer and reflecting
on it. "This kachina doll . . . I believe it's from the Hopi tribe . . .
or Zuni . . ." She's talking to herself more than to me, but I "mmm-
hmm" her and tease it from her hands as quickly as I can. The sun
sets and then rises again, and then days turn into weeks, months into
years, as we make our way through that one drawer.

I'm getting antsy as I wait for her to thumb through a bound
manuscript she's found. When she closes it, I see it's the screenplay
for the movie *Pulp Fiction*. There's an autograph scrawled across the
front that appears to be Quentin Tarantino's.

"That was a great movie," I say.

She grimaces. "He's so pompous, as if I'd want his signature. Do
be a dear, will you, and put this in the theater room?" She says the
word like the*atah*.

"The theater room?" There's only one room I haven't yet seen,
and that's Marva's bedroom—must be one and the same.

"One door past the office."

Glad for the chance to stretch my legs, I head down the hall that
leads to her office. There are only three doors: her office, a bathroom,
and what I'd assumed was her bedroom but must be the mystery theater room.

I struggle to push open the door. It's catching on a life-size golden
Oscar statue on the other side of it. Nudging it out of the way, I flick
on the light.

This is obviously the master bedroom. A bed shoved up against
the far wall is cleared off enough to be currently in use, and clothes
are strewn everywhere. But I can see why Marva refers to this as the
theater room. It's packed with movie posters and memorabilia and
thousands of DVDs and VHS tapes. There's a path from the bed to a
large-screen TV in front of a bank of vintage red velvet theater chairs.

He would love this room.

He'd go absolutely nuts in here.

Annoyed, I chase the thoughts from my head, but it's too late.

That's the problem: Most of the time I'm braced for missing Ash. So I'm on constant heightened alert for anything that might remind me of him.

But this isn't about Ash.

It's about Daniel.

Looking about the room, I find that the sadness isn't hitting me so much head-on as it is creeping up my legs, tendrils spreading over me. It devours me slowly, lazily, like those evil plants in *Invasion of the Body Snatchers*—a movie that Daniel has made me watch about five thousand times because it's his favorite.

Seven months ago now Daniel dumped me. I once read that for every year you're in a relationship, it takes half a year to get over it. So it looks like I have a couple years to go.

I met Daniel when I was working as a copywriter for McMillan Advertising and PR downtown. I'd been there two years when he was hired as a graphic designer. Only about forty of us were there. Normally there'd be quite a bit of speculation among the women about a new guy who was single and in his thirties. But we were all busy nursing wild crushes on the company vice president, Buck Henson. Buck had those sort of chiseled good looks that walked into a room before he did, and the charm that made it clear when he talked to you, you were the only woman in the world—even if five other flush-faced females next to you were feeling the exact same way. So in came Daniel Kapinski—kind of skinny, baby-faced, with a tendency to walk hands in pockets and slightly leaning back, as if always being blown by a strong wind.

He wasn't the sort you noticed.

But *I* noticed him. Though not right away. Not until we were thrown together on a project. I remember sitting with him at his Mac, going over drafts of an annual report. He'd been at McMillan only a couple months, but he'd already amassed such a ridiculous collection of toys and figurines there wasn't much desk space for anything else.

"You want to move Malibu Barbie there so I can put my folder down?" I said.

"That, I'll have you know, is an action figure of Brandon Lee in his role in *The Crow*. He was killed during filming by a faulty popgun. It's quite valuable. Great film."

"Never saw it. And this is lovely." I picked up a bloody, knife-wielding baby doll perched on the edge of the desk.

"Chucky, from *Bride of Chucky*. Sadly, not Chucky in *Child's Play 3*, which are harder to come by."

He took the doll from me and set it back in its place. Then he picked up a felt bowler hat and set it on my head.

"Don't tell me," I said. "The hat is from *Mary Poppins*."

"A *Clockwork Orange*. Just a replica though. Looks good on you." He smiled at me. Not Buck Henson's dazzling smile. More boyish. A sweet overbite.

"I never saw that one either. You know what else I've never seen? A James Bond movie, or *Rocky*, or"—I tried to list off the manliest films I could—"or any of the *Godfather* movies."

He faked being stabbed in the chest. "You're killing me here. Seriously. We need to work on your film education. I can't continue to work creatively with someone who has never seen James Bond. There must be some sort of HR policy protecting me from that."

What can I say? I was smitten.

We slipped so easily into dating I barely noticed that we were—except that eventually we started having sex. That I *definitely* noticed. Then Daniel started saying crazy things like "I've never felt this way about anybody before." I started doing crazy things like letting him store his collection of vintage movie posters under my bed—even though I *hate* having stuff under my bed.

We'd been at it for months when he said, "So, when am I going to meet this kid of yours?"

"Huh?"

"Ash? The son you claim to have? Eighth grade? Rumored to dislike pizza but love Lucky Charms cereal? Surely you've noticed him there in your house."

"I was wondering who that was."

"Seriously," Daniel said, "don't you think it's time you introduced us?"

In truth, I'd been stalling. One doesn't casually parade men in front of a boy whose own father all but abandoned him. I didn't want to see Ash get hurt again. "At some point," I said.

"Luce, I'm tired of sneaking around like a couple of horny teenagers trying not to get caught. I'll admit it was kind of hot at first. But it's getting old." He held my face in his hands the way they do in corny romance movies. "I'd like to meet the most important man in your life. I promise I won't embarrass you."

"I never thought you would."

"He doesn't even have to call me Dad on the first date. *Sir* is fine. Or maybe *Your Eminence*."

I gave in—how could I not? After a brief discussion, we decided some wholesome family fun such as putt-putt golf or a movie would be a nice, low-pressure way for them to meet.

Only, as luck would have it, the three of us had a chance to get together before that. It was a Friday, when Ash was spending the night at a friend's. Daniel and I, taking advantage of the empty house, were engaging in some fun of our own. Of the not-so-wholesome variety.

"Did you hear something?" I said, propping myself up on my elbows in the bed.

Daniel, busy kissing his way down my naked belly, impatiently tugging my panties down, gave a response along the lines of "Hmmph?"

"I heard a noise. Like a banging."

"Yeah?" He didn't break stride—we were almost fully naked and sex between us was still too new to worry about things such as noises . . . or banging . . . or bedroom doors bursting open or—

With the reflexes of a ninja, I yanked a blanket over us.

"Hey, Mom, do you know where the—" Ash stopped, hand on the doorknob. "What the . . . ?"

"You ever hear of knocking?" I snapped.

Daniel, his face inches from mine, mouthed, *Fuck*, which I'm sure accurately completed Ash's sentence.

"Oh, *gross*," Ash said in utter disgust, piecing together that two heads and four feet peeking out from his mother's blanket was about as cringe-worthy as it gets.

"Go," I said firmly, gathering my wits enough to take action. "I'll be out in a minute."

With only a grunt of contempt, Ash left. I fished around under the covers for my bra, as if, if I got dressed fast enough, this would never have happened.

"That's not the first impression I was going for," Daniel said. "I don't think he saw anything, though. You were pretty swift with the blanket. I had no idea you could move that fast. Impressive."

"It's not funny, Daniel. He saw his mother having sex. With a *stranger*."

"Technically, we weren't having sex. That was foreplay. If it were sex, we would have been—"

"Stop it!"

He stopped. "I'm sorry. What do you want me to do?"

"Just . . . I have to think." As we pulled on our clothes, I reeled with regret. Here was a guy I was falling for—but this just blew it. It was over. Ash would never want to have anything to do with Daniel after meeting him in such an awful way. As much as it might hurt, I had to respect that. Ash came first. "Let me go out and talk to him, okay?"

"Whatever you want," Daniel said, tugging his T-shirt over his head.

I finished getting dressed, then went to find Ash. He was in his room playing a video game.

"I'm sorry you walked in on that. I didn't expect you home."

He didn't glance up from his game. "Jordan's dad dropped me off—he forgot they had to go to his grandma's tonight."

"It was probably pretty upsetting to walk in and see me with a man, especially one you've never met. Especially one that's not your dad."

"Reeeeeally don't want to talk about it." His thumbs flew over the controller, his attention on the monitor. I could see the muscles in his jaw tighten, reminding me of how he was on the cusp of being a man, even though he was still my baby.

"Sweetie, we need to talk about it."

"Noooooooooo, we don't."

I was searching for the words to make this less—well, icky—when Daniel walked in the room. "Hey, I'm going to go out on a limb and assume you're Ash."

"Yeah."

"I'm Daniel. I'm your mom's boyfriend."

"Okay."

"I've been wanting to meet you. She talks about you all the time."

"Mmm-hmm." Ash didn't so much as glance up.

"Here's the deal. I love your mom. I'm crazy stupid in love with her. Like I can't believe I'm so lucky to have her in my life, so I hope to hang around." Daniel leaned against the doorframe, hands in his pockets. "You up for putt-putt golf? I'm thinking—and I say this man-to-man—that there could be an ass-whooping in store for you."

For a moment, there was nothing but the clackity-clack of thumbs on a controller. Then Ash said, "You *think*."

"What? You got skills?"

"Mad skills."

Throughout a game of miniature golf that I found utterly exasperating—they'd devised a scorekeeping system that rewarded banking the ball rather than getting it in the hole—I found myself pondering less what Ash may have seen and more what Daniel had said.

He'd never before told me he loved me. He was *crazy* about me. I was so *beautiful*. So *amazing*. So *lovable*. But never *I love you*.

By the time he dropped Ash and me off at home, I'd assumed that by unspoken agreement we were sweeping the earlier part of the evening forever from our memories. "Thanks," I said, opening my car door to get out. "That was fun."

Ash was already halfway up the front walk, but took a few strides backward to say, "Daniel, you coming in?"

"Nah." Daniel leaned over so he could see Ash through the open passenger door. "I'm going to go home and practice working a door lock. In the meantime, maybe your mom can sign you up for knocking lessons. I believe we can make this work."

Ash laughed and then trotted the rest of the way into the house.

I turned to Daniel. "Despite an absolutely mortifying start, I think he likes you."

"Good. I like him, too." Daniel brushed a strand of my hair back from my face. "And I love his mom."

Smiling, I pulled him toward me in a kiss. "She loves you, too."


Daniel and I didn't start living together right away. His spare toothbrush moved in first. Then the brand of shampoo he likes. Followed by enough clothes that I had to designate a drawer, then part of the closet. Then came the bike. Within a year he followed his stuff and gave up his old apartment.

We were already entrenched by the time I realized my mistake.

I'd let myself picture us as a family—the three of us.

Daniel, for his part, conspired in the lie: having the occasional "boys' night out" with Ash, seeming as relaxed with my son around as he did when it was he and I alone.

That's why it hurt so badly when Daniel eventually issued the ultimatum. When he said, "I can't take living here with Ash anymore. His drug problem is more than I can deal with. You have to choose— it's either him or me." He couldn't have cut me any deeper.

I chose my son. Of course I chose my son.

# chapter four

Owning a library of beautifully bound books doesn't make you a well-read person. You have to read them.

*—Things Are Not People*

After a weekend of hanging out with Heather's family, I'm glad to get back to work Monday. I'm exhausted. Ash was into LEGOs as a kid, whereas Abigail is all about imaginary play—and, may I add, bossily so. ("No, Aunt Lucy, you have to wear the pink. The pink! The *pink!*") Still, I gave it my all playing with her, and I insisted on babysitting so Heather and Hank could go on a date Saturday night. They've been so generous letting me stay with them. I do what I can to pitch in.

The morning is pleasantly sunny and warm. I've talked Marva into having her cigarette on the front porch so I can drag boxes out to present her choices to her there. Not exactly efficient, but I want to keep this job moving. If that means letting Marva sit like the queen while I bow before her, so be it.

"It's a heavy one," I say, sliding a box in front of her and opening the flaps.

Hmm. Books, mostly of the coffee-table variety I notice as I sift through the box. "Yard sale?" I ask hopefully, gesturing as if I'm moving the box as a whole to the side.

She gives me a withering look.

I stifle a groan. Book by book it is.

It's soon apparent the challenge I'm facing. Tucked in with books that could go for a dollar each at a yard sale are signed first editions. There's an art-house book on the history of the Barbie doll marked $500 retail. (Even I get sucked into sitting down and thumbing through that one.) There's also a brooch, one earring, and a $50 bill.

It's going to be like this through the whole house. Treasures mixed in with trash. I can't simply chuck a box into the bin unless I want to accidentally throw away a Picasso.

I start to panic at the thought of touching each and every object in Marva's house—of knowing that I'll eventually open the box or drawer or closet that contains the earring that matches the first one I found. That's how thorough I need to be. I'm not just looking for a needle in the haystack.

I'm also sorting the hay.

Will pulls in behind me when I arrive Tuesday morning. "Stopping by to give you your paycheck and see how things are going," he says, as we let ourselves in through the front door.

I wait nervously for his reaction. It's been a week, and even I have to admit the progress is less than spectacular.

"Is anything gone?" he says, gazing around the room. "In fact, is it worse? Did the two of you spend the week shopping?"

*Yeah, and then we got our nails done and had lunch at the Ritz.* I swear, he's such a jerk. "The mudroom is completely finished," I say, trying not to sound as peeved as I am, and not entirely succeeding.

I hear humming off the kitchen, coming from the laundry room.

I head over with Will to see that there's a woman in there, stuffing clothes into the washing machine—which means she had to have spent at least ten minutes moving boxes to get to it. "Finally, the housekeeper!" I say to Will. "I haven't had a chance to meet her yet." Although she comes by every day to deliver Marva's meals, she's in with the food and out with the previous day's containers before I show up in the mornings.

"She cleans Tuesdays," Will says, thumbing through a stack of mail on the countertop. "Name's Mei-Hua. Been with the family forever."

Mei-Hua glances up and nods in our direction. She can't be more than four feet seven, and while I can tell she's older than me, she could be anywhere between fifty and ninety. The massive 1970s-era headphones and oversize glasses she's wearing make her look more like a giant bug than a tiny lady.

"Hi!" I call out, giving a wave. "I'm Lucy! Nice to meet you! I've been hired to clear out the house, so I guess you and I will need to chat! So we can coordinate on what needs to be cleaned once it's emptied!"

She shakes her head and points at the headphones, so as to indicate she can't hear me.

Oh, for crying out loud. Are they nailed to her head? She can't take them off for a second? I'm obviously talking here! It's bad enough my own son ignores me—still no call, no letter—and now I don't even qualify for common courtesy from the housekeeper?

Will chuckles, clearly amused by my being snubbed, although he doesn't glance up from the mail.

"I'll discuss it with her later," I say with great authority in my voice. "I don't want to disrupt her work."

"Good idea. Seems you've got enough work of your own to worry about."

*Jerk.*

Over the next several days, Marva and I establish a routine. She goes where she wants and does what she wants. I follow her around like a spurned lover begging for attention. It's chipping at what little dignity I have left, but I don't have any better ideas.

It seems to be working at least. By Thursday afternoon, I feel I've done enough to bring Niko in.

"That's great!" he says when I call him. I'm in the bungalow, taking a break to catch up on calls and eat the sandwich and Fritos I packed for lunch—which I'd been looking forward to until I saw the shepherd's pie Marva was warming up for hers.

"Not your whole crew," I say. "You and one other guy with a truck. A small truck."

"I knew you could do it." He's so excited for me, I allow myself to feel a tinge of pride, and, hmm, perhaps even the vague stirrings of a crush. It's rather refreshing to have a man seem to think I'm doing everything right.

Before I make my next call, I have to take a few deep breaths. I chug a glass of water. I use the bathroom. I freshen my lipstick, brush my hair, and clean out my purse. Then I hurriedly press the number stored on my phone before I can come up with any other ways to stall.

When the receptionist answers, I ask for Dr. Paul. "Hold on while I transfer you," she says. There's no soothing music while I wait. Just an occasional beep, beep, beep that informs me I'm still on the line.

"Dr. Paul," he answers, his voice, as always, slightly raspy. I've never met him in person, but I read his profile on the Willows' website. He's quite young. Nonetheless, I picture Sigmund Freud when I'm talking to him.

"Hi, this is Lucy Bloom. Ash's mom? I'm calling to see how Ash is doing. And if he got my letter? Since he hasn't responded, maybe he never got it?"

"Ah, yes, the letter." He hesitates. I imagine him thoughtfully stroking his beard. "I gave it to him in our last session."

When Dr. Paul doesn't elaborate—probably writing on his pad the way the therapists always do on TV—I give him a prod. "So what did he say?"

"He chose not to read it. But don't worry. That doesn't mean—"

"He didn't read it?" I flop back on the couch. It's as if someone let the air out of me. It's all I can do to keep the phone to my ear, I'm so deflated.

"Not yet . . . no."

"It was only one page. How much must he hate me to not bother reading it?" I picture Ash glancing at the envelope, seeing my hand-writing on the outside, and sneering. Hating the cream-colored statio-nery I used. Hating the swirls of my penmanship and the way I folded the paper into three parts. Hating me.

"It's not that he didn't bother. And he doesn't hate you."

"Then why is he writing to some girl, but he won't even open a letter from his own mother? What did he say when you gave it to him?"

"I can't tell you what Ash and I discuss in therapy. But . . ." I hear him sigh. The sigh is a good thing. It means he's about to violate the therapists' code of confidentiality or whatever it is they swear to and spill dirt. I sit back up. "He was afraid you were going to be angry. Even when I told him it was a friendly letter—and that I was here to help him if anything you wrote bothered him—he said he didn't want to deal with it."

"He said that? He doesn't want to *deal* with me?"

"*It.* He didn't want to deal with *it.* The letter."

"Same thing," I say morosely.

I suppose in some ways I can't blame Ash for his avoidance. The last time he had a letter from me, it was the one I read to him at his intervention. That letter wasn't quite so upbeat—it wasn't supposed to be.

I'd worked on it for days, following the instructions e-mailed to me by the interventionist I'd hired (and I suspect if I'd done the num-ber of rewrites on my book that I did on that one letter, I'd probably have had a bestseller). The first part of the letter was easy enough, where I was to confront Ash with the ways his drug habit was affecting both him and me. It felt downright cathartic to scribble down how the fallout from his drug use had progressed—from his dropping out of classes at the community college to lately where I didn't dare leave the house for fear he'd be in trouble and need me.

But the part of the letter where I was supposed to let Ash know what he means to me had me stuck for the longest time. Maybe it was because I was actually sitting on a chair looking at Ash passed out on the couch as I wrote it. The grief settled into my bones so deep it felt as if I were penning his eulogy. As if I were being visited by the ghosts of Ashes past as I remembered little moments . . . how he'd build these intricate waterways for hours in the sandbox in our backyard . . . the sheer joy on his face the first time he mastered a two-wheeler bike . . . his determination to learn to make the perfect grilled cheese sandwich . . . the time he unself-consciously hugged me good-bye in front of all his friends before leaving for the eighth-grade overnight trip.

None of those by itself seemed significant enough to compete with the pull that the drugs had on him, but they mattered to me. All those little things made Ash . . . well, *Ash*. Maybe not needed by the world because he's sure to grow up and, say, discover a cure for cancer, but needed by me. Just to be my son.

Eventually I wrote about when our car hydroplaned off the highway on a road trip to Wisconsin. Stuck in the mud and shaken up, we spent a night curled up in clothes we pulled from the suitcase, playing cards by flashlight and eating the popcorn I'd brought to give as gifts. After we were towed the next morning, Ash excitedly proclaimed it our best vacation ever. Yet as I read the story aloud to a nine-years-older Ash at the intervention—wiping my eyes so I could see the words on the paper I held—it didn't seem to be stirring the same emotion in him as it was in me. Nothing had so far, and I was starting to worry that the intervention was a failure. I was too late.

"And so, here is what I will no longer do as long as you continue to do drugs," I said, moving on to the last section of the letter or—as I secretly thought of it—the giant pack of lies I probably couldn't actually follow through on if put to the test. "I'm not going to give you money anymore. And you can't live here with me. Not if you're using—and I mean anything. Pills. Marijuana. Anything."

Ash didn't flinch, just kept staring off sullenly at the wall, and I wondered if he had the same doubts about my resolve as I did — although I hadn't yet dropped the bomb on him. The part that *was* true.

"And I've sold the house."

That got his attention. He looked over at me for the first time. "You said you were only putting up the FOR SALE sign to test the market."

I didn't trust myself to improvise a response, so I just kept reading off the details of how the house was now in escrow and I'd soon be moving to a place that wasn't big enough for him. If he wanted somewhere to live, he'd need to go to the Willows.

There's a paper-rustling sound, and I am so deep in my thoughts I think at first I'm still clutching my intervention letter in my shaking hands. Then I realize it's Dr. Paul on the other end of the phone line. He clears his throat. "I know it's frustrating, Lucy. I'm going to ask you to give Ash time. It's only been, what, five weeks now? He's done excellent work since he's gotten here, but he has a ways to go."

"I don't get it. Before he left, as awful as it was, at least he would *talk* to me."

"Therapy stirs up all kinds of emotions. It takes a while to sort them out. So things often have to get uglier before they can get better."

As soon as he says the words, I totally get it. It's the therapeutic equivalent of "you have to make a mess to clean a mess." The man is finally speaking my language. I want to crawl through the phone and hug him.

After we wind up the call, I pull out the photo of Ash I carry in my wallet. I dig a straight pin from the mini sewing kit I keep in my purse and tack the photo to the wall.

It's my inspiration. It's the reason I'm doing everything I'm doing right now. It's how I put one foot in front of the other — and why I'm not going to let Marva bother me, no matter what she says or does.

▪ ▪ ▪

I had a dozen of these candelabras, and now there are ten," snaps Marva, leaning against the kitchen countertop. "They were right here. You threw them away, didn't you?"

Ugh. It's been days of this. Two weeks down, and I have little to show for it—which Will was quick to point out when he stopped by again.

"Marva, I did not throw away your candelabras. Either the others are here in the house, or you don't have as many as you thought."

She gives me a suspicious once-over, as if the moment her back is turned, I'm going to whip out two candelabras from where I've hidden them in my bra. "I know they're here." I'm twitchy and irritable at this point—and it's not merely due to Marva's rudeness. Because she's willing to work only in fits and starts, I'm here from nine in the morning until ten at night. If in that time I get in a few hours' work, I'm lucky. I'm worn-out from the boredom and from the low-grade stress eating away at me that the job is not moving as fast as it needs to be. I have no idea what that woman does all day. But I do know that for someone who is supposed to be a brilliant artist, she sure isn't creating any art. I have yet to uncover so much as a single tube of paint.

The front doorbell rings. "I'll get it," I say, grateful for the excuse to step away from Marva for a moment.

I open the door to a UPS deliveryman. Next to him are three large boxes. "Delivery. Sign here." He holds a signature pad out to me. I see him peeking in at the mess in the house. I block his view with my body.

"Marva, are you expecting packages?" I ask. "Is it okay if I sign?"

She's wiping her hands on a napkin and hustling over. "Yes, sign." For a moment she looks like a different person, and I realize it's because she's happy.

"What are they?" I ask as the UPS man walks away.

Marva calls to Niko out front. He's leaning against the bed of his truck, enjoying the sunshine since he doesn't really have anything else to do. "You there. Help bring this inside."

He jumps up and trots over. "Looking pretty crowded in there," he says, peering into the living room. "How about I put them in the mudroom instead?"

My heart sinks. My beautiful clean mudroom.

Marva nods, and Niko grabs a dolly from his truck. Marva trails after him, fussing at him to be careful as he wheels the boxes around back to the mudroom.

Once the boxes are set on the floor, I press Marva. "So what's in them?"

Instead of answering me, she kneels down and starts sawing at the packing tape on one of the boxes with a butcher knife. Then she yanks open the flaps, sending packing peanuts flying.

She gives a grunt of effort as she tries to wrestle out a large object.

"Let me get that for you." Niko lifts out what appears to be a glass bowl easily two feet in diameter—although it's hard to tell since it's so thoroughly wrapped in Bubble Wrap. He sets it on the floor.

"You bought a bowl?" I ask.

"Three of them," Marva says. "They're by Dale Chihuly—I've always meant to buy some of his pieces. He's amazing. Truly changing the way people think about blown glass." She snaps her fingers at Niko. "Scissors. I need a scissors."

Niko goes to the kitchen and starts digging through drawers.

I can only stand there. Stunned. Flabbergasted. My head is lifting off my shoulders . . . it's floating around the room . . . and now it's exploding into a thousand tiny fragments. *She bought stuff? I'm killing myself trying to clear out her house and she's bringing new stuff in?* "This is un . . . un . . . believable," I stammer.

Marva is picking at the tape with her fingers. "I know. These were too stunning to pass up. They're bowls within bowls. So innovative."

"What the . . . ," I say. "What on *earth* are you doing . . . *shopping* . . ."

"I realize I'm downsizing. But sometimes a woman has to splurge." She points to where Niko is holding the scissors he found toward me. "Be a dear. Pass me those."

I grab the scissors and toss them on the floor, away from Marva.

"What is the point of my being here? Why bring me in if you're going to . . . to . . . sabotage everything!"

"Heavens, it's a couple bowls. There's no need to get hysterical."

"I am not hysterical!" I notice Niko taking a cautious step back, away from the crazy lady, but I don't care. For once, I'm going to stand up for myself. "And for the record, it's not a couple bowls. A couple is two. This is three. That's a *few*. And they're big. And the entire point is that you can't—"

"You are not honestly about to tell me what I can and cannot do."

"Isn't that what you hired me for? Because you needed an expert to help you get your home organized?"

"Please. How *expert* does anyone need to be to throw things in a trash can. A trained monkey could do the job." She hoists herself up from her knees, casually brushing Styrofoam peanuts off her clothes. "At least a monkey would have been entertaining."

That's it. I'm done.

I'm done with her meanness, and her condescending attitude . . . and her plain insane hoarding. There's no getting through to her. She has no real intention of clearing out this house. I'm wasting my time.

"You're right. You don't need me. Good luck." With that, I turn on my heel and walk out.

Crap. My purse.

I head back in, grab it, and head out again. On my way, I stop at the bungalow for the blow-up exercise ball I'd borrowed from Heather so I could do ab exercises in my downtime, which I haven't, but now I never will. Oh, and my stapler. And coffee mug.

I'm shoving the ball into the back of my car when Niko ambles up. He flips the front seat up so the ball goes flying into the car. I stumble on top of it.

"Thank you," I say, getting up and smoothing down my shirt.

"You're not quitting, are you?"

"As a matter of fact I am."

"C'mon. She's a whack job. Don't let her get to you."

I climb behind the steering wheel and start the car. I'm about to pull away when I remember none of this is Niko's fault. Just because Marva has no manners doesn't mean I don't. "It was nice meeting you," I say, which is true—Niko's been the one nice thing about this place. Then I roll up the window and pull away.

I spend the next two hours driving around. The stereo is cranked so I'm basically a mobile boom box. There's nothing like a little Clash and Talking Heads to work off steam. Feeling the need for speed, I hit the freeway, only to drive smack into rush-hour traffic. I'm practically at a standstill, inching along at barely five miles an hour.

Doesn't matter.

I've got nowhere to be, and no particular time to be there.


It's two days later that I remember I left my photo of Ash pinned to Marva's bungalow wall. It's the only one I have of him. The rest are buried in storage, in a box marked PHOTO ALBUMS AND FRAMES that— according to my checklist of my storage-unit contents—is at the very bottom of everything. Left-hand corner.

So that settles it: I'm going back in to get Ash's photo.

I wait until the afternoon, when Marva usually naps. Cleverly, I park outside her property so my car won't alert anyone to my being here. Niko's truck is in the driveway. I glance around for him. Nope, no sign. I dart behind his truck and then tiptoe up the driveway to the bungalow.

When I step inside, Niko is there, sleeping on the couch. He's lying on his back, a nicely muscled arm flung over his forehead, his lips slightly parted. I have a crazy urge to run my finger over those lips, as if I were Princess Charming deciding if she wanted to awaken the sleeping hottie. Instead I push the door shut behind me.

*Ahem.*

He startles awake. "Oh, hey," he says, sitting up and rubbing his hands over his face. "You're back."

"I'm not back. I'm grabbing something I left behind." I unpin the photo of Ash from the wall.

"I noticed that picture. Your boyfriend?"

"Yeah, right."

"What?" His face is blank. He honestly doesn't see why a teenager couldn't be my boyfriend.

"It's my *son*, thank you, you sicko."

"Serious? Man, you must've had him when you were like five."

"I *was* a child bride," I say coyly. I was twenty when I had Ash, but that still made me younger than most of the other moms I knew. I'd been five months along walking down the aisle. Although Ash wasn't planned and the marriage was a step shy of shotgun, the moment the doctor held my new baby boy up—purple, wide-eyed, and totally pissed off—I was hit by the love truck.

I tuck the photo back into my wallet. "That's all I came for. I'll be off now."

"So you got another job?"

I wince, reflecting back on the fruitless e-mails and calls I'd made yesterday. "Not yet, but I'm sure something will turn up."

I'm about to reach for the doorknob when he says, "She never unpacked the other boxes."

"What? Marva?"

"After you tore out of here, she had me put the one bowl back in the box. Never touched the others."

That surprises me, I'll admit. But it could mean anything. "She probably ordered more of them and is waiting for the rest to arrive."

He shakes his head. "I think she felt bad."

"Oh, please. Marva has no feelings."

"Why don't you talk to her? I'll bet if you—"

"Talk to her? What would possibly be the point? She won't listen to anything I have to say."

"Maybe she won't. Then again she might. Did you ever ask why she bought all those bowls?"

"I don't need to ask. She's certifiably insane. That's why."

"You were doing more than any of the rest of us were able to. At least you got her to throw some things away. Besides"—he comes over to me and casually slides the purse strap back up my arm where it'd slipped—"I'd much rather look at you while I'm working than those ugly cousins of mine."

Is it me, or did the room get a whole lot warmer? I step outside the bungalow, so flustered that I forget I'm supposed to be stealthy. Marva is across the way sitting in the mudroom, having a cigarette. Even though I have to look through the oak trees, windows, and screens to see her, I can tell she notices me. Neither of us makes any sort of gesture of greeting.

Cranky old bag.

There is no way I'm coming crawling back to her.

She can rot in her own filth forever, for all I care.

I'm debating the best way to make my exit—should I strut boldly as if I don't see her, or give a friendly wave first, as if I don't care?—when I see the nurse, Nelson, come into the mudroom from the kitchen. He's dragging the IV pole behind him, chattering on as he bends over Marva and pushes up her sweater sleeve.

Crud.

I can't do it.

As much as my pride wants to, I can't.

I can't leave Marva in this mess.

As I stand here looking at Marva, I think about Ash, and how many people have been handling what I should have been able to do for him—first the interventionist, and now a team of teachers and therapists a thousand miles away. There's nothing I can do right now in regard to him but wait, and hope, leaving me feeling utterly impotent.

Yet before me is someone who desperately needs help, and it so happens this time around I've got the skills required. I can throw stuff away. And, sure, so can a trained monkey, but last time I checked, there aren't any of those here.

I turn to Niko. "Wish me luck." Then I walk up the path to the house and let myself in through the back door.

Nelson grins when he sees me. "Look what the cat dragged in."

I bend down so I can look Marva right in the eyes. "You and me," I say. "We need to talk."

# chapter five

Step one to eliminating clutter from your life is to confront it, scary though that may be.

—Things Are Not People

Have a smoke with me," Marva says after Nelson leaves.

"I don't smoke."

She pulls out a pack and shakes it at me. One cigarette slides forward. "Live a little."

"Really, I'm fine."

"If you're going to insist that I talk"—her lip curls up on the word *talk*—"the least you can do is have a cigarette with me."

I pluck the cigarette from the pack. "Just this once." If this is what it takes, fine. I'd set *myself* on fire if I thought it'd make this job any easier.

Marva lights her cigarette, then hands the lighter to me. It's one of those nondescript metal lighters, the refillable kind. I tuck the cigarette in my mouth and flick the lighter. Flick it again. Nothing. Again. Nothing. I hand it back. "It's broken."

"Have you *ever* had a cigarette?"

"I told you I don't smoke."

"Christ Almighty." She flicks the lighter, then holds the flame out to me. I lean forward and puff enough to ignite the tip. Then I hold the cigarette away from me, so the ashes will fall directly into the ashtray once they burn long enough.

"So, Marva . . . ," I begin, then falter.

I'm not prepared for this impromptu heart-to-heart. I'd only been planning to grab a photo and run, which would certainly have been the easier route. Because if there are some perfect words that will convince Marva that things between us need to change, they're eluding me.

She doesn't seem to notice I'm not talking. She's gazing out at the yard at what appears to be nothing in particular.

I take a puff on the cigarette, stalling.

Marva scowls. "What, are you planning to run for president? *Inhale.*"

I look at the cigarette in my hand. "I thought I was." I try again, this time sucking in. My throat feels as if a comet flew down it.

"So let's hear it. Hit me with the lecture," she says as I sputter out a cough.

I hack and harrumph more until I'm able to speak. "First, I have a question," I finally say. It's the one that's been eating at me. May as well ask it. "Why did you agree to clear out your house if you don't want to?"

"What makes you think I don't want to?"

"Do you?"

"Yes."

"Why?"

She looks at me. "You're asking why I want to clear out my house?"

I nod.

"I would think that would be evident."

"It is to me. It would help me if I could understand why it is to you. No offense, but you let it get this way. And you seem to be fighting pretty hard to keep it this way. I realize you're only cleaning out your house because Will is making you do it, but you still need to—"

"Will is not making me do it." Her voice is hard.

"Well, not *forcing* you"—I smile in an attempt at levity, since what I said apparently chafed her—"but since he's the one who wants the house cleared—"

Marva doesn't let me finish. "You are operating under a misconception, my dear. Will is merely helping move this project forward at my request." My disbelief must show because she adds, "Oh, he drones on about how things have to be done a certain way, but that's an annoyance I'm willing to bear in exchange for his handling—shall we say—the management tasks. It's been quite a while since I've had to hire handymen, and I wasn't eager to do it. When I mentioned to Will my intention to clean the place up, he gladly took the ball and ran with it."

"So you're telling me this actually is all *your* idea."

"That is correct."

Now I'm really stumped. "Then what brought it on? Why now? And why the strict deadline?"

"*Why*—it is the most interesting question one can ask, isn't it?" Her eyes light up. "It may be titillating to learn how a man was murdered, for example—especially if it was particularly gruesome—but *why*. Now that's what drives human existence. The motive!" Marva leans back, crossing her legs and holding her cigarette out in such a way that she reminds me of a 1940s Hollywood starlet, or a drag queen—one that happens to be hooked to an IV. "Will never once wondered why I wanted to organize my home. He was far too eager to get his hands on everything, I suppose. But that's Will. Only concerned with digging through to find what's of value—and by that, I mean what's worth money. If it were up to him, he'd take the fine art, sell it, and then gut the place."

"But it's not up to him, right?" I clarify.

"Oh, it will be his eventually—at least, what I don't choose to donate. But the day will never come when I allow myself to be mentally incompetent enough to put my life—or my possessions—in his hands. Lord only knows what would become of us."

"You don't really believe that, do you?" Will doesn't strike me as Son of the Year, but I think if Marva were to become senile and bedridden, he'd at least hire someone to stop by and flip her over now and again so she wouldn't get bedsores.

"I've never understood that boy." She absently flicks the ashes off her cigarette, half of them missing the ashtray. "I'd been willing to give him the world, quite literally. He traveled so many places with me as a small child, but when he got to be school-aged, he flat out refused. One time, there I was, ready to jet us to Paris—it was fashion week. Imagine the people he'd be exposed to! The atmosphere! And he dug in his heels and said no. I thought perhaps it was because he didn't understand what it was—he was only seven or eight. But, no, he didn't care. He wanted to stay home because he had *a book report due*. A book report! Over fashion week! Ugh, and those team sports he was always insisting on playing." She shakes her head.

Although I can't imagine too many eight-year-old boys choosing fashion week over a sports game, I figure Marva is simply expressing the frustration so many mothers experience in trying to split being a mom with being a person in their own right. "So you had to miss out on a lot," I say, nodding with understanding.

"Goodness no. He stayed with the nanny. But it goes to show that people are going to be what they are. And Will, for reasons I cannot fathom, is wholly determined to be ordinary. Tell me, do you have any children?"

Her question takes me enough by surprise that I don't let my twinge of pity for Will take root. After all, it's the first time that Marva's shown any interest in me, and I'm tempted to glance outside to see if there's a sudden frost on the ground as a result of hell's having frozen over.

"I do," I say. "I have a son. His name's Ash. He's nineteen."

"Off at college?"

I'm about to trot out a lie, but I stop myself. Here I am, practically rifling through this woman's underwear drawers—in fact I will be. It's downright stingy not to reveal something about myself in return. "He's in Florida at a drug rehab."

She nods, as if I said he was attending Harvard Law School. "What's his drug?"

It bothered me when Mary Beth Abernathy asked the same question, but for some reason it doesn't coming from Marva.

"He smoked a lot of pot. But it was mostly the prescription meds that were a problem. OxyContin, benzos . . . at first what he could steal from a medicine cabinet. Then anything he could buy from dealers. Occasionally meth. And then . . . it got pretty bad pretty fast. The guy who checked him in at the rehab called him quite the little pharmacist."

"It was coke in my day. I don't suppose anybody does coke anymore," Marva says wistfully.

I shrug.

"I certainly did my fair share of experimenting," she says. "Possibly someone else's share as well. No regrets about it, though." Her brow furrows. "Well, perhaps one . . ."

When she doesn't say anything else, I ask, "What was that?"

But she shakes her head. "No matter. Now, as for your most interesting question: I suppose it would be quite difficult for you to have this deadline, and yet not be able to move forth as you'd like."

"It is," I say, relieved that she's acknowledging it.

"To be clear up front, I am not going to return the bowls. It's an insult to the artist. However, I can assure you that I won't buy anything further."

"That would be great." While Marva is being so open-minded, I add, "It would also help if you'd let me make decisions on my own. Do presorting. Throw away what's clearly garbage. Use my time productively."

She stubs out her cigarette, then stands, wiping stray ashes off her sweater. "I'll require final approval, but I suppose at this point there's no harm in letting you ready things for me to look at. Now if you'll excuse me, I believe I'd like to rest."

After Marva leaves, I take one last pull on my cigarette, cough, and then bask in the glow of my victory. I didn't let her stomp on me this time! I told her what I wanted, and I got it!

But as I'm sweeping up the ashes from the floor, I realize—with a flush of humiliation—what a fool I am. Marva put up enough smoke and mirrors that I didn't even notice: For all our talking, she never answered why she has such a specific deadline.

Why do I *always* fall for that?

Ash used to do it to me all the time. When he was younger, it was kind of funny, the way he would bob and weave around any questions I might ask. I'd say, "Did you do your homework?" and he'd reply, "Really, Mom, what kind of son would I be if I didn't do my homework?" I'd catch on a few minutes later—force him to the table with his books—and we'd have a chuckle.

As Ash got older, however, it wasn't as funny. I'd say, "Ash, are you high? Were you smoking pot?" He'd snap back, "Why do you always think I'm smoking pot? You're so paranoid." The evasion was there, but also an underlying aggression—a subtle bullying that, I'm ashamed to admit, often worked to make me back off.

By the end, he still didn't answer questions, but there was no trickery about it. "Where have you been all weekend? I was worried sick!" I said after one of the many times he didn't bother coming home for days on end and didn't answer his cell. By this point, his responses were more along the lines of "None of your fucking business." Then he'd disappear into his room. I'd be left to shout through the door, "It is so my business! A door is a privilege, not a right!" Then I'd threaten to remove it from its hinges.

But I never did. Because at least when he was in his room, I knew where he was. He wasn't OD'ing or getting rolled for drugs or money or in any of the other scenarios that ran through my mind and kept me from sleeping at night.

I often wonder if things would have been different if I'd forced the truth from Ash—if I hadn't been so eager to be fooled. So willing to pretend that everything was okay.

I cringe at the memory of the first time I discovered a baggie of marijuana in Ash's room—which I found while rifling through his pockets and drawers while he was at school. Instead of waving it in his face and confronting him with it, I put it back. I knew I was being cowardly, but I wasn't ready for the fight I'd be in for invading his privacy. I figured I'd have a chance to "catch him" without having snooped, when he couldn't get indignant over *how* I found it. He'd be forced to accept his consequences.

"The problem is, teenagers are going to do this sort of thing. It's normal. I did my fair share of partying in high school," I told Daniel later that night while we were cooking a stir-fry for dinner—I chopped, he stirred and fried. "I used to sneak out in the middle of the night. Only my parents didn't have a clue. Sometimes I wish Ash would try harder to hide it."

"But now that you found it, you have to do something," he said.

"Like what? I hate to say it, but it's one tiny baggie of pot. I'm not condoning it, but I don't want to get freaked out about every little thing."

"Tell him you were looking for something he borrowed and you stumbled across it."

"Then what?"

He stared at me incredulously. "Then you take something away from him. Like his iPod or his computer. I'll back you up. You know I will."

I shook my head. "He'd never go for that. He'll get stuck on how I found it."

"He shouldn't get a choice on whether or not you punish him."

I started chopping furiously. "Yep. Everybody's a perfect parent when they don't have kids."

I regretted the words as soon as I said them, even before Daniel muttered, "Luce, that's not fair." He was right—it wasn't fair. I was so lucky to have someone such as Daniel, who seemed to appreciate Ash as he was, right down to my son's sarcastic sense of humor and quirky taste in music and movies. Yet, as grateful as I was, sometimes I couldn't shake my feeling of the need to protect Ash from Daniel. Even the most ordinary dustups that might occur with two men in the same house required me to referee. Daniel would say something perfectly reasonable like "Hey, Ash, you left the light on in the garage all night," and I'd bristle, as if Daniel were attacking me, via my son. As if what he were really saying was *Why couldn't you raise a son who knows how to flip off a light switch?* So when Ash's problems started getting bigger, and Daniel's prodding for me to handle them more direct, truth was, I didn't want to hear it.

Now I wonder if I'd listened to Daniel and cracked down on Ash, kept my eyes open to what was going on, if he'd be in college now, instead of where he is.

Or maybe Marva had a point: They're going to be what they're going to be.

I sigh. As tempting as it is to buy into that, I'm not going to let myself off the hook that easily.

Nor will I let Marva.

I toss the cigarette ashes into a trash can and then head to Marva's bedroom. Her door is open, and I hear the TV. I lean in and say, "Do you have a second? I have a quick question."

She's sitting in a theater chair, having removed the IV, and hits mute on the remote. "I'm afraid you've caught me watching some mindless television—sometimes I can't resist. It's the only vice I have left."

For a woman who only has one vice, she certainly does have a lot of them. "I realize I didn't get an answer earlier," I say. "Why does the job need to be done May fifteenth?"

"I didn't answer?"

"No, you didn't."

"Isn't that funny, I could have sworn I did." She picks up the remote as if she's going to unmute the TV.

I'm done falling for that trick. "Then please be so kind as to tell me again. Why the fifteenth?"

Her hand drops to her lap. "If you must know, I'd like the house to be in order before my birthday."

"Oh! That's wonderful! What a great birthday present to yourself!" Seems hard to believe she'd avoid such a simple answer. "Is the fifteenth your actual birthday?"

"A day before, but I'll need the day to prepare."

"Prepare for what? Are you planning a party?"

"Of sorts." Her mood darkens, and it occurs to me it's probably because she no longer has any friends to invite. Of course she's not planning a party. I've never seen her so much as talk to anyone on the phone, much less have people over. I'm struck with an image of Marva, sitting alone at a table in her otherwise empty house, blowing out a candle on a cupcake. Humming a pitiful rendition of "happy birthday to me." Without even any clutter to keep her company.

Turn here. No, left, left . . . *left.*" Heather gestures wildly to the left, in case Hank is unfamiliar with the word. I'm in the backseat of their sedan—squeezed next to Abigail's empty booster seat, spare blanket, and a pile of toys, books, and snacks. Impressive how that child manages to hog the space even when she's not around.

"Did you hear that, Hank?" I say. "Left? The opposite of right?"

"You ladies need to be nice to me. It's insulting enough I have to go to a baby shower."

"*You're* insulted—how do you think I feel?" I say. "A couples' shower! Do you have any idea how depressing it is to not have a date for a *couples'* shower? Worse, that I *do*—and it's the two of you again?"

"You still mad I didn't bring you a corsage?" Hank says.

Heather twists so she can see me. "It's not a couples' shower. It's simply not a women-only one. There will be plenty of singles there. Besides, it's very sweet after all they went through to get pregnant that Penny's husband gets to attend."

Penny Kramer is actually a friend of mine from where I used to work. She'd been trying for years to get pregnant—which is why I'd introduced her to Heather. It took Heather and Hank ten years to get pregnant with Abigail—several miscarriages, hormone shots, the whole deal. And that was after they'd had DJ without any effort. I knew Heather would be great at offering support, and she was. It's only mildly annoying that now Penny likes her better than she does me.

"So what did we get Penny?" I ask.

"Two blankets," Heather says.

"I picked them out," Hank says.

Heather gives a headshake to indicate, no, he didn't.

I pull my checkbook from my purse. "Thanks for doing the shopping . . . *Hank*. What do I owe you guys?"

"Don't worry about it," Heather says.

"I'd rather handle it now, before I forget."

"We were going to get her this anyway. It was no big deal to add your name to the card."

"I'm not that pathetic! I can afford to pay my share for a gift!"

Heather waves me off. "I don't remember what I spent. We'll figure it out later."

I put my checkbook away, both embarrassed and grateful. Later, when I bring it up again, Heather will make up some ridiculously low number for my "half." It'll be nice when I get that bonus from Marva so I don't have to accept charity anymore. Not that the bonus is a guarantee. Despite our recent chat, things are going as slowly as ever at the house.

When we arrive, a sign with balloons taped to it directs us to the backyard, where heaters are set up beneath a party tent, though it's a mild day.

"By the way," I say as I see the few dozen people already milling around, "if there are any of my old work people here, I never told them about Ash being in rehab."

"So I shouldn't announce it when we walk in?" Hank says from behind the wrapped gift box he's carrying.

"Hold off. I'll be issuing a press release."

Heather bustles off to hug a woman I don't recognize—I'm assuming Penny's sister, who is throwing the shower. Hank leaves to set the gift on a table. I feel that usual tinge of nervousness I get when I first arrive to a party. I glance around for an eight-months-pregnant woman or anyone else I know and, seeing neither, decide a canapé would be lovely. And a drink.

I'm pouring a chardonnay into a clear plastic cup when I hear the two Andreas say, "Lucy! *Omigosh!* It's been forever! You look fantastic!"

Actually, only one of them says it, but it might as well have been both of them at once. They're two women, both named Andrea, both secretaries, and—although they look nothing alike—no one's ever bothered differentiating between them. Someone would say, "Give this to Andrea," and you were free to go to whichever one struck your fancy. (They weren't offended and often got confused themselves. I was once at a group lunch where one of the Andreas launched into a story about the time she'd seen John Cusack walking along Chicago's Magnificent Mile, and the other one said, "That wasn't you that happened to, it was me.")

We air kiss in that jokey way we used to do at the office.

"Are you still at McMillan?" I say. "I'm terrible—I've barely kept in touch with anyone." I realize that Penny is the only one, and that's because of Heather. When Daniel broke up with me, he still worked there, whereas I'd been laid off a year before. I figured loyalty would lean his way.

"Yep, still there," Andrea says. "Although we'll see how long that lasts. They're doing more layoffs. We lost that big underwear account, and now everybody's pointing fingers. It's ugly."

The other Andrea nods. "You got out in the nick of time."

"Is anyone else coming today?" I believe I've pulled off noncha-lance—what I want to ask is *Will Daniel be coming?*

"No, we're the only work people invited," she says, to my relief. "They already had a big to-do for her at the office. We chipped in for a double stroller. Andrea and I got invited today because we had to answer phones while they ate cake and drank punch. As if we cared. It wasn't even spiked."

"So where are you working these days?" Andrea asks. "And are they hiring?"

I'd thought about how I was going to answer this question if it came up. "I'm doing a freelance gig, helping this insanely wealthy woman clear out her house."

"Because of your book!" Andrea says. "I should have you help me with my closets. They're out of control."

I don't want to say more about my job so I ask, "Where's the mom-to-be?"

"She's inside parked on the couch. Her doctor put her on total bed rest." Andrea leans closer. "And she's big . . . as a house. And it ain't all belly."

I'm not about to gossip about the weight of a woman having twins. "I gained fifty pounds when I was pregnant—and I only had the one."

"How is your little boy?"

I take a sip of my wine. I'd hoped to avoid talking about Ash. I brought this one on myself. "Not so little anymore," I say faux-cheerfully. "He's nineteen now."

"How is that possible? Oh, I feel so old. Is he going to school?"

"Uh . . . yeah."

"Where?"

*Well, Pinocchio, you should have seen that question coming.* "Out of state. Tiny school. No one's ever heard of it." I see Heather and Hank standing near a food table and frantically wave them over. "Look! There are my friends! I want you to meet them!"

I do brief introductions when Heather and Hank walk up. Hank doesn't skip a beat working his way through a plate piled with food to grunt a hello.

"I used to work with Andrea and Andrea when I was at McMillan," I say.

Before shoveling another bite of potato salad into his mouth Hank says, "Does Daniel still work there?"

I would shoot him a look that kills, only Heather is already doing it for me.

Andrea asks, "Daniel Kapinski? You know him?"

Hank now looks afraid to answer, but says, "Um . . . yeah. Through Lucy."

"Oh, that's right," Andrea says, and I can see the gears clicking into place. *They dated, he dumped her, and, oh, no, now what do I say?* "He's there, although he was on that underwear account we lost. He could easily get cut." She delivers the last bit like good news and gives me a conspiratorial grin.

Heather takes my arm. "I feel terrible—we haven't said hello to Penny yet. I'm going to steal Lucy here. Nice meeting you two."

That does it. If . . . no, *when* I get my bonus, the first thing I'm going to do is buy Heather an extravagant gift, like a pair of those shoes they're always carrying on about in chick-lit novels. Manolos? "What size shoe do you wear?" I ask Heather as she, Hank, and I head into the house.

"What?"

"Never mind." I'll look in her closet. Organize it while I'm in there.

The next half hour is spent in stress-free bliss, gathered around Penny (who, I have to admit, is shockingly large, to the point of being nearly unrecognizable). We chat about pleasant subjects for a change, such as baby names and breast pumping and dilating and placenta— nothing about me. I'm finally feeling relaxed when Penny's sister comes in to say we're about to open the gifts.

"I'm going to freshen my wine," I say. "Anybody need anything?"

"I'll take a couple more of those chicken wings," Hank says.

Heather shakes her head indicating not only *I don't want anything*, but also *Neither does he*. Hank deflates a bit but shrugs with the acceptance of a man who has high blood pressure and is content to let his wife police it for him.

"Pardon me . . . coming through," I say as I weave among the few people in the kitchen on my way to the yard. I squeeze against a countertop past some guy putting a bag of ice in the freezer.

He shuts the freezer door and turns around.

And I find myself face-to-face—and pretty much belly-to-belly—with Daniel.

"Hey," he says by way of greeting. "Luce, I didn't know you were going to be here."

I wriggle away to put distance between us.

"Hello, Daniel." I could be auditioning for a role in a Jane Austen epic my tone is so formal.

"They asked if I'd bring ice. They were running low."

"Yes, I see that."

He puts his hands in his pockets, which he does when he's nervous. "You look good."

"Thank you. As do you."

He does, too, look good. It's so not fair. Any man who's dumped you should automatically sprout horns and a paunch and go bald and—

"So . . . how is everything going?"

"Fine." I paste on a smile as I plot my getaway. Wine. I was going to get wine. I can't think of anything I'd enjoy more about now. "I was on my way to get something to drink. Excuse me. Lovely seeing you."

My heart is knocking in my chest as I make my way to the coolers outside. Okay. That wasn't so bad. Now it's over with. I'll simply grab my wine, sneak around the side of the house to the living room where Penny is, and then I'll—

"Are you working on another book?"

My heart stops its thumping and sinks to my stomach. Daniel

is next to me, pulling a beer from the cooler. He hands me an open bottle of chardonnay—of course he'd know my beverage of choice.

"I've been busy on a different project," I say, pouring a glass of wine, right to the top.

"What kind of project?"

I attempt to maintain a pleasant expression, but Daniel is doing that annoying thing he does where he looks all *nice* and *open* and *interested* in what I have to say.

"I'm helping this woman clear out her house. It's cluttered. Like insane-hoarder cluttered."

"You'd be great at that. I still line up my shoes in pairs, thanks to your fine teaching."

I'm trying not to picture how his shoes used to be in my closet when one of the Andreas leans between us to grab a Diet Coke.

"Oh, hello, Danny Boy," she says. "Surprised to see you here . . . figured they'd have you chained up at work trying to bring in new business. Since your account bombed out and all." She shoots me a significant look—maybe I was hasty assuming people would side with Daniel after the breakup. I clearly underestimated the bonds of sisterhood and scorned women everywhere.

Daniel takes a swig of his beer. "I'm a man at a baby shower. This is part of my penance."

"Then it's time to head inside for more," Andrea says. "Penny is opening the presents. Andrea and I can show you how to ooh and aah properly."

"There's a technique?" he asks.

Andrea rolls her eyes. "Men."

I'm picking up my wine to go, but Daniel says, "Save us a spot, will you, Andrea? We'll be there in a minute."

After she leaves, Daniel seems to take a great interest in peeling the label off his beer bottle. Finally he says, "How's Ash?"

I feed him my standard line: "He's great."

Daniel's eyes lift to meet mine. "Yeah? I'm glad to hear that." His voice is gentle. "What's he doing these days?"

I desperately want to lie to him—give him the same story about Ash's being away at a tiny college out of state. He'd see through it, though. Then I scold myself. Just because Daniel disapproved of how I handled things with Ash doesn't mean I should feel awkward. The great Eleanor Roosevelt once said that no one can make you feel like a total loser without your permission, or something along those lines, so I need to quit letting him make me feel uncomfortable.

"He's in Florida. At a rehab."

"That's great." Daniel seems genuinely happy at the news. For a second I fear he's going to hug me. He starts forward, and I stiffen, but he just runs a hand through his hair. "I'm so glad for him. It's great. Wow. It's going well, then? Which one is it? How long has he been there?"

This is nothing I want to talk to Daniel about. I take a step toward the house. "I don't want to miss out on the present opening."

"Sure. No problem."

He follows me to the living room, then sits down on the floor with the Andreas. I cram in next to Heather and Hank—a prime location since it's on the other side of the couch. If I lean back, I can't see Daniel over Penny's girth.

We leave as soon as the presents are open—Heather begs out with excuses of babysitting troubles but in reality is bowing to the combined misery of both her husband and me.

Not until we're on the road does Heather say, "I can't believe Daniel had the nerve to show up. Did you talk to him?"

"For a couple minutes. It was no big deal. I'm over it."

I assume that's the end of the subject. We move on to complain about the traffic, and how it shouldn't be allowed to be this bad on a Saturday, when Heather says, "Can I tell you something without you getting upset?"

"I guess so. What?"

"I'm not done being mad at Daniel. I liked the two of you together."

"If it makes you feel any better," Hank says, "his hair is getting thin on top."

It's not true—Daniel has the same wavy, unruly mop as always, and, damn it, it still looked as adorable as ever on him. But I can't say I don't appreciate Hank's effort.

# chapter six

**M**onday morning I'm enjoying watching Niko load the truck—both for the thrill of seeing the progress and the simple fact that he's easy on the eyes—when Will calls.

"Two things," he says, without so much as a hello. "First off, I'm making sure we're set for tomorrow, two o'clock, for when I bring the art expert by for a walk-through. It would be nice," he adds pointedly, "if we could actually *walk through*."

I glance worriedly around. Three weeks' worth of Xs on the calendar and—for all that's been removed—we've barely made a dent. "I'll do the best I can."

"That's what I'm afraid of."

That's rude even for Will. "This is not an easy job."

"If it's too much for you, let me know. There's a place—Organize Me I believe it's called—that submitted a very reasonable bid. Since you were already hired, I've held them off. But . . ." He lets the threat hang there.

Grrr. Organize Me!—yes, exclamation point—is like the National Guard of the organizing world. One phone call and they release a team of professional, snappy organizers that march into your home and whip it into shape. I hate them. They're so cookie-cutter. So overly polished. Plus I interviewed with them and they didn't hire me.

"I didn't say I couldn't do it—only that it isn't easy. That should come as no surprise to you."

"Remember, this man is not aware that Marva is the client. I intend to keep it that way. It's your job to remove any traces of her identity—paperwork, bills, and so on. I've timed it for when she'll be at a doctor's appointment. Which brings me to the second reason for my call. She's got some sort of tooth crisis. I need you to take her to the dentist today."

"Excuse me?"

He must realize he's overstepping, because he says, "Please, could you run Marva to the dentist? She called me to say she's in pain and has scheduled emergency dental surgery. Broke a crown off or something. Root canal. At any rate, I can't get away from work. Her usual nurse isn't available. I suggested a cab but they won't release her to one. Apparently she'll be doped up."

*Why don't you call Organize Me! if they're so great? See if they'll schlep your mother to a dental appointment.* "Today is a very busy day for me," I say, enjoying lording my power over Will for this brief moment. "It's not in my job description, but I *do* want to be flexible. I suppose that's one of the pluses of working with an individual, such as myself, over a faceless agency." Pausing long enough that I hope Will is squirming at least a little on his end, I finally put him out of his misery. "All right, then. I'll take her."

"Thank you," he says grudgingly, as if he's squeezed the words out from the bottom of a tube of toothpaste.

Sorry about that rattling noise," I say to Marva as I drive down Harlem Avenue. "I usually handle it by cranking up the music. Fixes it every time."

Having Marva in my car makes me realize how long it's been since I've given anyone a ride, and suddenly my beloved Mustang's faults spring to light. *Just a few more weeks and I can spruce you right up,* I silently promise, giving the dashboard a little pat of reassurance.

Marva seems unaffected by the rattling, which is accompanied by a clanging as I turn the corner. "I'd rather deal with noise in a car like this that has personality," she says, speaking slowly due to her sore tooth, "than ride in one of those dreadful SUVs." She gives a grunt of annoyance, her gaze on the shops and businesses as we pass. "Another yogurt shop. There must be five of them on every block. How much yogurt do people need to eat?"

It occurs to me how much of this is new to Marva. Even though she's lived here for so long, she's rarely left her home. Rather pitiful, actually. She used to travel the world. Now it's a big deal to go to the dentist.

After I drop her off, it takes two hours for Marva's dental surgery, which I fill with errands. When I get the call to pick her up, I'm at a yogurt shop, indulging in a chocolate frozen yogurt with raspberries (she gave me a wicked craving for it with all of her griping). Hurrying back, I escort her out of the office and quickly come to understand why they wouldn't let her take a cab. She's high as a kite. Goofy. Giggly. "What floor?" Marva asks when we get into the elevator, then apparently finds punching the buttons terribly funny.

"I've got it," I say, deftly blocking her hand with mine. "Don't feel like you have to talk if it hurts."

"Are you kidding? I don't feel a thing! Anywhere!"

It's like corralling a parade of kittens keeping Marva on track to the car, and I'm relieved when we're finally on the road, although tickled. One could assume Ash would have ruined for me any ability to see the humor in someone's acting loopy postsurgery, but I'm able to differentiate between a medical need and an emotional one—if only my problems with Ash had been limited to visits to the dentist.

"Chicago is such a great town," Marva says dreamily on the drive back, clearly seeing the route home more sparkling than on the way there. "You a native?"

"No, came here for college. How about you? How did you end up in Chicago?"

I'm just aiming for casual chat—I figure Marva's not capable of much more than that. But she says, "After the house burned down, this was all I had."

"You had a house burn down?" I'm stunned this has never come up before—but then again, Marva's never been this loose. "When? What happened?"

"It was twenty years ago . . . no, more than that. I was living in San Francisco—it was a terrific Victorian. As I said, I like things with personality, and that house had tons of it. At any rate, there's not much to say. There was a fire. I was away. I lost everything. Of course I didn't have insurance, not in those days. Fortunately, my parents had be . . . be—" She stumbles over the word *bequeathed* . . . tries again . . . and finally continues, "They'd left me the house here in Oak Park when they died. I came with nothing—had to start completely from scratch to re-create a home." She laughs far more gaily than the conversation merits. "You no doubt feel I got carried away."

I'm blown out of my socks. This explains so much—of course Marva can't let go of anything. To lose all she had in a fire—how shocking and life-changing that must have been.

"So your furniture . . . and clothes . . . and, oh, wow . . . any mementos you kept from Will's childhood?"

"Gone."

"Your *paintings*? Everything?"

"I was fortunate as far as that goes. I rented a studio, and I kept most of my own artwork there, along with a few favorite pieces. So those were spared. But, yes, everything else was lost." She closes her eyes. "Everything. Absolutely . . . everything."

Marva sleeps the rest of the short ride home as I try to imagine what it must have felt like for her to walk up to her house to find everything she owned destroyed. No wonder she's so insistent about deciding on each and every item—that choice was stolen from her once. It's not as if the flames held up, say, her midcentury end table and said, "Keep or donate?" They took what they wanted, and I wonder if that's how she sometimes regards me—as a wildfire sweeping through her home, trying to take it all away again.

"I promise I'm just here to make it better," I whisper gently with a wave of sympathy I've never before felt for her. She answers with such a loud, staccato snore that it nearly makes me swerve.

The next morning I get a later start than I'd planned to meet Will at Marva's. Wanting to pitch in wherever I can, I helped Heather prep for the book-club meeting she'll be hosting later. Then I made the mistake, after brushing my teeth, of patting my face with the hand towel in the upstairs bathroom. I hadn't realized Abigail had used it when she was playing with her Little Princess Glitter Gel. The only way to get rid of the sparkles was to remove my makeup entirely and start over.

Lucky for me there's not much traffic at this time of day. I'm zipping along the freeway. I start giving myself a pep talk about how great the day is going to go when I think, Why waste my energy coming up with positive things to say about myself when I can call my mom and make her do it?

I pull out my phone. There's a message on it . . . hmm . . . must've missed a call during the glitter incident.

As soon as I see the area code, my pulse quickens. It's a Florida number.

It's all I can do to stay focused on the road as I pick up my voice mail.

One message. It's from Ash's therapist.

"Hi, Lucy, this is Dr. Paul." I can't get a clue from his voice—it's the same modulated tone it always is. "Nothing to worry about. Everything is fine." The words don't soothe me as much as they should. Why is he calling? He never calls! And—ugh!—could he possibly talk any *slower*? Get to the point! "I have Ash with me. We're on speakerphone. He's here for his session, and he thought he might like to talk to you and say hello. We were hoping you might be there, but it seems we've missed you." There's a rustling sound—although that's possibly my pulse whooshing in my ears—and then Dr. Paul says, "Ash, bud, you want to say hello to your mom?"

There's mumbling . . . I can't quite . . .

Then Ash's voice: "Hey, Mom."

I don't see it coming, but I'm crying. Heaving, rocking sobs slam me with the force of an earthquake. It's as if the tears are being thrust out of me, against my will, and I'm making some sort of a noise, but . . .

Pull over . . . I have to pull over . . . I can't even see . . . I can't . . .

I manage to keep the phone to my ear. There's more hushed talking . . . I can't make out who is saying what, but then Ash says, "Talk to you later. Um . . ."—a long pause, throat clearing, then a reluctant, mumbled "See ya. Bye."

I missed it. Ash called me and I missed it. When the realization hits, I want to cry, but I'm already crying, so maybe I want to throw up.

I'm dialing Dr. Paul back as I veer over two lanes so I can take the first exit ramp. There's a chance it's not too late. The call couldn't have come that long ago.

The receptionist transfers me to Dr. Paul's office, where I get his voice mail. I hang up and try back. "Can you page him?" I plead. "He just called . . . well, I don't know if *just*, but he tried to call me and—"

"Hold on," she says. Again the beep, beep, beep tone. By the time she comes back on the phone, I'm parked at a gas station, gnawing on my fingernails.

"He's in session. It looks like he's booked up the rest of the day. You want his voice mail?"

"Sure," I say dully. "Thank you." I blew it—I missed my son's call. Crushed, I leave a message for Dr. Paul, telling him if Ash is willing to talk to me, he can call anytime. Day or night.

I hang up, but I'm not ready to go anywhere yet. I head inside the store and buy an ICEE. Brain freeze sounds pretty tempting about now. Mascara streaks my face, my eyes are red-rimmed, but the cashier doesn't appear to notice. This is a convenience store—I'm guessing he's seen it all.

When I get back to the car, I call my mom. She answers on the second ring.

Sure, *she* picks up. That's what mothers are supposed to do.

"Mom . . . ?" My voice comes out as a whimper.

"Oh, no, what's wrong?"

As soon as I hear the concern in her voice, the waterworks start again. "Ash finally called, only I missed it. I didn't hear the phone ringing and I missed it."

"I'm sorry. But he'll call back."

"I'm so mad I wasn't there."

Halfway across the country, I can feel her helplessness. "Sweetie, I wish I knew what to say."

But she doesn't have to say a word. It's selfish of me, but I feel better that on her end of the phone, she's aching because I'm aching. She'd probably been having a perfectly pleasant morning, and now she's sucked down into the depths with me. I keep her on the line while I cry, and I'm not sorry about it. Sometimes a girl just needs to unload her stuff on someone.

I manage to repair my makeup—again—but there's no hiding that my tongue is stained blue from the ICEE (plus refill) I downed while sitting in the gas station, playing Ash's message over and over.

Will's car is already in the driveway when I pull up. I feel a surge of panic, but I remind myself I'm not late—he's early. No need to apologize. There's an easy—I check my watch—three minutes before our scheduled meeting.

He's in the kitchen talking on his cell phone when I walk in. The housekeeper, Mei-Hua—who has not yet spoken one word to me—is attempting to scrub the kitchen sink, moving piles out of her way to do so. I give them a quick nod of greeting and then go directly to Marva's office to start hiding evidence of her identity.

"Don't bother, I already did it." Will followed me and is leaning against the doorframe, BlackBerry pasted to his ear, but it's clear he's talking to me, and not to whoever is on the other end. "It was my understanding you were going to—"

"Family emergency," I say. "I'll look upstairs."

"Did it."

"Did you get the—"

He shuts his phone off impatiently and pockets it. "It's done. Look, I expected this to be handled. Jameson Smithson believes he's scoping out the collection of a software millionaire, for whom I am a financial adviser. I intend to keep it that way."

"No problem."

"I don't want a soul knowing how my mother lives."

"Well *I* know," I say, figuring a bit of perspective might be in order. "And there's Niko, and his crew, and Mei-Hua, and yet none of us would ever—"

He waves off my words as if they're gnats. "I'm talking about people who matter. People in art circles. And the media. It would destroy everything I've worked so hard to build."

The doorbell trills, which is lucky because I'm about ready to smack Will. People who matter. Please.

We head through the living room and Will opens the door— which, I note with pride, used to be much harder to do because of all the stuff that was blocking it.

A petite man in a sailor-inspired ensemble holding a clipboard in one hand extends the other to Will. "Jameson Smithson—but everybody calls me Smitty!"

Will shakes his hand and then introduces me with a quick tip of his head and a "This is Lucy." Will's face has that pinched look it gets. This time I'm guessing he's bracing himself. It has to be tough ushering people through your mother's filth, even if you're pretending it has nothing to do with you.

"Splendid old house, this!" Smitty says as he enters. We're forced to stand in a line since there's no room to gather as a group. I'm picking up on Will's stress and am peering around him to gauge Smitty's reaction to the mess. It's not easy to tell. While his voice is boisterous, he's clearly no stranger to Botox—not a wrinkle or crease or sign of life on his face. I start to wonder where Will dug this guy up . . . literally. He's practically *embalmed*.

"And look around me here! It's a veritable treasure hunt!"

That's one way to put it.

"I'd like to just walk you through today," Will says. "Get a feel from you how much of this you'll be taking to auction or on consignment. Lucy here is in charge of selling anything else at an off-site yard sale."

"Tremendous!" Smitty says. "I'm eager to get a peek at the collection. You mentioned there's quite a leaning toward neo-Expressionism?"

"There are several pieces in that genre, yes." Hearing a reference to his mother's style of painting must be hitting too close to home—Will looks positively pained. I almost feel sorry for him.

"Any Ensor? Munch?"

"How about we get started and you can see for yourself," Will says.

He seems at a loss for a moment, so I say, "Let's start upstairs. Then work our way back to the office."

"Yes, right," he says. "Follow me."

As we make our way through the rooms, Smitty mostly mmm-hmms, taking notes on his clipboard. "Eclectic mix . . . ," he says, holding a vase upside down, I assume to look for a signature. "What did you say this fellow does?"

"Software," Will says.

"Really?" Smitty looks skeptical—how many software tycoons collect women's Easter bonnets?

I pipe in, "I believe he inherited a bunch of stuff . . . from a relative."

"Nutty auntie, eh?" Smitty says.

Will goes puce.

I quickly change the topic. "How about those chairs over there?" I point to two white chairs that seem chichi in a retro sort of way.

Smitty wrinkles his nose. "Yard sale."

"Oh, okay." *I* thought they looked cool—must've hung around Daniel too long. He would probably have loved them.

Will excuses himself to make phone calls, and I stay with Smitty.

After about fifteen minutes he says, "Not as much of value here as I'd been led to believe."

"The higher-end merchandise is on the main floor. But you'll be taking everything but yard-sale items, right? So antiques and collectibles and—"

"Shall we see what's downstairs then?"

"I want to be clear. You *do* handle more than fine art, right?"

"Hmm?" he says, already heading down the stairs.

I follow him, annoyed that he's ignoring my question. He's trotting through the house as if he owns the place, giving a friendly wave to Will—still on his phone—as he passes him in the kitchen.

"Aaah," Smitty says when we step into Marva's office. "Here we go." He's scribbling furiously now—poking and turning and touching. "Quite a few Meier Rios's here. I don't suppose he has *Woman, Freshly Tossed?*"

"Don't know."

"*That* I'd be thrilled to handle. Is this the last room?"

"One more." I take him to the theater room. "Here you'll see she . . . er . . . *he* has quite the collection of movie memorabilia."

Another nose wrinkle. "There's not the market for this sort of thing as there used to be. You're better off selling this at your yard sale."

I stare at him, incredulous. "Some of this is worth thousands! I'd never get anything close to that at a yard sale. People are *so* cheap at those things."

Not only that, but Marva would never allow that to happen. She's not going to let go of, say, her genuine James Bond golden prop gun if she thinks some eight-year-old is going to pay $5 so he can play cops and robbers with it.

Smitty crosses over to her shelf and picks up a drumstick signed by Ringo Starr in the manner one might a dead worm. "Why people feel the need to assign so much value to this sort of rubbish is beyond me. I enjoy the Rolling Stones as much as the next person, but do I need a stick with one of their signatures on it to remember their music?"

"Beatles," I mumble.

"Pardon?"

"Nothing. Will you excuse me for a second?"

"Certainly—I'll head back to that last room. I'd like to get a better look-see."

I scurry and find Will in the kitchen, texting. "Will, we have a problem," I say in a low voice.

He lifts his gaze from the phone to me.

"Smitty doesn't know who Ringo Starr is."

"Come now, that's not such a problem." Will opens his eyes wide in exaggeration. "As long as he's familiar with that dreamy Paul Mc-Cartney, we'll be fine."

"No, I mean, he has no clue about movies or pop culture or anything like that. He's only a fine-arts guy. He's not going to handle the collectibles. He insists there's no money in them."

"He'd know."

"But they *are* worth money. I can organize these things, but I don't claim to be an expert as far as pricing them."

Will goes back to texting. "So you figure it out. I'm not bringing anyone new on to this project. It's already out of hand."

"Marva is never going to let go of things that are precious to her if they're going to a yard sale." I harken back to the conversation I had with her, about how Will would practically *give* away her valuables if it worked out in his favor. This is exactly what she feared most.

"Then don't tell her—let her believe it's going up for auction. It's not as if she'll be stopping by the sale."

"You want me to lie to your mother?"

"If that's what it takes to get the job done, then yes."

My jaw drops open.

Will squints at me in disgust. "What's with your tongue?"

B̲y the time I get home, the book club is over and Heather and Hank are in the kitchen. She's wiping the counters and he's digging into leftover cake. "Sorry I missed it. Did you get my message? We ended up going to dinner," I say, which is a test-run for the lying I'll soon be doing. Actually, Smitty left soon after I talked to Will. I waited around for Nelson to bring Marva back from her doctor's appointment, then I put in a couple hours of work. It was better than coming back here. After the day I had, I couldn't face those women.

"You didn't miss anything," Heather says. "We barely talked about the book. And Eleanor McCabe drank too much wine and tried to get a conversation going about if you had to sleep with someone's husband in the book club, who would it be."

"Everyone chose me, naturally," Hank says.

"Naturally," I say. "Who did you choose, Heather?"

"I left to make a pot of coffee."

"Once you've had this sort of perfection," Hank says, patting his chest and sucking in his stomach, "the idea of anything less is almost vulgar."

Heather tosses the cloth in the sink. "How did your meeting go?"

"Fine, although it looks like I'm going to be in charge of more than I thought. The art expert was far too snooty to handle collectibles."

"Collectibles . . . like Beanie Babies?" Heather says.

"More like pop art, and tons of movie memorabilia. And I haven't the faintest idea what's of value."

"You know who knows everything about movies and could—" Hank stops himself. "Never mind."

You can't say Hank doesn't learn.

"You mean Daniel," I say, mentioning the name he knew better than to bring up. "I'm not that desperate."

"Although he certainly owes you," Heather says. "You *should* give him a call. He could go to that woman's house and give you advice. It's the least he could do."

"Thanks, but I'll bet there's all kinds of information online," I say, not telling Heather how tempting her idea sounds.

# chapter seven

As many as fifteen million people, or one in twenty, may be affected by hoarding.

*—Organize Me! website*

I'm deep into that dream I often have where my teeth fall out, so when I hear the noise, it confuses me.

What is—my alarm clock? No, wait. My alarm is more of a *bzzzz*. This is . . . ugh . . . what is that wet—? Abigail. She's climbed down onto the blow-up mattress with me and is drooling onto my clavicle. I ease her off and use the blanket to dry myself. The noise persists. *Bow, bow, wow, chicka bow wow.* It sounds like the music in bad eighties porn movies. It's vaguely familiar—not that I've watched a lot of porn—yet I can't quite . . . hmm . . .

What time is it? Except for the glow of a night-light, it's pitch-dark. And where—?

Finally, my muddled brain wraps around that I'm hearing my ringtone. My phone is ringing. My phone—

I jolt awake as if I've beer-bonged twenty cups of coffee.

Ash! It must be him!

By the time I scramble out of bed and reach my phone, which is charging on Abigail's dresser, the ringing has stopped. MISSED CALL shows on my screen.

When I flip the phone open to return the call, I see it's a local number. One I don't recognize.

It wasn't Ash—of course it isn't him. Why would he call in the middle of the night? Probably a wrong number.

As disappointed as I am, my body remains keyed up, as if it hasn't gotten the message yet from my brain.

The clock on my phone shows 2:24. The phone rings again in my hand.

Not wanting to wake Abigail, I answer in a whisper, "Hello?"

"What color is yard sale? I can't seem to find those little tags. I believe you took them when you went off in that snit last week."

"Marva?"

"I have a stack of quilts here I'm ready to designate for the yard sale, but I don't want you people getting it wrong and throwing them away. And where are the trash bags?"

"It's two o'clock in the morning. And it was not a snit."

"Two o'clock already? Time certainly flies," she says, ignoring the rest of what I'd said. "I'd like to start on my papers. Do you know how to work this shredder? I can't seem to get it to turn on."

"I . . . uh . . . hold on."

I feel my way down the hall to the bathroom, where I close the door before turning on the light. "Marva, it's the middle of the night."

"Yes," she says agreeably. "I find that's when I do my best work."

"I was sleeping."

"Then you're missing out on a lovely evening. Did you see that moon? Huge!" I'm struggling to find the words to express to her how inappropriate it is to call me like this when she adds, "You'll be pleased to learn that the duck statue is gone. I didn't care for the way it was staring at me from the shadows."

Interesting. Middle-of-the-night Marva seems to be more willing to let go than daytime Marva. And friendlier, too. It occurs to me: Here I am, awake. Why not go take advantage of the situation?

"I'll be there in half an hour."

When I get there, she's in her office. She's standing, hand on her chin, studying an Impressionist painting that is propped against a bookshelf. It feels strange—Marva and I are almost never entirely alone. Between Niko and his crew, the housekeeper, Nelson, and even Will's occasional pop-ins, it always felt as if I were reporting in to a workplace. This has the hushed intimacy of intruding on someone's home in the wee hours, which it basically is.

"That's pretty. Is it for the auction?" I say, pulling out the bag of supplies I took home the other day.

"This painting? Lord, no. It's atrocious. I don't even want it in the yard sale. I'd be afraid someone might buy it and hang it in their home."

"If it's so awful, why do you have it?"

"The frame. It's quite rare. I believe I paid ten thousand for it way back when."

See, this is why I could never do this job behind Marva's back. I'd have kept the painting and tossed the frame. It's a gold, ornate monstrosity that looks as if it belongs in a whorehouse.

By the time Marva calls the next night, I'm not so jumpy. Dr. Paul and I have already spoken. Ash and I are scheduled for a phone call during his next session, which to my frustration is a week away. So when the phone rings, I don't have any false hopes. I know exactly who it is.

The next two middle-of-the-night summonses, however, start to take their toll.

"Why don't you say no? Or not pick up?" Niko asks. He stopped by the bungalow to say hello Saturday morning, only to find me half-asleep on the couch. When he teased me about being a slacker, I'd filled him in on my midnight trysts with Marva.

"It's hard to resist." I'm sitting on the couch, curled up in one of the quilts Marva set aside for the yard sale. "She's so much more cooperative at night. And *nicer.*"

"That's not saying much."

"I want to bring this job in on time. If that means that I lose beauty sleep, so be it."

Niko sinks onto the other end of the couch. "Ah, so that's how you do it. Sleep. I thought you were born this beautiful."

"Very smooth." I aim for a note of sarcasm—although I'm horribly flattered. Men aren't exactly lining up to feed me compliments these days. I'll take even shameless ones, and I have to say, Niko is pretty darned generous in the flirting department. "Anyway," I say, trying not to read too much into the way he's grinning at me, even though it's deliciously unnerving, "I'm less worried about the bags under my eyes and more that I'm going to crash my car on my way over here. Last night I started to nod off while I was driving. I had to pull off to get one of those energy drinks before I dared get back on the freeway."

His look turns serious. "I was already not liking the thought of you driving around by yourself in the middle of the night. If you're tired, that's worse."

"It's sweet of you to be concerned. But I'm not worried. And there's nothing I can do about the drive anyway."

"Why don't you move in here?"

"Here? Oh, yes, Marva and I would be swell roommates. We can have a pajama party and do each other's hair."

"I mean it. The bungalow is private enough—she never comes out here. She doesn't even step into the backyard. I'll bet she'd have no problem with you staying here for a few weeks."

I look around. There's a shower in the bathroom, and an elf-size closet. I could set up a microwave. Bring in a minifridge. It's not a completely outlandish idea. And it would be pleasant to wake up without My Little Puppy accessories embedded in my face for a change. Although . . .

"The problem is the rest of your crew," I say. "It's one thing to have them tromping in and out of my office—it's another if it's where I sleep. That's creepy."

"They still come in here?"

"Every now and—" I stop myself. It's been a while, now that I think about it. "I guess they don't. Not anymore."

He nods. "I set up my Xbox in the basement, and there's a wet bar down there. And a bathroom. It's a regular man cave."

"You're kidding!"

"We have a lot of time to burn."

Niko's idea is certainly tempting, if for no other reason than it would get me out of Heather and Hank's way. They've always made me feel welcome, but there's that old adage about fish and guests stinking after three days. I'm well past my expiration date.

I toss off the quilt and get up. "I suppose it couldn't hurt to ask."

Partway into the house I realize that it could in fact be moderately painful. "Marva?" She's at her desk, reading glasses perched low on her nose, making notes in that book again, as if she were going to be tested on it.

"Working on a Saturday?" she says, as though *that's* strange, but reporting to work at 3:00 a.m. isn't.

"It's about that. Marva, I very much want to get this job done on time for you, and if that means working weekends or the middle of the night, I'm open to it. Only, the commute is killing me. I'm wondering"—I can feel heat rising to my face I'm so uncomfortable asking—"if I could move into the bungalow for the duration of the project."

"As in live there? Move in entirely? With your belongings?"

"I don't have much. Next to nothing!" She gives me a dubious look, so I try to explain my situation without revealing how strapped for cash I am. "I recently sold my house, and I'm not ready to buy a new one yet. So, there was no need to keep furniture. Or dishes. Or much at all for that matter."

She slides her reading glasses off. "I wonder. What's happened to you that you're this way?"

"Pardon me?"

"What went wrong? That you seem to have no attachment to things. It's not normal."

Funny, that's what I think about your hoarding. "I like *things*," I say. "I just don't get carried away by them. Ultimately, that's all they are. *Things*. In my book—"

"I'm not buying it," she says firmly. "Frankly, your refusal to give me an answer is insulting. You strut about this house, playing amateur psychologist with me—digging around in my psyche like you're going to find the umbilical cord that ties me to my possessions so you can snip it. I am simply asking why you are the way you are."

"I don't know, I've always been like this," I say, mortified that I was so obvious about analyzing Marva. "In fact there was this one time . . ." I start to laugh at the memory, but then say, "It's not really a funny story. It's quite awful, in fact."

"Oh, I love awful stories. Do tell."

"It's nothing. When I was five, my mother threw away my toys because I wouldn't put them away. On Christmas morning—and they were all new toys from Santa. You'd think I'd have gone ballistic, but I handled it quite calmly. My mom says *too* calmly."

"How so?"

"My memory is dodgy on it, but she says I'd been told I had to pick up my toys before I went over to a neighbor's house. When I started out the door with my new Tootsie doll in my hand and the other toys all over the place, my mother threatened to throw them away. Apparently—and honestly, I can't believe I was this big a brat— I said, 'Go ahead.' And then left."

"Nice to see you had some spunk," Marva says.

"When I returned, my toys were gone. Or at least that's what I thought. Turns out my mom had only hidden them in the attic. Once I'd begged and groveled to get them back, she planned to dole them out to me, one at a time, for doing chores or being a good girl."

"But you didn't."

"As she tells it, I simply walked up to her, held out the Tootsie doll, and said, 'Here, you forgot one.' As it turned out, she let me keep the doll. Said I never once asked about the other toys. Ever."

"Bravo," Marva says. "You may have lost the toys, but you won the battle of wills. Far more important."

"It's weird how I barely remember it."

"Well, perhaps you don't want to think of yourself as that brat. There are those times one finds that it's easier to alter the memory than it is to face the truth." She slides her glasses back on. "As for moving into the bungalow, I assume there won't be any wild parties? People coming and going at all hours? Sex, drugs, and rock and roll?"

I chuckle. "That's right, there was a time when Will was young that you had to worry about that sort of stuff. Glad you don't have to anymore?"

"Dear, when Will was young," she says, turning back to her book, "I was the one *doing* that stuff."

Heather backs her minivan into Marva's side drive and pops the hatch. "Great house," Heather says, climbing out of the van. "It's hard to believe it's as bad as you say on the inside."

"It is, although getting better. Thanks for helping me move," I say. I don't have much to bring, but my Mustang is built for beauty and speed—not so much for hauling bulky items such as the computer cart we stopped to retrieve from my storage unit. I lean in to wave to Abigail, who is eating Goldfish crackers from a baggie. She averages about a fifty-fifty ratio of how many make it to her mouth and how many surround her in her booster seat.

"Aunt Lucy, is this your new house?" she asks.

She's looking at the main house. "Mine is better," I say. "Because it's tiny—like a playhouse."

She nods and crams another handful of crackers into her mouth.

I can tell—that kid is going to miss me.

Heather and I start to wrestle the computer cart from the back of the van.

"Here, let me get that." Niko trots up and slips between us to pull the cart deftly out. "I take it this goes in the house out back?"

"Yeah, thanks," I say. "Oh, Niko, this is my friend Heather." He nods at her in greeting, then carries the cart away.

As soon as he's out of earshot, Heather starts laughing. "Oh . . . my . . . gosh . . . *This* is the Niko you've been working with? How come you never mentioned that he's so gorgeous? That body! Those lashes! Normally I'd say they're a waste on a man, but honestly, he is so—"

"Will you stop," I say.

She slides open the van door to let Abigail out. "Oh, come on. The man is so pretty it almost hurts to look at him."

We're both openly watching him as he walks back from the bungalow. He doesn't seem to notice—or maybe he's used to women gawking. As many times as I've enjoyed the view before, having Heather giggling next to me makes me remember again what a nice bonus came with the house.

Abigail climbs down from the van. She's clutching a naked Barbie. Niko bends down to her. "And what's your name?"

She's not so easily charmed as we are. A thumb goes straight into her mouth. "Babigwah," she says.

"Abigail," Heather translates.

"Hi, Abigail." As he shows Abigail a trick that makes it look as if he were pulling off his thumb, Heather leans to me and whispers approvingly, "He's good with kids."

"That's because he is one."

She gives me a nudge with her shoulder. "If you go for it, I promise I won't call you a cougar."

Yes, she would. Besides, nothing ruins a harmless crush like acting on it. We haul in the rest of my belongings, which doesn't take long since I don't have much. In no time, I'm saying good-bye to Heather.

"Thanks for everything," I say as she starts her van to go.

"It's been fun having you around. I'm going to miss you." She makes a pouty face. "You're like the sister I never had."

"You have two sisters."

"Yes, but I don't like them. That's why you're the one I never had."

She pulls away, and I spend the next hour unpacking and rearranging the bungalow, now my temporary home. It's not easy since I wasn't allowed to take any of Marva's junk out, but I pile it high so it takes up only half the space.

By the time I'm done, it's noon. I'm on my way out the door to check in with Marva, and I pause to take a moment to drink in my new space.

It's not much. I'm living partially out of a suitcase, and my bed has to be inflated every night. I'll have to do dishes in the bathroom sink.

Still, it's nice having a place to call my own.

Nurse Nelson is leaving Marva's room when I walk into the house. His scrub shirt today is a pattern of tiny sushis—which reminds me that I could use lunch.

"How is she?" I ask.

He gives the so-so gesture with his hand. "Bed rest for the next few days or that infection is only going to get worse. Don't want her to lose a foot."

A wave of guilt hits me, followed by a bigger wave of disappointment. I've pushed her so hard she's sick now. And because of it, it'll be days before I can get anything done. I noticed on the calendar posted in the bungalow that today is exactly the halfway point—timewise. We're nowhere near halfway done clearing the place out.

Nelson opens the refrigerator. "She needs to be more careful with her diet for a while. I just delivered a heaping tray of sugar-free Jell-O and toast. Decaf tea. Which means"—he pulls out a plastic container and pops open the lid—"she says I'm free to eat this. Mmm, looks like lasagna. I'd love to be rich enough to have a cook make all my meals. The microwave is . . . ?"

I point to where it sits on the counter. He walks over, pops the dish in, and starts randomly poking buttons.

"Can I go say hello to her?" I ask.

"Don't see why not. What do you suppose, two minutes on this?"

I leave without answering—if he gets lasagna and I don't, he's on his own.

"Marva?" I give a rap on the door, even though it's open.

"Come in."

She's propped up in her bed in the corner of the theater room. It's hard to tell that she's sickly because the vibrant color of her kimono and red lipstick seem so cheery. Although *she* doesn't. She sneers at the bed tray over her lap. The food is untouched.

"Take this away."

"You don't at least want a little something?"

The sneer moves from the food up to me.

Guess not.

I grab the tray and—not finding anywhere to set it in the room—walk out to put it in the hall. When I come back in, she gestures toward the bank of six red velvet theater chairs. "As long as you're in here, start with those."

"I'm not here to work. The nurse said you're on bed rest."

"And I'm in bed. Now, those chairs there. Listen to me. They came from the Bijou Theater in a tiny town by the beach in California. I had them restored and shipped here. The destruction of that theater made national headlines. They'll be quite valuable to the right buyer."

I cringe at the term *the right buyer* since Smitty won't really be selling these.

"Must be the lack of sleep talking," Marva says, "that I'm about to tell you to take them away for the auction."

My gaze is on my feet. "Got it. Auction it is."

"Now, that sled . . ." A wooden sled hangs from the wall. Printed on it is the word ROSEBUD. "It's the one they used in the movie *Citizen Kane*. The original, not a replica. I won it from Steven Spielberg in a poker game."

"Rosebud is a sled? I thought Rosebud was a horse. That Kane died yearning for the horse he'd always loved."

She grimaces. "Why aren't you writing this down? Where is that clipboard and those tags you're always carting about? I have spent decades amassing this collection—I don't want your carelessness sending a priceless film prop to the trash bin."

"Priceless?"

"Steve paid sixty thousand for it at auction. I nabbed it from him with a straight flush, but nonetheless. The sled is a difficult one to part with. The art direction in that movie was stunning. It changed my life. This art expert Will hired . . . what's his name again?"

"Smitty."

"I trust you'll be making sure these go directly into his hands."

I study my nails—anything but look her in the eye. "Uh-huh."

"Good, good. I suppose I'll need to let go of most everything in here sooner rather than later if I want to see it properly taken care of. Now the Oscar statue—"

"I'll be right back. I'm going to . . . look for my clipboard."

I pull my cell phone from my pocket as I head out to the kitchen. Nelson is sitting at the one cleared space at the table, polishing off the last of the lasagna. My stomach gurgles—now that I smell food, I'm starving.

I dial, and Will picks up directly.

"Hi, Will, this is Lucy Bloom. I need to talk to you. There's a problem."

"Now what."

I lean against the kitchen sink. Nelson is watching me as if I'm the dinner show. "You need someone who deals in collectibles. Your mom is only letting go of things because she trusts they'll go to a good home."

"I thought we went over this."

"It's not right for me to tell her these things are going to auction if they're being sold in a yard sale. Except if I tell her the truth, she won't agree to let go of them."

"Appears you're in quite a bind."

"So that's why you need to bring in an expert in this area that—"

"I'm not bringing in another outside person. Handle it. And don't bother me with this again. Do your job."

Will hangs up. Nelson doesn't even pretend he wasn't listening in. "So what's the problem?" he asks eagerly.

Ignoring his question, I pick up an individual pack of lemon Jell-O that's sitting on the island. "Is this leftover—can I have it?"

"Knock yourself out."

I open a few drawers until I find a spoon, peel back the lid on the Jell-O, and dig in. Will says I should do my job. He doesn't care if I lie, but it feels wrong to deceive Marva that way. I won't be able to even look at her.

But, it occurs to me, I could lie to Will.

Somehow the thought of that doesn't bother me one bit.

# chapter eight

I step up to the counter and hand the receptionist my coupon. The gym has the same muggy smell of sweat and chlorine as it did when I used to come here a year ago, before I let my membership expire. "Hi," I say. "I downloaded this. Free day pass. I already filled it out and signed the part that says I won't sue you."

"Great, let me call Javier. He'll give you the tour."

I lean closer. "Truthfully, I don't plan to join. I only want to work out this once. Can't I skip it?"

She picks up the phone. "Sorry. Gotta take the tour. Have a seat."

I sit. If Javier wants to waste his time on a woman who is (1) broke and (2) only here so she can ambush her ex-boyfriend into helping her on a work project, then that's his business. I have time.

Although I can't see the gym from the lobby, I know exactly where Daniel is right now. At least I hope so. He came to this gym every Monday, Wednesday, and Thursday after work as long as I knew him. Jogged the treadmill, then did weights—despite which he remained skinny and far from ripped (though I'd always make a point of swooning whenever he'd jokingly flex for me).

I tug to adjust my sports bra under the T-shirt I'm wearing. It would have been easier to call him. But what if he didn't answer or didn't call back? I'd be too humiliated to keep trying him. If he doesn't help me, I don't know where else to turn. As much as Daniel may have let me down, he's still a decent person. I can trust him to be honest about what Marva's collectibles are worth—and not to tell a soul about meeting her if I ask him not to.

So my plan is to sidle up next to him in the weight-lifting area, which is where he should be by now. I'll say, "I didn't know you still come here," all friendly like. We'll chat of course, with me deftly steering the conversation toward my job. Then I'll hit him with the bait: casually mentioning specific collectibles he won't be able to resist seeing. I won't have to admit that I need advice because he'll already be *begging* to come to Marva's.

A short man so pumped that he's almost as wide as he is tall comes up to me. "Hey, I'm Javier."

"I'm not going to join," I say, giving one last effort to avoid the tour. "I'm wasting your time."

"That's okay, I'm paid by the hour."

He leads me toward the main gym, which is packed with the after-work crowd—every one of the dozens of treadmills and elliptical machines is being used. I give a quick scan of the room for Daniel and, as expected, don't see him. Which is good—I want to take him by surprise, not the other way around.

"So what are your fitness goals?" Javier asks.

"To work out for one day."

He gives a deliberate glance to my backside. "You'll have to do more than that if you want to lift that any."

Oh, nice! "I happen to wear the same size I've always worn," I say, tugging my shirt down.

"And you look good. But as a woman ages, gravity takes a toll. You have to do more than diet and—"

"As a *woman* ages? What—men don't age?"

"I'm only saying, a few squats and the right machines could tighten all that up. Lift the tush. Flatten the tummy. Get those"—and he tips his head toward my chest—"up and out. Who doesn't want a perkier bustline?"

A familiar voice behind me says, "I know *I* do."

I want to die—right here in the middle of the gym. If an earth-quake caused the floor to crack open and swallow me whole, it would be a relief.

"Daniel . . ." I say, turning around. "Hi."

"I didn't know you still came here," he says.

Grrr, that's *my* line. This is precisely what I didn't want.

"I don't. I might rejoin."

Javier beams. "You have a friend here! A workout buddy is key to keeping your fitness goals."

I glare at him—it's his fault I was caught off guard. "I don't have any fitness goals."

"Of course not—not yet. That's where I can help."

"Actually," I say in sugary tones, although it's possible my expression is more grimace than grin, "I'd like to work out with my buddy here. Get all motivated. Then I'll come find you. How's that?"

Javier must figure Daniel stands a better chance at scoring him a commission than his own attempts to bully me because he says, "Super idea." He gives us a double thumbs-up as he leaves.

Daniel is wearing the BILLY GOAT TAVERN T-shirt I bought him. We liked to go there for burgers. "So how come you're not looking at a gym closer to your house?" he says.

My house. He doesn't know.

Where is a bolt of lightning to strike you dead when you need it?

"I don't have my house anymore. I sold it."

He doesn't say anything for a moment—the only sound is some techno song playing low on the gym's speakers and the thump-thump-thump of people's feet slamming on treadmills.

Finally he says, "How come?"

"I needed the money."

He nods—he's already figured out why I'd need cash. "So where are you living?"

And there I have it: the segue I needed to get my plan back on track. "Remember I said I was organizing that woman's house? I'm staying in her guesthouse."

"So it's near here?"

"Oak Park."

"Oh."

I can tell he's trying to piece together why I had to walk into this gym of all gyms. Before he has a chance to ask me again, I say, "You'd be amazed by the movie memorabilia she has."

"Yeah? Like what?"

I'd rehearsed this, but now nothing is coming to mind. Being face-to-face with Daniel again is throwing me. Since I can't recall a single item I'd planned to tempt him with, I improvise with something Marva doesn't in fact own but will sound impressive. "She has the ruby slippers Judy Garland wore during the filming of *The Wizard of Oz*."

Daniel frowns. "Those would be fake. The real ones are at the Smithsonian."

Shoot, now that he mentions it, I recall reading that in the newspaper once. I feel like a fool, but then I realize he's playing right into my hands, and I remember the rest of what I planned to say. "Really? See, I'd never know something like that. I'd probably sell them for thousands of dollars and then get myself sued for fraud."

"If they were real, thousands would be a bargain. They're considered priceless."

"Hmm. That's certainly valuable information." I step in closer, as if I have such hot news I fear being overheard. "She also has the robe from *Rocky*."

"*Rocky I*?"

"Mmm-hmm." I twirl a strand of hair. "Only I won't get much for it because it's used. Sylvester Stallone wore it during all that filming and they never even washed it."

He scratches the back of his head. "Um . . . that'd make it more valuable, not less."

"Oh. Gosh. I didn't think of that. There's so much in there that I get overwhelmed. I've had to sort through hundreds of those collectible figurines. Some date back to the 1940s. Now *those* will fetch a high price at the yard sale because I'm going to pull them out of those annoying boxes she's been keeping them in all these years and put them real nice on display."

He winces at the words *pull them out of those annoying boxes.* "No, you should never—"

I don't let him finish. "Luckily, most of what she has is in great shape. Except for that screenplay for *Casablanca*, which at first I was excited about—say, isn't that one of your favorite movies? Anyway, it turns out it's practically ruined because Humphrey Bogart scribbled these notes all over it." I exhale dramatically. "At least it's on white paper, so it's recyclable."

He's looking at me, stroking his chin, clearly at a loss for words. Perfect—right where I want him.

"Hey," I say, as if I had this swell idea. "Maybe you'd like to come see! For fun, before I sell it all. I could probably get you in, although I'd have to do it in the next couple days because everything will be out the door soon." I smile brightly.

Daniel grins back. "So, basically, you have no idea what you're doing and you need me to come there and help you price things and tell you how to sell them. Or even do it for you."

My smile fades. I am so busted. "Um, yes?"

"Is there really the screenplay with Bogart's personal notes on it or did you make that up?"

"It's there."

"You think she'd let me read it?"

"If you help me out, you can lick it for all I care."

He tosses his workout towel over his shoulder. "Then count me in."

Daniel and I make plans for him to stop by Marva's house after he's done with work tomorrow, meeting up with me first in the bungalow. I give him her address but not her name—I only say she's someone who used to be moderately famous. In case he changes his mind, that's one less person in the loop. Then I beg out of exercising and head directly to the locker room. My work here is done.

The next morning, I'm already getting a jump on dreading Daniel's visit when Marva calls me into her bedroom with uncharacteristic cheeriness. "I need your opinion on an ensemble. Be a dear and get it out for me. See it? The plum pantsuit hanging there in the closet." This instruction is delivered as if I can merely walk over and pull it off the rod—as opposed to what I'm doing, which is climbing over a dune of clothing, then attempting to pry it from where it's sandwiched so tightly that I fear one tug will bring the closet's entire contents with it.

Finally, I succeed in my quest and lay before her an elegant, silky pair of purple pants and a matching loose, flowing jacket.

"It's lovely," I say. And clearly expensive, not an outfit one wears around the house—certainly not in bed. She must be on the mend. I'm surprised at how pleased I am to realize Marva must be planning to go out. It's been bothering me that she doesn't seem to have a friend left in the world. "What's the special occasion?"

Instead of answering, Marva picks up the jacket and lays it against her chest. "How about the color? Does it make my skin look sallow? Hmm, perhaps a scarf . . . but I suppose it has to be the right sort of scarf."

"Right for *what*, exactly?"

After a moment's hesitation, she says, "I'm aiming for a look that says, 'Oh, this old thing?' I want to look like a million, but not as if I'm trying."

"Why, Marva!" I say teasingly. "Are you going on a *date*?" No wonder she's being so evasive.

"Don't be ridiculous. Now, upstairs in one of the rooms I have a basket of scarves—go fetch them for me. There's one that will be perfect for this." She scowls at me. "And wipe that smirk off your face. It's positively insufferable."

I look for a scarf for the next hour. It's a waste of time since I never find one, but it made me so happy to think Marva might have something special planned, I didn't want to let her down.

At six fifteen, Daniel knocks on my door, though it's already open. He's dressed in his version of work attire: polo shirt, jeans, and Vans shoes. He pauses to look around the bungalow. "This is cute. Cozy."

"That's a nice way to say crowded."

"I mean it. And the main house is unbelievable. You can see there's a lot of care put into maintaining it in the Craftsman style. It's so nice on the exterior, it's hard to believe there's as much crammed inside as you say."

"Believe it."

He perches on the arm of the couch. "You going to tell me who lives here now? You said famous. What—a producer? An actor?"

"No, she's a painter. I might have oversold you on the 'famous' part. You've probably never heard of her. I hadn't. Her name is Marva—"

"Meier Rios? You're working for Marva Meier Rios? Are you kidding me?" He gets up and starts pacing around, hands in his hair as if trying to keep his brain from exploding. "Do you have any idea how amazing that is?" He stops and looks at me. "You don't, do you?"

"Yes. No. I don't know. I mean, I looked her up on the Internet."

"Is *Woman, Freshly Tossed* here? Will I be able to see it?"

"I don't know if she has it here."

"You've been in this house for weeks now, and you don't know if you're in the vicinity of one of the greatest pieces of art ever created?"

I cross my arms—I didn't invite him here for a lecture. I invited him here to do my job for me.

He knows the arm-cross well enough to back off. "I'm excited, that's all. It's a big deal. *She's* a big deal. As far as I'm concerned, she started the neo-Expressionism movement, although she doesn't always get credit for it."

I manage to uncross my arms, but I can't shake off the defensiveness. "How is it you know so much about her?"

"What do you mean, how do I know so much? I'm a designer."

"A graphic designer. For advertising. Using computers."

His brows knit together. That's his version of the arm-cross. "So, that's my medium. It's still art. You wrote a nonfiction book about organizing instead of a novel. Does that mean you're not a writer?"

"Yes."

He's about to say something, but then he stops. He tips his head. "You don't think you're a writer?"

"Look, can we move on? Now, I've told Marva that you'll be—"

"No, I want to know. You don't think you're a writer?"

"If you must know, no, I don't. A book of household advice on how you should fill a trash bag every day with clothes for the Goodwill until you have a week's worth is not exactly Hemingway."

"But it's words on paper. That you wrote. That got published. And it probably helped a lot more people than *Old Man and the Sea* ever has."

"All five people who read it? Face it, I talked to experts, I gave examples about people with overstuffed closets and cluttered basements. But I had no idea squalor like that"—I gesture toward Marva's house—"ever existed."

"Most people don't live like that."

"Daniel, it's fine. I honestly don't care about the book anymore. Plenty of books never get off the ground, and it so happens mine was one of them. So come on—are you ready to meet Marva?"

"You bet."

"Fair warning: She can be . . . for lack of a better word, *eccentric*."

"Of course she's eccentric. She's a genius. I'd be disappointed if she was normal."

We start walking toward the house. "I'll give you the tour first. I'd like to get a sense from you whether there's anything that falls into that area between fine art and yard sale. Then we'll go to what Marva calls the theater room. That's where most of the memorabilia is. It's also her bedroom, so be prepared. As I started to say before, I've warned her you're coming. Hopefully she won't be lying there in her scanties."

"That might not be so bad. As I recall, she was quite an attractive woman."

"That was a long time ago," I say, realizing as soon as I do how uncharitable I'm being. "I didn't mean . . ."

"What is she now? Late fifties? Sixties?"

"I believe sixty-four."

"That's nothing. Look at the Rolling Stones—they're about that age, still banging twenty-year-olds."

"You want to bang Marva Meier Rios?"

He gives me a teasing nudge. "You think she would?"

It's testimony to how far I've come in my recovery over Daniel that I laugh, since months ago even the notion of that ridiculous pairing would have crushed me.

We go through the upstairs first. As I suspected, Daniel says there's plenty of value there. I feel utterly vindicated when we get to the white retro chairs that Smitty scorned and Daniel nearly births a cow he's so excited. "Do you have any idea how rare these are in this sort of condition?" he says, stomping over the Easter hats to pull one chair from its place (and nearly causing an avalanche in doing so).

"Be careful!" I scold, as though there's a big market for bonnets.

Daniel sets the chair in the hallway and spins in it as if it were a ride at Disneyland. Seeing him makes me remember how he could at times be a big kid. It's both his charm and his flaw.

There's no way he can see it all, but even at a glance, I have my answer. I'll be cheating Marva if I simply throw all this in a yard sale.

We pass Nelson in the kitchen on our way to see Marva. He's been staying during the day since she took ill. "How's she doing?" I ask.

"Good spirits," Nelson says. "When she threw the Jell-O cup at me, she wasn't even aiming."

I don't bother with introductions—it's not as if Daniel will be sticking around after today. He and I head to the theater room. He's repeatedly tucking and untucking his shirt.

"It's better out," I say. He pulls it untucked, staring at the door, which is slightly ajar. "Nervous?"

"Excited. Thank you for this."

"You're the one helping me."

"That's right. You're welcome."

With that, we head inside. Marva is propped up in bed, fully clad, in silky slacks and a caftan. "Marva, this is Daniel Kapinski. He's the memorabilia expert I told you about. Daniel, this is—"

"Marva Meier Rios," he says—and he must be worked up because he steps on a boxed figurine in his zeal to run over and shake her hand. Normally, he'd sooner step on his own mother. "I feel as if I should genuflect. I can't tell you what an honor it is to meet you."

She must approve of his goofy enthusiasm because she gives him a smile that from her is more rare than those chairs upstairs. "Nice to meet you, too. *Daniel* is it?"

He nods. I think I hear brain rattling. I've never seen him like this.

Trying to save him before he makes a fool of himself, I say, "Daniel, perhaps we should get started. If you want to come over here, I can show you the posters."

He doesn't so much as glance my way. He grabs the stool that Nelson uses when he's checking Marva's vitals and sits on it. "I'll never forget the first time I saw one of your paintings. I was ten. It was a class field trip to the MCA. They had one hanging with a few other artists' just off the lobby."

"Which painting?" Marva asks.

"*She Felt Herself Aggrieved.*" Marva nods, and Daniel continues, "I sat down on the bench in the middle of the room, just wanting to look at it for a minute. Pretty soon all the kids filed through, and the teacher started telling me I had to get moving. But I wouldn't. It was almost as if I couldn't. I'd never seen art like that in real life . . . ever. I wasn't prepared for the power of it. To see the actual brushstrokes. To have the energy of it right there in front of me—nothing blocking it. It was . . . the difference between looking at a girlie magazine versus seeing your first actual naked woman."

"There's no naked woman in that painting."

"Ah, but what a woman there was. Those eyes. I don't know what you were thinking when you painted those eyes but—" He stops—he makes a sound that's somewhere between a squeak and a gasp. "You're here! The artist is here right in front of me. Wow. Please. I'm begging. Tell me. What *were* you thinking?"

"Oh, that was so long ago. I haven't the faintest idea."

"I don't believe for a minute that you don't remember. But fine, you don't want to say. I respect that—although if you change your mind, feel free to shout it out at any time."

"Duly noted."

"Anyway, I wouldn't leave. One of the moms that was chaperoning said she'd sit with me." He gives a cheerful shrug. "I turned out to be the laughingstock of the fifth grade—apparently there were naked paintings further on."

"A shame you missed out."

"If only it was *Woman, Freshly Tossed* that was in that first room. I wouldn't have had to spend the rest of the year defending my manhood. Plenty of naked in that one." He's quiet for a moment, then he jumps off the stool as if it were spring-loaded. "And I'm taking way too much of your time."

Marva doesn't tell him to stay, but I get the distinct impression she was in no hurry for him to leave her side. She picks up her book. I can't imagine she can concentrate on her reading, though, with all of Daniel's carrying on. He's calling off each item to me as he sees it as if he were pitching As Seen On TV merchandise. A *banjo from* Deliverance! A *gen-u-ine* Willy Wonka *golden ticket!*

"Could you keep it down?" I whisper. I grab on to his arm and pull him into the hallway. "She feels bad enough about selling her most precious possessions without you rubbing it in."

"Sorry. You're right. But, man, if I was her, I couldn't do it. It hurts to know this is all going to be split up. I am feeling actual, physical pain right now. Believe me, if I had the money, I'd be buying everything in there."

"Unless you've struck it rich since the last time I saw you, that's not going to happen. I appreciate your input on this, but could you please bring it down a notch?"

He gives me his puppy eyes. "Got it."

Those eyes get to me every time. "Tell you what. Would it help if I let you look around without me for a while? So you can dig in without me standing over your shoulders?"

"Probably."

"Then have at it. I'll be in the kitchen." I start to go, but then turn back. "And please leave Marva alone. She really does prefer the quiet."

Nelson is sitting at the kitchen table. He's managed to shove enough aside so he can prop up a small, portable DVD player. He pauses what he's watching when I come in.

I lean against the island. "Am I the only one she doesn't like?"

"What, did she throw you out? Is she having wild sex with the new guy?" Nelson asks.

"I'm serious—she's friendly to you, right?"

"I wouldn't say friendly, but I've had worse. Sick people tend to be grouchy. And that's all I'm around all day."

I steal a cracker from an open box he has on the counter. "How sick is Marva? If they've brought you in, it must be pretty bad."

"Not really. For most folks, they'd have a friend or relative stop by, bring them food or run them to a doctor. But people who don't have anybody, they hire me."

"It's so sad. I mean, her son's worthless, but I don't see that she has any friends either. I wonder why she doesn't."

"Dunno." He clicks PLAY on the DVD player. "Want to watch the rest of this movie with me?"

I kill an hour watching an entirely forgettable film. The credits roll, and Daniel still hasn't come to the kitchen.

When I go to check on him, he has the stool pulled up to Marva's bedside again and he's shaking his head and saying, "I can't believe Karl Lagerfeld would *do* that." I feel jealousy rise to my throat like bile. It's completely irrational, but I want to shake Daniel and say, *Marva is* my *eccentric artist! You don't get to come in here and have her like you better.*

"So, Daniel," I cut in, "have you had a chance to look at everything? Maybe you could give me a few minutes and go over your findings?"

He jumps up and scoots the stool away back toward the wall. "In the nick of time, too. I've far overstayed my welcome." He picks up Marva's book and hands it back to her. "I can't thank you enough for honoring me with your time."

Oh, brother—could he be any bigger a kiss-up? What—is he vying to get in the will?

We head back out to the bungalow. As soon as we get there, Daniel plunks down on my couch. "I've got a plan."

"Oh, do you?" I say icily.

He gives me a perplexed look, which makes me realize how silly I'm being. I stamp the jealousy. He's being incredibly generous to help me. "You can take all the DVDs and VCR tapes for the yard sale," he says. "Pretty much everything else in there is worth selling online or straight to collectors. There's a place I know of that's supposed to be good. They'll take twenty percent off the top, but you'll still come out way ahead. You said there are guys that can move it all?"

When I tell him yes, he says, "Great. Oh, and don't touch anything that's behind the green chair. That's what she wants to keep. As for the rest of the house, I told Marva I'd come back to look again when I had more time. Worst-case scenario, you let me into that yard sale first and I'll check there's nothing I missed."

"That's a lot of work for you. What kind of commission are you thinking?"

"Don't worry about it. Glad to do it."

"That's not fair—I need to pay you something."

He rubs the back of his neck. "Well, if you insist, Marva could pay me in merchandise. Like that Bettie Page pinup calendar. If that wound up hanging in some horny college kid's dorm room, I'd hang *myself.*"

"The calendar I would have thrown away because it's out-of-date?"

"You're killing me." He gets up and heads toward the door. "By the way, how are you handling Marva's photos? I saw a snapshot in her room of her with Warhol. What are you going to do with that?"

"Whatever she tells me to."

"What if she tells you to shred it?"

"Then I'll shred it."

"You can't do that. That photo is a piece of history."

I shrug. "There's too much in there. Can't keep it all."

"But it *means* something."

"Daniel, some things have to go. If they're in the way, they're in the way. That's how it is."

My words seem to incite him because his voice is steel as he says, "You can't let go of everything. Some things are worth hanging on to."

I cannot believe that Daniel of all people would say that to me. He has the nerve to talk to me about hanging on—after he ran out on me when things got tough with Ash. Okay, *ran out* isn't entirely accurate, but he did leave. I'd dared to think we were forever, and I hadn't seen the end coming. I suppose if I thought back I could piece together when Daniel finally snapped, but I don't want to. I prefer to forget the whole thing.

Now here he is, in my life again, and it's dredging everything up. What was I thinking? I was a fool to believe I'd be able to work with him.

Daniel yanks open the door, his eyes not meeting mine. His voice is thick as he says, "I need to go."

It's all I can do to bite back the urge to tell him not to come back. As much as I hate it, I need him.

I'm just not sure I'm ready for all the mess that comes along with his help.

# chapter nine

The good thing about investing in people rather than things is that people don't have to be dusted.

—*Excerpt from* Things Are Still Not People, *unpublished draft of a sequel to* Things Are Not People

I manage to sleep in until 8:00 a.m. The first thought that pops into my head when I wake up is *I get to call Ash in mere hours.*

The very thought gives me jitters. It's my chance to reconnect with my son—to speak directly to him instead of having our conversation filtered through whatever drugs he's on. It feels more important than a phone call. It's a bridge. If I want him to be willing to talk to me again, I can't mess this up.

I'm mulling what I'll say to Ash the entire time I'm getting ready for work. Mostly, I want to ask him questions—and not about his drug problem or his recovery. I'd prefer to avoid those topics. All I want to hear is the mundane, everyday stuff. How does he like the food there? What's his roommate's name? Do they get along? What's his view from his room—can he see the ocean? I'll have ten minutes on the phone with Ash, and what I crave is ten minutes of *normal*.

Of course, they're not going to let me do that. I'm sure Ash has a list a mile long of the issues we're supposed to work on—all the ways I need to change so he can get better. Strange how I can look forward to and dread something simultaneously.

To pass the time, I check my e-mails, which I haven't done in several days. It appears my mom has discovered the FORWARD button. There must be fifty messages from her. I'm so busy sifting through them that I almost miss the e-mail from Daniel. He's sent me the address for where to drop off Marva's memorabilia. I feel a twinge of disappointment when it's only that and a brief note: *We're on. Talked them down to 15% on the fee. I'll supervise. Make sure it's all boxed and sealed so I can itemize.*—D.

Not sure what else I expected it to say. I grab a yogurt and a banana for my breakfast. By the time I let myself into Marva's house, it's after ten o'clock. Nelson is in the kitchen watching a movie.

"How's our patient?" I ask.

"Off bed rest. She's in her office. I'm hanging around today, but mostly because I add class to this place. And she pays me."

I give a knock as I lean into Marva's office. "Good morning. Glad to hear you're feeling better."

She's sitting in an easy chair, reading the newspaper. "Never felt bad. No idea what the fuss was about."

"So, Marva, as long as you're up, I'm going to have the—" I stop midsentence. I'm about to tell her I'll bring the crew in to clear out the theater room. Only the image of Marva with Daniel yesterday pops into my head—how excited he was to meet her. How different she was with him.

Maybe I've been too focused on business? It's why I'm here, and Marva's certainly made it clear she's not interested in establishing any sort of personal relationship with me. But still . . .

I lean on the edge of an antique writing desk. "I didn't get around to showing this room to Daniel yesterday when he was here," I say in what I hope is an inviting, chatty tone, borrowed from all those days I was laid off and watched *The View*. "So many beautiful paintings. I'm afraid once I bring him in here, I won't be able to get him out."

Marva doesn't look up from her paper. "Mmm-hmm. He was a nice young man. Seemed to know his stuff. How long have the two of you been sleeping together?"

"Wha—?" Didn't see that one coming. "I . . . uh . . . he and I aren't . . ."

"He strikes me as a considerate lover. Is he?"

"Daniel and I aren't—" Marva is now peering at me over the top of her thick-rimmed reading glasses, her expression politely interested. "That is, we aren't anymore. We *used* to be. He's an ex-boyfriend. We split about seven months ago. But, yes, as a matter of fact, he was."

"That's good. There's nothing worse than a man who wants a woman to do all the work. You'd be surprised at how many great men are dreadful in the sack."

I'm dying to ask her the juicy details: *What great men? Did you sleep with anybody I'd know? And what made you suspect there was something between Daniel and me?* Too chicken to do so, I instead say, "These paintings are stunning. Do you have a favorite?"

She gazes about, as if she can't recall what's in here. "I suppose that's rather like choosing a favorite food. It depends upon one's mood."

"How about *Woman, Freshly Tossed*? Is that here?"

"No." She picks up the paper again, briskly opening it with a snapping sound—a clear signal that our conversation has ended. "That one is not here."

My phone is fully charged. I'm sitting on the couch in the bungalow. Five minutes to go until I call Ash. I've told Niko—who has had the crew packing up the theater room all afternoon while I'd itemized—that no one is to disturb me from five o'clock to five ten.

When he cracked a joke about how it couldn't be that hot a date if it was only ten minutes, I couldn't resist telling him the real reason. Sort of. I may have edited out the part about rehab. The essence, anyway, is that I haven't talked to my son in a long time, and I will be. In five minutes.

*Four* now.

At last I call and get through to Dr. Paul. "I've got Ash with me here. I'm going to put you on speakerphone. The two of you can talk. I'll be here if you need me." There's a clatter, some clicking, and then Dr. Paul again. "Can you hear me?"

My mouth has gone dry. "Yes." I'd been anticipating a one-on-one with Ash. Now this feels like a performance, with Dr. Paul as both audience and judge. I'm playing the role of Mom, and I can't remember any of my lines.

"Hi, Ash," I say.

"Hey."

"It's nice to hear your voice. I'm glad you were willing to talk to me."

"Yeah. Okay." This is mumbled.

Now what? I was close enough to this boy at one point that I once licked melted Popsicle off his face when I didn't have a cloth—now I haven't a thing to say to him. Although I could start with an apology for licking his face.

"How is everything going?" I ask.

"Cool."

"How do you like the food?"

"It's cool."

"Do you have a roommate?"

"Yeah."

"Do you like him?"

"Yeah, he's cool."

I'm dying here. I'm covered in flop sweat. Only about twenty seconds into the conversation—one I've been looking forward to for weeks—and I can't wait for it to be over.

I put in an appeal. "Dr. Paul? What are Ash and I supposed to be talking about?"

"Whatever you'd like," he says.

Whatever I'd like. I'd like for our conversation to be less awkward. But it doesn't appear that's going to be happening anytime soon.

"Everything is going well here," I say. "I have a new job. I'm helping a woman clean out her home. It's super-cluttered." I give a weak laugh. "You remember what a neat freak I can be."

"Yeah. That sounds cool."

I decide to wait Ash out—if I don't say anything, he'll step up and do more than give me one- and two-word answers. A solid minute ticks by with neither of us saying a word. Finally, Dr. Paul takes pity on me. "Ash, maybe you want to talk to your mom about what we were discussing right before she called."

There's a low mumbling between the two of them.

"Lucy," Dr. Paul says. "Can I confirm for Ash that he's free to say anything to you?"

With loins girded, I say, "Sure."

We observe another near minute of silence. At last Ash says, "I'm starting to understand why it is I got into drugs."

"You are?"

*Please don't say it's because of me . . . please don't say it's because of me . . .*

"I do it—that is, I *did* it—because I didn't have a dad around."

*Whew. It's not my fault. Thank you thank you thank you . . .*

"And you weren't strict enough," he continues, "like a dad would have been. If I'd had one."

*Crap.*

"And you never noticed what was going on. Ever. Even when it was so frigging obvious."

"Like what?" I ask, though I'm already mentally ticking off a list of what I hope he doesn't say. The foil on his windows he said was because the streetlights bothered him . . . the white powder that was "caffeine" . . . his ability to stay awake for days on end . . .

"Come on, you didn't see a two-foot bong in my room?"

"Oh, I saw it." I sound defensive but, darn it, somebody needs to defend me. "At the time, it seemed the lesser of a lot of evils."

I hear more mumbling, and then "I guess what I'm saying is that I'm pissed I got into any of it at all. And when I did, that you didn't stop me."

"You're mad that I didn't stop you from doing drugs."

"If you had, I wouldn't be an addict now."

*Addict.*

It's the word I've been avoiding through all of this. Even as I was sending him away, it was for his *drug problem*, his *drug use*. At the time, Ash certainly didn't think he had a problem. *I* had the problem for not understanding that he was just a guy that liked to party. Now he's using the *A-word*.

He's faced it, and I suppose it's time I did, too.

Ash is an addict. I'm the mother of an addict.

"Ash, I *tried* to stop you. I did everything I knew to—"

"You tried too late."

Dr. Paul finally decides to earn some of that money I'm paying him and pipes in, "Ash, I'm going to challenge what you said. I don't believe you. You're here. Making progress on your recovery. So why would you do that if it's too late?"

I press my lips together, resisting the urge to answer for Ash, to supply the answer *I'd* like to hear.

"Nah, it's not too late," Ash replies at last.

We finish the call soon after, ending on what I consider a high note. In celebration, I grab a yogurt from my minifridge. Being cherry-cheesecake-flavored, it's the closest thing to a treat I have on hand. I pop it open and take a spoonful, immediately pitying anyone who thinks this is what cheesecake tastes like.

As I eat, Ash's words run through my head. *It's not too late.*

Until I heard him say it, I hadn't realized how badly I needed some acknowledgment from him that he believes he can succeed in rehab. Since sending him off, I've been shouldering the hope on my own. With those simple words, even with all the crap that preceded them, I at last feel that Ash has hope, too. He's the one that actually has to do the work—as much as I'd love to jump in and do it for him, I can't—so this feels like an important step.

I'm chucking the empty yogurt container in the trash when there's a knock on the door. I open it, and Niko is standing there, smiling so broadly that it's as if I peeled back the curtains to let in a ray of sunshine.

"I was leaving for the day," he says. "Thought I'd stop by to see how your call went. You were so excited about it."

Since I'm still enjoying that Niko doesn't know about Ash's situation—freeing me from having to worry about whether he thinks less of me because of it—I merely answer, "Fine, thanks."

"Just fine? You wanna talk about it?"

"Not really."

He nods. "You know the best way to not talk?"

"What's that?"

"Drinking. Come on, let's go. There's a great pub just a half a mile from here. I'll buy."

Out of habit I'm about to protest—tell him all the reasons I can't go with him. Then I think, why not? I'm a single woman—in fact, I'm an empty nester, although no one would ever call this cluttered bungalow empty, except perhaps Marva. I'm finally feeling freed of some of my fears about Ash, at least for the moment. He'll be back soon enough, and my focus will have to be on him again. I suppose there's no reason I can't squeeze in a little fun while I have the chance.

"Sounds great," I say. "Let me grab a sweater."

# chapter ten

Niko taps his beer bottle against mine. "Cheers!" He has to shout to be heard over the band. "Here's to not talking about whatever it is we're not talking about!"

I hoist mine before taking a swig. "I'll drink to that!"

After that, there's no point in attempting conversation. I sit back and pretend I'm enjoying the band. They're not bad—your typical rock-and-roll band of the quality one might find during happy hour at a pub located between a dry cleaner and a dog wash. I'd prefer that they either not play at all (so I can distract myself by talking to Niko) or play louder (so I can't hear myself think).

Unfortunately, I am left to my thoughts, which keep going back to Ash.

It's been months of ups and downs—although whom am I kidding? Mostly downs. Ever since that moment I realized Ash's problem was bigger than I could handle—and certainly bigger than I'd let myself see.

I'll never forget it. It was five in the morning—Daniel had moved out months before. I woke to Ash shaking me, telling me I needed to go pay a cabdriver. Grabbing my wallet, I stumbled outside, confused and muddled with sleep. At least Ash took a cab. I'd asked him to do that—told him if he was ever unsafe to drive, he shouldn't. Take a cab, I'd said. I'll pay. I knew plenty of parents who've told their kids the same thing.

The driver was a stocky, swarthy man wearing a Members Only jacket and a furious expression. Before I could apologize for taking so long—I was half-asleep, cut a gal a break—he said, "Fare's fifty-three bucks. Was that your kid?"

"Um. Yes."

"You have any idea where I brought him back from?"

I shook my head as I rifled through my wallet. I found three twenties and held them out to him. He grabbed the money from my hand and gave a snort of disgust. "Your son was in a place he had no business being. It doesn't bother you that he's in a crack house? You come out here and pay for his ride like nothin' happened?"

"I . . . uh . . ." *Crack house? Did he say crack house?*

"He's a sharp-looking kid. This is a nice neighborhood. And you're a damn fool," he said, climbing back into his cab while I stood there, unable to do anything else. "It's time you wake up, lady, before you find that kid dead."

I push the thought from my head, draining the last of my beer. That was then, this is now. In my new and improved now, the band is announcing that they'll be taking a short break. Niko excuses himself to go grab another round.

While he's at the bar, I give in to my inner twelve-year-old and text Heather.

I'M HAVING DRINKS WITH NIKO!

She texts me back within seconds: OMG! GO FOR IT!

Go for what, I'm not entirely certain. As I see Niko approach the table—the appreciative gaze of more than one woman on him—I suppose I could come up with a thing or two.

I feel myself flush. I'm so out of practice having sexy thoughts about a man—even one as blatantly attractive as Niko—I'm afraid that my doing so made a horrible, creaking noise as something rusty and unused in me gave way. Like the opening of an ancient crypt. And that was only because I'd noticed how his biceps flexed beneath his T-shirt as he held a pitcher and glasses. Imagine if I thought about him tugging off that shirt and . . .

*Creeeeeeeak.* Hmm, perhaps this isn't the time to entertain such thoughts. "A pitcher, huh?" I say. "What—you think you can come crawling in late tomorrow because the boss will be gone?" Marva is going to be at the hospital having some procedure done. As long as she's out, I've asked Smitty to pick up the first round of auction items.

"I'm gonna miss having her around," Niko says. "She adds such a nice touch of crazy to the place."

"You have to admit, it's never boring."

"How about yesterday when Torch found the broken statue?"

I groan at the memory of it. Marva was there in the living room when Torch, Niko's cousin with the muttonchops, unearthed a fertility-god statue—and let's just say, the part that broke off was key to its fertility. Torch fell apart laughing. That was, until I snapped at him to stop because I could see Marva was failing to see the humor. She stormed off, and it took me an hour to talk her out of insisting that Niko fire Torch. She was convinced his carelessness had broken the statue. "It was buried underneath a bunch of boxes," I'd said. "Frankly, it's a miracle we haven't found more that's damaged than we have. As we go on, we will." When that didn't get through to her, I said, "Look, it's a broken penis. There are worse things."

I say now to Niko, "Torch could have at least tried not to laugh."

"C'mon, even you were about to lose it."

"Okay, true. When she started waving it at him as she was yelling, I had to bite the inside of my cheek to hold it together."

Niko sits back and levels a look at me. "You're good with her."

"With Marva? Yeah, right."

"I mean it."

"She fights me on everything."

"But now sometimes you fight back."

We continue to chat until the band restarts. It's so easy being with Niko. I can't help but contrast it with my earlier talk with Ash. To be with someone and yet have no junk between you—except in the literal sense. It's making me feel almost . . . what's that experience I keep craving? Ah, yes. I take another sip of my beer. Normal.

I don't recognize the song being played, but a few brave (read: drunk) souls hit the dance floor. An elderly couple rocks out next to some blonde in a red halter top dancing by herself. I'm content to lean back and enjoy feeling buzzed when the band switches to a hip-hop song and Niko grabs my arm. "Old-school! We've got to dance to this one."

Old-school? I vaguely recognize this song—it can't be more than a couple years old. It packs the dance floor—and by *packs*, I mean a dozen or so people. Everyone knows the steps, such as they are, involving a crisscrossing and then leaping as though flying. Luckily, it's silly enough that everybody is as terrible as me, including Niko, who repeatedly crashes into me.

The song ends, and the band moves directly into a slow song. I start back to the table.

I've barely turned around when Niko's arm tugs at my waist, and his other hand clasps mine. It's so smooth I spin right into him, as if I meant to do it. His shirt smells of fabric softener. I wonder if his mom does his laundry.

"Where'd you learn how to dance?" I ask.

"I'm Greek."

"And . . . ?"

He looks baffled that I don't accept that as the entire answer. "So that's why I can dance."

He walks me home soon after that, steering me with a hand on my neck. It feels extra-nice because it's nippy outside. It's sweet, too. It may have been a long time since I've thought about romance, but I remember how guys do that—look for excuses to touch a girl when they like her. It occurs to me he might actually try to kiss me.

"Whew, I've had too much to drink," he says, when we get to the bungalow. "It might not be such a good idea for me to drive. I'm not drunk, but I don't need a DUI."

"Oh, okay . . . well . . ." I'm not sure what he's getting at.

"It'd probably be smarter for me to spend the night here."

Ah. That's what he's getting at.

Boy, he's smooth.

Kind of nervy, too. I mean, we've never even kissed. And he's hinting to spend the night? Sure, it sounds yummy, but my "going for it" is typically a whole lot slower than that.

Then again, I can't let him drive drunk.

"I guess I don't mind if you crash on my couch, but truthfully, Niko, I don't know you that well. This is all pretty fast. And I—"

"Whoa, sorry," he says, taking a step back. "I didn't mean sleep *here*. I meant at Marva's. In the man cave. I go in through the cellar entrance. I've done it before—she doesn't even notice I'm there."

I am instantly mortified. Of course he wasn't coming on to me. I'm so much older than him! I'm merely a woman he works for!

"Of . . . of course . . . ," I stammer.

He grins wickedly. "But, hey, if you're offering . . ."

"Nice try. Now off to your cave," I say, easing the door shut, no longer embarrassed. "And thanks for tonight."


The next two days are filled with overseeing Smitty's and Niko's crews. I'm exhausted, and my feet are killing me. It's my own stupid fault for wearing such high heels. To my shame, I am, as they say, peacocking—that is, fanning my feathers to attract the opposite sex. It seems to be working. There's enough sexual charge between Niko and me to light a small city.

Not that I'm acting on it.

I'm too busy moving the auction items out before Marva gets back from the hospital. The theater room has already been cleared of everything Marva approved to sell. My work hours have been long, but for the first time since I took this job, rather enjoyable.

Smitty flits down the stairs, clipboard in hand, following two workers carrying out part of an enormous art installation. I stop him in the foyer.

"This one's called *Umbrella* by . . . Imelda Elder, correct?" I say.

"Yesiree, and that's the last of it for now." Looking out toward the nearly full moving truck outside, he says, "Quite an interesting collection so far. Although I'll admit I'm a tad disappointed. We could've fetched quite the price for those Meier Rios's." Smitty had been particularly careful identifying the four paintings of Marva's tagged to go. He'd scrutinized her blocky MMR signature so long I had to fight the urge to offer to bring the artist herself to verify them. His enthusiasm had dipped greatly when I told him they weren't for sale. "Are you positive your boss wants me to arrange an endowment to a museum? It seems such a waste."

"Sorry, but *he*," I say, keeping up the ruse that this is the home of a software tycoon, "was adamant that they not go to private collectors."

"As I told you before, I could find a museum willing to buy. You'd have full approval."

"He said donate. Wants the tax write-off, I guess."

"Pity. At least *Woman, Freshly Tossed* isn't part of this collection. Giving that one away to a museum would be a travesty."

"Yes, imagine allowing ordinary people to enjoy a great work of art. Next thing you know, they're going to demand the right to vote."

"Sarcasm does not become you, my dear. I simply mean it would be thrilling to say I handled the sale of it. A moot point, since it's not here. I do wonder where it *is* housed. Have you any idea?"

"Nope." Given Marva's abrupt dismissal of the subject the one time I asked her, it's clear she doesn't have it. I got the distinct impression that she doesn't even know where it is—or if she does, she's not happy about its whereabouts. This is a woman who wants to make sure her spare flashlight goes to a good home—surely she wouldn't be happy about her life's greatest work being in the wrong hands.

"Let's work to discourage any more charity on the next go-round, shall we? A fellow's got to make a living." Smitty hands me the clipboard and a pen. "We're almost out of your hair. Need a signature on these."

As with everything he's taken yesterday and today, there's a ream of paperwork to pore over—release forms, verification of authenticity, it goes on and on. We're both being careful. Hundreds of thousand of dollars is making its way out the door. Possibly more than a million, but I can't wrap my head around that big a number. (Although it was fun seeing the look on Will's face when he stopped by and I told him Marva was giving her paintings to the art museum for free. There's nothing he can do about it, though. They're hers to give.)

It's twenty minutes before Smitty's semitruck pulls out. I shut the door behind him. It's quiet except for the faint strains of a TV coming from Marva's bedroom, where Niko is rearranging furniture. I take a moment to spin around the living room—I can do that now. It's still not empty, but it's getting there. Only, ow. My feet. I tug off my shoes. If I'd had any sense, I'd have gone the low-cut-blouse route.

Hmm . . . and speaking of the reason I'm tarted up . . . I head barefoot to Marva's room to give Niko a hand.

As I walk in, he's lying on her bed watching a basketball game.

"Hey! What's with the slacking?" I grab the remote from a dresser and click off the TV. "Marva could be here anytime."

"Has anyone ever told you, you're cute when you're bossy?"

"Surprisingly, no."

"Well, you are."

"Then I'm about to get cuter, because we need to move that bed to the middle of the room. Which means you need to get off of it." For some reason, with Niko this is my idea of flirting. Next I'll be pushing him down on the playground the way I did to Grant Smith in the third grade (who annoyingly didn't recognize it as the flirtation it was and ratted me out to a teacher).

Niko rolls off the bed. "Like I said, bossy."

"I'm not doing this for the fun of it." I crouch down and tug the bed while he pushes on it. It's a giant, four-poster number and weighs a ton. "This room looks too empty as it is," I say, huffing.

"So bring some junk back in." Niko throws muscle into the job, and it does not go unnoticed that he has lovely muscle with which to do it.

"Not a chance. I'm creating an illusion of fullness." We manage to shimmy the bed into place. "See?"

"Whatever you say."

I'm hyperaware that Niko and I are alone in the house. In a bedroom, to be specific. Standing on either side of a bed.

*Stay focused, Lucy.* "Help me move the shelf."

Once I get the furniture where I want it, I start unloading the remaining collectibles onto the shelves. It doesn't need to look pretty—just fluffed up. I want Marva to get the effect of having one room completed. I'd even had the guys put any clothes that didn't fit in the closet in the dining room to sort through later. She'll take one look at this room, beam with pride, and say, "I can't wait for the whole house to look like this!"

Hey, a girl can dream.

I'm reaching to place a decorative box on an upper shelf when I feel Niko behind me.

"I've got that," he says. He's brushed up against me as he sets the box on the top shelf. I don't move, although every nerve ending in me just stood on end. "Anything else up here?"

I point to—oh, I don't care what . . . magazines. He reaches down and grabs them, and I pretend to shuffle knickknacks about while I feel him setting the magazines on a shelf above me. My insides are buzzing and popping.

"You unload the rest," I say, wriggling out from in front of him. "I'll sweep!"

I grab a broom and start sweeping like Cinderella—that is, if she were really, really horny and had no idea what to make of it. I try to ignore Niko, stealing glances at me. In no time, the room is swept, unpacked, and looking . . .

"Not bad," Niko says, nodding approvingly.

"You think?"

He takes a step toward me and—did I mention how horribly out of practice I am romance-wise?—I step back. My foot knocks over a box filled with Styrofoam packing peanuts, sending them spilling.

"Can't have this mess here!" I grab them up in my arms as best I can, then look manically about the room, pretending to drink in my fine work. "Much better! Our first room! Done! And cheers . . . to the first of many!"

"Good job." Niko leans over and kisses me on the cheek. "To the first of many."

I'm debating if that was only meant to be a friendly kiss between coworkers when he cups the back of my neck and kisses me on the mouth.

Then another kiss.

Another . . . and . . . my lips part, and my arms reach up to go around his shoulders, sending packing peanuts flying everywhere, clinging to my shirt, my hair, and . . . *I don't even care.* I rise onto my tiptoes. Niko's hands roam over my back, and I tug him closer. If this is Niko being friendly, he may be the best darn friend I've had in a long time.

He walks me toward the bed, kissing me all the while. I lie down, and, oh, hot damn and hallelujah. He climbs over me, pausing long enough to give an *mmm*, his eyes flickering across my face. Then his mouth finds mine again, and I surrender to the crazy luck that this is, Niko, here, in this house—as if I'd dug through a box of fiber-rich nutritional cereal and found a toy surprise anyway. He's propped on one elbow, his other hand sliding deliciously along my side as he kisses me, maddeningly leisurely. As if he has all the time in the world. As if kissing me is his only destination. As if his mind isn't leaping and bouncing to nastier, more urgent places, like someone's I know.

As his tongue searches mine, I feel him hard against me. I'd almost forgotten it—this luscious feeling of being desired, of having a gorgeous man now kissing me down my neck. As we kiss, that hand of his is growing more audacious, and I think we're both highly interested to know just how bold I'll let it be. Niko's breathing is focused, his want evident, but he's waiting for a signal from me. Anything.

Could be shifting so I'm clearly more accessible . . . could be sending up a flare. Could be—

My cell phone buzzes in my pants pocket.

Niko gives a muffled chuckle against my clavicle. "Tell me you don't have to get that."

"I have to get that." Nelson is supposed to call to give me a five-minute warning so I can prep for his and Marva's return. Scooching from under Niko, I pull out my phone. "Hello?"

It's Nelson, telling me they're in the driveway.

"What happened to my five minutes?" I say, more snappish than I mean, but Niko is lightly running his fingertips along my waist and I'm not appreciating that it needs to end.

I hang up and reluctantly push him away. "They're here."

"*Here* here?"

"I'm afraid so."

He groans, but it's good-natured. Climbing off the bed, he says, "I suppose you need to deal with this."

"Yep." My brain is already at the front door—letting Marva in and touring her around to show her how much better the house looks—although my body wants to linger. I drag myself up. "Wish me luck."

"Luck. You need me?"

"No, you should probably go. I have no idea how she's going to react. I need to be ready for anything. In fact, go out the back door, will you?" After Marva so astutely keyed into the past romance I had with Daniel, I don't want to risk her running into Niko now and picking up on our makeout session.

Niko brushes crushed Styrofoam dust off my shirt, which is now all over his, too. "I could come back later. Check on things."

It's tempting because I know exactly the things he intends to check on—and they would *love* a visit, it's been so long since anybody's cared to stop by. But I can't see getting naked with him yet, and that's where this would be heading. Besides, I hear the slam of the door in the living room, which throws a bucket of cold water on my libido.

"Thanks," I say. "But that's not such a good idea."

"Really? Because I think it's an excellent idea."

"How about I take a rain check?"

He fixes me with a sizzling look that goes all the way to my toes, with a stop or two in between. "I'll hold you to that."

I find Marva with Nelson, standing in the living room. "You," she says. "Where's the Escobar?"

By now, I'm used to this—her naming an art piece by artist's name only (and addressing me as *you*). She should also be used to my replying, "The Escobar? What'd it look like?"

"Metal. Lady."

She's referring to what I call *The Angry Governess*. "Smitty's guys moved her into your office."

"I preferred it here."

Nelson gives me a conspiratorial wink. "C'mon, Miss Marva, you promised me I could have the food that was delivered while you were gone. I'm starving."

Marva slides a chair aside and starts digging through a box behind it. She's mumbling about how the hell is she supposed to find anything now that everything's been thrown God knows where by God knows whom that was trampling through her house all hours of the God knows when.

I try again. "We did quite a lot of work while you were away. It's probably a shock that so much is gone, but of course we only took what you—"

"What about the Baselitz?"

"Uh . . ."

She snorts impatiently. "Bright colors. Painted upside down. Tremendous use of brushstroke."

"About six feet tall?"

"Yes."

"Smitty took it. You said—"

"Took it where?"

"For auction. Per your instructions."

"Hmmph."

She starts up the stairs with a grunt of effort. Nelson says, "Marva, you might want to wait on stairs until you're—"

"Are you going to help me, or shall I risk taking a tumble because you're more concerned about getting free food than assisting your client?"

"Now, now." Nelson trots over to escort her up the stairs. "Let's not take it out on your loyal nurse. You have Lucy here for that."

Touring the upstairs goes similarly to how it did in the living room. Marva grouses about what's missing, though she can't give specifics because she has no idea what was up there in the first place.

When we get to the bathroom, she points to the toilet, which is finally visible now. "And *what*, may I ask, is *that*?"

"A toilet?" Is this a trick question?

"It's filthy. Get Mei-Hua to clean it."

Sure, if she'd ever take off her headphones long enough for me to give her instructions.

By the time Marva tromps back down the stairs, through the kitchen, and into the dining room, I'm a nervous wreck. I've managed to dodge every accusation so far, but we're not through the whole house yet.

Marva furiously pulls up a chair to the table and stands on it so she can reach the chandelier, from which she has a dozen or so necklaces dangling. Nelson is poised behind her, hands up so as to catch her if she falls. She yanks the necklaces down, hanging them one by one over her arm. "I'd best get these now before they walk off, too."

"Nothing walked off, Marva. There's not even that much gone. It only seems like a lot because you're not used to having any space to move around."

She struggles down off the chair, Nelson's hands hovering protectively over her but not daring to touch her. Necklaces clang and knock against one another as she sets them on the counter. "I suppose my office has been stripped to the floorboards as well." Marva bustles past me, limping slightly now but too focused on finding fault to stop and ask for her cane. She's grumbling under her breath. Although I can't make out what she's saying, I do pick up such words as "careless" and "sloppy."

I trail after her, keeping up a string of positive banter. My words bounce off her like bullets off an invisible force field. Her agitation builds as we make it through the office and on toward her bedroom.

*Her bedroom.* Why didn't I listen to Niko? How could I ever have thought Marva would react like a rational person and be happy to see her home looking so much better? As it is, it's still a pigsty, but you'd figure I'd gutted the place, the way she's carrying on.

As we approach the room, she stops in the doorway, as if to enter it would be to condone what I'd done.

"You moved the bed to the middle."

"Yes, I thought it—"

"It should be against the wall."

"Nelson and I will be glad to move it back." I shoot a pleading look in his direction. "But isn't it pleasant in here now? You can see your TV so much easier, and—"

"My book," she says, striding toward the bed. "It was right here. I was looking at *Grimm's Fairy Tales.* A very rare edition. Where is it?" She yanks open the nightstand's one tiny drawer, which I've left empty so she can put her personal items in there, and then twists around to face me. "Well?"

"I . . . I . . ." Did I really lose that? So much was going on, what with Smitty here, and Niko's crew running about, and me making goo-goo eyes at Niko. "You did say whatever wasn't behind the green chair could go. So if it was on your nightstand, I would have assumed—"

"You *assumed.*"

"But . . . but you said—" Ugh, could I be any more spineless? I stand straighter. "If it wasn't behind the green chair, then Niko took it to the collectibles distributor."

Marva keeps opening and closing the drawer, as if by magic it will appear. "If. *If* it's there."

"I'll check with Niko. Items from this room were only recently dropped off. We can always get it back."

She narrows her eyes at me. "Did anything in this room go to the trash?"

"Only if it was evidently garbage."

"What you're telling me is that the book is gone and you didn't see it go, so it could have been tossed in the trash."

"But it wasn't."

My decisive reply seems to push her over the edge she'd been teetering on. She is no longer Marva—she is a billowing storm cloud, and headed my way. "I entrust my precious belongings to you. Yet for all you know, this extremely rare *masterpiece* of *literature* is in the trash."

"It's not in the trash."

"How can you know? I'll answer for you: You can't. Lucy, you are fired."

Huh? Fired? Just like that?

She finally calls me by my name and it's to tell me I'm fired?

Surely she doesn't mean it. "Marva, you don't understand—"

"Get out."

"But—"

"Out. Of. My. Home." She points dramatically to the door. "Now."

"Look, I'll go to the warehouse myself and—"

"Out. And don't let me see you here again. I'll have to deal with retrieving the book myself. That is, if in fact it hasn't been carelessly destroyed."

"You're not even giving me a chance." I'm in the right here, and darn it, I'm going to defend myself. "If that book was so important, then you should have taken care to put it away properly. Now, I am willing to go—"

"If you are not off this property in five seconds, I will get my gun."

I stop, too stunned for a moment to say or do anything. Even if she's bluffing, threatening to kill me crosses a line I didn't know was there.

As I back myself out the door, the superior smirk on Marva's face makes me want to get in the last word. "I'm leaving, but not because I'm afraid of getting shot. I don't believe for a minute you could find your gun in this mess. But good luck. Maybe whatever poor sucker you hire next won't mind being constantly demeaned and yelled at and bullied. Me? I'm done."

Nelson's eyes are pie plates as I nudge past him and head to the living room to grab my shoes and purse.

My moment of bravado fizzles as soon as I step out onto the porch.

I'm homeless.

Jobless.

And my feet hurt.

Still, I'm about to walk defiantly out into the night and never look back when it hits me in a moment of blazing clarity that I've got no place else to go.

I flop down onto a porch step. A few minutes go by—although my mind is so busy spinning it could have been days—then Nelson steps out and sits down next to me. "You'll survive." He's using his nurse voice, and his pity shines a beacon on how pathetic my life is.

I lean my head against the railing. "I am such a loser."

"No, you're not. You did great. Which is probably why she fired you. If it makes you feel any better, she can't help it. Hoarding is an illness."

"Being a bitch isn't an illness. But she sure has a walloping case of that."

He nods agreeably. "So what are you going to do now?"

"I'm going to put on my shoes."

"I mean to fix the situation."

"What are you talking about? You were there—she threatened to shoot me."

"Big deal. She does that to me every day, and I'm still here, aren't I?"

"You didn't lose her precious rare-edition, probably-worth-a-zillion-dollars book."

"So go get it back."

"What's the point? It's not about the book. I'll spend hours digging through boxes to find it, and then she'll come up with some other excuse to fire me all over again."

"It's worth a shot, though." My face must reflect my hopelessness because he says, "Look, she needs to clean out her house, and she can't do it by herself. She got straight on the phone with that worthless son of hers and told him to call that other place. That . . . um . . . what's it called?"

"Organize Me, exclamation point," I reply dully. "And good. Let them put up with Marva's insanity."

"You don't mean that."

"Yes, I do. If she wants to replace me that fast, let her." I'm relieved to feel a surge of bitterness—it's so much more energizing than misery.

"But where are you going to go? Do you even have a place to live?"

"Yes." My mind flashes to Heather's house, and my bitterness congeals and turns into something murky and awful. I don't want to stay there again. If I have to drag myself along on hands and knees, I want to keep my life in a forward direction. Sharing a blow-up mattress with Abigail and smiling through dinners with Heather's perfect family is a one-way ticket to far too many memories of the worst of days after Ash left. I can't go back. "No. I don't know. I'll figure something out."

"Go get the book. Then come crawling back here, tail between your legs, and beg Marva to take you back. Do it before she figures out somebody else can do your job every bit as well as you, and probably better."

"Thanks so much. That's tremendously inspiring."

"I'm a nurse—sometimes that means giving people a shot in the ass when they need it."

# chapter eleven

It's raining as I pull into the warehouse parking lot. It's the next town over on a side street off Chicago Avenue, although it's not so much a warehouse as what appears to have once been a small business, like a flower shop or dentist's office. My back gets drenched while I fumble to open an umbrella. Then I scurry to the front door, dodging puddles as I go, and nearly run smack into Daniel, who is standing beneath a narrow awning.

"I didn't expect to see you here," I say. I'd called Daniel to get the address of the warehouse. (I have it in my files—I'm not completely incompetent, contrary to popular opinion—but I wasn't about to venture back to Marva's for it.) I'd ended up telling Daniel the whole story. He'd made the appropriate consoling remarks, but at no point did he say he was going to show up.

"Thought you could use a hand." He pulls a face. "Bad news, though. They closed at six."

"Oh, no."

"Won't reopen until Monday morning. I tried calling to see if they had an emergency contact. There was only a recorded message."

"It can't be closed. If I don't get that book, Marva's going to hire someone else." I'd given myself such a pep talk on the drive over that I'd already mentally handed myself the job back, along with a pay raise and a certificate for Employee of the Month—all contingent on finding that book.

I wriggle the doorknob, senselessly. Of course it's locked. "Did you try knocking?" I ask. "Maybe someone is still there who can let us in." I start rapping on the door. When that doesn't yield a response, I climb around bushes at the front to peer in the window. My feet sink into the mud, and brambles scratch at my calves. "Hello! Anybody there?" I cup my hands over the glass pane so I can see in past the fog I'm creating with my breath. There's a tiny reception area but nothing more. The merchandise must be housed in the rear. "I'm going to check the back."

I strut purposefully around the building, darkness and puddles be damned. I'm at the back door before realizing that Daniel has followed me. He's wearing a flannel shirt open over a T-shirt, and he's tugged the flannel up to shield against the rain in a manner that makes him at a glance appear headless. I wave him over so he can crouch under the umbrella with me, and I'm hit with a jolt of nostalgia when I catch the smell of the soap he uses. It makes me want to shove him back out into the rain. How dare he stir up memories when what I need to be doing is finding a way into this building.

Daniel takes hold of the umbrella as I knock. "Anybody in there?" I call out.

"It's a Friday. I'm sure they left the second it hit six o'clock. I do have an idea though. We can just buy an old copy of *Grimm's Fairy Tales* at a used-book store and fob it off on her."

"Marva's was a very rare edition. Are we going to find one of those?"

"Oh." Saying the words *rare edition* to Daniel is almost like whispering sweet nothings—he shivers from the idea of it. Or it could be the cold. April in Chicago can be mighty brisk.

I turn back to my knocking, my knuckles tender from the damp and cold. I'm at it for so long I might still have been there banging away at that door come Monday morning only Daniel says, "Nobody's there, Luce. You might as well give up."

He's right; I hate it but he's right. I pull my hand away, tucking it in my pocket for warmth, staring at the door. Perhaps I can will it open with the power of my mind. But I suppose for that to work, I shouldn't be letting myself be distracted by thoughts of Ash getting off a plane at O'Hare, fresh and hale after his successful bout of rehab, then wilting from the news that he has no home.

I've blown it. I've got no job, no money, and no idea how I'm going to move forward from here. My bag of tricks is empty. I don't even realize I'm crying until I hear Daniel groan, "Oh, man, don't do that. I hate it when you cry."

"I'm not crying," I snuffle.

"It's not so bad. Tell you what: We'll come back first thing Monday. We'll find the book. Then I'll go with you to Marva's and I'll charm the pants off her. She'll take you back."

"I'm afraid you overestimate your charm."

It sounds snottier than I meant it, but Daniel gamely says, "That's only because I usually rein it in. Don't want to make the ladies faint." He nudges me with his shoulder, trying to bump the misery out of me.

"You know what's pathetic? I'm so stupid I thought my luck was changing. Dumb, huh?"

"Not dumb." He rubs my back—it's an inappropriately intimate gesture, but I let myself sink into the comfort and familiarity of it. "We'll figure something out."

"Unless you've got a hidden talent for picking locks, then I'd say it's over."

"I am a man of many talents, but that's not among them. Although . . ." He thrusts the umbrella handle toward me. "Hold this a sec." He tugs his flannel over his head again and hustles to a window that's partially hidden by a large shrub. The window is about four feet high and a foot and a half wide. It's a slat window, made of strips of glass that twist open from a lever located—unfortunately for us—on the inside of the building. Daniel lays his palms on one of the glass panes and gives it a shove up—which to my surprise slides it free.

"Are they kidding me? That's their idea of security?" I say, aghast. "What kind of slipshod operation are they running here?"

Daniel easily removes another pane. "You should give them hell when you talk to them. On Monday. In your official position as a gainfully employed representative of Marva Meier Rios." He pauses to look over at me. "You want to give me a bit of that umbrella action over here? I'm getting soaked."

By the time I join him, he's removed a third pane, and I'm awash with anxiety. "I was only joking about breaking in," I say, whispering now since I'm an accessory to a criminal act. "We shouldn't be doing this." I glance nervously around. The back of the building is secluded enough that we're not likely to be noticed, but it's lit by spotlights. I've got enough troubles without adding breaking and entering to the list.

"Two seconds ago you're sobbing into your sleeve, and now you're chickening out?"

"I didn't mean we should *steal* it. What if we get caught?"

"We won't. Besides, it's not stealing if you're only taking what's rightfully yours." He pulls out another glass pane and sets it against the building. "You forget that I have a vested interest in this, too. If you get the ax, then there goes my chance to earn out a commission in merchandise. I've already cleared a space in my living room for a few of those movie posters."

I feel a twinge of disappointment—I should have known Daniel was only here for the collectibles. Not that it matters. It doesn't. Why should I care for a minute what motivates Daniel so long as it gets the job done? Hard to believe it was only hours ago I was lustily rolling around on a bed with Niko. Now I'm following Daniel as he crawls through the tiny opening he's made in the window, which is far less fun.

Although it's dark when I step in, enough light spills in from outside that I can make out we're in a storeroom. It makes up the bulk of the building, and it's largely empty, except for a pile of boxes, bags, and crates in a corner that I recognize as Marva's. On the far side of the room are several doors, which I assume lead to other storage units and the front reception area. A desk and several filing cabinets make up the only furniture. I kick off my shoes, which are caked in mud. There's nothing I can do about the rest of my wet clothes. Daniel is tugging off his flannel, but the T-shirt underneath is soaked, too.

"Don't turn on the overhead light," he says.

"I'm not an idiot."

"Didn't say you were." He flips on the tiny flashlight at the end of his phone and shines it in the direction of the pile. "Any idea where the book might be?"

"I'm guessing somewhere in that pile."

"Excellent. That narrows it down."

We head over, and he tugs open the flaps of a box. "This looks like as good a place to start as any." He tips his head toward the other side of the pile. "You want to work over there? We'll meet in the middle."

"I don't have a light."

"Your phone doesn't have one?"

"No. But my bra turns into a secret spy camera if that helps any."

He lifts one eyebrow, and I instantly regret the reference to my bra. Daniel mercifully must sense my discomfort, because he shoves a box toward me. "If we stick close enough together, we should both be able to work off of my light."

I'm on my third box when Daniel shouts, "Yes!"

My head snaps up. "You found it?"

"The book? No." He hands me the phone and pulls his T-shirt off over his head. "Glad to see you weren't lying about that robe from *Rocky*—I'm freezing." Daniel pulls a robe out of a box big enough to hold a washing machine and pulls it on and belts it at the waist. It's comically broad on his skinny frame. Then he dances around me like a boxer, throwing fake jabs.

"You realize that robe is losing value every second you wear it."

"Don't care! You know why?" Jab. "Because I float like a butterfly, sting like a bee." Jab, jab.

"Any chance there's another robe in there?" I grab at my pant leg, and the fabric makes a wet sucking noise as it pulls away from my skin.

Daniel bends back over the box. "I'm afraid not. But, this is your lucky day, my queen, because we have this!" He holds up a long, satiny medieval dress.

"Thanks, I'll pass."

"It's the best I have to offer unless you'd prefer the gold bikini in here. This dress weighs a ton, so at least it'll be warm."

"How about I wear the robe and you get the dress?"

"No way. Blue's not my color."

I trade him his phone for the dress. It occurs to me that I'm going to have to take my pants off before putting it on or I'll get mud all over it. "Turn around," I say.

"What?"

I make a twirling motion with my finger. "Around. I have to take these wet, muddy clothes off or they'll ruin the material."

He turns around but shines the phone's light over his shoulder so I can see what I'm doing. I unzip my pants and slide them down, then pull my blouse off over my head. I'm folding them neatly and setting them aside when Daniel says, "There's nothing you've got there I haven't seen before."

It does seem odd to be so modest when mere months ago Daniel would not only have been welcome to see me in only a bra and panties, he'd be an active participant in helping to remove them. Those days are over. I wrestle myself into the dress. It's got about five layers of fabric; it's also made for a woman about a foot taller and fifty pounds heavier. When I finally get it on, I face away from Daniel, gather my hair up, and say, "Do me up."

It takes him a couple awkward minutes to secure all the buttons. When I turn around, the top of my bra and straps are showing. The dress's waistline hangs to my hips. "You look enchanting," Daniel says.

"I look ridiculous."

"Yes, but in an enchanting sort of way."

I turn back to the box I'd been looking through. "Let's find a book, all right?"

We're not at it more than fifteen minutes when Daniel says, "Oh, wow!"

"You found the book!"

"No. Sorry. I'll quit doing that. But it's a baseball signed by Robert Redford, I'll assume from *The Natural*. Greatest baseball movie ever made—parts of it filmed right here in Chicago." He tosses the ball up and catches it. "Hey, remember that time we took Ash to that event on Wrigley Field? And he got to run the bases?" As soon as Daniel mentions Ash's name, I find myself bristling. Sure, *now* Daniel wants to reminisce about the good times, but when things started to fall apart with Ash, all he could do was point out the negative.

"I wasn't there," I say. "It was the two of you. One of your guys' nights out."

"That's right." Daniel lets the ball drop from his fingers into the box. "How's he doing?"

"He's good."

"Do you get to talk to him much?"

"Once in a while." That's close to the truth. At least the *once* part.

"What's he have to say?"

Most of my phone call with Ash wasn't anything I'd care to recount for Daniel. I'm still feeling hopeful after it, but I have a niggling fear that Daniel would tell me I'm in denial—that it wasn't good news at all. He'd probably only focus on the part of the call where Ash was complaining. Which, granted, was 95 percent of it. "He's making progress" is all I say.

"You must be so happy. How did you ever get him to—"

I cut Daniel off before he can finish the question. "We should get back to what we came here to do. We are here illegally, after all. We shouldn't dally."

My abruptness must have offended him because he says, "Uh, okay. Back to work it is. No dallying. I won't even dilly, if it makes you feel better."

"I didn't mean to be rude."

"No big deal. I get it: You don't want to talk about Ash. It's just that I care about the kid. And I—" He pauses, and I busy myself by opening the flaps of another box. Trying to do anything but look at Daniel. "I want to see him get better."

"It looks like he's on his way." *No thanks to you.*

"I'm glad."

We go back to work, and we're not at it for five minutes before Daniel says, "Hey, check this out."

Could his attention span be any shorter? "Now what is it?"

"Is that any way to talk to the man who has found . . . *this*?" He holds up a tattered copy of *Grimm's Fairy Tales.*

Without thinking I throw myself at him in a hug. "I can't believe you found it so fast! Thank you!"

"You're welcome."

I can feel the book against my back where he's holding me, and I reach to grab it. I flip to the title page. Daniel's hand lingers on my waist as he holds the light so I can see.

"She's written all over it!" I say. "I can't believe she put me through all this for a book she's ruined!" The spine is cracked and the pages yellowed, and a quick scan of its contents reveals Marva has scribbled here and there throughout—in margins, on blank areas at the end of chapters, right over the top of the book's text and illustrations.

"Are you sure it's Marva's writing?"

"Positive." It matches the signature on her paintings, and the crazy forward-scrawl of the *Do not disturb* note she'd taped to her door my first day of work. Plus I'm constantly seeing her writing in a book. I just didn't realize that was the one I've been on this scavenger hunt for.

"She defaced this rare an edition?" he says as if Marva had graffitied a national monument.

"Whatever. The good news is, now I have it. Thanks to you— credit where credit is due. I'll take this baby back to Marva and wave it in her face. She'll have to give me my job back."

"Let me see that for a sec, will you?"

I hand the book over and check my watch. It's not yet nine o'clock. Marva will still have time to cancel the services of Organize Me!, those lowlife interlopers.

Daniel slides to the floor, back against a box, and starts reading Marva's notes. I'm eager to get going, but it's only fair to give him time to look at the book if that's what he wants. I wouldn't have it if it weren't for him.

"Anything interesting?" I ask, gathering up my medieval skirts and taking a seat on the floor next to Daniel.

"It's strange. I figured these notes would be on the stories or the illustrations."

"They're not? Then what is it?"

"At first glance I thought it seemed to be a diary of sorts—I was so excited. To have a chance to read the deepest, most private thoughts of Marva Meier Rios would be unbelievable. But this is . . . it's a bunch of lists. Or random ideas."

I peer down the page he has open and read aloud what's scrawled down the side of the page. " 'Couch vs. bed. Bed's been done a million times—trite. Couch, might roll off. Don't want floor. Awkward.' Ew, do you suppose she's debating the best place to have sex?" That's nothing I want to picture.

"Beats me." He flips a few pages and reads, " 'Need to get purple pantsuit altered. Have the blond girl handle. Fits oddly when lying down.'"

"She doesn't even know my name? I'm the blond girl to her?"

He absently pats my knee, absorbed in the book. "Maybe she wrote that when you first started."

"I've seen the pantsuit she's referring to. She tried on outfits for me once. I can't imagine why she bothered since she never goes anywhere."

"How can she? You haven't gotten her only pantsuit altered." He flips to the back inside cover. "Now this is interesting . . ."

Before I can ask what, I hear the click of a door, followed by the overhead light flipping on. A jolt of terror runs through me. I start to fly to my feet but Daniel's arms grab on to me, and he pulls me so we're scooted behind a wall of boxes. I hear a woman's voice from the other side of the room. "Jeez, it's freezing in here."

A man answers, "I turned off the heat before we left. Didn't expect you'd make me come back here on a Friday night. I'll go kick it on."

"Thanks, hon."

I'm panicked that, even as still as I am, I'm trumpeting my whereabouts. Daniel's mouth is right at my ear. "Hide your face. While he's gone, we should make a run for it."

I mouth my words back to him, *She's still here.*

Daniel shrugs. Guess he figures we can outrun her. We quietly gather up our clothing, and we each get our car keys in our hands. He pulls the hood of the *Rocky* robe up, and I cover my face with the book. Then we leap to our feet and run to the window.

The woman gives a shout of surprise, but by that time I've already snatched up my muddy shoes and Daniel's shoving my skirts out behind me through the window. It's not raining anymore so I jump over my umbrella rather than take the time to mess with it.

"That must be Kathy, the owner!" Daniel huffs as we race around the building to our cars. "She's not following. I heard her calling for her husband." She must have been terrified to confront Daniel and me by herself, looking menacing as we must have in our robe and long dress.

I throw myself into the car, fumbling with the keys. My breath is coming in jagged bursts. I start it up and pull out. Daniel is behind me as I tear out of the parking lot, hang a right onto the first street, and start driving randomly, to put as much distance as I can between my car and the warehouse.

Daniel flashes his brights at me after we've been driving for a few minutes, and I pull over into a gas station. When we get out of our cars, he's laughing. "Holy crap, can you believe that? I almost had a heart attack!"

"You and me both." I lean against my door, finally letting relief flood in. "You think she recognized you?"

"They've never seen me; that was the problem. It's all been on the phone. I didn't feel like spending the night at Cook County while they figured out we're their clients. I hear that those strip searches aren't as much fun as they sound."

"Mission accomplished. Now I need to return the book to Marva, and you and I are back in business."

"Give it to me first. I want to take another look."

I grab the book out of my car. "Not too long. It needs to be in her hands before she figures out life is more pleasant without me around."

"No, it isn't," he says, not glancing up from the book.

All right. That's enough of Daniel's being nice to me. I endured seven months of grieving that he left me, and now he wants to get sentimental on the very day I have moved on to someone else. Instead of addressing what he said—which would only dignify it and, worse, encourage more—I say, "You looking for anything in particular?"

"I've figured out why she was so worried about this book. Look." He opens to the back inside cover, where she's squeezed a list in tiny letters.

## HOW

### Gun
*Pro:* Efficient. Have one. Not typical for a woman, so more powerful a statement.
*Con:* Messy.

### Pills
*Pro:* Like old times. No pain. Fun for a while.
*Con:* Risk of vomiting or if don't take enough, possible vegetative state.

### Hanging
*Pro:* Visually exciting. Could get workers to set up noose (call it art project).
*Con:* Not sure am the hanging type.

### Asphyxiation

*Pro:* Bag over head.
*Con:* Bag over head.

### Gas

*Pro:* No pain. No mess.
*Con:* Don't have car or garage. (Borrow blond girl's car?)

"Oh, for goodness' sake," I say. "How hard is the name Lucy to remember?"

"You're missing the point."

"Which is . . . ?"

"Think about it. All these notes—they're about getting her affairs in order. She has such a tight deadline for you to get the house cleaned. And a list of pros and cons for ways to die? It's obvious. Marva is planning to kill herself."

Marva? Commit suicide? My first instinct is to deny it, but that's only because suicide is nothing I'd ever do. It's hard to imagine anyone considering it, especially with such calm preparation. As soon as Daniel points it out, though, it all makes sense. It certainly does finally answer the question about why she's cleaning out her house when she's never wanted to before.

"That's horrible," I say.

"About as horrible as it gets." Daniel snaps the book shut. "Let me keep this for a while. Study it. I'll bet there's something we can do to stop her. The more we know about her plans, the better chance we have."

I can barely register what Daniel is saying, although it appears he's already formulating a plan of action. I'm still mired in the awfulness of it. Even as mean as Marva's been to me, I sure don't want to see her dead. Yet I am torn between finding it terribly sad, and downright infuriating. She has a *son*. Even if she doesn't want to live for herself, how could she do it to him?

"This whole thing makes me ill," I say after a while, reluctantly, but prompted by seeing Daniel tuck the book under his arm a bit too possessively for my comfort. "But it doesn't erase the fact that I need that book. It's the only way I'll get my job back."

"So you're just going to pretend you don't know?"

He's looking at me in disgust. It's déjà vu, Daniel judging me because I'm not dealing with a problem the exact way he would.

"Look, I can't do anything about it right now. And I certainly can't do anything if I'm not working for her anymore. So I'll return the book. Marva is not going to kill herself tonight, or even this week. She has things to do. For starters, clearing out her house."

"That brings up a whole other problem. If she's going to kill herself as soon as her house is in order, then you can't do it, Luce. She can't be allowed to finish the job."

"If it's not me, it'll be somebody else. And, yes, it bothers me that I'll be a party to Marva committing suicide, but it's her decision to make. Not mine."

"She's a creative genius. And someone you've gotten to know. It seems to me it ought to be worth a little effort on your part to save her life."

"I never said I didn't care. It's just nothing I am willing to deal with this very minute."

"It never is."

"What's that supposed to mean?"

"Nothing. Forget it. Here, take the book. Get your job back and don't say a word. Pretend everything is fine and it will be, right? That's how it works?"

I grab the book and storm back to my car. "It's easy to be a hero when you're not the one whose livelihood is on the line. If I'm going to do anything, seems to me it'd help if I had a damned *job*. If I was in a position to *talk* to her instead of out on the streets."

I'm furiously opening my door when Daniel says, "Wait. I'm sorry. You're right."

The apology seems sincere enough that I pause.

He leans against his car. "It's not always easy. You. Me. Working together."

Tell me about it. "I never asked you to come tonight. I'm lucky you did—I'd have never broken in on my own. Even with the book, there's no guarantee she'll take me back. But the sooner I get it there, the better my chances are. As we stand here arguing, the clock is ticking."

Daniel nods, but then we spend another few minutes deciding the best way for me to proceed with Marva. I'm calm and confident by the time I pull away. As much as Daniel's hurt me in the past, I'm left with the annoying reminder of how when he and I were together on something (which is how it was for a long time before it wasn't), it was really, really good.

# chapter twelve

The best way to honor someone who's passed on is not by keeping their belongings, it's by keeping their memory alive in the way you live your life.

—Organizing expert Claudia Marx, as quoted in
Things Are Not People

I s that my dress?" Marva doesn't seem so much angry as curious as to why I'd be wearing one of her costumes. She's in the mudroom—which means she'd have seen me if I'd snuck into the bungalow to change clothes. I was forced to gather my courage, along with my skirts, and march directly up to her.

"Here," I say, handing her the book. "*Grimm's Fairy Tales.* Although I'm a fool to have bothered. It's not worth anything. There's writing all over it."

That was part of the strategy I mapped out with Daniel: admit I'd seen the writing, but act as though I didn't look closely. Fool Marva into believing her secret's safe. Otherwise, she might be tempted to hide the evidence, and I want to be able to study her notes in the book later when I have more time.

She nestles it protectively in the crook of her arm. "Some things are of value, even if they aren't worth money. You'd be wise to understand that lesson."

"Then I'm delighted it's again in your possession. I'll see you in the morning." I say it boldly, as if we'd agreed that surrendering the book guaranteed me my job. (That's also per advice from Daniel: "Asking for the job gives her the power. Take it as your right.") I'll admit, the idea of playing a power game with Marva seems absurd. If this were Vegas, all money would be on her. "I'd prefer to start on the second floor if your knees are up to climbing the stairs. That's all for now. Good night."

She doesn't protest—plus she doesn't pull out a gun and shoot me—both of which I take as positive signs.

"By the way," I say before leaving, with as placid an expression as I can muster, "if you get a call about a break-in at the warehouse that may have occurred this evening, there's no need for concern. Only a few items were taken . . . of little to no value. All but one will be returned."

To my surprise, Marva throws back her head and erupts into a bark of laughter. I've never heard her laugh before—not heartily like this. "Princess," she says, her expression so lit up that I don't even mind the derisive nickname, "I didn't think you had it in you."


Hello?" My mom sounds breathless as she answers her phone.

"Am I calling too early?" Although it was all I could do to blow up the mattress last night before passing out asleep on it, I woke before dawn. First, I treated myself to a lovely flashback of making out with Niko, the delicious heat and weight of his body against mine as we kissed. But then my bickering with Daniel stole into the picture, followed by the idea of Marva's potential suicide—the last of which obliterated any daydreams I might have wanted to entertain myself with.

I'm entirely out of my depth. My gut says I should tell Will about Marva since he's her closest family. It'd be the decent thing to do. After all, if someone knew that Ash was suicidal, I'd want to be told. I'm still bitter that nobody tipped me off to how bad my son's drug problem was. I'd had to hear it from that cabdriver.

The problem is, Will is such a jerk. He might kill the messenger.

"It's not too early," my mom says. "I'm mall walking, but I can talk. Your father pooped out on me after the first ten minutes. He's already at the Starbucks having a muffin. What's up?"

"I need motherly advice. Let's say I knew of someone who was planning to commit suicide."

"Who is going to commit suicide?"

"I can't say."

"Not one of your brothers?"

"It's no one you know. She's older, and the son is grown, but she's keeping it a secret from him. I'd like to warn him in case he can talk her out of it, but I'm not sure that he will. It might make things worse."

"It's not my sister Joyce, is it?"

"*Mom.*"

"All right. Let me think." After a moment, she says, "Do you know *why* she's planning to do it?"

"Because she's depressed, I guess. Why else would anyone kill themselves?"

"You said she's older. Could it be that she's terminally ill and she wants to go with dignity? It wouldn't be an unreasonable notion. Nobody wants to be a burden to their children."

I mull it for a moment. "You might be onto something. She's only a few years younger than you, but she has a nurse come around regularly, plus she recently spent time in the hospital. It certainly is possible."

"There you go!" my mom says triumphantly.

"She's also a recluse and, other than the hospital, hasn't left the house in years. She could want to end what she considers her miserable life."

We debate the possibilities for a few more minutes until I'm more confused than when I first called. "Thanks, I'd better get going," I say.

"Did you decide what to do?"

"I suppose first I need to find out if she's dying and is simply speeding up the process. Although, while we're on the subject, if you're planning anything drastic at any point, you'd better tell me."

"You can count on it. I keep nagging your father about doing one of those living wills. If there ever comes a point that I'm going to be a vegetable, or completely doddering, I'd rather you pull the plug sooner than later. It needs to be in writing that my daughter will handle it if I can't."

"Not me. That's Mike's job. He's the oldest."

"No, it has to be you. Mike would never do it. He's responsible enough to be put in charge of the money, but when it comes down to the nitty-gritty, he'd wimp out. He doesn't have your strength."

When I end the call, I'm smiling. Even with all the mistakes I've made with Ash, that's my mom's gentle reminder that I'm stepping up and being strong in handling the situation. Even if I'm not entirely sure it's true, it sure feels nice to know that somebody sees it that way.

B y Monday morning I'm determined to intercept Nelson when he stops in to check on Marva. With God as my witness, that man is going to tell me whether Marva is dying. He's sidestepped my questions in the past, but I'm not letting him get away with that today. All weekend, instead of being elated anytime I pried an item from Marva's grasp, I wrestled with worry: Am I helping her take one step closer to the grave?

I've got enough mother guilt; I don't need to add to it.

As I stand in the kitchen waiting for Marva to emerge from her bedroom, I plot my strategy for when I confront Nelson. He's the type who'll withhold information to toy with me, so I need to be cagey. My thoughts are interrupted by a bang of the back door, and Niko walks in through the mudroom. "Hey, gorgeous," he says, "how was your weekend?"

If I had any concerns I'd feel awkward—after all, the last time I saw him, we were horizontal—I needn't have. He's looking at me as if I were three scoops high on a waffle cone.

"Busy," I say, tucking a strand of hair behind my ear in what I hope is a come-hither manner. "I've got a ton for you guys to clear out today."

"That woman works you way too hard. It's not healthy."

"I've got a deadline to meet." I neglect to mention I also don't have anything else to do.

"Haven't you ever heard that saying? All work and no play . . . ?"

"I'm a dull girl?"

"Not even close."

I feel that familiar rush Niko's flirting gives me. I'm searching a brain that's gone gooey for a clever response when my cell phone rings. When I pull it from my pocket to give it a quick glance, I see that Daniel's calling. Probably wants to report in on the warehouse— he texted me over the weekend to say he was going to stop there this morning to see what they had to say about the break-in.

Switching my phone over to vibrate without answering, I say to Niko, "From now on, I'll do my best to be interesting."

"To be on the safe side," he says, stepping closer, "you and I should—"

He stops when my phone buzzes in my pocket. Stupid Daniel—I can't believe he's calling again already. *If I wanted to talk to you, don't you think I'd have picked up the first time? I'm prying a date out of a hot guy here!* "I'm ignoring it," I say. "It's just the collectibles guy. What were you saying?"

"That we should grab drinks tonight after work."

I nod, trying to hide my giddiness. A date! Not just that, but potentially s-e-x. This very evening! I almost want to suggest to Niko that we skip the drinks and get straight to the fun stuff, but I'll need alcohol to fuel my courage. Not only do I usually go beyond the third-date-equals-sex rule but I have to be, if not in love, at least in a reasonable facsimile if I'm going to feel comfortable offering up the goods. In recent months, however, my life has been one dreary event after another. I deserve romance. Not to mention skin-to-skin contact. It's time for a whole new me, and it so happens this me is sluttier. "Okay," I say.

"I'll swing back here after I drop off the last load—like around seven?"

"Sounds good."

From there, I give him instructions on what he and his crew can start on. As he heads up the stairs, I can't help but watch him, thinking, *In mere hours, I'll totally get to tap that!*

Shortly after noon, I hear Nelson's van rumble up. I slam shut the drawer I'm sorting through and run out to greet him. He's pulling a duffel from the van as I approach. "Hey, Nelson. You have a minute to talk?"

"Not now, my love. I'm already running late. Why—what do you need?"

I don't want to blurt it out right there. "How about lunch? I'll treat."

He starts walking to the front door. "No can do. I'm on rounds today. Only here to do a quick procedure."

"Oh, really? What sort of procedure?"

"The usual."

"Which is . . . ?"

He pauses before heading through the door, which I've left open. "Which is none of your business."

"Come on, Nelson. Please? Tell me what Marva has—why she was in the hospital."

"I'm not going to divulge personal information about Marva's health for your entertainment. You may not believe this, but I have professional standards."

"Is that your opinion of me? That I only want to know for kicks?"

"What, suddenly you care about her?"

"Yes. As a matter of fact, I do." Oddly enough, I realize I mean it.

He pats the top of my head. "Sure you do. And I'm Mother Teresa."

I start to object, but Niko and Torch are carrying a couch down the stairs toward us. "Hold the door!" Torch yells. As I do, Nelson, that wily minx, manages to slip past me and into Marva's room.

Not wanting to risk being foiled again, I go out to Nelson's van and sit in the passenger seat. When he climbs in twenty minutes later, he greets me with "You've got to be kidding."

"Hi, honey!"

"Seriously, get out. I've got a man with late-stage liver cancer that needs his legs wrapped to reduce the swelling. You want to make him wait?"

"Do *you*? Look, answer my question and I'll leave you be. Is Marva dying?"

"We're all dying. It's only a matter of when."

"Nelson, I can't believe you won't answer a simple question for me. I thought we were friends."

He sits back and levels a look at me. "You want me to confide in you. Why should I? What secrets have you ever shared with me?"

"I would . . . if I had anything worth telling."

"Everybody has something worth telling. Come on . . . spill."

I'm dumbfounded. "You want me to give you a personal secret of mine, just so I can find out if Marva is dying?"

"Yep, that sounds about right."

"That's evil. Not to mention blackmail."

He puts a key in the ignition.

"Fine," I say, and his hand drops without starting the engine. "How about this. I've never told you this, and it's probably the worst and most personal secret in my life. My son is at drug rehab."

"Big deal. These days, who isn't? For that, I'm willing to tell you that Marva is a hoarder. There. Quid pro quo."

Ugh. I search my mind for a juicier piece of gossip—other than

Marva's suicide plans. There's no way I'd trust Nelson with that. Then the perfect thing occurs to me and I wilt. Surely there must be something less humiliating to reveal. But I struggle to figure out anything else. Nelson starts the van up. "I haven't got all day. Either get out or you're coming with me."

"Wait," I say, giving up. "Here's something. Friday, at work? Niko and I made out on Marva's bed. We only stopped because you and she came home."

He kicks the engine off in acceptance of my offering. "Now that's more like it. And here I was thinking you'd be a spinster for life. Was it good? Was there any removal of clothing and, if so, what exact pieces?"

"Forget it. I'm not giving you details. You haven't coughed up anything yet."

"Marva has diabetes. She was at the hospital for minor surgery to remove some infected tissue in her foot that was giving her trouble. Plus her knees are shot. She desperately needs replacement knees, but for reasons that elude me, she keeps putting it off. A lot of what I do is help her manage the pain."

"That's it? Diabetes? Bad knees? So you're telling me that it's not fatal?"

"Did Niko get any boob action?"

I can't believe I'm about to answer his question. "No. But there *was* feeling around."

"There now, that wasn't so hard, was it?" He lifts his brows suggestively. "Or was it . . . *hard* that is?"

"That's enough. Is Marva dying or not?"

"She's not. Other than the diabetes, some complications of arthritis, and those bum knees, that woman is healthy as a cow."

Marva holds up a sweater from a heap of clothes on the dining room table. "This is a keep."

Irritation rises in me like bile. *Why?* I want to ask her. *That's a*

*heavy winter sweater, and—as far as your plan goes—you'll never expe-
rience a winter again.*

Perhaps a better woman than me would feel sympathy for someone who has lost her zest for life, but I don't. It makes me furious.
Marva has so much talent and opportunity and *money*—not to mention a son—and instead of appreciating all she has, she's choosing to
have herself a pity party. One that—*grrrrr*—is forcing me to be a guest
of honor. "It's pilly," I say, taking the sweater from her and tossing it
into a pile for the yard sale.

"You've certainly got quite a bit of cheek today," Marva remarks,
although she doesn't retrieve the sweater.

"Trying to make your deadline." I realize I'm on the brink of acting insubordinate, but I keep thinking of all the people who *are* terminally ill—such as that cancer patient of Nelson's—and what they
wouldn't give to have a chance to live. Marva is throwing it all away. I
snort from the irony—the first thing Marva willingly throws away, and
it's her life.

She gives me a curious look. "Are you feeling well?"

Reminding myself how badly I need this job, I check my attitude
and offer a polite "I'm fine, thank you." We work in peaceable silence
until midafternoon, when the front doorbell rings. "I'll get it," I say.
"You can keep going."

When I open the door, Daniel is standing on the porch, holding a
sled under one arm. "I called earlier. Thought I'd try my luck at stopping by."

As he steps into the living room, I say, "What's with the sled?" I
recognize it as the movie prop we'd sent to the warehouse.

Daniel spies Marva in the dining room and calls a hello to her.
Then he says to me in a low voice, "I snagged it back when I went to
the warehouse this morning. If Marva changes her mind about—you
know—she'd be upset she gave it up."

"You're bringing things *back*?"

"Not things. *Thing*—singular. While I'm here, I can take a look
upstairs again. You said you wanted me to mark anything of value up

there, right? Plus," he says, leaning closer, "it'll give us a chance to talk all this over. Figure out what we're going to do to stop her."

He's being sweet—very sweet—but I don't want to deal with Daniel right now. Not when I'm on the brink of getting it on with Niko. Being around the man who broke my heart will only undermine my confidence, which is shaky to begin with. "Today's not so good," I whisper. "Marva's in a terrible mood, and—"

I'm interrupted by Marva's voice trilling across the room, "Your name's Daniel, isn't it? Is that Rosebud you have there?"

"Yes . . . on both counts." Daniel jogs over to her, explaining how he retrieved it from the warehouse, with vigorous apologies on how he'd *mistakenly* earmarked it to go when *clearly* no one in their right *mind* would ever part with it. Marva accepts the sled from Daniel as if it's a tiny blue box from Tiffany's and he's on one knee, instead of merely setting an old sled atop the pile of clothes on the table.

"Thanks for bringing that back," I manage to choke out as I join them, seeing no need to claim the role of the bad guy.

"My pleasure," Daniel says. He takes a moment to beam at Marva before turning his attention to me. "So if you have time, Lucy, let's hit the upstairs."

"I'd like to. But as you can see, Marva and I are in the middle of something."

"Oh, go," she says. "I'll be curious to see what this young man has to say. And I am certainly capable of sorting through a stack of clothing on my own."

"Great!" Daniel says, rubbing his hands together as if in anticipation of the many treasures he'll unearth. It's a gesture not lost on Marva, who smiles her approval. To love her stuff is, apparently, to love her.

I grab a handful of Post-its and lead Daniel upstairs. Halfway up, we bump into Niko, who is carrying a floor lamp. There's no getting around introductions. "This is Niko," I say to Daniel. "He's in charge of the work crew. And, Niko, this is the collectibles guy."

Daniel flashes me an annoyed look as he extends his hand to Niko and says, "Daniel."

So I *accidentally* forgot to say his name. What did he expect—that I'd give his life story? Introduce him as my ex-boyfriend? Suggest he give Niko a few tips on what I do and don't like in bed?

Niko shifts the lamp to his left hand so he can shake Daniel's. "Collectibles, huh?" he says. "Looks like a bunch of junk to me, but you'd know. You're the expert."

"That's the rumor," Daniel says.

Niko continues down the stairs as we walk up, and Daniel suggests we start in the room farthest down the hall so we can talk freely. I hand Daniel a set of hot-pink Post-its and tell him to tag what should go to the warehouse. "Speaking of which," I say, "what happened there today?"

He slaps a tag on a boxed Pee-wee Herman doll. "You're going to love this. I show up, and Kathy is there with her husband, Ed. They're excited about showing me how they spent the weekend itemizing everything—they did, too. Impressively thorough job. They had to have brought people to work around the clock."

"Like on a Friday night," I say drily.

He gives me that Daniel smile that's mostly a crinkling of the eyes. "I gave them plenty of time to fess up to the break-in. The rat bastards never said a word about it."

"Figures."

"So right before I left, I handed them the *Rocky* robe. Said, 'Add this to the pile. And fix the damned window. My client won't be happy if more of her memorabilia gets stolen.'"

This is the aspect of Daniel I've always marveled at—he seems like the most laid-back guy in the world, so it makes it all the more shocking when he busts your chops. He's funny that way. It tugs at my memory that it's not always such an enjoyable trait when you're on the receiving end, but before I can follow my thought, he says, "What are we going to do about Marva?"

I update him on my conversation with Nelson, minus the part

about the bait used to get him to talk to me. "It seems at any point after I'm done clearing out the house, she could possibly kill herself."

"Or before. There was a deadline date, right?"

"May fifteenth. You're right, it could happen even if the house is a mess, if she wants to do it on a specific day. And, wait . . . she told me her birthday is the next day—that she wanted the house cleared out before her birthday. Do you think she plans to do it then?" I flash back on how she reacted so strangely when I asked if she was having a party.

Daniel pulls out his phone and does a quick online search. "This says she'll be sixty-five. Does that mean anything to you?"

"No, other than she'll get the senior discount at Denny's."

We move on to the next room, which is nearly empty after the weekend's progress. Daniel pokes around silently and after a while says, "We can't let her go through with it."

"It's not as if I want her to, but I can't stop her. You may have noticed, she doesn't exactly bow to my every command."

"I wish I'd had more time to look through that book. I'll bet there's all kinds of clues in there."

"Like a secret spy code?"

He catches my sarcasm. "At least a *reason*. People don't kill themselves without a reason, at least not with such forethought. If we knew *why*, that'd give us ammunition to stop her. Remind her of why she'd want to live. Any chance you can sneak the book out for me to look at again?"

"Possibly. She keeps it in her nightstand. There's no real reason for me to go in her bedroom anymore since we've emptied it, but I'm guessing opportunity will present itself."

Daniel strokes his chin thoughtfully. "Or we could *create* an opportunity."

"Daniel, this isn't a caper. What—do you want to create a diversion, while I get lowered down into her room on cables?"

"You should create the diversion. All you have to do is wear that blue dress." He leans back against the wall, hands in pockets. "Believe me, it's very diverting."

I can't tell if he's teasing or flirting, but either way, it makes me fidgety. "Can you be serious about this?"

"I *am* being serious—at least about the part where we can't stand back and allow Marva to commit suicide. It would be wrong no matter who she was, but especially because she's . . . well, she's Marva Meier Rios. And, yes, I realize she hasn't done any painting in a long time, but she could be inspired again and—"

Hearing footsteps on the stairs, I shush him from saying any more. Seconds later, Niko comes into the room. "We've finished loading the truck. That'll be our last haul for today."

"Great, thanks," I say.

"So I'll pick you up at seven then?" Before I realize he's going to do it, he steps forward and gives me a quick peck, right on the lips. Then he nods to Daniel. "I'll be seeing you around, I'm sure."

"I'm sure," Daniel says, and while I don't have the guts to look at his face right now, his voice seems mighty icy.

Not that it's anything I should concern myself with—his interest here is in Marva, and her collectibles, and . . . siiiiigh . . . maybe a small part of me thought he might be having some regrets about me.

I look apologetically at him, deciding it'll be more awkward if I don't acknowledge what just happened. "About that. He's just—"

Daniel holds his hands up, as if in surrender. "Hey, no worries."

"No, but I—"

"You're free to do whatever you want. It's okay. Really." He holds a tag, looking with great concentration around the room, then plunks it on a stuffed dog.

"That's a collectible?" I say.

"I should know, I'm the *collectibles guy*."

"Daniel, I'm sorry about that. I didn't even—"

"No need to apologize. Frankly, it's a grander title than I deserve. I'm more of a hobbiest, but that'll be our secret, eh?" He slaps another tag on a glass vase.

He's acting so much the part of a spurned lover, I have to remind myself that *he* broke up with *me*. It's a pity that his male pride is

wounded by my finding someone new, but—and he said it himself—
I'm free to do whatever I want.

Still . . .

"I hope you realize how grateful I am for all the help you've been
giving me."

"I want to earn those posters I picked out," Daniel says perfuncto-
rily. "Cleared a space already on my wall. Don't want them going to
anyone else."

"Of course they won't."

"I'd better get to earning them then, huh?" He places several more
tags on items in the room, then moves quickly on to the other rooms.
When I try to make idle chitchat to warm some of the chill between
us, he tells me he's in a hurry and needs to concentrate. "In fact, I
should probably get rolling," he says, barely glancing in the last room.

"Thanks," I say weakly, my head a whir. I let him leave while I
stay behind to backtrack and remove several of the Post-its—there's
no way that busted TV is a collectible. When I head downstairs, I find
Daniel still here, talking to Marva.

"I was telling Marva," Daniel says as I walk up, his face not indicating any emotion, "that she might get quite a bit of notoriety if she
donated that sled to the Smithsonian."

Marva shakes her head. "I'm not looking for notoriety."

"Too late, you're already a name," Daniel says. "But it never
hurts to remind the world every now and again. I hope I'm not out of
line saying that." He starts to go on about some of his favorite movie
memorabilia the museum houses. In an attempt to look busy while I
stand there, I pull out my phone, figuring I'll delete those messages
from Daniel earlier.

That's when I notice they aren't both from Daniel.

One is from Florida—specifically, Ash's rehab.

In an instant, every nerve ending in me buzzes with anxiety. I'm
dialing Dr. Paul back as I remind myself that he could simply be
checking in. Everything is peachy keen. Ash wanted to say hello. Tell
me how nice the weather is. When the receptionist picks up, I turn

away and quietly ask for Dr. Paul, explaining that I'm Ash's mom and I'm returning his call from the morning. I expect to get his voice mail, which is what always happens, but she says, "He told me to get him if you called. Hold on."

I'm frozen in place as I listen to the beep-beep-beeps, and I cover one ear so I can hear over the drone of Daniel's carrying on to Marva in the background.

When Dr. Paul answers, I say, "I just now picked up your call." I realize I didn't listen to the message—just dialed him the second I saw the call was from him. "Is everything okay?"

"Lucy, I'd hoped we could have talked earlier." His voice is even calmer than usual. "I'm sorry to tell you, but this morning, Ash decided to check out of our facility."

"He's . . . he's going to leave?"

"He already has. He left before noon. Ash is a legal adult, and he was here voluntarily, so there's nothing we can do if he . . ."

I try to listen, but Dr. Paul's voice grows tiny, as does Daniel's, and some sort of noise swells, perhaps my pulse whooshing through my head. Before I can ask Dr. Paul to speak up, and Daniel to please shut up, I feel my knees buckle, and everything goes black.

# chapter thirteen

**D**aniel is slapping together a sandwich for me that I'll never eat, but he was in need of a job to do. Having already propped me up as I walked back out to the bungalow, settled me on the couch (feet elevated so the blood will flow to my brain), and talked to Dr. Paul on my behalf, he was fresh out of busywork. He thus proclaimed I needed food in my stomach.

It's a torment that I have no idea where Ash is, or if he's safe, or even alive.

According to Dr. Paul, relayed via Daniel, when Ash walked out, he had on his person the duffel we'd packed for him for rehab, along with roughly $80 in cash. This he'd earned doing extra chores in the kitchen—money most of his fellow rehabbers spent on chocolate or cigarettes, as if it were World War II. Ash refused to give specifics as to where he was going, saying only that he "had a plan."

I need to find Ash. The sooner the better, since every second that ticks by, the farther he can get from where he'd last been seen.

So far, all I can figure out to do is hop in my car, drive to Florida, and go up and down every street in the state until I see him. Which is ridiculous, but at least I'd be doing something, instead of lying here, feeling helpless. It's funny how I hadn't realized the small measure of peace that had crept into my bones until—with one phone call—it was gone.

It makes me recall back to when Ash first went away to the Willows, and at the suggestion of Dr. Paul I attended a local support group for parents affected by a child with a drug problem. The dozen or so of us there all had our own pathetic tales to tell, but the one who struck me most was a man with thinning hair and a cello-shaped face whose twenty-two-year-old daughter was addicted to heroin. "I have good news," he'd said during the portion where we were going around in a circle to either introduce ourselves or give an update. "I got a call from Sadie two nights ago. She was arrested, and she called me to bail her out of jail." As he told his story, I kept waiting for the good news, and by the end I realized that *was* the good news. His daughter was in jail. She wasn't out selling herself for drugs or getting beaten up or overdosing or dead. While she was incarcerated, she had a clean place to sleep and was forced to stay sober. I clapped along with the others as he said, "I told her, 'No, I won't bail you out, stay safe,'" but I never went to another meeting.

Daniel hands me a turkey sandwich on a folded paper towel. "I did the best I could with what little was in the fridge. I see your grocery-shopping habits haven't improved any."

"Says the man who still had a jar of mustard from college when I met him."

"It did come as quite the shock when you told me it was supposed to be yellow." He sits on the other end of the couch while I tug myself up to sit cross-legged. "So how are you holding up?"

"I vacillate between wanting to kill Ash and being terrified he's dead in a ditch somewhere."

He gives me a sympathetic look. "You have every right to be angry. Especially after all you've done for him."

Though Daniel has a point, I have to resist the urge to defend Ash. As I rearrange the turkey and lettuce leaf on my sandwich to stall on a response, there's a knock on the door.

"Looks like your date is here. I'm off. Keep me posted." Daniel's brows knit together. "On Ash, I mean."

As if I'd give him the dirty details on my date? As if there's still going to be a date? Besides, it's too early to be Niko picking me up.

"Come in," I shout before Daniel has a chance to get up.

The door pushes open, and it's Marva. She's holding a bottle of liquor, and she steps in, gazing around the room, which is heaped with boxes. "I like what you've done with the place," she says.

"I don't want to brag," I say, "but it was my idea to set the couch horizontally instead of vertically."

"It's been years since I've been back here. I used this as my studio."

"I wondered if you did!" Daniel says, then immediately looks guilty, as if he'd giggled at a funeral. "Please . . . here," he says to Marva, standing up. "Have a seat. I'll leave you two to talk."

Marva takes his place on the couch. "You needn't leave. I won't be long." She pulls shot glasses from a pocket in her sweater jacket. Setting them on a crate I've been using as a coffee table, she pours three shots.

"Thanks, Marva, but I don't know if I can—"

"This is fifty-year-old Scotch. Of course you can." She tosses her shot back. Daniel reaches down, grabs one, and does the same. I pick the last one up and—what the heck—down it in one gulp. Although I'd braced myself for the usual burn, this goes down warm and smooth. Guess that's the difference between half-a-century-old Scotch and Jose Cuervo.

Marva pours another round but leaves the shot glasses on the table. "So I gather that your boy checked himself out of rehab."

"This morning. Apparently he walked out the door like he was running to the 7-Eleven and not in fact throwing away all I'd worked for. And now I have no clue where he might be."

"You're planning to look for him?"

"Of course."

"Why?"

I stare at her, flummoxed. "*Why?*"

"Do you even know the reason he left the rehab center?"

"No."

Daniel leans against the wall, hands in his pockets, and sighs before speaking. "His therapist told me they'd been getting into some tough issues in therapy. That Ash didn't want to deal with it."

"You didn't tell me that," I say.

He shrugs. "Thought I'd wait until you weren't passing out all over the place."

"What kind of issues?" I ask.

"Don't know. He wouldn't elaborate."

"I'm not typically one to offer platitudes," Marva says, shifting about clumsily on the couch so she's facing me. "But perhaps all of this is meant to be. If your son feels that rehab isn't for him, maybe it's not. Some people have to carve their own paths."

"That would be fine," I say. "Except his path was going nowhere but down."

She scowls. "This whole war on drugs has gotten entirely out of hand. There's a reason people take them, and, frankly, it's because it's fun. At times even mind-expanding. Are you going to tell me you've never done any?"

Daniel shakes his head. "As much as I admire you, Marva, you're barking up the wrong tree on that one. Lucy here is the picture of innocence."

"I'm not entirely naive," I say. "I smoked pot here and there in college, but that's not the point. Ash isn't a guy who sometimes does drugs. There's nothing recreational about it. He's . . . well, he's an addict."

Though I'm responding to Marva, my eyes lift to meet Daniel's. He's staring at me with such surprise you'd think I'd popped naked from a cake. He opens his mouth to say something, but Marva pipes in, "People said that about me, too. What the hell do they know? They want to slap a label on you so they can shove you onto whatever shelf they want. Ridiculous. Yes, I did coke." Her face takes on a dreamy look. "And, oh, we used to take pills by the handful. They'd be out in bowls at parties. Like candy! I had a particular fondness for these little pink ones. Of course this was the seventies. And the eighties, too, come to think of it. At any rate, I suppose some people need to go to rehab and talk endlessly and join hands and sing 'Kumbaya' to move on with their lives. For others, they simply need to decide the party is over."

"And that's what happened with you?" Daniel asks. "You hit rock bottom?"

"Heavens no. That sounds so ugly. There was no rock bottom. I lost something important to me. That's what it took to decide enough was enough."

In my current state, my usual politeness filters are gone and I bluntly ask, "What did you lose?"

She studies me for a moment, then she claps her hands on her knees and hoists herself up. "It's not of consequence. And I didn't come out here to wax philosophical. I came to offer you the use of my private investigator." She hands me a piece of paper with the name Larry Mackenlively and a phone number scrawled on it. "I figured you'd want to hunt down your son. You strike me as the type."

"Thanks, Marva, but I can't afford a PI. Aren't they expensive?"

"He's doing work for me—he can do a bit of poking around for you. Tell him I approved adding you to my retainer. I'll consider it a business investment. After all, I've got a deadline to meet, and you won't be of any benefit to me if you're preoccupied fretting about your son." Even with her glibness, there's no missing Marva's generosity.

She turns to leave, but then stops. "Oh, what the hell." She picks up the other shot she'd poured herself and slugs it back. "My liver is going to hate me in the morning."

I'm already reaching for my cell phone to call the PI. Ash has a five-hour head start—which is entirely my fault, I realize with a flush of guilt. If I hadn't been finagling a date from Niko, I wouldn't have ignored my phone when Dr. Paul called. "I hope you don't mind that I won't be coming in to work tomorrow," I tell Marva.

"You worked all weekend, of course it's not a problem. Frankly, I was starting to wonder if you had any sort of social life at all."

"She does," Daniel says, his voice flat. "I'd better get going, too. Mind if I walk you out, Marva?"

"And they say chivalry is dead." She turns her attention to me. "Mackenlively is excellent at what he does, but don't worry if your son doesn't turn up right away. He will when he's ready. They always do."

"Not always," I say, punching in the phone number. "That's what scares me."

"My dear, I realize you're going to do what you feel you need to do. But you're constantly harping on me to let go. Perhaps it's time you learn to do the same."

Ash is not some old, wobbly dresser that I'm hanging on to for no good reason, I want to say, but I'm feeling too indebted to Marva at the moment to argue. I let her words hang there, as if she—of all people—has anything of value to say about parenting.

After she and Daniel go, I leave a message for the PI. I text Niko and cancel our date. Then I polish off the other shot, followed by the one Daniel left behind. While I'm at it, I pour another. My liver will probably hate me tomorrow, too, along with my head, but for now, I'm quite content to go numb.

Larry Mackenlively strikes me as too large to be a PI—heavyset, over six feet tall, with a rugged, angular face and thick mustache. Awkwardly perched as he is on the tiny coffee-shop chair, I can't imagine him on stakeout for hours at a time in a car, if that's what they do. He pulls out a spiral notebook. "Let me get some info from you," he says after we've exchanged pleasantries. "I've got a fellow nearby in the Tampa area who can do the footwork. Did you bring a picture?"

I slide across the table my one photo of Ash.

"Nice-looking kid," he says, picking it up. "Any changes since this was taken? Haircuts? Tattoos? Scars?"

"None that I know of." I feel myself blanch as I take a sip of my coffee. My stomach is none too happy after last night's liquor-fest. When Larry returned my call this morning at eight, I could barely get a "Hello" out as I dove for the phone. My mouth felt as if I'd swallowed the dust bunnies from beneath Marva's bed. For the next fifteen minutes, I fill him in on Ash's drug history, the intervention, and my conversations with Dr. Paul about Ash's progress.

Mackenlively leans back, and the chair whimpers beneath him. "So here's the part where I get you to do my job for me. Where do you figure he went?"

"I honestly don't know. With eighty dollars on him, he didn't go far."

"You'd be surprised. That could take him quite a ways on a bus. And if he's got a thumb, he could have hitched a ride. Which is the problem. He could be anywhere, or he could be fifty yards away from the rehab having a burger at a McDonald's." The discouragement I'm feeling must show on my face because he pats my hand. "I'm not saying it's going to be impossible to find him. Just pointing out the challenges. So tell me, is there any chance Ash is coming home?"

I wince at the word since we don't really have a home anymore. "I don't know."

"Does he have a girlfriend here?"

"No. Although . . ." I remember my conversation with Samantha at the bowling alley. "There is a girl here he wrote to while he was in rehab, but they only dated briefly, and that was a while ago."

"That could be important. Here's the thing. I'll have my guy check hospitals, jails, bus stations—the usual. He can interview businesses right around the area of the rehab. See if anyone remembers seeing your son. What would be ideal is if we can hone in on his location. Otherwise the area we're searching is the entire United States of America. That's a big net to cast."

Fighting tears, I stare outside the window at a harried mom wrestling her toddler into a stroller. "You're not sounding hopeful."

"We'll do what we can do. We could get lucky. It would help if you could put out feelers on your end. Call the ex-girlfriend and see if she's heard from him. Call his friends. I'll do what I can, but your contacts may prove more valuable than mine. There's a very good chance Ash is going to get in touch with somebody. They usually do. To get money. For a place to stay. To buy him a bus ticket. Eighty dollars isn't going to last long."

"Especially if he's used it to buy drugs," I say glumly.

"That's a possibility, but I'm a glass-half-full sort of person myself. So we're going to proceed as if he's simply a young man that you'd like to find. Does he have a Facebook account by chance? Maybe he's logged on. Some of these kids are so dense, they post their whereabouts right there on their status."

"He won't friend me."

He nods. "My daughter unfriended me. Apparently I commented on her wall too much."

As he scratches something in his steno pad, I make a mental note to ask Heather if she'll have DJ check Ash's Facebook page. Beyond that, I'm feeling utterly impotent. "This might sound crazy," I say, "but what if I head down to Florida? Poke around myself."

"Not crazy, but if you're asking my opinion, you're better off staying here. Put his friends to work spying for you. Some won't do it—that annoying way teenagers feel they have to protect one another—but his true friends will be concerned about him. Hey, your son might surprise you and contact you on his own."

"Doubtful," I say, but I nonetheless feel for my phone in my pocket.

"Stranger things have happened. If he calls, try to get him to tell you where he is. An address. At least a city. The best you can hope for is that he'll ask for money. Whatever you do, don't deposit it into an account. Buy him a plane ticket home, and book it yourself. That way you can meet him at the airport so he can't wriggle away. Or if he wants money, say you'll wire it. He'll have to give you an address. Then call me right away."

"Then do I wire it?" Larry's coaching is making me nervous, as if I were being asked to pose as a spy to draw secrets from the Russians.

"No, but tell him that you are so he'll stay put. That'll give you time to—" He stops. "What do you plan to do once you locate your son?"

I feel myself blinking at him. It's a simple question, yet I don't have the answer. "I just want to talk to him. First off, to see that he hasn't done anything drastic. Tell him I love him, that I'm proud of his progress but that he needs to go back to rehab and finish up."

"Will they take him back?"

"If they have an opening. They told me this morning they'll try to hold it, but they can't guarantee."

"So you'll send him someplace else if they don't?"

"If I win the lottery. Otherwise, I don't have the money to pay for a new one. The Willows was cash up front. Ash stayed long enough that we don't get a refund, but not long enough to make it through recovery."

"Then let's get to work finding your boy ASAP."

After that, Larry gives me my homework of contacting Ash's friends—a clear case of be careful what you wish for. Although I'd desperately wanted a task to do, I was hoping for one with less humiliation. As we get up to leave, he says, "If you hear anything—even if it seems irrelevant—call me. That's what I'm here for. Got it?"

"Got it. By the way, Marva spoke very highly of you."

"Send her my regards. I've never met her. All our interaction has been by phone. Interesting lady, though."

"What are you doing for her that she has you on retainer? Must be a big job."

He winks. "Top secret. Real hush-hush."

"In other words, none of my business. Can you at least give me a hint? Who's she having you locate? An old lover? The one who got away?"

He gives me a mock scolding look. "If Marva wants you to know, she can tell you herself."


When I walk into Marva's kitchen the next morning, she's pulling a bowl of oatmeal from the microwave.

"Any word from your son?" she asks.

I'm touched—and a tad surprised—that she'd mention Ash. Of course, most people who know that your drug-addicted son has abandoned rehab and is wandering the countryside with no real plan would certainly ask, but this is Marva we're talking about here.

"None yet," I say.

Yesterday, I made as many phone calls as I could bear, starting with my brothers and my parents, then moving on to a handful of Ash's old friends, including Samantha. Mercifully, Heather took on many of the calls—or, that is, she put DJ on the task. He checked Ash's Facebook page—nothing new there—then put out the word among his friends to contact him if they heard any news. So far, zip, zero.

"He'll turn up," Marva says, as if I'm fumbling through couch cushions for a lost TV remote. "Which reminds me, I need to borrow your car, if I may?"

"My car? Why?"

"I find myself in the unusual circumstance of being in need of one, and yet you may have noticed that's one thing I haven't hung on to. The damned car-rental agency I called was no help. They kept carrying on about how I need a valid driver's license."

"Wait. You want to borrow my car, and you don't have a license? They can impound it for that."

"Only if I were caught, which I wouldn't be. I happen to be an excellent driver."

"Marva, as much as I'd like to help you out, I can't loan you my car if you're not legally able to drive it. Where do you need to go anyway?"

She frowns. "It hardly matters if I can't get there, now does it?"

I silently curse the deal with the devil I made when I accepted the help of her private investigator. Hoping she won't take me up on my offer, I say, "I'm wondering if it's somewhere that I can take you."

"Hmm, that's a thought. My knees *have* been bothering me. Ten hours behind the wheel could be taxing. Better to have someone else do the driving, although I was looking forward to hitting the open road solo."

*Ten hours?* The woman has barely left her house in years, and now she wants to go on a road trip? "I thought you meant close by. With all that's happening with Ash, I shouldn't be that far away . . . in case he calls and I need to be somewhere quickly."

"I'd pay you, of course," she says, as if she didn't hear what I said. "Chauffeuring is above and beyond your job description. Nelson could always do it, but the last time I asked him to run me on an errand, he got all worked up, saying he's a nursing professional, not an errand boy. And to be honest, I doubt his ability to be discreet. This venture is hardly anything I'd want him to go blathering on about to others."

My curiosity piqued, I say, "Where is it exactly you need to go?"

"Grosse Pointe. It's in Michigan, outside of Detroit."

"I'm familiar. What's in Grosse Pointe?"

"I'm looking at Friday," she says, ignoring yet again what I said. "Day after tomorrow. If we get an early start, we can be back by early evening."

"No."

The decisiveness of my response startles her into paying attention. "Pardon me?"

"I'm not going to take an entire day to cart you to another state — especially at such a stressful time for me — when you can't be up-front about where we'd be going and why."

Marva regards me, hand stroking her chin, as if I'm a painting she's evaluating and not finding to be a great work of art, but a piece she'd at least consider hanging in an upstairs hallway. "It could be handy to have you in the loop, I suppose. You can't imagine how irritating it's been coordinating this on my own."

She continues unabashedly staring at me, so I sort cutlery as a distraction — Marva must have a dozen different sets, probably not one of them complete. After a moment, she says, "As you are aware, Larry Mackenlively has been doing investigative work for me." I perk up immediately — am I about to hear about the love that got away — or whoever it is she's been looking for? "I'd hired him to locate something I'd lost, something of value to me." She takes a deep breath, and I realize she's stalling. It's the first time I've seen Marva visibly nervous—snarky, annoyed, bored, yes . . . but nervous? Never. "He recently located it. That's what's in Grosse Pointe. What he found. I'd like to go see it."

"What is it?"

"A painting of mine. In particular, *Woman, Freshly Tossed*. It's in the home of a private collector, and I've arranged for a viewing. And don't start fussing at me—I'm not going to buy it and bring it back here. It's not even for sale, so far as I'm aware. This is a bucket-list sort of thing. I want to see the painting one last time before I die."

*Before I die*. There it is.

# chapter fourteen

That evening I'm moving boxes off the washing machine to use it—I'm tired of laundering my underwear in my sink—when Will walks in. He's handsomely dressed in a tux, but he ruins the effect by wearing his usual sour expression. "What's this crisis that's so important you couldn't tell me over the phone?"

Glancing around for Marva, I say, "I'd prefer to go out to the bungalow to talk." Marva has been in and out of her office all day, and I don't want her overhearing the conversation. While she didn't actually admit earlier she was going to kill herself, it was close enough that I realize it's not right to keep her plans entirely to myself. As her nearest relative, Will needs to be told—thus, I find myself with the unenviable task of being the one to do it.

"Let's keep it brief," Will says, as we weave through the kitchen. "I'm on my way to a fund-raiser. You had my hopes up this place had burned to the ground."

A woman's voice chides, "Will, that's not funny," and then I see a tall brunette walking in from the mudroom—very pretty, very pregnant.

"I told you I'd only be a minute," he says to her, but his voice doesn't have the hard edge it always does with me. "Just wait in the car. Please."

"I'm not going to sit outside of my own mother-in-law's home, like I'm not good enough to come inside."

"You know that's not what it is."

"I don't care what it is. I'm not waiting out there." She finally takes notice of me. "Hi. Are you the one who's clearing this place out?"

"Yes, I'm Lucy." I step forward to shake her hand. "Nice to meet you."

"I'm Padma. Will's wife." She gazes around. "She here?"

I assume the *she* refers to Marva. "In her office, I believe. You want me to get her for you?"

"Yes, please," she says, just as Will says no.

He gives her a flinty look. "We don't have time for this. We're running late."

"So we'll miss a soggy Caesar salad. I can't have a damned glass of wine anyway. I'm in no hurry."

I can almost see the battle being waged in Will's brain like a movie projected on a screen as he resists his wife's request. Eventually he acquiesces. "Fine, I'll go get her."

After Will leaves, Padma starts poking around the kitchen, opening drawers and cupboards. "It's worse than I remember it. And you've already cleared a lot out, right?"

"Right. When's the last time you were here?"

"Years. Will and I were still dating at the time . . . so at least four. Even then I had to beg him to let me meet her. He kept stalling, but I insisted. I mean, how can you be sure you love a man if you don't know how he treats his mother? That's the measure."

If that's her criterion, I'm curious why on earth she married Will, but he's walking in with Marva so there's no time to ask even if I could. Marva is complaining to Will about how he needs to find her a new gardener. The current one's leaf blower is too loud—can't he find one that uses a rake, for Christ's sake?

Padma straightens, jutting out her chin. "Hello, Marva."

Marva stops short, surprise registering on her face. After a moment, she says, "I see congratulations are in order."

I'm dumbfounded. She didn't know Will's wife is pregnant? They live only fifteen miles away! Marva and Will talk all the time!

"Thank you," Padma says. "We're very excited."

Will takes his wife's elbow and says to Marva, "We stopped by to check on the progress while we were in the neighborhood. Lucy, you wanted to show us the bungalow?"

That's it? He went to get Marva for a three-second exchange? Is it me, I wonder, or does anyone else in the room find it strange that Will never mentioned to his own mother that his wife is about to birth a baby? Marva's *grandchild*.

I hesitate, figuring that there'll be more, but Padma—for all her bravado before Marva arrived—is already heading for the back door. "Nice seeing you, Marva," she says, all cool politeness.

"Likewise."

Apparently it *is* me.

I follow, giving a last beseeching glance at Marva—surely she'll want to chat further, ask about the baby, show some enthusiasm—but she's already busied herself fitting together the pieces on a broken bowl.

"That went well," Padma says in wry tones when she and Will settle on my couch a minute later.

I take a seat on the spare chair. It never ceases to be humiliating to host people in what is currently my home amid Marva's squalor—and I'm struck again how badly Will must feel every time he has to bring anyone here.

He cuts to the chase. "So what's the big emergency?"

I'd hoped to speak to Will alone, but Padma doesn't look as if she plans to go anywhere soon. "It's about your mother. It's okay to tell this to the both of you?"

"Nothing you could say about Marva would shock my wife," Will says.

I take a bracing breath. I'd thought earlier about how I might broach the subject, but all I concluded is that there's no easy way to tell a man his mother is going to kill herself. "I found some information while going through Marva's things that's . . . disturbing."

"What, that she's a pack rat?" Padma says.

I smile to acknowledge the joke, then say, "She wrote some notes in a book." I look at Will. "Does *Grimm's Fairy Tales* have any significance for your mother?"

"None that I'm aware of. Why?"

"That's the book she wrote in—I was surprised because it was such a rare edition, worth a fair amount of money."

"She probably couldn't find a blank sheet of paper," Will says without irony, and it occurs to me he's probably right.

There's no use stalling, as much as I'm tempted, so I continue, "Her notes at first glance seemed random—some lists, to-do items, and so on. But it quickly became clear they were all on the same topic. Will, I'm sorry to have to tell you this, but I believe they were notes planning how and when to commit suicide."

I pause to let those words sink in. They must not have because Will's expression remains impassive. Padma says, "Are you sure? Can you show us the book?"

"She still has it. I couldn't reveal I'd seen it, or, frankly, she'd fire me. I had no business looking at it, but it sort of happened by accident. Anyway, yes, I'm sure." I go on to describe specifically what I'd seen. The more I talk, the more the color drains from Will's face.

When I get to the part about how she wants to make sure it's not the housekeeper who finds her body, he stands abruptly. "Give me a minute," he says, and walks out the door.

"He needs to process it," Padma says, looking worried. "It's a lot to take in."

"Of course. You sure I can't get you anything? Water?"

"I'm fine."

"So how far along are you?" I say, deciding to break the tension by switching to a happier topic.

"Seven and a half months. I'm due June tenth."

"That's so exciting. Your first?"

"Mmm-hmm."

"Boy or girl?"

"We've decided to keep it a surprise."

I nod, although personally I couldn't wait to find out my baby's gender. Finding myself pregnant was enough of a surprise. "Do you have names picked out?"

"Lullabelle if it's a girl, and we haven't decided on a boy's name. We can't seem to agree."

"There's always William Junior."

She regards me carefully for a moment, and I wonder if I've offended her—if she considers it antifeminist to name her child a junior. Then she says, "Why are you telling Will about Marva? What are you hoping he'll do? Stop her somehow?"

"I felt he ought to know. And, yes, I am hoping he'll want to do something about it. She's his mother after all."

She makes a face that suggests she finds my last point debatable. "My husband would hate that I'm about to tell you this, but you should know what we're dealing with here. The sort of mother Marva is. You see, Will's given name isn't William. That's a name the nanny started calling him when he was a baby. The actual name on his birth certificate is spelled W-f-f-p-h-b-t-w-z-g. Your guess is as good as mine as how to pronounce it."

"I don't understand . . ."

"Marva thought it would be amusing to name her son—her only child—some sound no one can pronounce. She picked random letters. Thought she was so clever. But he's the one who had to live with that name until he was legally old enough to change it on his own."

"That's terrible."

"That's Marva. I told you earlier that I could only marry a man who treated his mother well. In my opinion, he does—more than she deserves."

"What about Will's father?" I ask.

"A brief fling with a waiter. Marva doesn't even remember his name." Padma shifts irritably on the couch. "Actually, I will take a glass of water. When you first get pregnant, everybody talks about morning sickness—nobody mentions the nonstop heartburn."

I get up to grab a water from my minifridge. "I'll admit, I was shocked that she didn't know you were pregnant. Why didn't Will tell her?"

"It's hard enough on him dealing with clearing out this house. The less he has to talk to her, the better. Up until she called to ask for referrals when her basement flooded back in January, they hadn't spoken in three years. Ever since she didn't show up for the wedding."

"Ouch."

"It's not like that was the first time she let him down. He's used to it, just tired of it. It's so sad, because when he was a boy, he worshipped her. She was so exciting, so beautiful, so larger-than-life. But I suppose that was the problem."

My mind flashes to Marva mentioning how Will didn't want to go to fashion week and the way she'd spoken with scorn about his school and his sports—things that were important to him. That would have to wear a boy down. Ash certainly trailed after *his* absent parent's approval. Even back when Billy and I were still married, he wasn't interested in being a father. At least Ash had *me*. I constantly ran interference so his feelings wouldn't get hurt when his dad pushed him away to watch football on TV or work on his car or any of the sort of activities fathers and sons often share. By the time Ash was older, he told me it didn't matter that his dad didn't want him around. "It's boring at his house anyway," he said, giving an indifferent shrug. "The new baby cries too much. My stepmom's food is way too healthy—I mean, would it kill her to buy a potato chip?" That all translated to me as a boy who was protecting himself against the hurt of rejection, and I'm forced to recognize that perhaps Will is simply doing the same. Before I get a chance to ask Padma anything further, Will comes back in, plunking down next to her. He looks more weary than upset.

She clasps his hand. "Honey, maybe there's nothing to worry about. There's always a chance we're interpreting it wrong."

"We're not," he says. "She's been getting her affairs in order. Working on her will. Ensuring that all she holds dear—her precious stuff—goes to good homes. I'd wondered what the rush was."

"Why would she do it?" Padma asks. "Why now?"

They both look at me, as if the answer might be inscribed on my forehead. "Sorry, no clue. She doesn't have much of a life, but that's her own doing." I hand Padma the bottle of water and sit back down. "There is one more thing I need to tell you. She wants to see *Woman, Freshly Tossed* once more before she dies. It's at a private home just outside of Detroit. She's scheduled a viewing on Friday, and she's asked me to drive her there."

"Are you going to do it?" Will asks.

"I think *you* should."

Padma attempts to cross her arms over her belly. "Wouldn't it be better to not take her at all? If that's something she wants to do before she dies, under the circumstances we should hardly be helping her accomplish it."

"She'll just hire a driver," I say. "She's determined to go—so my thought is that her first big trip out of the house in years shouldn't be alone. Will, if you're with her, you can talk some sense into her."

He gives a mirthless chuckle.

"It does seem rather unlikely," Padma agrees. "But, still, I see Lucy's point. Who else does Marva have? Who else could possibly have an influence on her? If I'm being honest, Will, I'm not at all scared your mother is going to kill herself. I'm scared for you—that you'll never forgive yourself if she does and you didn't try to stop her."

He rubs the back of his neck as we sit in quiet contemplation. The only sound is the gurgling of what at first I thought was water pipes but then realize is Padma's stomach. Then Will gets to his feet. "All right, I'll drive her there." He extends an arm to his wife to hoist her from the couch. "Give me a minute to go deliver the joyous news. I'll meet you out at the car."

"Poor Will," Padma says after he leaves, more to herself than to me. "It'd be so much easier if he could hate her."

■ ■ ■

Although Will arrives promptly at eight o'clock Friday morning, he and Marva don't make it out of the house until nearly nine. I'd been starting to wonder if this trip was going to happen at all. When Marva lit up her third "last cigarette for the road," it was through gritted teeth that Will said if she'd prefer to stay home and smoke all day, she was welcome to. He had plenty of things he could be doing instead. At that, Marva snubbed out the cigarette and got up, muttering under her breath that if she were allowed to smoke in his fancy car, they wouldn't be having this problem.

They aren't gone a minute before Daniel is at the door. "I thought they'd never leave," he says when I let him in. "I was sitting in my car out front forever, bored out of my skull. It must suck to be a PI if that's what they do all day long."

The reference to a private investigator makes me wince, reminding me of Larry Mackenlively's call this morning to say he's holding off the search for Ash. When I gurgled a helpless "You're giving up?" he said, "Holding off, not giving up. Until we can narrow in on an area. Between the calls you made and my guy in Florida, we've got plenty of hooks out there. It's only a matter now of which one gets a nibble."

I shove away a box of silk ribbons I'm earmarking for the yard sale. "We still have plenty of time," I tell Daniel. "They'll be gone at least ten hours."

"Did you get the book yet?" he asks in hushed tones, and his gaze shifts to where Niko is sealing a large box in the dining room. "You didn't tell *him* about it, did you?"

"About Marva's notes? You can't possibly believe I would do that," I say, incredulous.

"I wasn't sure how close the two of you are."

Give me a break. "Just come help me look." I spin on my heel to head to Marva's bedroom. Passing Niko on the way, I say, "You can put that with the others outside."

"You got it." He nods a hello to Daniel before hefting the box up onto his shoulder.

When we get to Marva's bedroom, Daniel shuts the door behind us. "Boy, he sure jumps when you give a command, doesn't he."

"Are you going to be like that all day?"

"Like what?"

"Never mind," I say, crossing over to the bed. "Let's just find the book, okay?"

"That's what I thought we were doing."

I tug open Marva's nightstand drawer and am disappointed to find the book isn't in there. We look around the area of the bed—under it, through the covers, behind the nightstand. I'm starting to get nervous we might have to expand our search when Daniel slides his hand between the mattress and box spring and—with a "Ta-da!"—emerges with Marva's copy of *Grimm's Fairy Tales*. "I knew all those years of stashing my *Playboys* in that same spot wasn't in vain. I feel sorry for kids today—there's just not the same thrill in erasing your history on the Internet to hide your porn viewing."

He opens the book and sits on Marva's bed, but I insist we leave the bedroom—I don't want so much as a stray hair falling from my head to tip her off we've been in there since we have no reason to be. We walk out to the front porch, taking advantage of the unusually warm spring day.

"If this indicates the inner workings of Marva's mind, what a bizarre place it must be in there," I say after we've looked at some of her notes. We're seated on the bench, Daniel holding the book while I peer over from beside him.

What we have managed to glean thus far: Marva wants to be cremated. She wants her ashes tossed from the Golden Gate Bridge, which I'm quite sure is illegal. (Perhaps among her notes we'll find a list of shady funeral directors willing to perform such a task for the right fee.) Quite a few references are to someone named Filleppe— all written as if she's talking directly to him. *Oh, Filleppe, how clever of you to leave me to do the dirty work, and how typical.*

"You ever hear her mention this Filleppe guy?" Daniel asks.

I shake my head.

"He's the only name mentioned here other than her son."

"And me," I say, annoyed, pointing to another notation of how she's concerned the blond girl might not be done on time. "I'll have her know, if I'm not done on time, it's through no fault of my own."

As I'm busy being defensive, Daniel starts flipping more quickly through the book.

"Slow down," I say, "she's written on some of those pages."

"I'm skimming for dates. I want to know when she plans to do it."

After a few minutes, he finds it. Atop an illustration of Rapunzel's hair, Marva has written a to-do list by date, backing up from . . .

"May sixteenth," Daniel says. "Her birthday, right?"

"Yep. Happy birthday. Although it doesn't specifically say that's the day she plans to do it."

"But her checklist ends there—that's a mighty big clue."

We're still piecing together Marva's plan—we've got *when*, but it'd be helpful to add *how*—when I hear a car pulling into the drive. Upon glancing up, my insides turn to ice. "It's Will!" I gasp. "They're back already!"

Daniel, wide-eyed, turns to me and mouths, *Fuck*, and I barely have time to register the déjà vu before he's slid the book up the back of his shirt and is backing into the house. "Stall them," he says.

I hurry over to greet Marva as she and Will get out of the car. "What happened?" I say it brightly—of course I am, as always, delighted to see her!

"I should have known this wouldn't work," she says.

Will snaps, "I have a GPS. You haven't been out of the house in years. Which one of us do you think is best capable of getting us onto the Ninety-Four?"

"I'm telling you, it's faster if you bypass the expressway altogether." She slams the car door using her cane and starts toward the house, only I'm in her path. "You care to move? You're blocking me."

"I am?" I say, not moving.

Marva shoots me an irritated look, then steps around and marches with such purpose that I fear for her knees—not to mention my own safety were I to dare to get in her way again. As an attempt to distract her, I call after her, "So, Marva, now how are you going to get there?"

She ignores me, not slowing stride.

In a panic—if she catches Daniel in her room, I may be joining her off the side of the Golden Gate Bridge—I blurt, "I'll take you!"

It works to make her stop, and she turns around, slowly, as if considering my offer—as if she hadn't already asked me to do it.

I prattle on about how I'll get directions from Will, that I'll need to fill up my car, and, hmm, it could use tidying, and I'm boring even myself with the pointless details but keep at it until I see Daniel walking casually up the drive from the back of the house. "Marva, what a pleasant surprise!" he says. "Just here helping Lucy—what a bonus this is!"

Her face softens. For a woman as bright as Marva is, she falls for his kissing up every time. Although it may be because he's being sincere.

I used to fall for it, too.

"Lucy," Marva says, "I would be delighted if you'd drive me. Thank you."

"It's settled then," Will says briskly, nearly diving headfirst back into his car. "I'll be off. Good luck."

As Will turns over his engine, Daniel frowns in the direction of my Mustang, which is parked in front of the bungalow. "You're taking her in that?" he says, as if I'm offering to ride her sidesaddle on my donkey.

"Yes, I am. Marva happens to find my car quite snazzy, right, Marva?"

"Not the word I would have chosen, but sure."

"When's the last time you had it tuned up?" Daniel asks, then turns to Marva before I answer. "Never mind. Ladies, I'd be proud to be your chauffeur for the day. I'll borrow my friend's SUV—you'll love it. What it lacks in gas efficiency, it makes up for in a vulgar display of comfort." He pulls car keys from his pocket, secure in the knowledge that he's made an offer nobody is going to refuse—not when our other choice is being squeezed into a tiny Mustang of questionable reliability. "Back in half an hour."

We're almost to Detroit before anyone broaches the subject of *Woman, Freshly Tossed*. We've talked little on the drive. As soon as Marva directed Daniel to the freeway (which *was* rather grating, I have to side with Will on that one), Daniel cranked up classical music on the XM radio. To my relief, Rachmaninoff filled the space of conversation so I could settle back and spend my time fretting instead of talking. For the past four hours, I've bounced between wondering about how on earth we're going to convince Marva not to go through with her plan and what I'll do if Ash calls needing me urgently while I'm on the road. I'm moving forward on autopilot. Otherwise I'd crumple into a ball and cry. Motion—no matter what the direction—at least keeps me occupied and provides the illusion that I'm doing something.

We pass signs for the town of Ann Arbor, prompting Marva to remark, "Home of the University of Michigan. They used to have a marvelous art fair every year—I believe they still do." Then suddenly she blurts, "Take this exit!"

Without hesitating or asking why, Daniel veers across three lanes to rocket off the freeway while I cling to the door and watch my life flash before me (annoying, as I was hoping to never revisit this past year).

"Take a left when you get to the light," Marva says before turning around to me. "You're in for a treat—the best corned beef outside of New York City."

Lunch meat? We risked my life for lunch meat? With the GPS chirping warnings that we are now off course, Marva directs us to Zingerman's, a funky brick deli and market in a quaint downtown area. It's bustling even though it's rather late in the day for lunch, and being in proximity of food reminds me that I'm actually quite peckish. We place our orders at the counter. I get a Reuben that turns out to be larger than my head, and we elbow our way to an open table.

Once we're settled, Marva takes a bite of her sandwich and then closes her eyes in apparent bliss as she chews. "Mmm, this constitutes my sodium intake for a month, and it is absolutely worth it," she says. "I hope one of you knows CPR."

"We both do—took the training back when we used to work together," Daniel says, and I'm slammed with the memory of how for weeks afterward, Daniel would tackle me anytime we were out of sight of others at the office and perform mouth-to-mouth, plus chest compressions if he was especially frisky. "So feel free to live it up," he adds, smiling at Marva. "Have the pickle, too."

"I believe I will. You have no idea what it's been like to subsist on such a restrictive diet," she says grimly. "It's not right. We're hardwired as humans to desire food. Eating is meant to be a sensual experience. We're supposed to taste and feel and *experience* what we're eating, not ponder fat grams and carb content and sodium."

I picture her kitchen that's so cluttered it's a challenge to wash a dish, much less cook a meal. "It's interesting to hear you say that. You've never struck me as a foodie."

"Not anymore. Oh, Mei-Hua does the best she can under the circumstances, and her food tastes adequate, but it's soulless. I swear anytime I eat it I'm emptier afterward than I was before. Although I believe that very soon I may give her permission to go wild with the food. Ignore all the restrictions. See what she comes up with. I've experimented a bit in the kitchen in my day. Perhaps I'll give it a go again, so long as I decide I can use all the butter and salt I want. As you said, Daniel, live it up."

"That's great," Daniel says. "Living is a good thing, don't you agree, Lucy?"

I get where he's going with this—starting to plant the seeds with Marva that there are plenty of reasons to hang in there, but I'm not sure this is our moment. She's willing to go off her diet because it doesn't matter. As far as she's concerned, these are her final days. I wouldn't be surprised if on the way back to the car she proposes skydiving or a rousing game of Russian roulette. "I'd love to see you be able to cook," I say, attempting a slightly different tack. "In fact, when we get back, the first thing we can do is focus on clearing out the stove area."

"You can't ever let it go, can you," she says.

"What? I'm simply agreeing with you and saying that—"

"That if I achieve the proper level of sparseness and scarcity, that I'll be happy. Just as *you* are, is that right?"

*Ow.* What did I do to deserve that? I'm still struck dumb when Daniel says, "Marva, you're pretty darned lucky to have Lucy. She's a hard worker, and she's brilliant at organizing. If you want a kitchen you can cook in, believe me, our girl can hook you up. By the way"—he lifts his gigantic sandwich to his face so I can't even see him anymore—"the food here is incredible. I may ask this pastrami to marry me. How do you know about this place?"

With that, Marva launches into a story about the brief time she spent lecturing at U of M before she finally settled in Chicago. I sit quietly and only half pay attention, no longer miffed at Marva because I'm so awash in gratitude for what Daniel said. As much as he idolizes Marva, he risked irking her to defend me. While it's no knight slaying a dragon, it feels nice to have someone have my back.

We finish our meals—I ate until I was ready to burst and still didn't make a real dent in my sandwich. Once we're back on the freeway, instead of putting on music, Daniel says, "So, Marva, I'll confess to an ulterior motive for offering to drive today."

"What might that be?"

"Are you kidding? The chance to stand next to an artist of your caliber as she views her most famous work? This goes straight to the top of my list of exciting life events. I'd put it above losing my virginity."

She shakes her head, chuckling. "You might want to prepare yourself for a letdown."

"Nah, this is going to be great. Although that's probably what I should have said to the girl I lost my virginity to."

I have to lean forward to join the conversation. This vehicle is so huge I'm in backseat Siberia. "How long has it been since you've seen *Woman, Freshly Tossed?*"

"Let's see. I sold it in the mideighties, so, what's that then? My, a long time, isn't it?"

"It must have been hard to let go of it," Daniel says, which isn't saying much—this is a woman who can't even part with an empty tissue box. "How'd you wind up selling it?"

"Lucy here may find this difficult to believe, but there was a time I didn't place much stock in what I owned. I didn't sell the painting. Rather, I offered it in trade to a fellow by the name of Echo for a rather large amount of cocaine."

"You traded a million-dollar painting for drugs?" I say, not even trying to disguise my horror.

"The painting wasn't yet appraised anywhere near that high. I'd no idea its worth at the time, but I found myself strapped for cash. So a thing's value becomes—let's say—more malleable based on what else you find yourself needing. It was testimony to my growing notoriety that Echo would take merchandise at all. As a rule, he preferred cash. Insisted on it, in fact. But I was a loyal customer, and, truthfully, he got it for a song. Velvet paintings of dogs playing poker have sold for more."

I'm trying to read her expression. It must bother her that she let her greatest life's work basically go up her nose, but Marva could play poker with those dogs and win every hand because she is inscrutable.

Then something occurs to me. "You traded it for drugs. So . . . where exactly are we going now? We're not going to a drug den, are we?" If I'm going to go charging into a building full of drug lords and ne'er-do-wells, it's not going to be for Marva.

"Don't worry," she says. "According to Mackenlively, the painting has changed hands. As I recall, Echo ran his business out of Detroit. I've never been to Grosse Pointe, although I hear it's lovely. Rather upscale. I'm assuming we'll be treated to quite an impressive art collection today."

"Sounds great," Daniel says. "Although it's yours I'm dying to see.

Lucy tells me you don't want to buy it from them. Aren't you at least kind of tempted to see it come home?"

"Not one bit."

He glances sidelong at her. "I assumed, since you wanted to see it . . ."

"I recognize that it is my most lauded work."

"You're being modest," I say, recalling my Internet research, where Marva is regarded as a pioneer of sorts. In the same way I could never understand why someone would be so impressed with a painting of a can of soup, I can't say I see what's so outstanding about a nude woman leaning against a bed, even if she is blue. Still, I'm here to inspire Marva, so I keep laying it on thick. "That painting set an entire style of art in motion. That's no small achievement."

"That particular point is up for debate," Marva says.

Daniel shakes his head. "Not among people with any sense. Or any grasp of art history. It's a shame how you don't fully get credit for your contribution to neo-Expressionism."

"I don't need credit."

Marva seems chatty enough that I dare to challenge her with the big question. "Marva, so why do you want to see it? Why *now*?"

She gazes out the window. "Call it a sentimental journey, but don't read too much into that. I'm not being reunited with a long-lost love. More like . . . oh . . . meeting a former coworker for a drink. Possibly pleasant, but more likely tedious."

"For you maybe," Daniel says cheerfully, although I can tell by his expression he's as bothered by what she's saying as I am. She's supposed to be eager. Ripe for suggestion. Ambivalence does not create fertile emotional soil for us to work with. "I have no doubt it will be a life-changing experience for me—and unlike my first life-changing experience, lasting longer than a minute and a half."

"Perhaps," she says vaguely, and any attempts after that to get her to talk are politely rebuffed.

It's not quite five o'clock when we pull up to our destination, having grown increasingly perplexed the closer we got.

Grosse Pointe is famous for its grand, sweeping mansions and waterfront property, so that's what I expected to find. This, however, is a fifteen-hundred-or-so-square-foot ranch-style house, painted white with blue shutters. It's not exactly the slums, but it is in no way remarkable. We pull in behind an older-model Ford Taurus that's parked in the driveway.

"Are you sure this is it?" Daniel asks.

"This is the address Mackenlively gave me," Marva says, squinting at the house.

We amble up to the door, and Marva rings the doorbell. From inside, a woman calls out, "Hold on! Let me just . . ."

As the door jiggles open, Marva turns to me. "By the way, I didn't mention I'm here to see the painting. I said I was a reporter for *House Beautiful* magazine interested in featuring their interior decor. Go with it."

# chapter fifteen

Before I have a chance to ask Marva why she lied about the painting and whether she actually expects me to play along, the door swings open. In front of us stands a middle-aged woman with vibrant auburn curls swept into an updo with lots of makeup on. She's wearing an apron over a sweater set and slacks.

"You must be from the magazine," she says. "I expected you earlier."

I pause to let Marva handle this—it is, after all, her big fat lie—but she's too busy peeking past the woman into the house to say anything. Once again, it's up to me to do her dirty work—as if I don't get enough of that already. "Sorry we're late," I say.

"It's nearly five o'clock. You said you'd be here at two."

"Traffic was awful, but we're excited to get started now!"

"Gee, I don't know. I've had to start dinner, and now the kitchen's a mess. I can hardly let you put pictures of my dirty kitchen in your magazine, can I?" Her words come out in a rush. "Besides, I was hoping to get this done before Gil—my husband, Gil?—before he gets home from work. He's due anytime." She starts to push the door shut. "Maybe it'd be better if you came back on Monday."

Daniel blocks the door with his foot and says, "That's a great idea. The light's better earlier in the day. Monday it is." I'm about to throttle him—there's no way I'm schlepping back up here next week—when he adds, "But I'd like to see what we're working with here. How about giving us the fifty-cent tour."

She looks skeptical. "How long is that gonna take? It's just that Gil—my husband, Gil?—he likes his peace and quiet when he comes home."

"We'll be fast," I say.

"Well . . . I . . ."

"Just a quick buzz through the rooms," Daniel adds.

"You see, I didn't exactly *mention* to Gil that—"

Marva turns to go. "No problem. We'll pick another house to feature in our magazine."

Daniel and I remain rooted, unsure of what to do. Marva nearly makes it to the SUV before the woman calls out, "Wait! Fine. Come on in."

"Delighted," Marva says, then strides past us and into the house. As we follow, the woman introduces herself as Lynette. Although none of us offer names in return, she doesn't seem to notice.

"Welcome to my humble home!" Lynette says with a sweep of her arms.

We're standing in a foyer that's wallpapered in a busy, faded floral. I glimpse a dining area and a family room beyond. So far as can be seen, the decor is middle-class Americana—not expensive, a bit dated, but clean and well cared for. Seeing it cements the nagging feeling in the pit of my stomach that there's been a mistake: Mackenlively got it wrong. An edgy, stylistic painting such as Marva's can't possibly be in a house that has a bench in the foyer with needlepoint pillows bearing such slogans as BLESS THIS MESS and THE BEST THINGS IN LIFE AREN'T THINGS.

"I can't tell you how excited I was to get your call—I don't even remember entering that contest! So is one of you the gal I talked to?"

This would be an ideal time for Marva to pipe in, but she's already walking toward the dining room. She's not even pretending to be concerned with Lynette, who has obviously gone to a fair amount of trouble for us today. It smells freshly Windexed in here, and there are telltale vacuuming tracks. Plus it's doubtful she usually wears pearls while hanging around the house.

"We're only the crew," I say, deciding that playing dumb under the circumstances will require the least stretching of my acting talents.

Daniel, however, is fully embracing his role. He pulls out his phone and snaps Lynette's photo.

"Oh, don't get me wearing this old thing," she says, whipping off her apron as if it's caught fire. "I thought you said no pictures today."

"These aren't for print." He fires off random shots—snapping a photo of the corner of the ceiling, the floor, the edge of a light fixture. "But since we're not doing the shoot today, I'd at least like to get an idea of what's here. Do some poking around. See all the rooms. Right down to the basement if need be."

"The basement?!" Lynette seems scandalized—although nice job on Daniel's part planting the idea. If the painting *is* here, it's quite possibly in storage.

She bustles us through a living room and into a dining room. There was a time, I muse—while pretending to assess a tchotchke-filled china cabinet—I'd have called this house cluttered. Tromping through Marva's mess day after day hasn't merely altered my standards; it's buried them alive. All I require now is a path and a less than 20 percent chance of something falling on me and causing a concussion and I'm happy.

"So in this room," Lynette says when we reach the kitchen, "I decided to go with a color scheme of peach. I wanted a food color, what with it being a kitchen and all." Marva appears pained by Lynette's nonstop chattering. Our hostess has rightfully identified Marva as the alpha in this group and has nearly been tripping over herself pointing out what to feature in our fake magazine profile. Although grating for Marva, it's allowed Daniel and me to trail after to peek behind credenzas and in closets and under couches.

At one point Daniel tugs open a door, and Lynette startles. "Goodness, that's the pantry!"

"Sorry . . . just making sure we see it all." He gives her a look of a puppy trying to get itself adopted from the pound. "They give us such grief back at the office if we aren't thorough in our research. Almost got fired once because I came back after scouting a location and I hadn't gone up into the attic."

Lynette falls for it. "Then let's not get you in trouble," she says decidedly. "You help yourself to whatever it is you need to see. Although if we can keep the pace snappy, I'd appreciate it. Gil could be home anytime now."

"No problem. You two ladies lead the way," Daniel says, nodding toward Marva. She's passed right through a formal living room and is leaning her head into a den that's sectioned off by glass double doors.

Upon noticing where Marva is, Lynette trots after her. "That's my husband's den!" she calls out. "Can't imagine there's anything worth seeing there, it's so plain." She catches up and joins Marva in the room. "You know how men can be. You set so much as a pretty doily in their man caves and they get afraid they'll have a mad urge to start sipping tea with their pinkies in the air."

As Lynette laments to a visibly strained Marva about how her husband makes fun of her decorating efforts—if he had his way, they'd have nothing but shelves made of lumber held up by cinder blocks—Daniel leans close to me. "You thinking the same thing I am?"

"That if that woman keeps talking, Marva may not wait to see her painting before killing herself?"

"She does look miserable. But, no, that's not what I'm referring to."

"So what then?"

"Do you think there's a chance in hell that the painting is hanging anywhere in this house?"

"Not really."

"Me neither. The way I figure it, if it's in this place at all, our best bet is an attic or basement. So I say we divide and conquer. Keep Lynette busy with Marva in the main house and the yard. That will give you and me time to dig through storage in peace." Without waiting for a response, he says in a loud voice, "Lynette, in the interest of time, how about you two tour the house—and please, hit on all the landscaping in the yard. We're quite interested in foliage. I'll check out the basement, and my buddy here"—he puts an arm around my shoulder—"she'll look in the attic. That okay with you, Marva?"

Marva nods—although I'm sure she'd rather swap places with one of us—and Lynette eagerly agrees. "That *would* save us some time. Although we don't have an attic. And don't you worry. I'll sign something that says so that you can give to your boss."

"That's very kind of you," Daniel replies. "And the basement is . . . ?"

She directs us to a door near the back entrance. We click on the light and head down the stairs.

"I feel awful," Daniel says as soon as we're out of earshot. "She's going to be crushed when we don't show up on Monday, and I'm just egging her on. I'm such a dick."

"I know."

He pauses, hand on the railing. "You think I'm a dick?"

Unfortunately, no—things would be so much easier if I did. "I mean I feel sorry for her, too. Which is annoying. That's all I need is to add somebody new to the list of people I'm worried about."

We reach the bottom of the stairs and Daniel squeezes the back of my neck. "He's going to be okay. The number one on your list. He's a smart kid."

"Let's hope so," I say, touched that Daniel's mind leapt so quickly to Ash, but not wanting to get into it at the moment. Rather than let thoughts of my runaway son into my head, I shove them back down to where they usually are. It's hard to remember a time when I didn't have this dull ache inside me, and I wonder if that's how it is for people with a chronic illness—if after a time they can no longer recall what it's like to feel healthy and whole.

Hands on hips, I take in my surroundings. The basement is a large, open room that runs the length of the house and is smattered with shelves, piles of boxes, old furniture, a pool table—the usual basement fodder. "Now let's find us a hidden treasure. How big is this painting?"

"Pretty large—like three feet across. So if it's here, it won't be hard to spot."

After we've been sifting through for a few minutes, Daniel says, "This is déjà vu, huh? We seem to enjoy sorting through other people's junk together."

"And to think we used to enjoy . . . uh . . . dancing together."

He pauses to look at me, perplexed. "We didn't dance. Except for when you made me at weddings."

Thank goodness it's poor lighting down here because I can feel myself going hot with embarrassment. I started to explain what I meant by *dance*, but realized midway how weird that would be. "Well, I should have made you dance more often."

"I'd have danced with you," he says, his voice serious. "Even without you shooting at my feet. You only had to ask—just said, 'Daniel, dance with me.' I don't read minds."

Wanting off this awkward subject, I walk over to a floor-to-ceiling pile of boxes and bins across the room. "We haven't looked over here yet."

Almost immediately I'm excited that we've hit pay dirt since there's a stack of pictures and paintings against the wall behind the boxes. Alas, it turns out none of them are *Woman, Freshly Tossed*—or anything of remotely the quality that might lead us to believe these people have an inkling about fine art.

"It's not here," I say, surprised at how crestfallen I am.

"No worries. If it's not in the basement, it must be upstairs."

"If that's the case, then what are you doing down here?" I aim for a teasing tone, as much to cheer myself up as anything. "You could be having your big moment with Marva—basking in the glow of the famous artist. You are missing out on it *right now.*"

He shrugs. "She doesn't need me with her for that."

"What? Isn't that the whole reason you came?"

"No."

"All right, for that and to find out details about how and why she plans to kill herself so we have ammunition to stop her."

"Not entirely."

I search my mind for what he's getting at. "And to see a famous painting that's been missing to the world for years?"

"Luce, I thought you got it."

"Got it?"

"The reason I came here today. I'm here for *you*. You were stressing about Marva, in part because I was making you stress. It wouldn't be fair to make you handle it by yourself. You shouldn't have to handle things alone so much."

It's as if something inside me pops open, and without giving myself time to overthink it, my hand goes up to his neck to pull his face closer. "Daniel, kiss me."

He blinks once—and I wonder if he's going to make a quip—but only the tiniest bit of a smile registers before he presses his mouth to mine. We kiss, and then again, and then our lips part slightly—and as many times as I've kissed Daniel, it feels as sweet and tentative and as tingly as the first time.

He pulls away, then leans his forehead against mine. "See, that's what I'm talking about. I'm not that bright. You've got to spell it out for me. Although sooner or later I'd have had to kiss you anyway. I've been dying to do it for a long time now. In fact, why am I talking?"

His lips barely have time to find mine again when there's a commotion upstairs, then Lynette calls down, "You two? I need you to come up . . . please?" It's followed by a man's voice shouting, *"Now!"*

He sounds so angry that we snap apart and immediately scurry toward upstairs. "Guess we're in trouble," I say.

Daniel gives me a mock concerned look. "You got a jealous husband you neglected to tell me about?"

As much as it would be habit to do so, I'm unable to formulate a snappy comeback because in that moment it catches up to me: Daniel and I kissed. I have no idea what it means, but it definitely means *something.* He grabs my hand to squeeze it, which tells me I'm not the only one who feels that way.

When we get to the top of the stairs, a tall, balding man in an off-white workman's uniform is there with Marva and Lynette, glowering at us. "Lynette," he snaps, "you want to explain to me again why you invited total strangers into our house and let them run around pell-mell?"

"Gil, they're not strangers!" she says in a perky tone that doesn't entirely disguise her nervousness. "This was supposed to be . . . a surprise. I won a contest and they're going to put pictures of my decorating in a magazine!"

He barks such a mean laugh that I immediately want to establish a publishing company so I can start a home magazine for the sole purpose of printing a big, glossy, multipage photo spread of this house, just so his wife can roll it up and smack him in the head with it.

"What magazine would care about your decorating, huh?" Gil says. "*Too Many Stupid Fluffy Pillows Everywhere* magazine? Or *I Spend All Day Making Silly Quilts While My Husband Brings in All the Money Fixing People's Sinks* magazine?"

Lynette's mouth forms into a stubborn line. "It's *House Beautiful.* And these people appreciate my artistic sense."

"And for that they gotta snoop through our basement?" Gil narrows his eyes at Daniel. "What sort of trick are you trying to pull here?"

"No trick. Just doing my job, man," Daniel says, hands in his pockets. He is the picture of nonconfrontation.

"You even got ID? Lynette, you think to ask for ID? Or a business card?"

"As I told you," Marva interjects in the manner one talks to a naughty preschooler, "we are simply here to see what might be worth photographing. Every month we do a story on clever ideas from real people. It's a very popular feature. You would have final approval, of course. Now there are a few more rooms to see before—"

"No dice," Gil says. "Might as well put an ad in the paper, telling people what they can come and steal. I ain't a fool."

"But, Gil!" Lynette whines.

As they go back and forth, my phone buzzes in my pocket. I pull it out and see a Chicago number I don't recognize. On the off-off-off chance it's Ash, I hold up a finger in the international symbol for *I'll be just a moment* and quietly answer, "Hello?"

"Lucy? It's me. Mary Beth."

Mary Beth Abernathy—ugh, it's her turn to host book club. She's probably calling to warn me she'll be able to tell if I only watched the movie.

"I'm kind of in the middle of something," I mumble so I won't interrupt Marva's incensed tirade that there is simply no *trust* in the world anymore.

Mary Beth replies, "Call me back when you get a minute. It's about Ash."

"Wait. Ash? What about Ash?" Fireworks go off on my insides at the mention of my missing son.

"I have information about where he is. So I should be home for another—"

"No, wait, I'll—oh, hold on." I point to the phone and say to Daniel, "I need to take this call. I'm going to step outside."

He mouths, *Who is it?*

I wave him off and run out to the front porch. "Mary Beth, what is it?" I ask as soon as I'm alone. "What about Ash?"

"You can't tell anyone where you heard this," Mary Beth says in an ominous tone.

"Why? What's going on? Is Ash in any sort of trouble?"

"Katie will pitch a fit if she finds out you heard it from me."

"All right."

"Because I promised her I wouldn't say anything, and if she finds out I did, she'll never trust me again. And with all the pressures on kids these days, I need to keep communication open."

*Cut to it already!* "Mary Beth, *please*. What did you hear?"

"As you know, Katie is very close with Samantha Peterson," Mary Beth says, now in brisk tones. "So she told *me* that Samantha told *her* that Ash called her soon after he left the rehab facility."

Samantha. That little snot. Since she'd told me at the bowling alley Ash had written to her, she was one of the first people I called to ask—no, make that *beg*—to be told if she heard from him.

"Is he okay? Where is he?" I ask.

"From what I hear, he's fine." Upon hearing those few words, my entire body instantly unclenches. "He's still in Florida, in the Tampa area. He's staying with a guy he met in rehab. According to Samantha, this friend already completed the program, and he's taken Ash under his wing. He's going to help him find a job. They've been attending those meetings together . . . not AA . . . what's it called when it's drugs?"

"NA. Narcotics Anonymous."

"That's right. Anyhoo, that's the skinny."

He's okay. From what Mary Beth says, he's clean. But if that's the case . . . "Why hasn't he called me?" I ask, barely caring that I must sound pathetic to Mary Beth—even though later she'll certainly recount my angst to the other moms in her circle. *(She was quite choked up, but who wouldn't be? Snubbed by her very own offspring!)*

"He didn't say specifically. Although he did tell Samantha he wanted to show the rehab people he could do it on his own. So maybe that includes you, too."

That sounds like Ash. Stubborn. Willful. And—thank God—still sober. "As long as he's fine, that's what matters," I say, though it's not true. He should be back in rehab. He should call his mother—not hide from her as if she were the enemy. "It's strange Samantha wouldn't have called me to tell me that herself. Or at least tipped me off in some way."

"She's scared her mother will find out. Delores wouldn't be wild about her daughter associating with a drug addict. No offense."

Offense taken, but whatever. "So does she have a contact number for him? Can you get it for me? Because I'd like to—"

"I can't do that!" Mary Beth gasps, as if I'd asked her to drive the getaway car while I rob the bank. "As far as anyone is concerned, we never had this conversation. If I go back to my daughter and say you want a phone number, she's never going to come to me with her problems again."

"But isn't there some way you could finesse it out of her, or ask her to have Ash call me . . . ?"

She exhales sharply. "I'll see what I can do."

"Thank you. It'd mean the world to me if you could."

"It's challenging enough raising teenagers in this world today. We moms have to stick together."

"So true," I say, watery with unexpected gratitude. I've been too harsh on Mary Beth. She's not as snooty and obnoxious as I've always thought her to be. Why in fact, she's quite—

"It's the least I can do," she says, interrupting my thoughts. "I count my blessings every day that I have these wonderful children, so I owe it to the less fortunate to help them out when I can."

*Or* . . . perhaps Mary Beth is exactly as I thought. No matter. I'll gladly suck it up and take what charity she's tossing my way. Mary Beth has told me that my son's not dead or back on drugs. Even if I am a pariah—both to Ash and to society—I'm a pariah with a son who is, at least at the moment, alive and well.

I'm in the midst of giving one more plea for her to find out Ash's whereabouts and ending the call when Daniel comes out onto the porch.

"Was that the PI? Did he find Ash?" he asks as I tuck my phone back in my pocket, still stinging from having to hear the news from another mom. If only it'd been Mackenlively—then I wouldn't be feeling so inadequate on top of everything else.

I give Daniel the short version of Mary Beth's call, noticing as I'm speaking that instead of feeling the sensation of unburdening myself, it's as if I were admitting my shameful story to yet another person.

When I'm finished, he crooks an arm around me in a hug. "Thank God, huh? You must be so relieved."

I wriggle from his embrace. "Where is everybody else? Is Marva seeing the last of the rooms?"

"They're still arguing. You're happy, right? That Ash is safe?"

"Yes, of course, but *happy* might be too strong a word. So why won't that guy let Marva see the rest?"

"He suspects we're casing the joint. That we're going to come back later to rob them blind. Is there something else about Ash you're not mentioning?"

"I told you all I know, which obviously isn't much. So why is Marva putting up with that idiot? Why doesn't she go look at the rooms whether he likes it or not?"

"He's brought up more than once that he has a shotgun—and he strikes me as the type who's itching to use it." Daniel tips his head, openly studying my face. "What's going on, Luce?"

"How would I know? You're the one who was in there."

"I mean, what's going on with you? You seem upset."

"You'd think they'd be out here by now."

"Was it the call? Are you upset about the call?"

Daniel's refusal to let it drop finally breaks me. "Of course I'm upset about the call. Who wouldn't be? Just because Ash isn't dead doesn't mean that everything is peachy. Not that I would *know* how things really are with him, because he can't be bothered to contact me."

"Yeah, that is pretty rotten," Daniel says, nodding. "Can't say I blame you for being mad about that."

Here it is again, the feeling that I need to defend Ash, even though I couldn't agree with Daniel more—it is rotten of Ash. I don't need Daniel pointing it out, though. I'm well aware of my son's faults, as well as my own. "I'm not mad. I'm concerned. I'm sure Ash has a good reason for not calling, but—"

"Yeah, like there isn't a single pay phone in the entire state of Florida, right? Or the dog ate the paper where he wrote down your number? I tell you"—and I'm amazed at how agreeable Daniel's tone is, as if he and I were on the same side of this argument, which we most certainly are not—"now that you know he's alive, you must want to kill him."

"You know, I'd appreciate it if you wouldn't make light of this."

"I didn't mean to—"

"It isn't funny."

"I know it isn't. But you told me yourself, he's got a place to stay and a few bucks in his pocket. He's going to NA meetings. *He's* having a fine old time. Meanwhile, you're up here worrying yourself sick, and he can't make a call? Sorry, but that's shitty. You can make excuses for him all you want, but it doesn't change the fact that he owes you more than that."

"I don't care what he owes me. It's not like I'm keeping score."

Daniel presses his lips together, and for a moment I'm hopeful he's going to drop the subject, but he continues, "You're allowed to be mad."

"Oh, believe me, I am," I say, hoping he picks up my hint.

He does. "At Ash, I mean. He has you walking on eggshells again. You're scared anything you do or say is going to send him back to using drugs, and he knows it. It's just . . . it's hard to watch him do this to you."

"Nobody said you had to watch. In fact, please don't."

My words hit their mark. "What the f—," Daniel says, his face flushed with anger. "That's what I get? Because I'm being honest and telling you I don't like the crap he's pulling?"

"This is not *crap* he's *pulling*. You act as though he's a normal teenager who's breaking the house rules by staying out after curfew or sneaking a beer. Ash is an addict, and now he's dropped out of rehab and is just stumbling along on his own. He could backslide. He could overdose. He could *die.* I'm not simply going to ignore that, as much as you might think I should."

Daniel doesn't even try to keep his voice low. "Don't twist my words. I'm not suggesting you ignore Ash. That's the last thing I'd ever say. You may recall that *I* was the one who—"

The door is swinging open, and I want to get in one last word as the others step outside. "Daniel—you asked me before if I get it?" I say barely above a whisper. "Well, I get it. I'm Ash's mom. He's my problem. Not yours. Not anyone else's. *Mine.* This job with Marva is almost over, so don't worry—I won't be *bothering* you with having to look at me and my annoying crises anymore. In fact, consider it over now."

I'm waiting for the rush of satisfaction to hit at seeing the pain flash across Daniel's face, but it feels more like that sandwich I ate at lunch doing handstands in my stomach. It all catches up . . . Ash . . . Marva . . . the painting . . . the job . . . the kiss . . . Daniel's hurt expression . . . my rolling, tipping stomach . . .

"Hon, you okay?" It's Lynette, pausing in her litany of apologies to Marva to stare, concerned, inches from my face.

"Yes . . . but I may be about to throw up."

"For Christ's sakes!" Gil bellows. "Not in the bushes! I just trimmed those!"

Lynette ushers me back into the house and chucks me into a bathroom inside a hallway. After assuring her I don't need her help— I'm already starting to feel less queasy—I head to the sink and splash water on my face. The bracing cold calms me. After a short while— with my hairline and part of my shirt soaked—I turn off the faucets and use a hand towel to dry my face.

That's when I see it in the mirror's reflection.

*Woman, Freshly Tossed.*

It's hanging directly across from the toilet, partially obscured by a shelf containing towels, spare toilet paper, and magazines. Hesitating only briefly—do I dare reveal to Marva that her life's greatest work is on display in a *bathroom?*—I open the door and start shouting for her, claiming that I need her help.

She approaches in the manner one might a car they suspect contains a decomposing body. "I'm not good with sick people," she says grimly. "You should ask that Lynette gal."

I beckon her inside. "There's something here you need to see." I'm too emotionally exhausted to even hope to fawn over her brilliance the way Daniel would have, but I'm also not about to leave her alone in the bathroom for what may turn out to be a huge disappointment. There are razors in here.

As soon as I click the door shut, she sees it and then softly laughs. "How very apropos."

Setting the carpeted toilet seat down for her, I say, "You wanted to see it. Make yourself comfortable."

She sits down. The space between the toilet and the painting is so small that she has to tip her head up to get a good look. "So there she is."

I lean against the sink and decide to take on the elephant in the bathroom. "Sorry it's in such an awful place. That must be infuriating."

"On the contrary, I find it rather amusing."

Though I don't believe her, we've come all this way for her to visit it, so I shut up and let her do so. Her eyes flicker over the painting, and I wonder what she sees. That is, besides the obvious. Like all of Marva's paintings, the colors in *Woman, Freshly Tossed* are bright, the lines bold. The image is simple: a nude woman in blue tones leaning against a bed, behind her a ghostlike image of a man. Then there's some squiggly stuff. It's powerful, although seeing it in person, I'm surprised everybody says it's so sexy. It strikes me more as melancholy, although that could be attributed to my current state of mind.

Eventually, Marva breathes out a sigh, still looking at the painting. "You couldn't go away, could you. You had to drag me through it one more time, didn't you."

Is she talking to me? "Are you talking to me?"

My voice pulls her from her reverie. "I'm not sure who I'm talking to." She pushes on her thighs to stand. "The lucky news is, you're the only one that responded. I'm not quite as crazy as rumor would have."

"You're not crazy," I say, trying to rally with at least *some* gushing. "Except in the way that brilliant people are, but that's allowed. That painting shows what you're capable of, that's for sure. It's amazing. Of course you know that, but I'm telling you in case you forgot. About how amazing your painting is, and, by extension, how amazing you are."

She doesn't say anything, but opens the medicine cabinet and starts rifling through. "God bless Lynette," she says, pulling out a plastic prescription bottle. "There's enough here to take down a dinosaur. Can't say as how I'd blame her. I'd need a lifetime supply of painkillers, too, if I had to live with that man."

*Pills! Why didn't I check for pills! I'm a fool. I bring a suicidal woman into a bathroom chock-full of narcotics.*

"Marva . . . don't . . ."

"She won't miss them," she says, struggling with unscrewing the childproof cap. "I'll be long gone before she even comes in here."

*Oh, no . . . long gone.* "I can't let you do it. You mean too much to the world. If you don't care about yourself, think of your *son.*"

"What are you carrying on about?" She pops off the cap and shakes some pills into the palm of her hand.

I snatch the container away. "Marva, don't do it. Give me those in your hand. I'm prepared to call a paramedic, and—let me assure you—getting your stomach pumped is *not* a pleasant experience."

"Please," she says drily, "I used to take these by the truckload with no ill effect." She opens her palm, where I see only two pills before she swallows them back dry.

Well, this is awkward. "You're only taking two? What *are* those?"

"Valium—the generic. I'd like to nap on the way home. Now do you want to explain what this fit was about?"

"I know about your suicide plans. I accidentally saw your notes in the book." The words come out in a rush before I lose my courage to say them. "We were hoping that seeing your painting today would remind you about why you should live. Only we figured it'd be properly displayed in some mansion, and now I'm afraid we've made things worse."

"I see," she says in measured tones. "Does Will know?"

"Yes." She shoots me a murderous glance, and I exclaim, "I *had* to tell him! He's worried, Marva. We both are. It may seem that ending your life is the answer to your problems, but it's not."

"And how is it you've got the answer to my problems when you haven't the faintest notion what my problems might be?"

I open my mouth to rebut, but she shushes me. "Here I was believing that we'd come to an understanding, but you're still busy playing out all your busybody, fix-it schemes on me."

"That's not it at all, I'm only trying to—"

"Well, don't. Don't try to do anything other than what I've hired you for, which is to clean out my home. Otherwise, you may quickly find yourself without even that job to do—if you catch my drift."

"Marva, this is your life you're talking about throwing away. I can't sit back and pretend I don't know."

"Of course you can," she says, gingerly retrieving the pill container from my hand and placing it back in the medicine cabinet. "In fact, I'd imagine you're quite skilled at it."

"What is that supposed to mean?"

"A son with a drug problem, living with you right under your roof? I believe you know precisely what I mean."

"That's low," I say, my voice quavering.

"I'm not saying it to be cruel—simply to point out your abilities to carry on in spite of tragedy unfolding all around you," she says, her hand on the doorknob. "Frankly, I find it to be an admirable quality that you possess. And I suggest that if you want to continue working for me, you use it."

Marva leaves the bathroom without another look at the painting, and I take a moment to pee before we hit the road. I have every intention of curling up in the back of the SUV and sleeping all the way home, so I don't want a full bladder waking me up from blissful escape. On my way out, I pass Gil, who is sitting at his desk in the den. I'm in a lousy enough mood to hold up my hands and say, "See? I'm not stealing any towels."

"Yeah, I'm a son of a bitch," he says matter-of-factly. "But you try living with a woman who trusts every door-to-door salesman and preacher and lying nut job that she comes across."

Being the third among his categories, I almost feel sorry for the guy for a moment. Then it occurs to me I can at least walk out of here with the answer to one of the questions plaguing me.

"That painting in your bathroom, it's interesting. Where'd you get it?"

"Funny story." Gil seems less cranky than he did earlier, perhaps owing to the beer he's holding. "Years ago, back about '94 I'd guess, I get this call from a fellow I sometimes do work for. Got my own plumbing business. My buddy, he manages this apartment building—real swank place. One of the tenants got busted for dealing cocaine, so my bud's got to clear out the apartment, right? And the toilet's all backed up, right? So I go to snake it, and that thing's so full of pills and plastic baggies and syringes and whatnot, I had to take apart half the pipes to get everything out. Asshole that lived there must've tried flushing a million bucks' worth of drugs before the cops got him."

"And he paid you with the painting?"

"He threw it in on top of my fee. I told him I liked it, and he said take it then—that's one less thing I got to toss in the trash."

I cringe at the thought of Marva's painting getting thrown away—although that's not much worse than where it is now. "That's nice he gave you a painting you liked."

"Oh, I don't like it. The thing's uglier than my sister. But it might be worth something. I asked for the leather couch first, but he said no. Figured nobody'd want the painting so that's why I snagged it."

"If you hate it so much, why do you have it hanging up?"

He takes a swig of his beer. "Because my wife hates it more. A man's home is his castle. I should at least get to decide what goes in the room with the throne."

I leave him yukking it up at his own joke and pass Marva, who is pressing several $100 bills into a stunned Lynette's hand, claiming it's a location fee that she gets even though we can't shoot. "Don't feel you have to tell your husband about this," Marva says. "Every woman needs a little mad money."

Daniel is behind the wheel as I crawl into the back of the SUV. He tips his head toward Marva outside. "She told me she saw it. In the bathroom. Those people don't have a clue what they have. She could've *bought* the painting off them for next to nothing."

"She doesn't want it."

"It's a waste." He's staring straight ahead and starts the engine as Marva approaches the vehicle. "It's all a damned waste."

# chapter sixteen

Sometimes the clutter gets to be too much, and you need help.
There's no shame in that. The only shame is if you don't take the
help that's being offered.

—*Organize Me! welcome letter*

Three days later, Niko is passing me carrying yet another handful
of bulging trash bags to his truck. "Whatever you did to her on that
trip, she can't get rid of stuff fast enough now." He's slightly damp
from the on-and-off rain, which makes his hair curl slightly by his
neck and his clothes cling to him in a way that looks mighty fetching.
"This is my third haul to storage today. We may finish this job yet."

It's true—as much as I feared that seeing her painting might have
depressed her, if anything Marva seems galvanized by the experience.
It's starting to seem we might actually meet the deadline. For once,
instead of expending my energy fighting Marva, I'm organizing and
packing and doing what I was brought in to do. I've scheduled the

yard sale for Saturday—only five days from now—and then after that
I have one more week to finish the rest of the job. Amazingly, I've
talked Will into bringing in Organize Me! to run the yard sale. Sure,
they're the enemy, but I'm willing to wave a white flag if it means I
don't have to price twenty thousand items myself. This morning I met
them in the storage unit to go over the job. Niko drove me there, then
laughed at me when I gasped at the sheer volume of merchandise.
He's been seeing the place fill up day by day, whereas this was my first
visit—guess I wasn't fully prepared to witness what had once been
stacked to the ceiling in Marva's house now stretched out on tables
across a cavernous floor. Once buyers are unleashed into the place,
it's going to be madness. The furniture section alone is several normal
household's worth; there are enough chairs to pack an entire living
room with nothing *but* chairs.

Turns out, insulted though I may have been by what Marva
said, she was spot-on about my ability to pretend nothing's wrong.
I'm pushing forward on the job with an almost manic energy, even
though once I'm done, another item will be checked off her bucket
list. I can't even claim ignorance. I'm fully aware that I'm helping
Marva take one more step toward killing herself—possibly the final
step.

I am, however, also stupid enough to believe I can still stop her
somehow, even though I no longer have Daniel by my side to plot
and scheme with me. (He sent a curt text the day after our road trip
to say he assumed his services were no longer required, which they
aren't. I texted him back saying that I'd still give him the memorabilia
items that were to be his payment, as we'd agreed. Then I applied the
time formula for getting over a breakup: six months of grieving for
every year together. Since we kissed for about a minute, I gave myself
thirty seconds to pout about how I'd foolishly brought him into my life
again, and then it was time to move on.)

Anyway, I don't need Daniel's help. I have an idea or two of my
own on how to handle Marva. Okay, *an* idea. One. It's better than
none.

I grab my keys, leave Niko with instructions on what to do next, then spend my afternoon at an art store buying supplies. (Now I understand where the term *starving artist* comes from—I could have bought a month's groceries for what I'm paying for a few blank canvases, paints, and brushes. It didn't help that I had to ask for the top-of-the-line items, but how could I possibly inspire Marva with the cheap junk that I can really afford?) Yes, somewhere between stumbling groggily from the SUV Friday night and reporting in to work Saturday morning, it dawned on me that Daniel has had me going about this all wrong. Marva doesn't need to be reminded of how she used to love to paint—she needs to understand that the passion for painting is still in her. All she needs is a bit of prompting to rediscover the great artist she still *is*—and I seem to be the only one willing to give her said prompt.

I'm in Marva's office, arranging paints on a table and propping a blank canvas on one of several easels I found in the house, when she walks in. "What's this?" she says, eyeing the canvas with about as much enthusiasm as one might a basket of dirty laundry.

"Surprise!" I paste on a grin while bracing myself for what I can already tell is going to be a tough sale. "It's an early birthday present. We haven't come across your personal art supplies yet in our cleaning, but I didn't want you to have to go any longer without." Holding up a hand, as if her only objection is going to be the quality of what I've brought her, I add, "Now, you undoubtedly have a preference as to the types of paints and brushes you like, so this is only to get you started."

I once made the mistake of giving Ash clothes for his birthday when he was little—his face looked quite similar to how Marva's does right now.

"You shouldn't have," she says.

"My pleasure!"

It quickly becomes evident this "don't ask, don't tell" policy we've established goes both ways: She's aware of what I'm doing here, yet to say so would be to bring up the taboo subject of her suicide plans.

Finally she says, "You forget that you have me very busy going through my belongings. I hardly have time to sleep, let alone pick up a paintbrush. I'm afraid you've wasted your money."

"Marva, you're an artist, and far be it from me to allow my duties here to stand in the way of your artistry. Of *course* you need your tools. Frankly, I'm astounded you've managed this long without them. Imagine a pilot without a plane! Or . . . or . . ."

"I get the analogy," she says. "You needn't strive for another. But this pilot"—she points to herself—"is perfectly content to walk." Picking up a stack of papers, she turns to leave. "I'll be in my bedroom if you need me."

"And I'll leave this here, in case you find yourself with the urge to paint."

"I won't."

"You might."

"It will just be in your way."

"I don't mind."

"Fine then," she says. "Suit yourself."


It's Tuesday afternoon when the call finally comes.

I'm splayed on a floor rug in an upstairs room doing my best impression of making a snow angel for the simple reason that I can. There's finally enough room! In just days, we've cleared out the entire upstairs, leaving only the most basic furniture and decor (although the Easter-bonnet collection somehow survived the cut and fills an entire closet). The upstairs rooms can serve as guest rooms as soon as Mei-Hua does a thorough cleaning, which is sorely needed. It's astounding how filthy a room can get even when it's only being used for storage. It's as if Marva's stuff somehow got together to breed more tiny stuff that can only be cleared away with a broom, a bucket of Pine-Sol, and a lot of elbow grease.

"Guess I'm the only one who's bothering to work around here," Niko says with a smirk. He's changing a wall sconce and wearing the hell out of a pair of Levi's, so I've been enjoying a view of more than just an empty room. In our catch-up chat this morning, Heather suggested that the best way to get over one man is to get under another. As I recall, I had quite a lot of fun beneath this particular man not that long ago—and that was with clothes *on*. So imagine if . . . Mmm, I'm in the midst of imagining when my phone rings from where it's lying on a dresser.

"I need to get that," I say. As I do every time it rings, I silently pray that it's Mary Beth with more news about Ash. So far the poor person on the other end has been treated to my obvious disappointment when it isn't.

Niko reaches for my phone. "You're looking too comfortable down there. I'll grab it for you."

Assuming he's going to hand it to me, I'm startled when he instead flips it open and answers, "Lucy's phone." After a moment, he holds it away from his ear. "You willing to take a collect call?"

"Yes!" Without asking from whom—who else but my son would call collect?—I snatch the phone from Niko's hands saying, "Yes, yes, I accept," and am galloping down the stairs so I can talk in private. An operator asks for my credit card information, followed by a click-click as the call goes through.

"Hello? Ash?"

"Hey, Mom, it's me."

"Hey me." My tone is so casual you'd never guess I'm pacing nervously in a tiny clearing in the living room like a duck in a shooting gallery. Mackenlively's advice careens through my head. Get Ash to reveal where he is. Don't give him cash unless it's to wire to an address. No yelling or lecturing or anything that will scare him off. Hearing Ash's voice at least assuages my most nagging concern: Was Mary Beth wrong and my son is dead? "I'm glad you called," I say. "I was upset when I heard you left the Willows."

"Didn't mean to upset you. I'm fine."

"Where are you calling from?"

"Pay phone. It sure wasn't easy finding one. And then it wouldn't let me call collect to your cell phone. I had to use one of those 800 collect calling numbers." He sounds peeved, as if the process of dialing a few extra numbers was more effort than I'm worth. Still, I'm not about to waste this call with Ash now that I have him on the line and am paying good money for it.

"I mean what city are you in? Do you have a place to stay?" Aiming for perky and fearing I'm on the brink of what he'd consider badgering, I press my lips together to prevent any more questions from tumbling out. That's when I notice Marva, sorting through things in the dinette the next room over, but I'm too focused on Ash to care.

"I'm staying with a buddy of mine I met at the Willows," Ash says. "Cool guy. And don't worry, he's real straight. Totally clean. He's helping me get a job."

"Where?"

"He works for this company. They might have an opening."

Gee, Ash, could you possibly be any more vague? I attempt a different tack to pin down his location. "What company? Is it near where you are . . . in Tampa, right?"

"I don't know. Anyway, I know this call is expensive. I wanted to let you know I'm okay. I was talking to a girl I know from high school and she said she heard you were kind of freaking out like I might be dead or something, but I'm not. Obviously."

So Mary Beth came through after all and got Samantha to put in a plea to Ash. The motherhood underground is alive and well. It would be too time-consuming to take back every snarky comment I've ever made about Mary Beth, but I vow in this moment never to utter another.

Ash clears his throat. "Somebody's waiting to use this phone, so I'm gonna—"

I cut him off before he can get to the good-bye. "How come you left rehab? You were making progress, but they tell me you still have more work to do. I'm scared, honey, that you're risking a relapse. You need to go back and finish the program. They still have a bed for you, but they're not going to hold it forever."

"I'm not going back."

"Why? Did something happen?"

"I just don't need it."

"Yes, you do, Ash. This isn't the sort of thing you do on your own. Besides, why not? It's paid for, and—"

"Look, I'm sorry. You spent a lot of money sending me there, but I wish you didn't. It sucks. Maybe the first couple days I probably got something out of it, but then it was all bullshit. I don't need that place. I can do this on my own."

"You might think you can, but—"

"I gotta go."

"Is there a number where I can call you? Your friend's cell phone? Or—"

"I'll try to call back again another time."

"Ash, please, I'm begging you, give it one more chance to—"

"It's all good, Mom. Don't worry."

I'm telling him how I can't help but worry when I realize he's no longer on the phone and I'm rambling on to no one.


Unsure of whether Ash hung up or the call was lost, I glumly tuck my phone into my pocket as Marva calls me into the dining room. "I'm nearly ready to go through these piles with you," she says, not giving me a moment to digest the call. "Per your request, I've put like items with like. And, for the record, you can't get anywhere by begging him. It's undignified."

It takes me a second to realize she's talking about Ash. "You listened in on my call?"

"You of all people are going to lecture me on poking one's nose where it doesn't belong? Besides, it was impossible to ignore, what with you stomping back and forth, carving a hole in the floorboards."

There's no denying the stomping. "I didn't beg."

"Yes, you did. You said so—I'm merely quoting. And it's not going to do anything but give you gray hairs. Why so many mothers these days can't seem to detach their grown children from the tit long enough to let them stand on their own is beyond me. I am genuinely happy for you that you've found him. Now leave him be."

She can't possibly be lecturing me on parenting—Marva of all people! She has absolutely no relationship with her son, and she's going to tell me how to be a mother? "Let's stick to the sorting, shall we?" I say.

"The kindest thing you can do is set him free to be what he's going to be."

That does it—I tried to be nice, but she won't let it go. "Like you've done with Will?"

"I didn't have my personal situation in mind, but, yes. I did that for Will."

"More like did it *to* him. And still are. He doesn't want his freedom. Your son wants his mommy."

"That's ridiculous." She picks up a teakettle and chucks it in a box with a sweater (what category those two items might make is beyond me). "Although I can't say he and I are close, I must have done something right. It's not the path I'd have chosen for him—far too conventional for my tastes—but Will is a fully functioning adult with a well-paying job, a wife, and a baby on the way."

I can't resist the dig. "A baby that you didn't even know about until a week ago." The darkness that passes over Marva's face instantly takes the fun out of winning this argument. "I'm sorry. That was out of line." I realize I'm about to plead for the second time today. At least with Marva, I have an opportunity to get through to her—if for no other reason than she can't hang up on me while I'm standing in front of her. "Maybe Will doesn't have the words to tell you, but he wants you in his life. If he doesn't ever get the chance, it's going to break his heart. It doesn't have to be too late for the two of you. If you only were willing—"

My phone rings, and although I want to push my point further with Marva, having a chance to talk to Ash trumps that. "This might be my son calling me back."

"Well, hell," Marva says, suddenly cheery. "What is life but a glorious chance to make mistakes and never learn from them? What are you waiting for? Answer it!"

"Hello?" I run out to the porch and close the front door behind me. Better to brave the sideways sleeting rain that's been going on all day than Marva's ridicule.

"Hey, it's me."

Wrong me. "Oh. Hi, Daniel."

He clearly picks up on my disappointment because he says, "I'm only calling to tell you that I promised I'd do a run-through for collectibles at the yard sale, so I still plan to be there."

"You don't have to do that."

"I keep my promises." The edge to his voice makes it clear he's as eager to get this call over with as I am.

"Okay. I'll see you then."

He gives an irritated huff. "There's one more thing. I did some poking around on the Internet. Did you know Marva once had a house burn down?"

"Yes, she told me she lost almost everything."

"Did she mention that somebody died in the fire?"

"No. That's awful! Who was it?"

"Rumor has it he was her longtime lover. Officially, he was a business partner. Name of Filleppe Santiago. Ring a bell?"

I tug my sweater tighter around me against the cold. "Filleppe. From her notes in the book. What was it she wrote?"

"She'd written his name quite a few times. And it was always like she was talking to him, and not necessarily in a positive way. Something about him leaving her to do the dirty work. That one I remember specifically."

"That's right. How strange that she told me about losing her possessions, but not that a person had died."

"I'm guessing she doesn't want to talk about it."

A lover, dead in a fire. As I quickly wind up the call with Daniel with a set of good-byes so overly polite they were almost F-you's, I peer in through the foggy window at Marva and try to imagine what she used to be like. It's impossible to picture, she's so cranky now, but maybe once she was a softer, sweeter Marva.

Maybe once she was a girl in love.

# chapter seventeen

W hat are you doing here?" I eye Nelson suspiciously, unable to figure out why a nurse would be called in for a woman who intends to kill herself in days unless it's to assist her with it in some way.

"Oh, how I've missed you and these delightful chats we have." He plunks a duffel bag on the mudroom floor and looks around. "Someone's been a busy beaver! This place almost looks habitable. And speaking of beavers"—he tips his head toward Niko, who is in the yard with Torch finally emptying Marva's things out of the bungalow—"how's our office romance going?"

"Seriously, Nelson. Why are you here?"

"The lovely Miss Marva is having knee pain. I'm going to see if I can provide a bit of relief. So, as I recall from our arrangement, this is where you now offer up a juicy detail or two about your sex life in exchange for that information. And don't be afraid to be graphic—I can take it."

"You'll have to find your kicks elsewhere. Nothing's happened."

"No fair holding out on me."

"That's the truth."

"Hmmph. Pity."

Couldn't agree more. As I watch Niko muscle a box out of the door—*muscle* being the operative word—it's hard to fathom I've let over a week fly by without following up on what was such a promising start between us on Marva's bed. I blame the bout of temporary insanity that caused me to kiss Daniel. It messed up my judgment and made me miss out on what was right in front of me. Not only is Niko a sweetheart, but he's willing to accept me as I am. Or, even better, as I purport myself to be. Why am I *not* giving myself the pleasure of being with someone who thinks I'm competent at my job? Who doesn't question my abilities as a mother? And, I'll admit, is also fun to look at?

Niko must sense my gaze on him because his head lifts and he winks a hello. I wave back.

"Ah, young lust," Nelson says, fishing through his bag. "So where's the patient?"

"She's been holed up in her office all morning working on something top secret. Won't let me in when I knock."

Nelson frowns. "If her knee is giving her problems, she should be lying down."

"She might be busy painting," I say, which is what I've had my fingers crossed for, ever since she yelled at me through the locked door to go away. "If she is, that's more important than resting. So don't give her any lectures."

"You say that now. Nobody appreciates knees until they're gone. She's at least going to lie down for a while if I have any say in the matter, and—as luck would have it—I do."

"How long will you be?"

"It depends . . . why?" he asks.

"No reason."

It's Nelson's turn to eye *me* suspiciously, and justifiably so. As soon as he disappears with Marva into her bedroom, I steal toward her office. I'm dying to see if my scheme is working, and this may be my brief opportunity for a peek. Even if she hasn't started a painting, maybe she's dabbled with mixing paints or played with a few strokes or . . .

Or nothing. The canvas is untouched. A light layer of dust may even be forming.

Siiiiiigh.

Sullenly, I pick up a box and start filling it with items for the yard sale, no longer being sneaky since Marva's obviously not hiding anything in here. It's when I'm piling some old *Life* magazines into the box that I notice it: the copy of *Grimm's Fairy Tales*. Sitting right on the desk.

*Yes!* When God closes a door, he opens a window, as a wise nun-turned-singing-governess once said. Maybe now I can find out more about Marva's suicide plans. Possibly there's something more about this Filleppe guy.

I peek out into the hallway to verify that Marva is still in her bedroom before snatching up the book. Underneath it I see a letter written on monogrammed stationery: MMR. My blood turns to ice as soon as I read the opening line in Marva's familiar handwriting:

*To Whomever May Find Me*

First off, it's *whoever*—but that's not the point.

It's Marva's suicide note. Or at least a draft of it—crumpled papers are in the trash can next to the desk, so this isn't her first attempt. This is what she's been laboring at all day while she banned me from the room. She's scratched out some of what she's written, but as I pick the paper up and read, her intention is evident. She's going through with it. This letter is for the poor slob who stumbles across her body. For the first time it occurs to me that it could be *me* who finds her—definitely outside my job description and the thought of which has my hand shaking as I read on.

> *They say you can't take it with you. And so, I leave it all behind as I venture into—as Emily Dickinson once wrote of death—"a wild night and a new road." I've had everything I wanted in this lifetime and now would only face that which I don't, and swore I never would.* ~~To my son, I'm sorry. To Will,~~ ~~know that this has nothing to do with you. Will, you are the~~

*one thing I will miss.* Will, I won't insult you with sentiment
at this juncture, other than to say I admire your courage to become the man you were meant to be. As for you, F, hope you've
been saving me a deck chair in Hell.

The note is signed with the same signature Marva uses on her
paintings, the blocky MMR, as if this is a work of art she's created
here and not a horror. Although I'd wanted to pore through the book,
now that I realize what she's been up to, I know she'll be furious if
she catches me in here. I hurriedly set the note back on her desk
beneath the book, arranging everything exactly as I found it. Then I
scurry from the room, feeling as dirty as if I'd stumbled across photos
of Marva in flagrante delicto. And frustrated: She finally says sweet
words to Will, and he won't see them until she's gone?

In the kitchen I nearly crash into Niko, who is carting a box of
paints and brushes he'd told me earlier that he'd found in the bungalow. "We're done out there—come take a look," he says.

After I have him drop off the box in the office, he takes my hand
to lead me through the yard to the bungalow. That simple gesture
is the comfort I need right now. I wonder if he'd find it strange if I
curled up and asked him to carry me.

"Did you mean for us to remove so much? It's pretty empty," he
says as we step inside.

"It's perfect."

"At least now there's enough room to bring in the rest of your
stuff."

I shake my head. "I'm going to be moving out once this job is
done so there's no point."

"Then what?"

"Then home," I say, though I have no idea what that even means.

He sits on the edge of the couch. "So, when are we going to go get
that drink? I haven't forgotten. You busy tomorrow night?"

"Boy, am I!" I say, and launch into a list of all the things I still need
to do at Marva's before it occurs to me that I am in essence rejecting

an invitation—for an actual date. From a hot, eligible man. Niko is getting up and backing out the door, probably having barely scraped his ego up off the floor. It's now or never. "So what I'm getting at," I say quickly, "is that I'm pretty wiped out. How about we hang out here? I'll download a movie. Or now that I have all this room, we can turn cartwheels if we want. Do jumping jacks. Practice the long jump."

He laughs. "I'm sure we'll come up with something."

What are you going to wear? Not the polka-dotted dress—no offense, it makes you look hippy," Heather says. She and I are grabbing a quick lunch at Red Hen Bread because she had a hankering for their cranberry chicken sandwich. Though I suspect it's more she's craving adult company. I'm coloring with Abigail as we chat. Marva must be rubbing off on me, because I'm purposely going outside the lines.

"We're watching a movie at my place. Sweats will be fine."

"They are not! This is a date!"

"Kidding—I'll probably wear jeans and that sequined T-shirt you gave me."

Heather sneaks off a piece of Abigail's PB&J. "You're going to wear nice underwear, right? A date at home means s-e-x."

Abigail pops up her head. She's learning her letters, but luckily for our conversation here, she hasn't yet figured out how to string them together into words. It proved to be a veritable spelling bee telling Heather how Ash hung up on me again (a-s-s-h-o-l-e) when I refused to transfer money to his ATM account and instead said I needed an address to overnight a money order. Then we talked a bit more about how Daniel and I k-i-s-s-e-d but now aren't speaking.

"If things go as I anticipate they will," I tell Heather, "nobody's going to be in their u-n-d-e-r-w-e-a-r all that long." I pull out a blue crayon and begin to color a princess's face with it, just to see if I can get a rise out of Abigail, which it appears I will. Her brows shoot down in disapproval.

"Good for you," Heather says, "after all you've been through, you deserve this piece of happiness."

"Or a piece of something."

"I still can't believe Daniel, though, being so rude like that. It goes to prove, there's no going back."

"Forward motion only," I say. "From now on, I don't care where I'm headed, as long as it's not anywhere I've been."

Abigail can't take it any longer and yanks the crayon from my hand. "Princesses are not *blue*," she scolds.

Heather absently retrieves the crayon from Abigail. "I understand how you feel, Lucy. Although the time may come when you'll need to pick a more specific destination."


You look nice," Niko says, handing me a six-pack as he steps into the bungalow. "Hope beer is okay."

"It's great. Thanks for bringing it."

For as much as we've been around each other these past weeks, suddenly I'm feeling shy. Niko is wearing his usual jeans and a T-shirt, but he smells soapy, indicating a shower. I may have snuck in showering myself—plus shaving, loofahing, hair blow-drying, reapplying makeup, changing my outfit five times, and winding up in what I started out with.

"What's the agenda?" Niko says, twisting open the beer I hand him and then handing it back to me. "A movie, or should we get straight to the cartwheels?"

"Definitely cartwheels. But you first."

He surprises me by saying, "All right." Shoving my couch back with his foot to make more room, he turns out a pretty reasonable cartwheel, his shirt sliding up around his chest while he's upside down to reveal taut abs leading into a muscled V of hip bone. Hoo-ya. This whole date thing? *Excellent* idea. When Niko is again upright, he says, "Now your turn."

"Gosh, I'm worn-out from all the cartwheels I was doing before you got here," I say, plunking down on the couch.

Niko grabs a beer and sits next to me. "I'll let it slide this time. What movie did you pick? Hope there's killing in it."

"Nope, total chick flick," I tease. "Nothing but endless talking and kissing."

"That's cool." He lightly brushes back a strand of my hair. "I like talking and kissing." I'm all for getting directly to the latter, but he says, "Man, you should've seen how bad the damage was in that closet today." We then launch into what would be a monumentally dull conversation to anyone else, but I'm riveted to hear how many floorboards Niko's crew has to replace due to the rot caused by the sheer weight of Marva's belongings.

I'm having a perfectly enjoyable time when out of nowhere, Niko asks, "Hey, who was that collect call you got the other day?"

"That? Oh, it was my son," I say, hoping I'm not asked to go into any details.

"Yeah? An uncle of mine once took a collect call, and, man, it was expensive. Like fifteen bucks for a one-minute call. And that was just from across town. You're not gonna be happy when you get the bill. I hope it was important."

"It was. He—" I'm not going to stoop to lying, but I also recall how the last time I told someone that Ash walked away from rehab without bothering to call me, it didn't go well. Somehow, I doubt Niko would ever tell me that my son was being shitty, as Daniel did, but why get into all that if I don't have to? "He didn't have his cell phone."

"Bet you'd like to kill him, eh?"

I'm momentarily taken aback at how similar Niko's words are to what Daniel had said—although he was referring to Ash's not calling, versus his calling collect. Not that I want to be thinking about Daniel right now. A swift change of subject is definitely in order, so I say, "I can't believe we're almost done with this job!"

"You think you're going to make your deadline? Seems like a lot still to do in a week."

I glance at the calendar taped to the wall, nearly filled with Xs. "Don't remind me. To be perfectly honest, with that stupid yard sale day after tomorrow, the last thing we should be doing is hanging out on this couch. We should be in there packing boxes. Only . . ." I lean against the couch and smile at him so he knows I'm not really cracking the whip. "I've been working so hard the past few days, I'm so sore I can barely lift a pencil right now, much less a box."

"Well, that's not right. C'mere." Just like that, he tugs me closer to him on the couch, my back facing him. "Bet you could use a shoulder rub."

Oh, yes, indeed, I could. Is there anything more universally beloved than the shoulder rub? And this isn't some cheesy, halfhearted effort—he's giving me a real massage. I feel so much tension ease out that I'm a puddle within seconds. His hands move firmly up my neck, digging between my shoulder blades, down my back. I'm so blissfully relaxed that—when he lifts my arms and tugs my shirt up and off—I don't think twice about it, other than to give an *mmm* of happiness before I shift to face him and pull his mouth to mine.

We're soon rolling around on the couch. I quickly divest Niko of his shirt—fair is fair. He's kissing down my neck, and my hands are roaming over his firm, smooth chest, when he lifts away and gazes around the room. "I just noticed, you don't have a bed."

"Nope."

"You sleep on the couch every night?"

"I have an inflatable."

"Cool." Then he takes a great interest in my bra straps and, specifically, sliding them downward. That is, as best he can on this cramped couch. I hadn't thought about that for a while, how pathetic it is I don't have a bed. A hot guy has his lips sliding toward the curve of my breast, a hand fumbling with the button on my jeans, and I can't even show him the courtesy of a bed? Niko probably thinks I'm one of those free-spirit types who is *choosing* this lifestyle rather than what I really am, which is broke. No, not true—I am merely in transition. I will have my life together again, and soon. Then I won't have to be embarrassed about my pitiful living circumstances, or about how I've screwed up my life in other ways. Just as soon as I get the bonus. If I get the bonus. Correction: I *will* get that bonus.

Shifting so he can get better leverage—that button is a stubborn one—it strikes me as kind of funny that Niko was so easily distracted when I switched the topic from Ash's call earlier. Unlike *some* people, Niko is obviously willing to go with the flow. It's what I find most attractive about him, really, that he's so laid-back and sunny. Every minute with him is so easy and—

"You're *so* hot," he murmurs, disrupting my thoughts. He's temporarily given up on the button and moved on to unhooking my bra, which he does with remarkable skill. He eagerly goes about enjoying the goodies he's released, and I must say, it feels incredible. What am I doing, letting my mind wander? Here I am with a gorgeous man's mouth on my breast and his hand gripping my ass and I'm barely paying attention? I don't need to wait for some bonus to start my life—it's starting now. Right here. Although quick mental note—not to distract me from that thing Niko is doing with his tongue, which is, in a word, *yum*—but I need to spend the day tomorrow focusing on yard-sale items only. Making the deadline is so closely within reach. It seemed hopeless there for a while, but—

*For crying out loud, Lucy, focus!* Just look at Niko, will you? In fact, have a good feel! Wrapping my arms around his back, I grasp the taut ripple of muscle, let myself sink into the sexiness of his soft moan as I tug his body closer to mine. It makes me feel so . . .

So . . .

What is it exactly that I'm feeling? I search myself for the right words and . . .

Huh . . .

I do believe I'm bored.

That can't be—I'm out of practice, that's all. Niko is hitting all the right notes—really, I can't say enough good things about his dogged determination to conquer that button—but, well . . .

*Meh.*

It seems impossible—I mean, it's been so long since I've gotten any action and I've had a crush on Niko for weeks—but there's no getting around it. As good-looking as he is, as nice, as eager to please—I'm not into him. I'm not really even here. I'm off somewhere else, worrying if Ash is okay, and if I'm going to get this job finished, and Niko doesn't know any of that. And I don't want him to know. I want him to be at arm's length where he can't see the real me . . . but arm's length is pretty distant for what I'd originally planned for the evening's activities.

God help me, but I want a man who would love me in spite of everything—possibly even because of everything. I've already had that once, and I'm still not over it.

"Niko . . . wait."

"Wha— Huh?" He's breathing heavily as he looks at me lustily through those impossibly long lashes of his. "Something wrong?"

"I can't do this."

"Too fast?"

I reach for my bra, slipping it on as I search for the right way to tell Niko I'm sorry for leading him on, but I need more than a pretty face and a buff body. I need someone who *knows* me, and the primary appeal of Niko is that he doesn't.

"I thought I was ready, but I'm not. I hope we can still be friends?"

*Yeah, right*—that's what a guy wants to hear from the seminaked woman that he was moments ago dry-humping.

He doesn't answer, just pulls his shirt on over his head. Then he reaches for the remote. "Hey, you got any food?"

I wake to my phone ringing. Niko is gone, and I'm on the couch with a blanket thrown over me. It takes a moment of fumbling in the dark before I find the phone and answer it. It's Ash again.

"Yes, I'll accept charges." After I again provide credit card information—and I'm starting to wonder just what sort of charges I'm racking up—I greet my son with "It's after midnight."

"Is it? Shit. Sorry. I need you to put money in my ATM account."

"As I told you last time, I'm willing to mail a money order. Give me the address where you're staying."

"See, that's the problem. My buddy is, uh, getting the place fumigated, so I need to get a hotel room for a while. Just until, uh, we can go back to the apartment."

"And he threw you out into the street without a warning? What kind of friend is this?"

"Uh . . . it happened kinda fast. So can you put the money in? Like a few hundred bucks? It's freezing here. And I'm tired."

Does Ash believe I'm that stupid, or have I in fact been so stupid in the past I would have fallen for such a fishy story? Then again . . . if he does need a place to stay, and I say no, I'm leaving him to sleep in the streets.

After mulling the options, none of which are good, I go with the one that will at least buy me time to come up with something better. "Tell me roughly where you are." I head to the computer and log on. "If you truly need a place to sleep, I'll book you a motel."

"But I'm hungry, too."

"Tough luck. You should have thought of that before you left the Willows. I hear the food there is excellent."

A light is on in Marva's kitchen. Since I'm wide awake after Ash's call, I decide to see if she'd like to get some work done. When I walk in, she's sorting a set of dishes into stacks of pink, blue, and yellow. "Decided I could let go of the Lu-Ray after all. Surprised to see you up and about."

"My son called."

"Ah. I take it then you didn't get him to go back to rehab."

"No, I didn't. He called saying he needed a place to stay, so I booked him a motel."

"That'll show him who's boss." When I slump down defeatedly onto a chair, she says, "I'm joking. Don't take everything so seriously."

"All I've been through and he still has me wrapped around his finger. But I'm scared if I don't help him, something awful will happen."

"That's the problem with love—it's too closely tied to fear. But you can't be afraid of your own son. That doesn't help him. As you've seen, he simply uses it against you."

"I wish I could *talk* to him."

"So talk to him."

"He keeps hanging up on me."

"You've booked the hotel. You've got an address. Go there. Do what you feel you must. Twist his arm, beg, plead, knock him upside the head."

"I thought you said it was stupid."

"It is! But sometimes stupid is exactly what the situation requires. I'll bet you can be on a flight first thing in the morning."

"I can't do that. Tomorrow's the last day before the yard sale. I need to be here."

"You think I can't carry on for one day without you? That you're the only person in the world who can place things into a box? You certainly do have an overinflated sense of your own importance."

"But there's so much left to do."

"It's not as if I have to do any heavy lifting—I have that Niko fellow to do that sort of thing. That is," she says, smirking as she reaches into the cupboard for another stack of plates, "if you didn't tucker the poor boy out tonight."

I don't even bother to be embarrassed or try to make an excuse for why Niko was over; I'm too busy contemplating Marva's suggestion. It's ridiculous, of course. I can't possibly leave the day before the yard sale—there's too much left to do, and Marva can't be trusted to do it. I could just see her sending Niko to retrieve things from the warehouse the moment I left, then Will refusing to give me the bonus as a result. Still . . . the whole reason I'm doing this job is for Ash. Earning that bonus isn't going to mean a thing if he's back on drugs.

I heave a sigh and say a silent prayer because—as bad as the timing may be—I don't see how I can afford *not* to go.

After giving Marva instructions on what to pack up tomorrow, which I suspect she'll ignore, I head back to the bungalow and schedule a 7:00 a.m. flight. Then I curl up on the couch, but I'm so stressed out it's hard to sleep. It's going to be next to impossible to convince Ash to go back to rehab. It wasn't easy the first time, and I had a professional interventionist there who knew how to close the deal.

Eventually I manage to drift off, knowing I should be figuring out what I'll say, but lulling myself instead with the thought that, in mere hours, I'll get to see my baby.

It's shortly before noon when I pull the rental car up to the motel, which looks as if it's worth the $30 a night I paid and not a penny more. It's close enough to the airport I could have taken a cab, but my goal is to get Ash to come with me. I'll drive him straight to the Willows, less than an hour away. As a step toward earning his affection, I stopped to pick up a deli sandwich in case he's as hungry as he said. I actually practiced my side of any argument the entire flight over, and I'm coming in with a plan to be firm, unafraid, and—beyond that—to wing it.

I show the clerk my credit card to get a key, and in minutes I'm at Ash's room, sliding the key card in and opening the door.

"Ash, it's me, Mom," I say once the door is open a crack. This motel looks dodgy enough he might have slept with a knife by his side, so a little warning would be prudent. The blackout curtains make it pitch-black in the room. The only light is what I'm letting in, and it illuminates my son's sleeping shape. He's on his side, curled up with a pillow as if it were a teddy bear. His hair is going in about twelve directions at once, and he has several days' growth of facial hair, the usual blond peach fuzz that's more scruffy than manly. He doesn't stir. He's snoring lightly, and the sight of his tangle of legs and arms and kicked-off blankets wallops me with a wave of nostalgia. As when he was a colicky baby, I take this moment to feel the rush of fondness for my son in slumber—before he wakes up and starts squalling and wrecks it all.

It's when I open the door farther and step in that I see the empty baggies and open prescription bottles on the nightstand—and, ugh, *not using anymore, my ass.* Instantly furious—both at him and at myself for being so gullible—I step in, slam the door shut, and flick on the light. "Ash, wake up. It's your mother."

"What the f—?" He scrambles to sitting, confusedly grabbing pillows and sheets around him, as if I haven't seen him in his boxers a million times. "What are you doing here?"

I toss the bag with the sandwich in it onto the bed. "Bringing you breakfast."

He seems to accept this answer, sleepily scratching his head. I set my purse on a table and pull up a nasty, stained chair. Debating for a few seconds whether I dare sit on it, I finally sink down directly across from him. We're going to be a while. "You're using again."

"Wha—? No, I'm not, I . . ." He at least has the decency not to bother continuing with the denial, what with the evidence right in front of us.

"It wasn't a question. You need to get up and put some clothes on. I'm taking you to the Willows." Whoever I'm channeling right now sounds firm and assured, so I go with it.

"No way."

"Ash, you told me you were clean, but you aren't. It's obviously not working to do this on your own. You need help. There's no shame in that. The only shame is if you don't take the help that's being offered." I'm impressed that I managed to pull out something so wise to say, until I realize I'm quoting the welcome letter I received from Organize Me! after I hired them.

"I only did it to take the edge off. It was a onetime thing—I was stressing about not having a place." He opens the takeout bag and pulls out the sandwich, examining it with a grin. "You remembered. Ham and cheese. Mayo, no mustard. Lettuce, no tomato."

"I believe I can still manage to recall my son's favorite sandwich."

"Not entirely—you forgot I like the Italian bread more than the plain wheat. It's got these seeds on it—".

"Get dressed. You can eat in the car."

"I'm not going."

"Yes. You are."

"No. I'm not."

Here's the problem—being tough is impressive and all, but doesn't work with Ash. It never has. Cajoling, tricking, pleading . . . all potential successful actions. But try to tell my stubborn boy what he has to do, and all that happens is that he sits right where he is and infuriatingly bites into the sandwich you were kind enough to bring him, chewing as if he's got all day and his mother doesn't have a non-refundable flight back to Chicago at six o'clock. Still, I stay focused on the goal: Get him back into rehab. Don't be afraid. I've risked too much coming here to back down now.

"So then what is your plan?" I ask.

"You say that like you assume I don't have one." He leans over the bed and digs through his duffel bag. "But I do. Here." He hands me a glossy brochure. It's for the Betty Ford Center in California. "Got this from a guy in NA. Bet you thought I didn't really go to any meetings here, did you. This guy says this one's the best. They all say it. It was started by the wife of a *president*."

Is he serious? I look at his proud expression. Yes, he is. He honestly believes that I'm going to pay for an entirely new stint in rehab. "Ash, I can't afford this. The Willows is already paid for."

"The Willows sucks. It's boring."

"It's rehab! It's not supposed to be a thrill a minute—it's *work*."

He sets the sandwich down directly on the bedspread, which makes me shudder—it's probably years since it's been cleaned. "I'm not scared of work, but that place is bullshit. Once I got through the first couple days, they couldn't tell me anything I haven't already figured out. And you didn't even say you were happy that I'm talking about going back to rehab—that I'm not giving up."

"I *am* happy, but I have to be realistic. The Willows is a respected facility. It certainly wasn't cheap. Who's to say the Betty Ford is any better?"

"Everybody," Ash says excitedly, and it's so achingly sweet to see him enthusiastic about anything that I allow him to show me the brochure, to explain about how its program is better suited to his type of addiction. Though there's not a chance I'm sending him there. I don't even know if I'm going to get that bonus anymore. Even if I do—and please let everything be going okay back at the house—paying for the Betty would take every bit of it. It'd completely wipe out the future I'm working so hard to create from the rubble. I can't do it, which is what I tell him.

As soon as the words are out of my mouth, he's back to his usual pissed-off self. "Can't . . . or won't?" he challenges.

I don't take the bait, but instead say, "What will help is that I'll be driving you personally to the Willows, so I can talk to them when I check you in. We can tweak the program so it works better for you."

"They'd have to fire all the staff and change the whole place. That ain't going to happen. But at this other one—"

"Ash, I'm not paying for another rehab."

He narrows his eyes at me, and if eyes are the windows to the soul, then his soul is looking pretty tired and bloodshot. "So you're going to do nothing—just let me slide back. Because you're too cheap. I'm not worth the money. Real nice."

He may as well have slapped me. I can practically feel the marks across my cheek. What is most painful, however, is that it's working. I'm not angry, as I should be—I gave up everything to send him to rehab, and now he's calling me cheap?

But I'm not mad. I'm scared.

He may as well be holding a gun to his head, daring me to tell him to pull the trigger.

I take a calming breath. *Don't be afraid of your own son.* "Nobody is letting you slide back. If it happens, it's of your own doing."

"I don't *want* it to happen. You said it yourself: I can't do this alone. I need you. Please, Mom," he says, taking on a pleading tone that is my personal kryptonite—I'm aware of it, and, unfortunately, Ash is, too.

"Sweetie, as much as I may want to, I can't."

He goes in for the kill: "Don't leave me to do it alone."

"Then come home with me," I say, grasping for a way to fix this, though there's technically not a home for him to come home to. I'll figure it out. "You can do an outpatient program there and live with me. That'll be more affordable."

"Outpatient? Living with you? That's worse than the Willows!"

It takes a second for what Ash just said to sink in, and when it does, I nearly choke on a laugh. His outrage is so absurd that it lifts the curtain of fear I've put up between us, and in that moment I can see him clearly. It appears that my boy—my sweet, beautiful, but troubled little boy—is a spoiled brat.

The realization takes me by surprise since I've always prided myself on not spoiling him. He could throw a tantrum to get a new toy until he combusted and I wouldn't give in. But that I didn't buy him things doesn't mean I haven't given him too much. I must have. Because I can't believe he'd let me do it—he'd gladly let me wipe out everything I've done, *again,* and for the sole reason that better me be uncomfortable than him. This goes beyond his addiction—which I don't think he can entirely help—to something that's in his control.

Now it's time I took control. "Outpatient is your only other choice," I say, having found my spine, right there in my back, holding me up. "So it's that or the Willows. I suggest the Willows."

Grumbling under his breath, he gets up and slides his legs into the pants that are in a heap on the floor. I can't believe it. He's getting dressed. I've done it! I held tough, and he's going to go back to rehab. It's all I can do not to grab him and smooch his face as he glares at me. "What's your deal—you take bitch lessons or something?"

"As a matter of fact I did. From the master." *Thank you, Marva.* I bend down to hand him his shirt, also from the floor. "You need to shower before we hit the road?"

"I'm not going anywhere, except to take a piss."

"I thought . . ." I don't bother finishing. We're back at square one.

While he's in the bathroom, I throw away the empty baggies and containers so they'll quit mocking me. They're winning, and I'm a big loser. Short of clubbing Ash over the head and dragging him unwillingly back to rehab, which he'd walk away from again anyway, I'm fresh out of ideas of what to do.

I spend the next couple of hours trying to sell Ash on the Willows—even getting Dr. Paul on the phone, but Ash refuses to talk to him. It's Dr. Paul who eventually breaks it to me that I'm wasting my efforts so there's no need to miss my flight home. If my son won't go willingly, they can't take him.

As Ash polishes off the rest of his sandwich (I have to force myself not to imagine the germs on it since I have no other food to offer), I try one more strategy. "Can I at least meet your friend?" With a few hours until my flight takes off, I have enough time to make an ally. If he's off drugs as Ash said he is, then the two of us can gang up on my hardheaded son.

"That fell through."

"So there's no friend going to NA."

"Not anymore."

"And no couch for you to crash on."

He shakes his head.

This just gets better and better. "So where are you planning to live?"

"Haven't worked that out yet. I was hoping you could float me some cash."

And it's official: This trip has been a total failure. May as well skulk home before I somehow make things worse. In the time before I catch my flight back, I buy Ash groceries and a bus pass, and book the motel room for another week. That probably makes me a sucker, but one whose son at least won't die hungry and homeless in a gutter.

At the airport, I call Phoebe, my contact at Organize Me!. She tells me that ads, e-mail notices, and signs have been posted, so they're expecting crowds in the hundreds tomorrow. Bigger-ticket items are already priced, and staff will be on hand to haggle the rest. They're ready to go! Hanging up, I can see why Will had once threatened to replace me with these people. Talking with them offers the reassurance of being held close to your mama's warm, yet very organized, bosom.

It's after midnight when I get home, but as is often the case lately, Marva is still awake. I pop in the house to tell her Ash didn't go back to rehab, and while I'm there, I'm so wired that I decide to look for any last-minute items for the sale. After only a few minutes she kicks me out. "You're driving me batty! It's like having a bird accidentally fly into the house, fluttering about and crashing into windows."

"I suppose I should get some sleep. Big day tomorrow."

Marva grabs a pack of cigarettes off the counter. "Might turn in myself after I have a smoke—thought I'd stop by your little sale in the morning."

Although I summon great verve to tell Marva she needn't bother—we've got it under control!—she insists that it sounds "fun."

Oh, yes, tomorrow is going to be a regular laugh riot. When I get to the bungalow, I don't bother inflating the bed and just collapse on the couch. Between having to face Daniel at the sale, and now Marva's possible guest appearance, whether things sell will be the least of my troubles. I close my eyes, trying to get *some* sleep, but now that I'm no longer busying myself with work, all I can think about is Ash—there in that hotel room, teetering on the brink of a backslide, or worse, and his own mother without a clue of what to do about it.

# chapter eighteen

If you love something, set it free; if it comes back, it's yours. If it doesn't, it never was.

*—Poster about letting go that cluttered the walls of millions of homes in the 1970s*

The sale is due to start in an hour, and already I feel as if I've put in a full day (especially since I *have* been here since six). Everything is set up in the warehouse: the cash registers, shopping baskets, and endless rows of tables, racks of clothes, and items laid out on the floor. The staff (eighteen of them!) are dressed in red polos and khakis, so I feel as if I am at the world's weirdest Target store and we're about to open doors on the busiest shopping day of the year. I'm strapping on a fanny pack so I can handle money when I hear Niko behind me. "Here she is." I turn around to find him walking up with Daniel. "Security wasn't going to let him in, but I recognized him as the collectibles guy," Niko says before taking off—inadvertently reminding Daniel of the time I'd introduced him so rudely.

It doesn't go over Daniel's head. His face flashes annoyance, but he doesn't say anything. A few seconds later he's over it and is turning in a circle to take in the full effect of the warehouse. "Wow. Her stuff looks so much bigger stretched out."

"Doesn't it?"

"I should've come earlier. I'm going to have to sprint through here to look at everything before they let people in."

"You don't have to do this. They've already done the pricing, and—"

He cuts me off. "I said I would. Don't want to see Marva get ripped off if something slipped past you all. No sense selling for a dollar what's worth a thousand."

Having exhausted our desire for conversation, Daniel grabs a rolling cart and starts making his way through the aisles. At first I keep tabs on him out of curiosity, but soon I'm absorbed in the frantic preopening activities. A few minutes before nine, I go to peek at the line outside, which, shockingly, snakes around the warehouse. And coming up the side of it, right toward me, are Marva and Will. She's a walking billboard for the style of clothes people can purchase inside, wearing a geometric-print caftan and dark glasses. Her hair is in a turban and she's back to leaning on her cane. Will—to my delight—is unwittingly in the staff uniform of a red polo and khakis.

Waving them past security, I escort them in, being especially watchful of Marva as she steps into the warehouse. My arm is at the ready to catch her if the trauma of seeing the sheer volume of her possessions splayed out makes her faint. One would suppose her son would be concerned, but he's got his arms crossed, swearing to himself in obvious disgust.

Marva's breathing seems shallow, her mouth formed into a thin line.

"You okay?" I ask. "Do you need to sit down?"

"Of course I don't," she snaps. "I just got here! Is this all of it? Only this one room?"

*Only this one room?* Don't play coy with me, sister—it's the size of a basketball stadium and there's not a chance it's unimpressive.

"This is it," I say. "You must be proud to have given so much up."

"Hmmph. As much as I'd enjoy staying here so you can patronize me, I believe I'll have a look around." She heads in the direction of the furniture area, and when Will starts to follow, she points her cane to stop him in his tracks. "I hardly need a babysitter!" Then turning away, she exclaims, "Wait a minute, is that my art deco armoire I see there? I don't recall saying that could be sold!"

She bustles away as Will turns to me. Through a jaw so clenched I almost want to take a can of WD-40 to him, he says, "This is going to be terrific having Marva here. So glad you suggested it to her."

"I didn't suggest it. All I did was remind her the sale was today."

"You should have talked her out of it."

I throw up my hands. "*I'm* not the one who drove her here!"

At that, he has the decency to look chagrined. "She's going to cause a ruckus." We're both watching her. She's already corralled a worker into following her with a cart, into which she's plunking merchandise with the wild abandon of a sweepstakes winner let loose in a store for an all-you-can-grab-in-sixty-seconds prize.

"Not to be crude," I say, "but why is she so worried about keeping things if she doesn't expect to be around much longer anyway? What sense does that make?"

"What sense does it make to own a hundred umbrellas? My mother is a crazy hoarder, and now she's running around, waving her hands in the air, telling everybody in the world that this is all hers. The entire reason I wanted this off-site was to avoid this very sort of a scene."

"If it's any consolation, she's not waving her arms." The bad news is, that's because they're too filled with merchandise.

Customers begin to file in. I pull off my fanny pack, handing it to Will. "Here, you can make sales. I'll deal with your mother."

He holds the pack away from him in the manner of a man being asked to hold a woman's purse. "What? Me? I'm not here to work."

I can't resist giving him a once-over as I say, "No? You're dressed like you are." Then I head over to Marva and attempt damage control.

She's clutching a brass standing toilet-paper holder when I reach her—to my annoyance, one of the few items that I *did* sneak out. Figures. "Whoa, Marva, what's going on? Why are you shopping at your own sale?" Hoping a bit of levity might distract her, I add, "You angling for a family discount?"

"I've half a mind to close this sale down. Did you honestly believe I wouldn't notice how much you've brought here without my permission?"

Her accusation—even if it *is* true in this instance—riles me to produce my most powerful weapon: sarcasm. "What? A toilet-paper holder? Seriously, you're telling me that this is a prized possession? A family heirloom perhaps?"

The worker Marva had nabbed—a scrawny kid with the pasty complexion of a World of Warcraft addict—clears his throat. "Um, I'm supposed to be helping at the registers?"

"You can go," I say as Marva commands, "Stay."

He's frozen in place, hands clutching the cart. I feel sorry enough for him to take control. "Go. I'll handle this."

"I hardly need to be *handled*," Marva says after the boy scurries away. "I have simply voiced a legitimate objection to seeing my personal property up for sale against my wishes."

It's seeing the cart heaped with what she *did* approve that keeps me focused. "There's no point in arguing about what you did or did not agree to sell. It's here now. As we speak, people are shopping."

She tips her chin up defiantly. "Perhaps then I *shall* cancel this event."

"It's your call." She's hardheaded enough to do it. I could see her with a bullhorn, chasing out the crowd of at least a hundred people who are now dashing through the aisles of this one-woman flea market. "Of course, Organize Me! would need to be paid. And this is the last weekend before your deadline, so I don't see when else it could be scheduled. You'd be out a lot of money. But if you are truly worried—"

"Oh, cut the crap—I don't care about the money. I care about what's *mine*."

"Why?"

"Wha—" She blusters for a moment, tripped up by my searing inquiry. Finally she says, "Everyone cares about what's theirs."

"Not everyone. I don't. I was able to let go of everything I had and barely flinched." I raise a hand to ward off her objection before she can say it. "I am not implying that makes me morally superior."

"It makes you a fool. Or a liar."

"Because I'm not a pack rat?"

"Because you haven't any idea what's of value to you, so you claim nothing is." She sets the toilet-paper holder down. "Is this your clever strategy—to tie up my attention with a silly debate while half of Chicago walks away with my belongings?"

A barrel-shaped woman immediately snatches up the toilet-paper holder. "You know what they're asking for this?"

"Ten dollars," Marva says.

The woman sets it down. "Too much."

After she leaves, Marva sighs. "I believe I paid several hundred for that at an antique store."

I seize the opportunity. "Marva, it's clear that everything here at one time was worth something to you, but that doesn't mean it has to be forever. They're holding you back from the *life* you could have." For good measure, I'd emphasized the word *life*. "Let it go."

"You sound like an infomercial."

"So are you buying what I'm selling?"

She surprises me by laughing. Then she does the same slow spin Daniel did, drinking in her surroundings. "So this was all in my house. Tremendous. Clearly I have a gift for managing spatial relationships if I was able to fit all this in there. But . . . I suppose there is no point in dragging it back. That wasn't the purpose of my visit today."

"Why *are* you here?"

"I thought I'd enjoy having one last chance to bid it all adieu, say a final farewell. I hadn't anticipated how annoying it would be to see people pawing through my valuables." She slides a cutting look to a group of women trying on her clothes over the top of what they're wearing. "Nonetheless, I'd like to peruse what's here. So pardon me, will you? I'll do my best not to bring anything back home, although I can't make promises."

"I'll go with you."

"I'm certain you have other duties more pressing," she says, which is her nicer version of *I don't need a babysitter.*

I watch her walk away, at least leaving the cart behind. I have a brief moment to reflect sadly on how she's giving a more personal good-bye to her stuff than she is to her son before I spot Daniel making his way down a nearby aisle. Oh, swell. Here's my chance to face all my demons before lunch.

"How's it going?" I say, walking up to him, and then I notice his empty cart. "So you haven't found anything that shouldn't be here?"

"Not really. And they seem to be on target with their pricing. I'd have done a few things differently, but nothing major. So I'm about to get going. You don't need me."

"Good. Well. Thank you. For checking. That was. Sweet of you." We're walking side by side past a pile of several dozen beanbag chairs, on which a couple kids are wrestling. I consider telling them to stop but one of their parents beats me to it.

"So what's going on with Ash?" Daniel asks, keeping his eyes on the merchandise and off me.

"Um. Look, I should get back to the sale. It's a long story, and I don't have time—"

Daniel's voice is hard as he says, "Alive? Dead? Can you at least spare me a couple seconds for the upshot?"

His reaction shames me into answering. "He's in Tampa, but the guy he claimed to be staying with doesn't seem to exist. I put him up in a cheap motel for now, and I'm trying to convince him to go back to rehab."

Daniel nods, picking up a glass bowl and then setting it down. "That's all I was asking."

We continue walking in silence, and it strikes me that—for the first time in a long time—Daniel's asking about Ash doesn't feel like prying but, rather, something quite different. Something more along the lines of what I'd found missing with Niko, and it makes me realize how unfair I've been. "I'm sorry. It's very considerate of you to ask about Ash."

"It's *considerate* of me? I'm not asking to be polite. I'm worried about him—I've *been* worried about him. I happen to love the kid."

The word *love* irks me. Sure, maybe Daniel does care—I'm willing to admit I haven't given him enough credit for that—but if he really loved Ash, wouldn't he have stuck by him? By *us*? I'm not in the mood to let this one slide. "You sure had a funny way of showing it."

He stops cold. "What's that supposed to mean?"

I distract myself pretending to look at a poncho on a clothes rack. "I mean the fact that as soon as things got tough, you took off. Tried to make me choose between Ash and you. Well, I chose my son. Of course I chose my son!"

Daniel grabs my arm, spinning me to face him. "What the hell are you talking about?"

Pulling myself from his grasp, I say, "When you broke up with me, I—"

"When I broke up with you . . ."

"Yes, as I was trying to say, when you broke up with me—"

"What the *hell* are you talking about 'when I broke up with you'?" His voice is low and even, but he seemed to be shaking with a quiet rage.

"May I finish please?" I snap. "All I'm saying is that when you broke up with me—because I wouldn't choose you over my son—I believe you demonstrated how deep your caring for him went."

There! I finally said it, and, whew, it feels positively liberating to call Daniel on his bullshit.

He starts several times to respond, stops himself, then finally says,

"I've always believed in you as a writer, only now it's become clear to me that your talents were wasted writing that book on organization. You should write a novel. Because, Luce, what you said there was truly the most remarkable piece of fiction I've ever heard."

"Excuse me?"

"I didn't break up with you. *You* dumped *me*."

"What—that's insane. Why would I do that?"

"You tell me. You told me to get out of your house. You *threw* me out."

"Sure, after you already said I had to choose between you and Ash."

"I *never* said you had to choose. Ever! All I said is that I couldn't stand by and watch you not doing anything—because I loved the both of you. I'd simply given you the hard truth, that Ash isn't someone who does drugs. He's an addict. The next thing I know, you're screaming at me to go and pitching my albums into the yard like they're fucking Frisbees."

An elderly man reaches nonchalantly between us for a pewter candlestick, making me suddenly aware that while we're having our lovers' quarrel, we are doing so in the midst of a group of shoppers.

"There are people here," I say. "And what you're saying . . . it's not what I remember."

"Well, it's what happened."

The image of the *Pretty in Pink* sound track sailing through a blue sky tugs at my memory, but all I say to Daniel is "It doesn't make sense that I'd react that way to you simply giving your opinion that Ash is an addict."

"Sure it does. You shot the messenger." He taps his heart, an indication as to where the bullet went. "It doesn't matter, though. It's ancient history. I'm over it, and I'm not mad—but do *not* tell me that I didn't care." He takes a step away from me. "You've got work to do, so I'll leave you to it."

■ ■ ■

Not until two o'clock do I have a chance to think as I sit down outside and eat a slice of the now room-temperature pizza Organize Me! brought in for the workers (*dang*, those people are good—they think of everything!), washing it down with a Diet Coke.

Marva has caught a ride home with Niko because, sadly, the truck was needed, as she had a change of heart about parting with the armoire she'd noticed earlier. Will is still inside working. My tiff with Daniel is playing in my head, and it's forcing me to revisit the day we broke up, which isn't easy. I've buried the memory so deeply that to dredge it up is on par with attempting the raising of the *Titanic*.

Did *I* really break up with *him*?

I thought I remembered clearly what happened—I'd tortured myself during enough sleepless nights. It was a Saturday afternoon, and I'd just told Daniel I couldn't go with him to his brother's birthday party. Ash had crawled home a few hours before in pretty bad shape. Although it wasn't worth taking him to a hospital, I was on duty poking him every few minutes in case he was worse off than I thought. That's when Daniel said it: *I can't take living here with Ash anymore. His drug problem is more than I can deal with. You have to choose—it's either him or me.*

But now that I'm forcing myself to look at it, is it possible that all this time I've conveniently edited what he said?

*It's either him or me.*

An image of Daniel floats up, red-eyed, miserable, and he's pleading with me, and now that I let myself really look at it, I realize he's not saying, *It's either him or me.* There was more to it.

*It's either keep pretending there's not a problem with him or have the courage to listen to me. . . .*

*He's an addict.*

*Luce, baby, I know this is hard to hear, but your son is an addict.*

In desperation, doing anything I could to fight off the possibility that Daniel could be right, I grabbed on to what he said about Ash's problem being more than he could deal with and used it to beat him senseless. "It's too much for you?" I said, looking wildly about the room at anything other than Daniel's eyes trying to catch mine, look-ing at me with a compassion I wasn't willing to accept. "That's too bad, because I already have enough to worry about with Ash. I don't need to mollycoddle you, too."

That's when I did it. I tore into the living room, flipping madly through his collection of albums, grabbing the ones I knew would cause the most pain because I wanted him to hurt as much as I was, to feel as helpless as I felt. "You don't want to look?" I shouted. "Then get out." And I chucked the records into the yard, while Daniel stood mutely by, not stopping me, but simply watching them sail into the air, one by one at first, then handfuls at a time.

He'd only tried to tell me the truth, but I wasn't ready to hear it. I'd pushed him out, then I changed the story—for myself more than for anyone else—so the truth couldn't find me. It had taken a couple more months, and an irritated cabdriver, to shake me into reality. But by then, I'd already lost or thrown away everything that mattered.

You didn't buy anything?" I joke to Will as we walk together to our cars. The sale is closed, and the storage room looks as picked over as a Thanksgiving turkey.

"Not a chance. I'd only planned to pop in, but turns out I was dressed for work," he says sheepishly. "It felt great getting rid of so much of my mother's junk. I've been wanting to roll up my sleeves and do that for years."

"Whatever didn't sell is going to charity, so you'll never have to see it again. Nothing is coming back into that house unless it's over my dead body."

"I suggest you don't give my mother that option unless your will is up-to-date." We're at my car, which is in dire need of a trip to the car wash, when he says, "Say, what's with the paints and the canvas? I saw it in Marva's office when I picked her up this morning, and she said you bought them. Why'd you do that? Isn't the point to take things out?"

I tell him about my plan to inspire Marva, fully expecting he'll make fun of me, but he says, "Interesting."

"It hasn't worked. She hasn't so much as looked at the paints."

He gives me a friendly pat on the back, which is such an un-Will-like gesture I'm tempted to feel his forehead for fever. "It's not a terrible idea, getting my mother to paint. It certainly *is* the love of her life, her art. All she ever cared about."

"That's not true. She cares about you."

He gives a wry laugh. "Anyway, nice job on the sale."

A compliment? Now I *am* sure he's ill.

"Will, have you talked to her yet? About . . . you know . . ."

"Wouldn't do any good. Besides, I'm starting to wonder if we've misunderstood those notes you saw in the book. That they weren't about suicide. Maybe it's something else entirely—we're misreading it."

As much as he finds comfort in pretending nothing is wrong with Marva—if anyone understands how tempting that is, it's me—he needs to face it. He won't get a second chance if he doesn't. "I found her suicide note." His expression grows bleak as I continue, "She was working on it in her office, and I came across it."

"What did it say?"

"Mostly that she was done living. She mentioned you in it. She kept crossing things out because she was trying to find the right words, but she said she was proud of you, of the man you are. So see? You do matter to her more than you know. You can get through to her."

"You said it's only a draft. Let's see if I make it into the final," he says with a sigh of resignation.

"Do you want to wait to find out? It can't be easy having a mother like Marva, but she's the mother you've got. You may find this hard to believe, but she's tried to do what she feels is best by you. Maybe it's not what you wanted, or needed, but it's what she knew how to do. Parents make mistakes." I pull open my car door, embarrassed in front of Will by the creaking noise it always makes. "It'll ring true when you're a dad. You do the best you can."

I slide into the driver's seat, looking forward to cruising around and being with my thoughts for a while.

I take the long route back to Marva's, driving along the tree-lined streets, enjoying the signs of spring. As much as I wish I had the money to fix my car so I could be riding top down, that's going to have to wait. As I told Will, there aren't always second chances. I won't forgive myself if I don't do the best I can by Ash. As hard as it's going to be, I know what I need to do now.

I've done so many hard things, what's one more?

# chapter nineteen

W hat's that noise?" my mom says as soon as I tell her it's me on the phone. She still doesn't have caller ID; my dad doesn't believe in it.

"Car wash." I'm sitting on a plastic chair waiting for my car to make it through the wash. Between the whir of traffic on the nearby street and the car wash itself, I'm practically forced to shout.

"Any news on Ash?" my mom says.

"Sort of." I've been keeping my parents updated with quick calls, but—not wanting to stress them out or admit the depths of my problems—I've candy-coated the situation when I could. Now is when that stops. Done hiding from the truth, I tell her about Ash. I don't skip the gritty details—though I cringe when I confess he's possibly using again, and how he claims he's going to NA meetings but how even that's probably a lie. "He already backslid once," I say, "and I don't dare risk it happening again. He won't go back to the Willows so . . . I'm sending him to the Betty Ford."

"In California? That's the one where the celebrities go, isn't it? Didn't that one girl, the one who was in all those movies, you know who I mean, didn't she go there?"

Strangely, I know precisely whom my mom means. "Yes, several times."

"But, sweetheart, isn't it expensive? Those people are rich. How are you going to afford this?"

"I'm counting on getting the bonus for this job. I'm almost finished, and it'll just be enough."

"But that's your money for a house! Where will you live?"

"Funny you should ask." Once I decided that I wasn't going to risk having regrets about helping Ash, the plan fell easily into place. As of Friday I won't have a job, I'll be out of money again, and there's nothing holding me to Chicago. I may as well move someplace where rent is free, and where I'll be only a four-hour drive from my son. "How would you feel if I moved in with you and Dad for a while?"

"We'd love it!" She shouts away from the phone, "Roger, guess what? Lucy is going to move here and live with us!"

I hear him say, "Good." From my dad, that's practically gushing.

"So why Betty Ford?" my mom asks.

"It's a place he'll go."

"Well, that's a start, isn't it?"

We talk for a few more minutes about the plan I've been working on all morning. I'll book a flight for Ash to California, where a representative of Betty Ford will meet him at the airport. That'll take a couple days. I called Ash's motel room last night, and he's excited, or as excited as Ash gets. As for me, after the job with Marva ends— barring the need to stick around for a funeral—I'll pack everything into a trailer, including what's in storage, and haul it to Arizona.

"By yourself?" my mom asks.

"I'll be fine."

"You're not driving the Mustang, are you? I don't like the idea of you driving so long a distance in such an old car."

"I already thought of that. I'm selling it. That's why I'm getting it washed."

Already grieving the loss, I watch as a team of cloth-wielding men descend on my awesome, gleaming cherry-red Mustang to wipe it dry now that it's been spewed from the mechanized wash. Niko knows a guy who'd kill to buy it off me and, more important, is willing to pay top Blue Book. I'll use the cash I make from selling it to buy a boring, sensible car.

Fishing in my purse to find a dollar for a tip, I say, "We'll get into the details later."

"We're going to have *so* much fun. What a wonderful Mother's Day this has turned out to be."

"It's Mother's Day? I completely forgot—and you let me get through the entire call without reminding me! Happy Mother's Day!"

"You've got a lot on your mind, honey. And happy Mother's Day to you, too. I know Ash is running you through the wringer. You've been so strong through all of this. He might not show it now, but someday he'll appreciate everything you're doing for him."

"Thanks, Mom." I hurry off the call because a car-wash worker is waving a rag to signal I'm done, and I don't feel like crying in front of him.


It's ten o'clock and I'm finishing up for the night at Marva's. The deadline is Friday, and the X-filled calendar on my wall shows a mere five days left. I should really keep working, but Marva is cranky and has bandied about the term *slave driver* one too many times for my taste. As if *I'm* the one who came up with the strict deadline and then dragged her feet for weeks.

I'm leaning into the refrigerator, deciding whether Marva would notice one of her apples missing, when the door bangs open in the living room. In walks Will, carrying a large, brown-paper-wrapped package the size of a mirror or a frame.

"Where's Marva?" he asks.

"Office. What's that?"

"A gift. Do me a favor—go in there and take the canvas off the easel. Hurry—this thing is bulky."

I give my customary knock that I do when I enter Marva's office—even if the door is open, which it is. Will follows, setting the package on the easel as soon as I take the canvas down.

Marva looks up from where she's sifting through a box of loose photos at her desk. "What's this?"

"Happy Mother's Day," he says, and tears the paper off. Even before he steps aside, it's apparent what he's brought her.

"How on earth did you get *Woman, Freshly Tossed*?!" I exclaim, figuring somebody had better show excitement, because Marva's expression is blank.

Luckily, Will isn't noticing because he's beaming as he says, "I still had the GPS coordinates to that house in Grosse Pointe, so I hopped in the car today and drove up there. Made them an offer they couldn't refuse."

"What'd you pay for it?" I ask. He had to have gotten it for a song since those people had no idea of its value.

"Didn't your mother teach you manners? You don't ask what a gift costs," Will says. "But I paid a fair price. Apparently, my interest in it so soon after it caught the eye of a certain decorating-magazine writer tipped them off that it might be worth something. They did fast homework. Damn that Google."

"What a thoughtful and generous gift." I look leadingly at Marva. "Isn't it?"

"It is," she says evenly, getting up from her chair. "Whatever possessed you to do it, Will?"

"You've given up so much. You should have it. And . . . uh . . ." He pauses, and I quietly begin backing out of the room so he can be candid. This is his moment to finally open up to Marva in a way that will get through to her that she's making a huge mistake. To tell her what he's been holding in all these years. He clears his throat. "It's a good investment."

*Ugh. Will.*

"Thank you," Marva says.

Hoping to prompt a more heartfelt conversation between them, I say, "I'll get going so the two of you can talk further. Will, I'm sure Marva would love to hear more about what inspired this gift."

Staring back at me is a Will-in-the-headlights who mutters, "I've got to run, unfortunately. Left Padma alone all day on a Sunday." He hurriedly sets up one of the other easels I'd left in the office and sets the blank canvas on it. "Here. In case you feel like, um, creating another masterpiece."

He's gone within a minute, leaving Marva and me alone in the office. "He bought it for you because he loves you," I say. "You realize that, don't you?"

"I suppose I have to keep it displayed here."

"Yes, you do."

She grimaces, finally showing some emotion. "It's like getting an ugly sweater from someone that they expect you to wear."

"Only this isn't ugly. It's remarkable." Side by side with the blank canvas, it nearly leaps from the easel. "Why don't you like it, Marva?"

"It isn't a matter of whether or not I like it."

"What is it then?"

"Complicated."

"I've got time."

She puts the lid on the box of photos and leans over to click off the light, leaving us with only the hall light spilling in the room. "I don't."


Over the next two days, the plan for my future takes shape, as does Marva's house. Tuesday afternoon—bumping elbows with Mei-Hua as I clear the last items from the dining room and she's giving the kitchen a scrub-down—I finally come across the memorabilia that Daniel had set aside as his payment.

Although he'd told me he doesn't want it anymore, I owe it to him. Truthfully, I owe him more than this bag of boxed figurines, a popgun, and a couple of rolled-up posters, but it's a start.

Before I can lose my nerve, I grab all of it, hop in my car, and head to my old digs of the McMillan offices.

One of the Andreas greets me at the reception desk. "Lucy, what brings you here!"

"Dropping this off for Daniel," I say, holding out the bag.

"Great! I'll see that he gets it."

She reaches out a hand for it. I'm tempted to do a drop and run, but I didn't come this far in rush-hour traffic for that. "Is he here?"

"He was saying something about a meeting, but he might be. Go back and check his office. If you don't find him, I can try to hunt him down."

Thanking her, I make my way down the once-familiar halls, hoping I don't run into anyone on my way. There's only one person I'm hoping to see, though my stomach is flipping nervously as I pause outside his office.

"Luce? What are you doing here?" Daniel comes out of the doorway across from his.

So much for taking a moment to compose myself. "I brought this." I hand him the bag. "Your payment."

"I thought I told you that you didn't have to. But, hey, I'll take it."

We stand awkwardly for a moment, and he flaps a hand toward his office. "You want to come in?"

"Okay, sure."

As I walk into his office, I see he's managed to cram even more movie knickknacks onto his walls and desk—it looks like a theater lobby in here. "Why do I have a sudden craving for popcorn?" I say.

"So what's going on?" This is delivered not so much as an invitation for a chat as a desire to understand why, of all the offices in all the world, I had to walk into his.

He doesn't sit, so I don't either. "I wanted to give you an update on Ash and, well, say good-bye. I've decided to send him to Betty Ford. It's the one place he's willing to go, so I'm taking my bonus money and sending him. He flies there tomorrow night, and then after that, I'm going to move in with my parents. Get a fresh start. They're still in Sun City. I'll be closer to Ash there."

"Big changes. Sounds like you've got a plan in place."

"I do."

He picks up a paper clip from his desk and starts twisting it open. "Well, good luck."

"Thanks. And, um . . . I also wanted to tell you that you were right. About how I was scared to admit the truth about Ash. So I took it out on you. I'm sorry." My eyes don't dare meet his, so I'm making this apology to his Sex Pistols T-shirt.

"I told you, it's ancient history."

"It took guts for you to confront me, and I wished I'd listened. I guess I couldn't, but I'm different now. Less scared. Or at least I'm trying to be. Anyway, I didn't want to leave without letting you know that I appreciate what you tried to do."

"Okay." Then his arms go around me in a hug, pinning mine to my side. "Next time you see Ash, give him this from me."

The following morning, I'm saying good-bye to another dear friend: the Mustang. Niko leans in close as we watch his friend walk up, who took the train from downtown to get here. "I talked to him last night—it's exactly what he's been looking for," Niko says. "So your top price? I told him three hundred higher than that. Don't back down. He'll pay it."

"I hate selling cars. Thanks so much for helping me."

"Hey, what are friends for?"

I search his face for sarcasm, but it's as guileless as ever, and, yep, just as handsome. And those *lashes. Such* a waste on a guy.

The friend's name is Skeet, and he's gangly, with a thin ponytail and those ear piercings that create a hole the size of a quarter. I can look through them and see my car behind him. The sale goes remarkably easily. Niko's right—Skeet is wearing his desire for the car pinned to his chest. I'm so effortlessly staying firm to my price, I'm almost proud that Marva is watching the whole thing from where she's having a cigarette on the porch.

The title is exchanged for cash, and Skeet hops into the driver's seat. "Woo-hoo! I'm gonna treat this baby right. She is one sexy beast."

"Enjoy," I say. "I sure have."

He smacks the steering wheel. "Can't wait! How about those keys?"

"Oh, gosh, almost forgot!" I pull my keys from my pocket and start to detach the key from the ring. "You know, I originally bought this car to piss off my ex-husband, but then I grew to love it."

"I'll bet."

"When I'm driving this car, I feel . . . free. Like even a trip to the grocery store is an adventure. Although I never did get around to fixing the top."

"First thing I'm gonna do."

Still wrestling with the key, I say, "Lucky you. I didn't have the cash to do it once it broke. I'm getting a big bonus for this job I'm working here, and I was going to spend part of it to make this into a convertible again."

"You want me to get that off for you?"

"I've almost got it. Anyway, I'm driving cross-country, so I'm going to have to buy a more sensible car. Which is no big deal. It doesn't matter what I drive. This car was great while it lasted, but it's time to move on."

"I'd be glad to give that a shot if you're having a problem—"

"Got it!" I hand him the key. "There you go."

He puts it in the ignition and starts the car. "Glad you don't want it anymore."

"It's not that I don't want it. And I wish I'd gotten a chance to drive it again with the top down, wind in my hair and all that. But I can't . . . it's not practical, and besides, what's important is—"

"Okay! I'm sure whatever made you give up this baby was worth it."

"Definitely. It's for my son. I'm moving to Arizona for him, and that meant the car needed to go, which again is no big deal because—"

"Awesome! See ya." He slips into reverse and backs out the driveway.

I fully expect to raise my hand and wave so long, so imagine my surprise when I'm running after him, banging on the hood and shouting for him to stop. "Wait!"

He's partway down the drive when he brakes, looking through the windshield at me expectantly. I run over, gesture for him to roll down the passenger window so he can hear me. "It's not for sale," I say, breathing heavily from my quick sprint after him.

"What are you talking about? You just sold it to me."

"I changed my mind."

"Too bad, because it's already done. You got the cash, and I got the title."

I pull the wad of money from my pocket. "Here."

"No chance. This is my baby now." He slips it into reverse. I yank the door open and start to jump in as he taps the accelerator. The door's swinging and my leg is dangling as I say, "You can't have it!"

Skeet slows to a roll but doesn't stop. "Get out!"

"No!" My heart is thumping out of my chest, and I feel as if, if I don't stop him, it's the final scene in every romantic comedy where the plane is pulling away and it seems lost for the young lovers . . . only I want the plane, not the guy inside it.

"You wreck my door, you pay for it!" Skeet yells.

"No way! Give it back! You can't have everything! Not all of it again! This car belongs to *me*. It's not fair to ask me to give up everything I've worked for—not when you haven't done jack-all yourself!"

"What the . . . ?!"

"Just because *I* want a life doesn't mean I've abandoned you, so quit making me feel that way! I'm not doing it again! I won't!"

Skeet hits the brake, throws the car into park, and starts shoving me out the door. "Get out of my car, you crazy bitch!"

"It's *my* car," I shout, reaching for the keys as he keeps pushing at me. I manage to at least turn off the ignition, and then it degrades quickly into a tussle. There's further shoving, some ugly name-calling, and possibly hair pulling, then I notice the hood snap up.

"What the f—?" Skeet says, and by the time he jumps from the car to check out what's happening, Marva is standing there holding some sort of a hose and a couple wires.

"If the young lady says the car is not for sale, it's not for sale," she says.

"I can't believe you pulled that from my car!" Skeet says, but it's clear that he's unnerved by Marva's calm authority—I sure am, and I don't have a stupid name like Skeet.

He starts yelling and feather-ruffling at Marva, who seems bored by his display. It at least draws Niko over.

Skeet makes an appeal to him. "I bought this car fair and square, and your psycho friend here starts screaming crap at me that doesn't make any sense."

Niko looks at me. "What were you saying?"

"All the right words," Marva says, handing Niko the wires and the hose, then clapping the grit off her hands. "Wrong person."

From there, the sale is quickly undone. Niko drives Skeet to the train station, promising to return to fix my car. I join Marva on the porch, enjoying the view of my shiny, freshly washed Mustang beneath the oak trees on this fine spring morning.

Marva leans back in her chair. "So it turns out Miss Free Spirit is attached to something after all."

"Guess so," I say, since there's no point denying it. "Oddly enough, it's not the car itself so much as the *idea* of it—how it makes me feel to have it."

"Precisely. Welcome to the human race."

A few more minutes of listening to the sound of wind rustling the leaves and then I say, "It's not only that I want to keep the car—I want to keep my life, here in Chicago. I don't want to start over again."

"I gathered that from your wild ranting."

"Ash is going to be disappointed. He's going to feel I'm letting him down."

"Are you?"

I ponder her question. It's not as if I believe California is the perfect solution, or I would gladly pay anything. But it's no more certain than the other choices I've already given him, either going back to the Willows or moving home and doing outpatient rehab. I'd be giving up all I've earned more as a show of what a loving mother I am rather than truly doing the loving thing. "No," I say, "I'm not."

Not until late afternoon, when I've called more than a dozen times, does Ash finally pick up the phone in his motel room. When he answers with a sleepy grunt, I say, "Ash, it's your mother. There's something I need to tell you."

# chapter twenty

Task: Practice saying no. It's too many yeses that got you into this mess, so look in a mirror, hold firm, be tough, and say, NO! It may seem strange at first, but it gets easier.

—*Things Are Not People Workbook* (proposal)

Later that night, I'm in the office with Marva, again annoying her with my darting about. It's just that there's so much left to do. It's the only room that's still a hoard-level mess, and I'm not about to let it prevent me from getting my payoff on Friday. Truthfully, only a total jerk wouldn't give me the bonus for all I've accomplished, but Will's the one in charge of the checkbook, and only recently has he demonstrated being anything *but* a jerk.

My body may be hard at work, but my mind is in Florida. I can't stop thinking about Ash, who is not happy with me right now. (As opposed to my mom, who was only disappointed for a second, then brightened at the realization she doesn't have to clean out the spare room.)

I have handed Ash his choices and given him until tomorrow to decide: the Willows or come home for outpatient rehab. After that, I told him, the motel goes away, and so does my other financial support. To deliver that news with believability, I harkened back to how I was able to stick firm to my price when selling the car earlier today and reminded myself that, as in that situation, I have the upper hand here. Specifically: I have the money. And—though I'm terrified that Ash is going to choose neither, that he'll be willing to be penniless and homeless in Florida rather than take the help I'm offering—I'm not going to go running after him changing my mind. It's his turn to step up. *Please, Ash, I'm begging you, step up.*

Carrying a stack of yellowed newspapers to be recycled, I knock into the canvas for the millionth time, sending it wobbling. Which is not entirely my fault. Both the canvas and Marva's painting are parked smack in the middle of the room, but neither of us is willing to move them—me, because I still hope they'll be an inspiration, and Marva, because they may as well be invisible. She doesn't even glance in that direction, as if she's a bat able to avoid them by sonar.

"Slow down," Marva says, "I do have a few things of value in here."

"Yes, and that reminds me, Smitty is eager to get his hands on the rest of it. He's coming tomorrow, don't forget. You'll need to stay in your room so he doesn't see you."

"Shall I wear a dunce cap and face the corner?"

"Hey, I'm not the one worried about people finding out how your house was so cluttered—that's you and Will."

"It's Will," she corrects.

I balance carefully on a stack of old magazines to pull a hodge-podge of vases and urns from the top of a shelf unit for Marva to sort through later. "The house is certainly something you can be proud of now, don't you think?" I say, reaching for an urn decorated with what appears to be flowers from a distance but at closer inspection is a fairly graphic depiction of an orgy. "If Smitty hadn't seen your house before, it wouldn't matter now if he knew it was yours."

"Careful!" she shouts. "That urn happens to be extremely precious! So don't—"

Too late—I'd been fine, but her outburst threw me off-balance, sending me sliding on the magazine covers. Clutching the extremely precious urn to my chest to protect it, I tumble to the ground, aiming for a pile of papers to cushion my fall. I land with a crashing thud—I missed—which jostles the lid off the urn, sending its contents flying. Soot and dirt get in my face and hair and on my clothes, and spill out over the floor.

Sputtering in annoyance, I sit up and dust myself off. "What *is* all this?"

"Filleppe."

It takes about a half second for what she's said to register, and another half second for me to go completely hysterical. *"His ASHES!?"* I scream, wiping frantically at my face, shaking out my hair, and swatting it from my clothes. *EEEEEEEyaaaaa, I'm covered in the ashes of a dead man!*

"Calm down," Marva says. "It's not literally his ashes."

"What—what do you mean 'not literally'?"

"They're merely representative. They're ashes from my house that burned down. He was inside when it happened, but it wasn't possible to recover his ashes specifically. These have had to suffice."

"Oh." I sit, trying to regain a semblance of composure. When my breathing is back to normal, I say, "Sorry. I didn't mean to be disrespectful of the deceased. It just freaked me out." I get up so I can get a dustpan from the kitchen and rinse off my face, feeling worse when I notice her rueful expression. "I'll sweep it carefully—I'll bet we can get most of it back in that urn."

When I return, Marva is on hands and knees, using the side of her hand to gather the ashes on the floor.

"Let me. You've got those bad knees."

She nods and pulls herself up. I glance up at her as she sits in her chair, wiping her hands carefully on a tissue. Her face is such a kaleidoscope of emotions that she looks like a different person—yet oddly familiar somehow. It's as if she's peeled back a mask to reveal . . .

The painting behind her.

*Woman, Freshly Tossed.*

"That's a self-portrait," I say.

The features aren't Marva's entirely. Marva's cheekbones are far more striking, her brow more arched, plus she's not blue—but the face, right now, is absolutely Marva.

"Only egotists do self-portraits," she says, echoing her words from when I first met her, but now I realize she's being facetious.

"The man in the background, then, is that Filleppe?"

She turns to regard the painting—the first time I've seen her look at it since her horrified reaction when Will unveiled it. "He'd always tell people, 'Don't let a woman paint you when she's angry. She'll take it out on the size of your nose.'"

"So that's why you don't like it. It's a reminder of someone you lost."

It wasn't a question. I don't expect an answer, but she says, "That painting is said to be my greatest work. It certainly established me as an artist, and one on the cutting edge . . . an innovator. Which is ironic, because when I look at it, all I see is a reminder of how very *ordinary* I am. Through some feat of illusion with paints and a canvas, I managed to trick the world into seeing brilliance. Yet all the while, there I was—the great Marva Meier Rios—nothing but a silly girl willing to make a fool of herself for love."

*Boy, and I thought I could be hard on myself.* "But you painted it. It still inspires people."

"It's a fake."

"Wait . . . you didn't paint it?"

"Oh, I did, and many others like it afterward. Although it bored me to tears, limiting myself to a particular style, even if it was my own. But I was so afraid of losing Filleppe. He was my lover, but he also handled the business end of things. He created me, my *brand*. To abandon it and try something new was to risk it all . . . my reputation, my standing . . . Filleppe . . . everything.

"And then he left me anyway." She sets down the tissue. "We were so young. We'd sworn we'd never get old . . . never lose our edge. But fear made me play it safe. That's why he walked out on me—said that he intended to carry out our bargain, to only bother living if it was on the edge, and he'd do it with or without me."

I shake my head. "Damned if you do, damned if you don't. But wait. If he left you, why was he in the house when it burned down?"

"I'd begged him to stay . . . pleaded. Not my finest hour. Said to hell with my dignity and went crawling after the man. And I wonder now why my knees are shot? I was so in love, or thought I was, and determined to prove myself to him. I left to pull an all-nighter at the studio. Everything I painted was complete garbage, of course. Never confuse desperation with passion. At any rate, I wasn't home to re-mind Filleppe not to smoke in bed when he'd been drinking. And that was that."

"How awful," I say, again trying to picture the moment Marva walked up to her burned-down house, knowing now it was more than a house and her things that she lost. "But it wasn't your fault, you real-ize that, don't you?"

"I do, but I sometimes wonder if it was no accident—if Filleppe wanted to go out on a high note."

"You think he set the fire on purpose?"

"He always did have a flair for the dramatic. They say you can't take it with you. He managed to, in a sense, take everything I had."

*They say you can't take it with you.* The reference to the first line of her suicide note is a Taser to my insides. "If that's true," I say, and darned if my tough-mom voice doesn't get trotted out, "then it's not flair, it's selfishness. And cruelty."

"I'm only speculating."

I drop the broom. "Marva, I can't do it anymore—I can't pretend everything is all right when I know you're planning to do the exact same thing yourself. Whether you like it or not, I care about you—so do a lot of people, including your *son*. So big deal—you had your heart broken. As a wise woman once told me, welcome to the human race."

She stands and sets the lid on a box of photos she'd been looking through. "Not so wise, only older. Apparently the two don't always go hand in hand. And I wish you wouldn't waste your concern on me. You have plenty going on in your own life to keep you occupied, I would assume."

"Yet here I am, concerned all the same."

"Fair enough. Now if you'll excuse me, I believe I'll retire for the night."

Although I try to convince her to stay—"I'll drop it, let's talk some more about anything you want!"—she says she's tired. If I want to do some shredding, she adds, the noise of the machine won't bother her.

After she leaves, I finish sweeping up the ashes. I scoop them back into the urn and set it on a lower shelf. My mind reels with the things I wish I could say to convince Marva that her life's worth living, but I hold no sway. The one person who possibly does seems unwilling to take the risk. If I could, I'd use Will like a ventriloquist's dummy, hand shoved up some orifice, making him speak words of need and love and hope until Marva broke.

I sleep later than I mean to, and my phone wakes me up shortly before 9:00 a.m. My first instinct is that it's Ash calling with his answer, only when I look at my phone, I'm surprised by whose number I see there.

My voice still has its morning frog when I answer it. "Daniel?"

"Did I wake you up?"

"That's okay. I needed to get up anyway."

"So you don't know then."

"Don't know . . ." *Oh, no . . . She killed herself last night. Why did*

*I let her go to bed depressed? And I ran the shredder—probably her trick to cover up the gunshot noise! But, wait, how would Daniel . . .* "What? What don't I know?"

"Marva," he says, and at her name, my worst fears are set alight. "I was on Yahoo! news, and I noticed she was trending. Somehow it got out that she plans to kill herself, and that she's a hoarder. They've got pictures. And a suicide note. They're crediting a reliable source close to the family."

I'm flooded with such relief that I'm giddy. "Oh, thank God!"

"You're glad about this?"

"The way you led into it, I thought you were going to tell me she's dead."

"Hmm. I could see why you'd take it that way. Then allow me to deliver the happy news. She's not dead, but she is a scandal."

"But how?" I'm up and flipping on my computer. "Who could have leaked this—and what would be the point? We're nearly finished!"

"There are a lot of guys working there. Not suggesting your little friend did it, but *you* didn't . . . did you?"

"You're not seriously asking that question . . ."

"No, I'm just—" He pauses. "I wanted to give you a heads-up. Thought you might need the warning."

I barely have time to enjoy the idea that Daniel would care enough to call after all that's happened between us because an image of a pinched, angry face floats to my mind. "Will is going to be *furious*," I say.

"He wasn't what I was worried about—although you're right. I meant the media. It's a pretty sexy story. Hoarding. A possible suicide. Even if Marva isn't a name a lot of people know anymore, she's about to be. You might want to think twice before you answer the door."

"They wouldn't come here, would they?" I ask. As I do, I leave the computer to check, walking out of the bungalow and starting up the drive—only to stop short because news vans are there and I'm in my jammies. "Crap, they would. Gotta go."

■ ■ ■

Y*ou*," Will says when I let him into the bungalow, having confirmed it's him and not a reporter. "You let this happen!"

"I'm glad you're being reasonable."

"I thought you understood the importance of discretion. I hear there are photos all over the Internet showing every room in the house. You know where I heard that? From a Channel Seven news reporter parked outside!"

"What makes you believe I have anything to do with this?"

"Please—who else has that kind of access?"

"Lots of people—and people *you* hired, not me." As I'd poked through the Internet coverage while getting dressed (and it's definitely an inside job, nobody could have gotten such detailed shots of the rooms through a window), I'd tried to imagine Niko doing this and can't. He's too sweet. Torch, however, is another matter.

"I hired *you*," Will says. "Big mistake."

"It wasn't me that leaked it, I swear. With all I've gone through to help your mother, you must know I'd never hurt her this way. Besides, look." I pull my phone from my pocket. "I don't even have a camera."

Will takes my phone and looks at it, appalled. "I didn't realize they made phones like this anymore."

Snatching it back, I say, "They don't. I'll be able to afford a better one as soon as I get my bonus."

"You might want to hold off on shopping. I've seen that mess of an office."

"You'd better not be implying you'd stiff me because of one lousy room. Besides, I have all day today, and Smitty is coming, isn't he? He'll be taking much of what's in there."

"He's due any minute, which is why I'm here. What a lovely surprise to be greeted at my mother's home by the fine representatives of the local Chicago news media asking me how I know Ms. Meier Rios and if she hoards animals, too, or if it's only the garbage."

"What'd you say?"

"'No comment'—what do you think I said? Then I made them get the hell off the property." He notices my computer, which is open to a news item on Marva, complete with a shot of the living room as it was on my first day on the job. "So how bad is it?"

"You haven't seen any of it?"

"I only found out two minutes ago when I got here. I was just swinging by to double-check that all signs of my mother's identity were out of the way so Smitty wouldn't figure anything out. Guess that cat is out of the bag."

"At least it's only the one cat, and not a hoard of them," I say, and Will's steely look reminds me he's not one to joke in times of pressure. Or ever. "You can use my computer. I've bookmarked some of the stories, or feel free to browse around online. I'll finish getting ready. Then we can figure out what to do." As Will takes a seat, I remember the suicide note. The leaked version is a different draft from what I saw. In the leaked draft, Will actually gets an *I love you*. But that's crossed out and replaced with *I wish I could have loved you the way you wanted to be loved*. Only *wanted* is crossed out and replaced by *deserved*. Then Marva signed it, apparently crumpled it in a ball, and tossed it into the trash—only to have it retrieved and fed to an Internet news site, where soon her poor son will have to see it.

"Wait a minute," I say, and dig out the Scotch left over from Marva's visit. Before heading into the bathroom, I pour Will a shot and hand it to him.

"Drinking on the job?"

"Not me, but you may want to."

Will intercepts Smitty when he arrives and fills him in on the situation, shielded from the media by Smitty's massive truck and aided by Smitty's diminutive stature. Then Will leaves directly for his office, never having said anything to me about the suicide note other than to acknowledge he saw it and giving firm directions to let no one in. He's already canceled Niko for the day.

I search for food in Marva's kitchen that I can pilfer for breakfast and settle on a banana. As I peel it, Smitty bustles through the mudroom door and clasps my arm, jittery with excitement.

"Will told me she's here, but I'm to leave her alone," he says. "Surely you can arrange a meeting, can't you?"

"Yes, but in a while. You're bound to run into her anyway. Only a quick hello, though. She's very busy." I neglect to elaborate that she's busy on the Internet and flipping through the TV looking at the coverage after Will broke the news to her. It's like getting to rubberneck your own freeway accident, and she's watching it with a ghoulish and yet detached fascination.

"Is *it* here?"

I play dumb, solely for the fun of toying with him. "It . . . ?"

"*Woman, Freshly Tossed.* Is it here? In this house? Which, by the way, looks fabulous. Can't believe it's the same place I was in before."

"It does, doesn't it," I say, pleased to receive a compliment on my work, since they're not being handed out by anyone else around here. "And, yes, it is."

He brightens. "Any chance I'd get the chance to represent that particular—"

"It's not for sale."

"Can't blame me for trying." Smitty leaves to get his workers under way, who will use the back entrance to avoid giving a free show to the cameras outside. I scarf down the banana and then check in on Marva.

She's at her computer, which rarely gets used since I came here and put the kibosh on her online shopping habit. "It's time to shut that down and stop torturing yourself," I say.

She points at the screen at a picture of one of the upstairs rooms taken during its previous state. "Did I keep this mirror?"

I study the photo. "No."

"What a shame. It would look so nice over the credenza."

Blinking in disbelief, I say, "That's it? You're sad about a mirror? But you're not upset that this is all over the Internet?"

"I'm not *thrilled*, but it's not as if anyone remembers who I am anyway. Frankly, I'm surprised it's getting so much attention."

"People clearly remember who you are."

"Yes—*now*—but not as an artist. Merely as a suicidal hoarder. Today's freak show."

Without asking if she minds, I turn off the screen. "Then prove them wrong."

B̲y the time Will calls in the afternoon, Smitty is finishing up—his progress slowed by his repeated fawning over Marva and pausing to longingly sigh over the dream of including *Woman, Freshly Tossed* among his acquisitions (which I encourage—if love or logic can't save Marva, maybe appealing to her ego can). The reporters, having no luck talking to any of us, have moved on to neighbors. None of them have met Marva, but they speak of her in the serial-killer stereotype of keeping to herself but seeming like a nice lady. Who knew she was hiding such a shocking secret? Despite my efforts to cut Marva off from the news and keep her focused on clearing out the office, she keeps going back to check updates.

After telling Will it went well with Smitty—and doing a PR pitch about how *great* the office is starting to look—I ask him how he's holding up.

"Other than a senior VP hugging me this morning—*hugging* me—it's been relatively a nonevent."

"I'm not surprised. Everybody is so tied up in their own problems, they don't have the energy to pay attention to yours as much as you fear they do."

"Or they're being polite to my face and gossiping behind my back."

"There's that possibility."

"My only consolation," he says, "is that this will blow over the next time some politician gets busted texting pictures of his man parts, so I'd say a day or two."

"Or"—I say, deliberately being blunt so as to slap reality into him—"it'll be an even bigger story Saturday, if there's news on her birthday of a tragic suicide."

"Yes. About that. I'll be over tomorrow evening at some point to spend the night and all day Saturday. If she plans to do it on her birthday, I intend to be on her like stink on a goat so she can't."

"I'm so glad!" It's such a relief that Will is taking over, since I'll be distracted with Ash tomorrow. He's agreed to come home, and I'm due to pick him up at O'Hare at noon. It's not how I imagined my last day on the job. I assumed I'd be hanging out, perfecting the last few details, but I've got to tend to Ash, and the job is passably finished. "Marva's not going to make it easy on you," I say to Will. "It's going to drive her nuts to be followed around. She'll fight you on it tooth and nail."

"Well, then I suppose I'll have a taste of what you've been going through these past several weeks, now won't I?" He exhales loudly, letting me know he's aware of exactly what he's up against.

# chapter twenty-one

In the morning, I let myself in through Marva's front door. I still can't believe the project is done, and right on time. Just for the satisfaction of doing it, today I wrote the final X on the calendar, amazed at how many days I've been here. It feels both like yesterday and a year ago that I first met Marva, and it's strange to think I won't be back except to gather the rest of my things.

Although I'm about to leave for the airport, I want to say good-bye. Before heading to find Marva, I give myself the reward of doing a walk-through of the house—a much more understated celebration than I feel the occasion merits. For all I've been through, there ought to be popping champagne corks and brass bands—or at the very least a beribboned finish line that I bust through—but it's unusually quiet today. Niko and crew are still banned until Will can figure out the identity of the mole, and the news reporters have drifted away. Apparently, a famed local artist is only saucy enough to warrant one day's attention, even if she is a suicidal hoarder.

I start upstairs, where the rooms were once so cluttered I had to climb garbage mountains to see them. Hard to believe this is the same house I wedged myself into mere weeks ago. Now it's open, airy, and decorated in an eclectic style that's cozy without being overly cluttered.

Soon I'll have a home like this again. Okay, not this enormous. And I can't afford Oak Park. In fact, I'll rent for a while—some crappy apartment, but it'll be *my* crappy apartment. The idea sends a warm rush through me. When I head back downstairs, I find Marva in the kitchen, making coffee. "I didn't expect to see you today," she says, scooping grounds into the filter. "The job is done. Haven't you heard that means you don't report to work anymore?"

"Ha, ha. And did you really think you'd get rid of me without a good-bye? I'm about to head over to the airport."

"So you got what you wanted, your son back."

Is that what I wanted? "I want him off drugs, working on a future. So hopefully this is a step."

"Well, you did a fine job here. It can't have always been easy."

"Nah, piece of cake. Will is coming by later for the final inspection," I say, although I don't add he'll be spending the night and all day on her birthday so she doesn't do anything to hurt herself. I only pray he has the guts to follow through. "Don't buy anything between now and when he gets here, okay? I need that bonus check."

"Rest assured, I won't. I plan to spend the day in quiet reflection."

There's no escaping she'll be reflecting on her life. Isn't that what you'd do the day before it's ending, if you knew? Sure, I'd probably eat a giant tub of Garrett's cheese popcorn and wash it down with Cristal chugged straight from the bottle, but all the while, I'd be reflecting.

"Spend some time thinking about how people care about you," I say.

"Do they? You'll notice the media is gone. I'm yesterday's news. Just Marva Meier Rios the clinically depressed hoarder who, according to some reports, is raising chickens in her living room," she says, chuckling.

It's alarming how it doesn't bother her—as if she's already checked out so nothing matters. But it does. "You can't let that be your legacy. Not after all you've achieved in your life. Don't let that be how you're remembered."

"At least I'll be remembered." Her tone is joking, but this isn't funny.

My voice is trembling as I say, "It's not too late. You can create something new. Please . . . stay around to do it." Then, though I expect she'll hate it, I throw my arms around her in a hug. She stiffens, but she at least gives me a couple pats on the back before pulling away.

"Best of luck to you," she says.

"I'll be back in a few days to pick up the rest of my things, and to make sure you haven't dragged a bunch of junk back the moment my back is turned." Tears are welling in my eyes. "I very much look forward to seeing you then."


I allowed for traffic, but the freeway didn't get the memo that rush hour is supposed to be over by now, so I'm racing to baggage claim to meet Ash. According to the monitors, his flight arrived eight minutes ago. Standing at the spot that divides me from the secure area, I wait, catching my breath. There's plenty of time. Ash still needs to disembark and get down here.

It's going to be tough, but I'm allowing myself only a minute or two of gushing over how happy I am to have him home, and then it's on to business. I've got a bag packed in my car that'll see me through the next few days. We'll get a hotel, then we'll immediately sign him up for NA and look into local outpatient rehab programs. Heather and Hank offered to let us stay with them—mind-blowingly generous of them considering they have a toddler and an impressionable teen—but it's important that Ash and I have time alone. I'll need one-on-one time without distractions to get him ratcheted into the new rules—the new *me*—from day one. He needs to understand that it's not going to be how it was before.

After a few minutes go by, I unfold the piece of paper on which I've written ASH and stand holding it jokingly as if I'm a hired driver, staring with a mix of excitement and fear at the escalator that will transport my son to me and into his—our—new future.

After thirty minutes and no sign of Ash, I decide to give it ten more. Still no Ash. I find my way to ticketing, where I wait in line another twenty minutes before being waited on by a woman who looks quite a lot like me—granted, me on a good day, when I've bothered blow-drying with the round brush. "My son was supposed to be on a flight from Tampa, and I'm meeting him at baggage claim. He hasn't shown up. Can you check if he was on that flight?"

"A minor?"

"No, he's nineteen, but he doesn't have a cell phone."

"Good for you," she says. "I'm embarrassed to say my eight-year-old has one."

After verifying my ID and collecting a confirmation number, she consults her screen. "According to this, he got a boarding pass . . . but didn't check in for the flight."

"How could that be? He went all the way to the airport and then didn't bother getting on the plane?"

"He might have cut it too close, gotten stuck in security. Or you'd be surprised how many people stop for Burger King and miss their chance to board—happens all the time. He's probably trying to get on another flight standby."

*Or he changed his mind and left.* "Is there any way to check?"

"Sorry, no. Don't worry, he'll get ahold of you somehow." She gives me an encouraging smile—mom to mom—and I leave, crumpling up the ASH sign and tossing it in a trash can on my way out.

Honey, I'm *hooooome!*" I shout as I poke my head in through Marva's mudroom door a few hours later. I'd stopped for lunch and to make phone calls to tell my family and Heather that Ash didn't show. With each passing hour, I'm forced to face the ugly reality. He didn't miss his plane. Nope, that little shit just changed his mind.

Marva comes out from the hallway. "You don't get it, do you. The job is over. You can go home."

"He never got on the plane."

"Ah," she says. "Sorry to hear that."

"So I might as well do more work on the office before Will gets here for his inspection—especially since, technically, I don't have a home to go to."

"You're free to stay in the bungalow if you wish." She grabs a pen from the counter and turns to leave. "But I prefer to be alone today."

Now that I'm no longer an employee, I can hardly wander around as if I work here, so I leave. To kill time until Will arrives—which I expect will be as close to the birthday deadline of midnight as he can cut it—I start packing my things and cleaning up. About seven o'clock, Will storms into the bungalow, slamming the door behind him. He startles when he sees me. "What are you doing here?" he says irritably, as if I were the one bursting in on him.

"I thought I'd stick around in case you needed me," I say, meeting him scowl for scowl. "Pardon me for trying to help."

He does that thing he did the very first day I met him, pinching the bridge of his nose in frustration. "It's not you—sorry. I came out here to blow off steam. You took me by surprise. My mother. She just—*ugh.*"

"What's she doing?"

"Acting like nothing's wrong, that's what. And meanwhile, I'm a wreck, panicking that anything she touches might be what she'll use to off herself tomorrow. She's ironing, and I'm wondering, 'Is she going to take that in the tub and electrocute herself?'"

"What is she ironing?"

"What? Uh . . . a top or something."

"Purple?" I can't help it—I'm curious if she is going to go with the pantsuit I helped pick out.

"What difference does it make?"

"None, really, only I thought she might be preparing what she wants to be . . . er"—no point in being delicate—"found in."

"That does it, I'm done pussyfooting around. It's time to be proactive. Whether Marva likes it or not, I am combing every inch of that house and confiscating anything she could possibly use to kill herself."

"Could be tough. She's pretty creative."

"Are you going to help me or not?"

"Sure, I'll help. You want me to distract her?"

"I don't care if she sees what I'm doing—in fact, I hope she does. Let her call the cops on me, but she's not going to be able to stop me otherwise. I need to make it clear I'm not taking this lying down."

Once we're in the house, Will grabs a garbage bag (blue, which technically is for recycling, but I'm not foolish enough to say anything). I follow him to the bathroom, where he throws open the medicine cabinet and begins chucking its contents into the bag with noisy abandon. "Check the shower," he instructs me, his eyes wild with a mounting fervor.

I whisk open the shower curtain and am snapping up the plug when Marva arrives. "What on earth are you doing?"

"Childproofing," Will says, crouching down and opening the cabinet doors. "If you don't have any razors"—he holds up a pack of old-fashioned single-blade razors—"then you can't slit your wrists, now can you?"

"Why, of all the cheek! Put those back, and get out of my bathroom."

"No."

"William, I insist you stop this instant."

"Nobody in this room named William. Call me by my real name. Go ahead, say it!"

"Are you still angry about that? It was a whim!"

He stands, grabbing up the trash bag and brushing past her toward her office. "A whim I lived with for eighteen years. How long am I going to have to live with this latest whim, huh? You go off, doing whatever you want to do, and don't give a damn how it affects me. So long as it suits you. And I pick up the pieces."

She follows him into the office, her cane thudding on the floor,

and I trail behind, willing myself invisible, which seems to be working. "None of this is your affair," Marva says to Will.

"Of course it's my affair! You're my *mother*!" He snags up a mug
filled with pencils, considers it, and, apparently finding it dangerous,
dumps it in the bag.

"You have no right to dispose of my things."

"What's the difference? You're not going to be around to use
this . . . this . . ." He looks around and snatches up a stapler. "This
stapler!"

"That is *enough*."

"You want me to stop? Then tell me—what's your plan for offing
yourself? Put me out of my misery. Let's play Clue—will it be with a
dagger in the library? Or the candlestick in the billiard room? Or . . ."
Will is frenzied, jittering with the same out-of-the-lines energy that
has made Marva's paintings famous.

Marva finally looks at me. "This is your fault."

"Leave her out of this," Will says. "You think it's okay with me that
you kill yourself? Think again. I'll find how you're going to do it, and
I'll make sure it can't happen until I can talk some sense into you, not
that I believe that's possible."

"I don't care for being bullied," she says, but for all the bravado of
her words, she seems flustered. "I have ironing to do."

Will runs a hand through his hair, about to leap from his skin.
"That book . . . *Grimm's Fairy Tales* . . . I'll bet you've written in it
what you're going to do. If I can find that . . ."

I lean toward him. "Between her mattress and box spring," I say
quietly.

Marva gives me a look that dissolves my bones so I'm barely standing as Will bolts toward her bedroom. "So this is how you thank me,"
she says.

I swallow, but don't reply. In a moment, Will returns with the
book, waving it defiantly at Marva. "I guess now I'll find out what way
you plan to torment me," he says, but before he looks through it, a
piece of paper falls out. Picking it up and unfolding it, he reads aloud,

"'To Whomever May Find Me . . .'" His eyes flit over the page, and I expect Marva to snatch it from him in outrage, but she collapses onto her chair, surprisingly mute.

He looks at her crossly. "How dare you write that you love me." Grabbing a pen off her desk, he thrusts it at her. "Cross it out."

She waves him off.

"Cross . . . it . . . out," he says through gritted teeth.

"Stop it."

"Stop it? It's a little late to start telling me what to do. As I hear it, most parents set rules when their kids are . . . are *kids.*" Turning his attention to me, he says, "You know what she did when I snuck past the nanny in seventh grade so I could go make out with a girl at the park one night? Offered me a *ride.*" He snatches up a pack of cigarettes from her desk, pulls one out, and shakes out the matches tucked into the pack. "Although I do recall you have one rule. No smoking in the house," he says as he lights the cigarette. "Guess it's a sore subject, huh?"

"Since when do you smoke?" Marva says.

He sucks the cigarette, then blows out a cloud of smoke. "Since now. Right here in the house! Breaking your one rule! What are you going to do about it?"

"What is it you *want* me to do?" she snaps.

"What I want is for you to be a parent! For once . . . in . . . your . . . life. Which, as I understand it, is nearly over." He continues puffing madly.

"Oh, yes, I was such a terrible mother, and that's why you turned out so poorly, is that it?"

"I adored you, and you didn't give a damn about me. You still don't. Tell me," he says, flicking ash deliberately onto the floor. "Tell me, why would you do this? What could be so awful in your life that you would end it, without any concern for anyone else—how it would humiliate me. Hurt me. *Why?*"

Marva's defiant expression falters. "It's not important."

"The hell it isn't!"

I flash back to when Marva told me that she finds *why* to be the most intriguing word in the human language. "He's right, Marva. You owe him that—the reason why," I say, though I fear my intrusion may turn her wrath on me.

It doesn't—in fact, she seems to wilt. "If you insist on knowing . . . I made a promise." Her gaze flickers to the painting but goes back to Will. "We both did. Filleppe and I. We promised we'd never let ourselves grow old, that we'd die before we'd let that happen. If I hadn't been failing at the promise already, hadn't been playing it so safe at the time, Filleppe would still be alive. He'd be here with me for this. Going out with me. The two of us together. When I turned sixty-five."

"Right. The two of you together," Will says, although his voice has lost its anger. "Do you really believe, Marva . . . Mother . . . that that son of a bitch would have ever kept this promise?"

"Honestly?" she says, her eyes moist. "No."

"So why are *you* keeping it?"

She gives an almost helpless laugh. "I . . . I'm not entirely certain. It's an idea I've held on to all these years, and I . . ." Her voice trails off.

This is supposed to be Will's battle, but with what Marva just said, I realize the situation may require my particular area of expertise. "Then it's time to let go of that idea," I say, and she looks alarmed for a moment, as if I'm going to whip out Post-its and apply the N-Three test. "I'm simply saying, it may be an idea that used to fit, but it doesn't anymore. There's no need to keep it because you've always had it. You just don't have room for it anymore—not if you want to bring in something new."

Will hands Marva the cigarette and holds the suicide note toward its burning tip. "She's right. It's time you said good-bye to all that . . . junk."

She hesitates, takes a deep breath, then holds the cigarette to the paper in Will's hand until it slowly catches and then burns. Once a flame gets going, Will tosses it into a nearby metal trash can, to my alarm not bothering to notice that other papers are in it. Flames rise up quite spectacularly.

Marva picks up *Grimm's Fairy Tales*. "Let's make it a bonfire," she says, adding it to the fire, where it's accepted with a whoosh.

"Um, you guys? We might want to handle this," I say. The flames are climbing, in my opinion dangerously close to the easel holding Marva's painting. She and Will are so entranced by the flames they're not paying attention to how close they are to possibly catching . . . "I'm going to get an extinguisher!" I say. "Will, move the trash can!"

I bolt out of the room—luckily, per my place-for-everything-and-everything-in-its-place dictum, the extinguisher is under the kitchen sink where it belongs. When I return, Marva is holding the orgy-decorated urn—the remains of her house, her last piece of Filleppe. "I've got this," she says, and dumps its contents out onto the fire, the ash effectively damping the flames.

A trail of smoke rises up, making curlicues that lick the edge of the easel but otherwise leave the painting untouched. I look at it, thinking of all those years of pain and disconnect that Marva and Will passed through to make it to this new path they've wound their way to find. As much as I'm happy for them, it makes me ache for Ash and me. We've missed out on so much of the normal stuff that families get, but I still cling to the hope that we'll make up for lost time. Someday, I'll send him care packages to his dorm room at school. He'll call me, nervous about a term paper he has due. I'll come up for parents' day and take him and his adorable girlfriend out to dinner. He'll stand at the podium—elected by his classmates to speak because of how he overcame his drug addiction—and address his fellow graduates, saying how he owes it all to his mother . . .

"What's she crying for?" Will says to Marva, tipping his head toward me, making me aware I'm full into the ugly cry and hadn't even noticed. "Maybe you should've let her use the extinguisher."

I'm freshening up in the bungalow before joining Will and Marva for the birthday cake he brought when I remember I'd left my phone charging when I followed Will into the house. I retrieve it and see there's a message on it from a Florida number.

I'm in no hurry to listen to it.

There's no way it's good news. I'm not going to hear, *Hey, Mom, sorry I didn't get on the plane, but I decided to go to the Willows instead.*

Only after I've brushed my hair and reapplied powder to my face do I pick up the message. "Mom, it's me, Ash. Crap, why aren't you there? Uh, I got stopped up in security. TSA popped me for syringes, found some junk on me. This is my one call—been in friggin' jail all day. They're saying I was acting wasted, which I wasn't. I only did enough to take the edge off, 'cause I don't like flying. So I need you to make bail. Like, soon. Guy here says I could go to prison. Crap, why aren't you *there?*" He goes on in the same vein for a while, at last giving me information on the jail and how to contact them.

Which I'll do.

Tomorrow.

Tonight, however, I believe I'll enjoy the peaceful feeling of knowing my son is safe and, while I'm at it, have myself a big, fat piece of cake.

Minutes later, I'm standing at the kitchen counter as Will cuts into the cake—Marva wouldn't let me sing, citing bad luck since her birthday doesn't start until midnight (a superstition I suspect she made up).

After I shovel down not one but two slices of cake—lemon, hooyah—I tell them about Ash's phone call.

"If he'd only gone back to rehab, none of this would have happened," I say. "Now he might go to prison."

"Doubtful," Will says, "especially if there's a rehab lined up and it's a first offense. Chances are they'd just make him go back and finish it out."

For the first time ever, I look at Will and genuinely want to hug the stuffing out of that man. "Really? They can do that?"

"I suggest you get a lawyer."

Marva holds out her plate to Will. "Just a sliver more. I shouldn't be having this at all. And, Lucy, you can use my lawyer. I have one on retainer."

Of course she does. "Thanks, but don't they charge a fortune?"

"Consider it a bonus to your bonus. You've earned it."

My bonus! After all of this, I can't believe I nearly forgot it. At the reminder, Will reaches into his shirt pocket and pulls out a folded check and hands it to me.

"Woo-hoo!" I say, unfolding it and giving it a loud, smoochy kiss. "Hello, lover . . . hello, future. So nice to finally hold you."

I kiss it a few more times, then say, "Thanks for the cake and the cash. I'm going to go—you don't mind that I spend one more night in the bungalow?"

"Stay as long as you need. But don't get carried away," Marva says. "I'm not looking for a roommate."

"Just for the night is fine. And, Will, tell Padma how much I enjoyed the cake."

"Yes, do," Marva says. "In fact, let me cut off one more piece and I'll send the rest back home with you tonight. Wouldn't want to bring an extra plate into my perfectly clean house."

"I'm not going home tonight," Will says. "I intend to stay by your side until your birthday is over."

"There's no need. I give you my word I'm not going to do anything drastic. Besides, you have it wrong. The promise was that we'd never let ourselves become senior citizens—so by midnight, it's too late. I'll be sixty-five. 'Crisis'"—she air-quotes the word—"is over."

Even though I believe her—looks as if Daniel and I were one day off on our guess—I'm glad to hear Will say he's staying anyway.

"And I'll pop in here around ten tomorrow," I tell Marva, and that I feel the need to let her know before coming in cements that I'm done here. "You two have fun."

A full moon lights my way as I head through Marva's yard to the bungalow, creating a pretty glow through the trees. It's my last night here, and—though I have a whopping check in my pocket—the future is uncertain. Ash could be sent back to rehab—or prison, or be released, and then who knows what he'll choose to do. What I do know: I'm no longer willing to put my life on hold for him. He's my son, and I'll do what I can for him, but that no longer includes giving up everything that *I* want. It's *okay* for me to have things. It doesn't mean I care about Ash any less—only that I care about me, too. I want that pretty picture I imagined in my head, what feels so long ago—the one that includes a home and a job and friends.

This time, however, I add to the picture something I didn't even dare think about before, but I realize that I really want it—I deserve it.

As soon as I get into the bungalow, I grab my purse, then head out to my car. Now that I'm finally clear about what I want, I don't want to wait a minute longer than I must to try to get it.

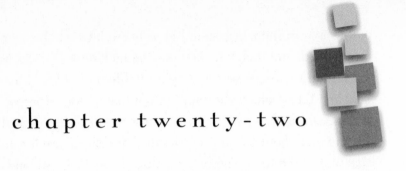

# chapter twenty-two

The street parking near Daniel's apartment is a nightmare, so I pull into the huge subterranean garage, hoping there are visitor spaces. There aren't, but as I drive around, I notice Daniel's car. He's in the front of a tandem space, so I take a chance and pull behind him, happy to see he's home on a Friday evening.

Getting out of my car, I pause, not sure how to get to his apartment. I've never been here before—just did some drive-bys to torment myself after he and I broke up. Correction: after I broke up with him. I'm glancing around for an elevator or stairs when Daniel's car loudly chirps itself awake and unlocked, the noise bouncing in the cavernous garage. I'm already jumpy enough over what I plan to say, so this nearly sets me clinging spiderlike and terrified to the wall.

Daniel comes around the corner. He's dressed nicely in a polo and black jeans, carrying a bouquet of flowers. "Luce? What are you doing here?"

"Oh, hey. You're probably afraid I'm stalking you. First the office and now this." I wait for a laugh—I mean *stalking*, that's funny stuff—but Daniel just seems baffled and, possibly, mildly irritated. I couldn't have expected I'd be given a hero's welcome. I once threw the man's original-run Beatles' *White Album* into the yard. It's a miracle he's speaking to me at all. "I'm wondering if you have time to talk."

"I was on my way out." He gestures slightly with the flowers, and I don't miss the meaning. He's going out on a date, and one that he's excited enough about to bring flowers, even if they are from the grocery store. I bite back a swell of disappointment. I'm too late. He's moved on. Sometimes when you throw something away, you can't get it back—somebody's already gone to the secondhand store and snatched it up, probably at a bargain price since it's tattered and worn from all the abuse you gave it.

On the chance that my shopping competitor is not yet at the cash register but still browsing around, leaving her item untended in her cart . . .

"Just a couple minutes?" I say.

"Okay," he says without enthusiasm. "What is it?"

I clear my throat. A car rumbles past, emitting a wave of exhaust fumes, and on the other end of the garage, a group of twentysomething girls emerge giggling from a stairwell, dressed tartily for a night out, their stilettos tap-tapping on the concrete floor. This is not the atmosphere I imagined for delivering my declaration of love. "Maybe we can go for a walk?"

"I'm already running late—you said a couple minutes, and I—"

"No problem. But at least let's sit in my car where it's quieter. Do you mind?"

It's obvious he wishes he'd said no, but he sets the flowers on the trunk of his car and climbs into my passenger seat. Once inside, as I'm taking a second to gather my thoughts—which are scrambled by his wearing aftershave, not intended for my appreciation—he says, "What is it you want?" in the manner of someone who can't get a dreaded task over with fast enough.

Hoping to at least get Daniel's attention, I start with news about Ash. "First off, I thought I'd tell you that I didn't send Ash to California." I'm talking to his shirt again—a polo that has an insignia of a tiny monkey head where the polo player would normally go. "It seemed like a waste of money—he didn't strike me as being that serious, and I was right. He got busted for drug possession today, so he's in jail in Tampa."

"Wow," Daniel says quietly. "Sorry to hear that."

"Oddly enough, it might be a good thing. There's a chance they'll send him to rehab instead of prison. On the other hand, they might release him on bail. I'll find out more tomorrow."

"All right, thanks for the update." He reaches for the door handle. "You've got my e-mail, so keep me posted."

"Wait, that's not all," I say, agitated by his disinterest. Did I not start this conversation with the words *first off*? Does that not imply there will be a second point? At least he lets go of the handle. "I wanted to tell you again how badly I feel that I threw you out of the house like I did. It was a terrible thing to do. Really, really not fair. And I'm sorry."

"I keep telling you, it's ancient history."

I finally dare look at his face, into his puppy-dog eyes, which I search for some sign of possibility. But it's as if he's pulled down a privacy shade that lets me see in, but only shadows and light, so I'm forced to forge ahead blindly. "What if I don't want it to be? What if I wish it wasn't ancient history—that we weren't over. You and me."

The sound of my swallowing nervously booms as if I were holding a microphone to my throat. After what seems forever, he turns away to face the dashboard. "But we are."

The finality in his tone sinks any hope I might have mustered. It's over. I had him, I messed up, and—in this case—there aren't second chances.

Alas, in an unfortunate turn of events for my pride, my heart has gotten the message, but my mouth, it appears, won't give up quite so easily. To the monkey-head insignia, I say, "I understand, although I'm not going to lie, it breaks my heart. I'm so mad at myself for blowing it with you. For some reason I was compelled to make this past year so awful. It's like I felt so guilty about letting Ash get into drugs, I needed to punish myself, and I dragged you into it. What's worse, I'm fully aware that if I'd let you, you would have been there for me, a hundred percent. You always were—always." I barely stop to take in a breath. "So, anyway, I get it—I wouldn't want me either. Especially since my life is still the same crazy mess it was before. Although *I'm* different. I really am. I'm no longer afraid to face things—believe me, I've been put to the test enough in these past weeks. That's why I'm here. My feelings are what they are, and I'm not going to apologize for them, and I'm not going to hide from them. I love you. I'm stupid, crazy in love with you. And, though it's clear you've moved on, I'm asking if you'll consider making room for me somehow in your life. I hope you will. That you and I"—I take one more breath, having reached the end of my monologue—"can be friends."

An endless number of aching, awkward seconds pass by, then Daniel says, "No."

I nod, crushed. All that's left is for me to go and let Daniel move on in peace, though I selfishly don't want to. I'm searching for a way to say it without quoting that poster about setting something free and hoping it comes back when I feel Daniel's lips on mine. "I don't want to be friends," he says, and kisses me again, then again. "I'm afraid that's not acceptable." He continues kissing me, softly, sweetly, and things inside me are popping and tingling and buzzing, and the kiss deepens, and I'm going to go out of my mind with happiness that this is happening, until eventually he pulls back. He looks into my eyes, and this time the shade is up so I see the sparkle in them that makes me go squishy inside. "But if you're willing to come up on your offer, we can figure something out."

Things progress pretty quickly after that—this is a man I've known for years and have slept with many times before, after all. I don't exactly have to worry about seeming slutty as—tongues meeting, hands groping—we attempt to slide into the backseat and . . . ugh . . . erf . . . well, maybe if . . .

"Love this car," Daniel says, panting with both lust and the effort of wedging himself through the tiny opening to the back, all the while working the buttons of my shirt. "But I'm thinking we need to move to a roomier location."

"Good idea. Your car's bigger."

He laughs, his mouth warm against my neck. "I was referring to my apartment."

"That'll work, too."

When we get out of the car, buttoning and retucking, I remember the flowers, still sitting on Daniel's trunk—and apparently, so does he. "Shoot, I forgot. I'm supposed to be at Andrea's."

*Andrea? He's dating one of the Andreas?* I'm torn between jealousy and curiosity over which Andrea when he says, "Oh, well, her bridal shower will have to go on without me." He hooks a finger in the waistband of my jeans and pulls me along as he walks backward toward the stairwell. "It'll be my way of protesting. This trend of inviting men to girlie parties has got to stop."

It's after midnight, and I'm lying next to Daniel, who fell asleep on his back with me nestled in the crook of his arm but then shifted as he always does in his sleep to his stomach. I'm wearing his reversible Cubs/White Sox jersey, Cubs-side out. I can't sleep, but I don't mind. This isn't the insomnia of the stressed-out lunatic that I've been for months now, but a woman who isn't ready to let what's turned out to be an incredible day end yet.

When we got into the apartment, Daniel started the tour in the bedroom. We kissed madly all the way there, loosening clothes as we went, and collapsed on the bed together in a heated frenzy. "Mmm, a bed," I said, giving a good bounce on it. "An actual bed! Like real grown-ups have. I can't tell you how excited I am to be on a *bed.*"

We then dispensed with the talking and got down to the business of picking up where we left off—and not merely where we left off in the car. It may have been months since Daniel has had access to my body, but he clearly remembered his way around the place, showing me in no uncertain terms and with great enthusiasm that he knows exactly where I keep things and where I like everything to go.

The streetlight from outside casts a grayish glow in the room through the closed blinds. I have no idea what tomorrow will bring, but I do know that—though I could face it by myself—I don't have to. I stare at Daniel's face for the longest time until, tugging up a blanket, I finally give in to my body's demand for slumber. As I drift off, I burrow closer to Daniel, an arm possessively thrown over him. It is with pure greed and joy and comfort that I think, *Mine.*

I'm back at Marva's house shortly after ten, a little later than I'd told her I'd check in with her. I hadn't realized at the time I'd be coming from Daniel's place. He sent me off with an egg breakfast in my belly—cooked on a stove! in a real pan!—and wearing a borrowed Foo Fighters T-shirt, which I needed because several of my shirt's buttons didn't survive last night's activities. We've made plans for me to be back in time for a *late lunch*, which I hope is code for "sex."

Will is at the kitchen counter, drinking a cup of coffee and texting, when I let myself in. "I see you've let her out of your sight. You must be feeling confident."

"Exhausted is more like it," he says, not glancing up from his phone. "I slept on the floor next to her bed—the woman snores like she swallowed a running chain saw."

"But otherwise it went well?"

"She's alive."

"That's a start. Where is she? I want to get the phone number of her lawyer." I've already talked to an officer at the jail where they're holding Ash. Although I could bail him out now, if I'm hoping to strong-arm him back into rehab, the officer said it's to my advantage to leave him there and get a lawyer in ASAP to propose the deal.

"Office," Will says, and it's like old times, Will texting and barely bothering to talk to me. I'm already getting nostalgic about leaving this place.

I'm at the office doorway, about to give my usual knock announcing that I'm there, when I stop short. Marva is standing, her back to me, stirring a large brush in a can of paint set on a tabletop. This must

be from the box of old supplies Niko brought in because I bought her
only tubes of oils, but no matter. She's going to paint again! I barely
want to breathe for fear of disturbing her, and I'd stop the whooshing
of blood through my veins and arteries, too, if I could. What a moment this is. After all Marva's been through, she's going to start fresh,
creating this new painting and, in daring to do so, creating a new life
for herself.

"As you can see, I am still here," Marva says, not turning around.
"As promised."

"Oh, I'm sorry, I didn't mean to disturb you. Please, keep on with
what you were doing. I'm just stopping by to get the lawyer's phone
number, but it can wait."

"Of course it can't," she says, leaving the brush in the can as she
crosses to her desk. Bending down, she rifles through an old-fashioned
Rolodex and tugs out a card, handing it to me. "I've already called
and told him to take good care of you. Now if you'll excuse me, I have
work to do. I woke up itching to get to this but held off, figuring you'd
want to be here for the big moment." She goes back to the paints.

"I do!" I say, grateful she thinks enough of me to allow me to be
there when she sets brush to blank canvas. I watch as she steels herself, lifts the brush, then turns and sets it down to create a large streak
of white—right across *Woman, Freshly Tossed.*

*Whaaaaaat?* "What are you doing?!" I bolt up to her, wanting to
snatch the brush from her hands but fearing the splattering would
cause further damage. The streak runs across the middle of the painting, directly over the chests of both the man and the woman.

"What does it look like I'm doing? I'm painting," Marva says
cheerily. "Well, this is only primer, but it's a start." She dips the brush
again and strokes it across the painting—this time covering their
faces—as Will rushes into the room in a panic, drawn by my cry.

"What the—," he says, letting us fill in our own expletives.

"Will, look at what your mother is doing!" I say, sounding like a
tattling little sister. "Stop her! Talk some sense into her! If we act fast
enough, maybe it can be fixed. Maybe—" I stop talking because he's

not moving but, rather, has collapsed in laughter, leaning against the doorframe, as if watching his mother ruin an extremely valuable painting—which he bought for her—is the funniest thing he's ever seen.

"Am I the only one around here who hasn't lost her mind?" I say, throwing my hands in the air.

"Now, now," Marva says, "I thought you wanted me to paint again, and here I am, painting. There's no reason to waste this perfectly good canvas."

"But there's a blank one right next to it! Please," I plead, "I understand all you've been through with that painting, and that it brings back sad memories, but that doesn't mean you have to destroy it."

"Oh, I'm not destroying it." She lays down another sweep of primer, then steps back to admire her handiwork. "I'm giving it a second life."

I hand my car keys to the valet driver.

"Wow, is this a '71?" he asks. When I nod yes, he says, "It's a beauty. Mind if I keep the top down while I park it?"

"Knock yourself out," I say, grabbing my purse from the backseat before heading up the street to the restaurant where I'm meeting my editor for lunch.

The two months since I watched in horror as Marva painted over *Woman, Freshly Tossed* have been a whirlwind—although I have to say, I'm liking the new painting quite a lot. Much softer than her old style, and surprisingly sexy.

I've moved out of the bungalow entirely and am subletting an apartment on my own, not that I'm ever there. Ever since Daniel proposed—oh, did I mention I'm engaged?—I've been moving my stuff bit by bit to his apartment. I suppose eventually we'll get a place together, but I was homeless for so long I'm fine with having two homes. They both have beds. Bouncy ones.

As for Marva, the hubbub over her hoarding and suicide may have died down for TV news, but the Internet kept churning out new stories until she couldn't stand it anymore. The story about her hoarding used adult diapers did her in. Marva at last invited the queen of daytime talk herself to tour the house and see that she is—indeed—very much alive and living a noncluttered life. The house, naturally, still looks lovely thanks to once-a-week check-ins with yours truly. She has me on retainer.

Being Marva Meier Rios's personal organizer has had other benefits. As soon as my agent realized I was the one behind Marva's transformation, she worked a deal to release *Things Are Not People—and* an accompanying workbook. The initial print run is twenty times what it was the first time. In fact, that's why I'm here today, to talk to my editor, who is in town from New York, about expanding it into a series. I'm glad we could squeeze in a meeting before I leave for my trip down to Florida tomorrow to see Ash.

He's at the Willows, thanks to a deal worked out by Marva's lawyer in less than twenty-four hours from the time I called him. There's no guarantee, but Ash is so much more committed to the process this time around. It helped that his other option was prison—suddenly the Willows didn't seem so bad. I've been down to visit him two times already, and each time I've seen more and more of my boy emerge. He's taking an online class at the community college, and the goal is to segue him into being a full-time student, living in a drug-free dorm. We're going to talk about that further on my next visit, when I'll be there with—ugh—Ash's father. I have to hand it to Dr. Paul on that one—he wore the man down until he finally stepped up to his obligations.

Besides painting, Marva is considering teaching a course at the university on the impermanence of art. They'd no doubt be appalled to learn she painted over *Woman, Freshly Tossed*, but that's a secret that only three of us are privy to. She also recently recorded an anti-suicide public-service announcement that has nearly a quarter million hits on YouTube.

Although we know that Marva was going to kill herself, she won't

reveal *how*. Will—a proud dad of a baby girl named Lullabelle—
badgers Marva regularly, trying to guess what it might have been.
Oddly enough, it's turned out to be a strange joke between the two
of them. He'll say, "Hanging from the bathroom curtain rod?" while
Marva insists the truth will go with her when she kicks the bucket
naturally. No shortage of gallows humor in that family.

As for who blew the whistle to the media—it turned out to be
Mei-Hua, who was found out after Will put Mackenlively on the job.
She did it for some fast cash since she, too, found Marva's suicide note
and realized she was soon going to be out of a job. Marva didn't fire
her, though. She says it's because of Mei-Hua's eggplant Parmesan,
although I suspect Marva has other skeletons in her closet that Mei-
Hua knows about.

At the crosswalk, a woman is selling necklaces from a cart. She
hands one to me that's pretty in a flashy sort of way, with lots of multi-
colored beads. "On sale just for you," she says, "twenty dollars. Goes
with your blue eyes." I'm tempted to buy it if for no other reason than
to celebrate this moment—I'm about to be published again!—but
then I run the necklace through the N-Three checklist. Though it's
quite sparkly and cute, I don't need it. It doesn't match anything I
own, so who knows when I'll get around to wearing it. And, truthfully,
nothing bad will happen if I say no.

I hand the necklace back. "Wrap it up. I'll take it."

"There are those things you keep, things you let go of—
and it's often not easy to know the difference."

—*Marva Meier Rios, from the foreword*
*to the newly updated* Things Are Not People

# a c k n o w l e d g m e n t s

First off, I'd like to thank my boyfriend, John Cusack . . . oh, wait, this is the part of the book that *isn't* a work of fiction. In that case, forget the boyfriend thing, and let me start by giving a very real thanks to my amazing editor, Sally Kim, as well as to Allegra Ben-Amotz and the entire team at Touchstone for all the support and enthusiasm they've given this book. I'm also endlessly grateful for my agent, Kirsten Manges, who always knows when it's time for hand-holding and when it's time to throw a good scare into me, and a big thanks to Jenny Meyer for helping my characters get to speak so many different languages.

This book wouldn't be what it is without the help of those who slogged through varying drafts along the way to give me feedback (and some much-needed cheering on), including Jen Catalano, Carol Snow, Candy Deemer, Sandra O'Briant, Mary Jo Reutter, Shelly Smolinski, and Linda Keathley-Stamey. I also have plenty of friends and family who didn't read any of the pages but still had supportive things to say—believe me, it was always appreciated.

To Daniel Storm: Nobody knows movie memorabilia like you do—thanks! To the "organizationally challenged" people I talked to when trying to learn more about the hoarding mentality: Don't worry, even under the lamp of truth, I will never reveal your identities. To my son, Daniel Elder: Thanks for tolerating my need to bounce ideas off you (and for being such a great son).

While I worked on this book, I had the honor of calling in to "join" hundreds of book clubs, and every one of them helped me remember why I love to do what I do. Writing can be a lonely business, and these great readers helped me rediscover my enthusiasm for my craft . . . so many, many thanks.

Oh, and it turns out that not everything in this book is fiction: Lucy's parents are entirely supportive of her as she's struggling to pull her life together, and that comes 100 percent from my real-life experiences. Thanks so much, Mom and Dad, for always being there for me — I love you.

# about the author

Jill Smolinski is the author of the novels *The Next Thing on My List* and *Flip-Flopped*. Her work has appeared in major women's magazines, as well as in an anthology of short stories, *American Girls About Town*. A transplanted midwesterner, she now lives in Los Angeles with her son. Find her at www.jillsmolinski.com.